Blood
for
Honor

Blood
for
Honor
Emma Lee Joy

RHR
Red Hawk Ridge

Published by Red Hawk Ridge.
www.red-hawk-ridge.com

Cover Designed by Emma Lee Joy
Printed in the United States of America.

[1. Psychological—Fiction. 2. Dystopian—Fiction. 3. Science Fiction—Fiction. 4. Mind Control—Fiction. 5. War—Fiction.]

ISBN: 979-8-9866078-0-1 (pbk)
ISBN: 979-8-9866078-2-5 (ebook)

To those struggling to conquer their demons, whatever they may be.
The past shapes us, but we choose who we become. Die to your past so that you may live for your future.

Acknowledgments

I would like to first and foremost thank my husband for the many hours he graciously allowed me to ignore him to complete this book.

I want to give major props to my mother, who contributed significantly to this process, and my father, who influenced my life more than he knows, even when he couldn't be there.

I want to thank those that donated money to help me publish this book on my own terms. You know who you are, and I am eternally grateful and still in awe that you believed in me enough to give me money.

Much thanks to Virginia Pierce, who has been a huge supporter and source of encouragement in this process.

And, of course, I have to thank my God for his revelation over the years that spilled over into this book as I grew as a person.

PART 1
The Catalyst

CHARON

One

It has been a very dry end to summer. Long, hot days and cool, brisk nights are devoid of moisture. Even the humidity has been scarce, a rarity for the Piney Woods that I have called home my entire twenty-four years of life.

The void left by the moisture is now filled with all-consuming flames.

A cacophony of screams coats the night air as thick as the smoke hovering over my wooded village. A faint orange glow illuminates the trees in the direction of the more densely populated area. Still, the extent of the damage hides from my secluded shanty cabin behind my father's larger cottage.

My knees weaken under me as the shrieks and yells grow in volume. I attempt to slow my breathing to quell the anxiety building in my chest, but the smell of smoke sets my nerves on edge. Though deadened through a distance, I might as well be in the midst of hell with them.

The village garden is shrouded in darkness through the window over the sink, untouched by the violence this night holds. I can only pray to whoever might be listening that the fire does not reach it. Nearing the final harvest, we cannot afford to lose our crops. The deer have become sparse over the last few years, and we can no longer depend on their meat to feed us, cutting down our food supply significantly.

My husband is conspicuously absent, and my village is under attack. I have resigned myself to pacing the narrow patch of earth between the empty fire pit in the center of the cabin, and the water pump against the wall, chewing on my thumb anxiously. My leather-clad feet make no sound against the rabbit skin rug covering the sandy floor as I wear a path in the soft fur.

Unsure of what to do, my anxiety threatens to overtake me. I can do nothing except gnaw violently on the calloused skin of my thumb and continue pacing with intentionally deep breaths to try and calm myself.

My thoughts run rampant despite my efforts.

Tonight's attack is entirely unprovoked. We have had a tense ceasefire with Charon for some time since the new Chief took power, but we have had no intentions of breaking it on either side—or so I thought. After decades of constant fighting, I thought we were finally making headway toward peace despite our differences.

I can fight, without a doubt. I could swing a sword before I could read, but the thought of missing my husband somewhere in the fray keeps me within the four walls of our home. Danny will come here to look for me first unless he needs my help.

Or he is dead.

We parted on a sour note this morning, and I cannot help but fear that negative words may be the last thing I ever said to him.

I should go look for him.

The thought evokes a strong sense of determination, forcing itself through the fog of anxiety clouding my mind. It makes it easier to process my thoughts, and I finally make my decision.

A raucous banging against the cabin's doorpost sends my heart beating erratically in my chest, flooding my body with adrenaline. Danny would not knock, but neither would intruders.

"Iylara! You in there?" Damian's voice bellows through the barrier in his deep, southern cadence. Impatience lurks at the edge of his tone.

My older brother's familiar voice from the other side of the door calms my racing heart—to an extent.

The Damian Vance from my childhood would be much more welcome to hear. That Damian was more accepting of me. Now he harbors resentment against me because of who the man I married is—or rather is not, which is Blackthorn. My brother is not the only one who disagrees with my decision, but I can't think about that right now.

I mentally shake myself, shoving the bitterness brought on by the thought aside to deal with later. I take the three steps between me and the door, inhaling a deep breath and releasing it before slinging the thick woven door open.

My six-foot-tall brother stands outside under the thatched awning with a worried look. The lines of his furrowed brow crease his forehead, uncovered by the long, black hair braided down his back. His tear-drop-shaped clan mark stands out stark against his skin in the light of the torch he carries. It curves over his chin and down his neck, the tip ending at the hollow of his throat, identical to my own.

"Danny here?" he asks, dark brown eyes searching for my husband over my shoulder. Crow's feet are unmistakable at the corners of his eyes as he narrows them at Danny's absence.

I shake my head, trying to keep the frantic fluttering in my chest at bay. I glance over my brother's shoulder, but there is no movement in the courtyard behind him.

Where is Danny?

"I haven't seen him since he left to help the blacksmith this morning. What is going on?" I ask, my anxiety clawing its way out of the cage in my chest more and more by the second.

"Charon," Damian says shortly. "We need to go."

My heart thuds vigorously against my ribs. "Not without Danny," I say, shaking my head. "Of course, who else would it be? You know I mean, 'Why are they here?'"

Damian ignores my question. "Grab your bag, Iylara. *Move,*" he orders, trying to coax me into action with the venom in his voice. He uses fear and malice to get what he wants, but it does not work on me. I do what I want, for the most part.

I do wish to hear my brother call me by my affectionately given nickname, Ray, one more time. It's like a stab in the heart every time he calls me by my birth name. He was the first to call me Ray, after all. It may have been a joke at first, but it stuck, nonetheless. But now, his voice always has an undercurrent of disgust when he speaks my name.

I give Damian a shaky huff and turn on my heel, strutting for the antique armoire in the far corner of my home with more than a little attitude. I pull out a long hooded cowl from the wardrobe. It covers my olive green overdress with gentle ochre waves, hiding the two short swords hanging from my weapons belt on either hip. I procrastinate in joining my brother by adjusting my belt's position languidly.

It only takes a moment before an impatient Damian finally yells at me from the door. "Hurry up, woman! We don't have time for this! The fire is getting closer to the courtyard!"

Damian's patience with me is running thin, but I am stalling on purpose. I can only hope the extra time will give Danny a chance to make his way home. Damian is only moments away from dragging me off to the safe house, per our doomsday plan in the event that something like this night ever came to pass. The fact that Danny does not know how to get there by himself does not escape me.

My father never entrusted the location to him, much to my chagrin, and I never went against my father's orders to withhold it from him. It is on me if he is lost tonight because of that.

A deadly virus swept through three years ago, killing a third of our population, including my mother and older sister. Now, the ruling bloodline of Blackthorn has had to take some precautions to ensure the clan always has a leader. But it entails running away from a fight like cowards if you ask me. That opinion is frowned upon, so I keep my mouth shut if I can help it.

"I'm coming," I say over my shoulder.

I pull the hood of my cowl over the dark, auburn red braid hanging halfway down my back, casting my sun-kissed face in shadow. My leather rucksack and quarter-staff wait for me beside the door, and I meet Damian outside after grabbing both.

I adjust the strap of my bag on my shoulder as I speak. "Are we holding Charon off at all?"

Worry gnaws away in my chest for our people like a starved beast, and I cannot help but feel less of myself as I prepare to run away from the inferno and battle to save my own life.

"So far, but Charon was more organized than ever before. If you can't tell, they got through the South Gate," Damian says, lowering his voice as we head for the smaller North Gate, near the Orchard.

Of course, they did. We wouldn't be evacuating if they didn't.

"Dad ordered me to fetch you and Danny—bring you to the safe house," he says, cutting off my thoughts.

I glance back at the pine wood, scavenged metal, and animal skins pieced together in a haphazard yet functional design that is my home. "But Danny isn't here. I should be looking for him, not coming with you. I can fight, you know," I say bitterly, wishing I had gotten myself together and gone looking for my husband before Damian showed up.

"Dad won't allow that," Damian says, grabbing me roughly by the arm to stop me as I take one step in the opposite direction. He knows I am seconds from bolting off into the darkness after a man he hates, if not to help defend our people.

He tugs on my arm with a snarl, and I let him pull me along against my better judgment. It is quieter on this side of the village, and we make it to the North Gate without interference. The sounds of battle shrink away with the ever-increasing distance our feet carry us.

We slip through the North Gate, mainly used for exporting extra food from the gardens to the trading post. It is only wide enough for a small supply wagon to fit through. I am sure if Charon knew about it, they would have utilized it tonight, but it is nestled under cover of dense forest and overgrown trails, well hidden from anyone ignorant to its existence.

"Our father doesn't allow much," I mumble, trudging behind Damian with a bitter attitude. "I should be fighting, not running," I add, righteous anger rising inside me.

I don't know how much longer I can continue to do nothing. I helped train many of the people we are leaving behind to fight for their lives. I should be by their side, but being an heir to leadership, I am begrudgingly withheld from participating in the name of preserving Blackthorn's ruling bloodline. I don't understand why it matters so much. Surely others could lead just as well, but tradition runs deep in our clan.

"You should be thinking about the bigger picture," Damian spits at me, poking at my anger while simultaneously acting as though he has heard my thoughts.

I should not poke back, but I don't listen to rationalizations on the best of days when it comes to my brother. "You mean saving ourselves," I throw back at him, unable to hold my tongue. "Our people are dying, and all we can think of are our own lives."

Damian turns, towering over me. "You need to watch your tone, Iylara." I do not cower from him like I know he wants.

Damian likes to throw his weight around from time to time. Since our older sister died, making him the next in line to be Chief, he has let the thought of power go to his head. If he had it his way, he would have talked our father into stepping down long ago, but extreme stubbornness runs in the family.

I came by mine honestly, that is for sure.

"Don't even. You know good and well that I am right." My words only make Damian angrier, as I knew they would, but I enjoy poking the bear from time to time.

Damian brings his hand up, striking me on the cheek with the back of his hand. I hiss, my hand automatically covering my stinging skin.

I glower at him as he points his finger in my face. "You forget who you are talking to," he says with a growl, shoving me forward roughly. *"Walk."*

I grit my teeth against the stinging his hand left behind and concede. Picking a fight with him right now might not be the best life choice, so I submit, falling into step beside him with a defeated sigh to avoid his wrath. Damian may very well beat me if I run off to search for Danny with the mood he is in now. He has only ever slapped me once before, on my wedding day, and it isn't something I like to remember.

Damian does not act like this in front of our father. Surely Leeland Vance would find his son's behavior distasteful, but he would never believe me if I told him about it. Being the only son, Damian has always been our father's favorite.

"You aren't as superior as you think," I mutter. I shrug off his hand to walk ahead of him, determined to have the last word, as childish as it is.

Damian's anger pulsates outwards from him like hot tendrils waiting to burn me, much like the heat of the flame smoldering at the end of his torch, but he does not answer. He grabs my arm once again to ensure I do not run off, and his long legged-strides surpass my shorter ones as he drags me closer to our destination through the wooded forest.

***

The family safe house is not much, but it has withstood the test of time for over a century. It is one of the best-kept secrets of our age, or so it seemed when my mother talked about it. She was very prideful, it being her great-grandfather who built it.

Inset underground in the rock of an old abandoned quarry, the hazardous pathway down into the pit deters most passersby, but our trained feet glide over the loose ground with ease.

I vault a new addition to the crumbling stone near the bottom with the help of my quarterstaff. I land on the hard stone floor of the quarry pit with a flourish and arrogant bow, trying to lighten the tension between my brother and me.

"Show-off," Damian mumbles grumpily, but there is the faintest sound of amusement in his voice—a shadow of times past. It is the best I can hope for.

I grin meekly with satisfaction but say nothing, opting to turn my attention to the stone wall in front of me. I place a hand on the stone inside of a chest-high indention and hold it there. The surface remains cold even in the heat of late summer. At my touch, it burns hot for the briefest moment.

I wince as the stone pricks each of my fingertips all at once, soaking up the singular droplets of crimson instantly. The stone sighs and slowly slides away to reveal a tunnel entrance that opens the way to a hallway. Sucking on my fingertips, I step through the hole, and follow the path with the sharp taste of iron on my tongue.

The winding hallway opens up to a large cavern. The expanse in front of me is complete with a wellspring surrounded by dark-dwelling plants that glow dimly in the low light of the cavern. The foliage thrives on the minimal amount of light at noon that comes through the skylight positioned directly above the pool.

I glance around the rocky cavern, my eyes stalling on the light of the fireflies flickering amongst the flora surrounding the pool, but only for a second. Looking around the room, I frown at my husband's absence. A part of me hoped that a member of my family had already found him and brought him to safety. It would have saved me from the worry rising in my throat that threatens to choke me now.

Keena, Damian's wife, and their eleven-year-old daughter, Ysabel, sit by the fire pit in the center of the cavern, nestled under blankets on the overstuffed couch. They ignore our entrance, for the most part, their matching raven hair shining in the firelight.

I catch Ysabel's glance, but she diverts her eyes before her mother notices. A look I cannot place envelopes her sharp features, but my father interrupts before I can ask what is wrong.

"Where is Danny?" he asks, knocking the cherry from his cigar as he stands up from his spot next to the water. He places the nub of tobacco between his teeth as he ambles over.

I make my way to the small fire pit, trying to ignore Keena's derisive glare that has taken me captive with my father's acknowledgment.

The cavern is chilly, much colder than the air outside, and goose flesh appears on my arms where my skin is not covered in fabric. I push my hood back. "I don't know," I answer with a slight shiver.

Familiar energy in the air puts me on edge, and I cannot ignore it. I begin to gnaw on my thumbnail nervously again, anxiously waiting for whatever is to come.

"Then he did do it!" Keena says with an accusing tone as she stands, her malice directed at me.

"What are you talking about?" I ask, glancing between her and my father in confusion.

"It isn't Aunt Ray's fault, mom," Ysabel tells her mother in her songbird voice. It chimes around the room like music, but it does not do much to tame the chaos swirling in the atmosphere around her mother.

I look at Ysabel with questioning eyes. Keena looks down at her daughter and waivers. After a moment, Keena turns to me, eyes smoldering. She is dead set on blaming me for something, as always, and there is betrayal in the sharp look in her eyes at her daughter's defense of me. Thankfully, she cannot bring herself to take her frustration out on the girl, but I am a different story.

"Of course it is," Keena hisses at me. "Someone opened the gate and let Charon in. How else could they have gotten past the guards?" Keena says with a flourish of her hands. "And now your *Charon-born* husband is missing."

Her accusation is as clear as day. Loyalty lies with your clan, and turncoats are one in a million. No one ever entirely leaves their clan—unless you are Danny Rekkon. But I am the only one who believes that.

But I trust my husband implicitly.

"Don't even go there. He would never betray us," I say.

How can she have the gall to pin this on Danny?

Keena was a forest rat, a clan-less outsider in her own right before Damian found her half-dead in the middle of nowhere. She was not born Blackthorn either, but we took her in as our own, all the same.

What a hypocrite.

"I don't believe that," Keena says, standing up straighter as she challenges me.

Standing as tall as she can, Keena is still several inches shorter than me. To make up for her stature, her chocolate eyes, made lighter by the mocha tone of her skin, shine bright with determined anger.

"Enough," my father's low voice rumbles through the cavern with authority. "We have enough problems without you two at each other's throat." His green eyes are stern as his gaze bores holes in the two of us.

"Yes, sir," I say, bowing my head and submitting immediately to my father's authority. The need to fight still radiates from Keena, but she manages to restrain herself after a moment.

"Let's go get ready for bed," Keena tells Ysabel stiffly, trying to divert her anger before she does something to enrage my father.

"I can't go to bed. I need to talk to Aunt Ray," Ysabel tells her mom, sounding more like a miniature adult than an eleven-year-old.

"No, you don't. Come on," Keena chastises, tugging gently on her daughter's arm.

Ysabel looks at me, but rather than give her mother more reason to hate me, I side with Keena for once. "We can talk in the morning, alright?" I say as Keena steps between us.

Ysabel ignores her mother's scathing glare as she takes her arm back. "It could be too late by then," she says but gives into her mother's threatening glare.

I want to stop Ysabel and find out what she means, but Keena does not offer the chance. She grabs her daughter roughly by the arm, pulling her along as they head off toward the arched hallway by the water where the bedrooms are. Ysabel gives me one more glance over her shoulder before her mother turns her back, and they disappear down the corridor.

I cannot quite make out the look my niece gives me. Something in her translucent brown eyes hovers between fear and anger that is not directed at me but somehow *for me*—like she knows something I do not.

With the duo out of earshot, my father walks over as Damian towers over me, pulling my attention away from his wife and daughter. "Do you always have to antagonize her?" he asks in his favorite domineering tone. "Especially with Ysabel around!"

"Antagonize her? Keena started it," I say in disbelief. "How come you always blame me when she starts something?"

Encounters between Keena and I are usually tense, and she is eleven times out of ten the one who starts it. Somehow I still get blamed for disturbing the peace—every time.

Damian huffs as our father places a hand on his shoulder. "Lay off your sister," he says, looking at me in concern.

"What are we supposed to do about Danny?" I ask. I need to search for my husband, but I know my father will never let me.

A dark look crosses my father's lined face, but it is Damian who speaks. "Danny can take care of himself," he snaps, seemingly coming to some conclusion since we arrived that I am still in the dark about.

"I have to go look for him," I say, glancing between the two men with pleading eyes. My mother would understand if only she were here. Meredith Vance was the only person who ever understood me in this family.

My father takes a deep breath, hesitating to answer my question. "Iylara, there is a very good chance Danny *is* the one who let Charon in."

I stare open-mouthed at his words. "No, there isn't," I argue. I will not stand by and let them pin this on Danny. They have wanted to get rid of him since day one and would have succeeded if my mother had not been the one with the final say in my marriage.

"He has been on the run from Charon for a long time. You think he couldn't have finally given in and made a deal to save his own skin?" Damian asks.

Are they all in on this? My own family is attacking me.

"No!" I almost yell. "He would never do that. Charon would never take him back! You have to believe me. I know it is hard for you to put aside his past and trust him, but I will not stand around and listen to this!"

I make for the entryway, but Damian steps in front of me, stopping me in my tracks. "Get out of my way, Damian."

My brother shakes his head as my father says, "No."

I turn back to my father. "I am going to go look for him," I say with finality.

"I cannot allow that," my father says, shaking his head.

I clench my jaw in anger, withholding the retort that will get me reprimanded. I look up into my brother's eyes. I see a challenge in them, but I am wise enough not to take the bait.

I stalk off toward the bedrooms as calmly as possible, but every part of me wants to scream. The dim light of the corridor embraces me, and I slink by the partially closed door to Keena and Ysabel's room. They whisper, but I restrain the urge to stop and listen, continuing down the stone hallway. My path is lit only by large candles mounted on iron plates bolted into the walls every few feet.

Ignoring my room altogether, I make my way further down the corridor. There is no way I can go out the front, so I head for the back exit, knowing what I have to do. My father may think he is always right, but I cannot see how he could be anything but wrong now.

Crouching to pass through a low crevice, I inch my way out into the darkness. I shrug off my pack as it catches on the stones above me and abandon it behind me. I drop down from the outcropping of rock into the dense bushes below that conceal the exit from view.

No turning back now.

Looking both ways through the bushes, I find my path clear and make a beeline for the village.

Smoke permeates the air even this far out, like a roaring chimney. I can imagine that if it were daylight, I would be able to see the smoke billowing from the southwest side of the village like a fountain. The stars are nowhere to be seen, and the invisible haze blots out the light of the full moon above me. I should have brought a torch like Damian's.

I spin around, sensing a shift in the atmosphere behind me. I bring my staff up in front of me in self-defense, squinting into the dark. I cannot see anything until Damian steps out of the densest shadow, that damned torch of his flaring to life. I do not lower my staff as I face him, and he frowns.

"Go back," I tell him, committed to fighting him on this if he does not concede. I cannot go back to the safe house. Not without Danny. I have to prove my husband is not to blame for this mess we are in.

"I can't do that, little sister. I'm sorry."

As Damian speaks, a sharp sensation in my neck sends me staggering. I reach up, fingertips brushing against a small, feather-tipped cylinder. I shudder a breath, the effects of the dart protruding from my neck, kicking in instantly. Even with the support of my staff, I cannot stay upright as the world fades, and I sink to my knees as my legs give out.

Three figures appear out of the trees and diverge on Damian from all sides, swords raised, but he has not seen them.

My warning cry is lost to the darkness as I fall into oblivion.

Two

The tinkling of chains echoes off metal walls, and I jerk awake with a helpless yelp. Darkness conceals my prison, blinding me, and my fingertips tingle from the weight pulling against my wrists. I blindly grip the chains connected to the cuffs restraining me, tugging against them while praying for the chain links to give way.

My effort proves futile, and the noise made by the chains against the metal wall is unbearable in the silence surrounding me. I give up the struggle, saving my wrists from the abuse while trying to get my feet under me. The smooth leather soles of my boots slip on a slick floor, and I fall back against the wall with a grunt of pain.

The sound of rustling next to me tells me that I am not alone and is possibly the source of noise that woke me up in the first place. The individual in question either cannot talk or chooses to remain quiet.

The sound of heavy boots on concrete meets my ears, and dread pools like a weight in the pit of my stomach. My heart thuds painfully in my chest. I know instinctively that the sound is coming straight for us. It will not pass.

The footsteps stop, and the jingle of a lock echoes around me for one heart-stopping moment. Then the door is thrust upward, filling the room with mid-morning sunlight. The light bounces off of the silvery walls of my prison cell, and the room glows orange. Squinting, I turn my head away from the glaring light to find Danny gagged and chained up next to me in a ray of sunlight, staring at me with amber eyes void of emotion.

At the sight of my husband, I forget how to breathe. With a pitiful whimper, dread constricts my heart in my chest. I only look away when Danny does to take in the smugness of our captor as Charon Chief Carnegie Lysander waltzes in with an air of overzealous joy about him.

Carnegie's X-shaped Charon mark is on a prominent display on the side of his neck above the stiff collar of his red vest. It triggers the memory of Danny publicly burning off his own Charon tattoo. It was my mother's one request as a show of loyalty before Danny could have my hand in marriage. Much to the rest of my family's disdain, he went through with it.

Danny deserted his family and clan to be with me, deeming himself a traitor to his kin, all in the name of love. Yet he was never worthy enough to be marked as a Blackthorn. Anger still rises at the thought, and I cannot help but drop my gaze to the ragged scar peeking out from the top of Danny's shirt.

I am starting to regret dragging Danny into my life if it is what gets him killed. I know Carnegie will not let Danny Rekkon, *Blood Traitor,* leave this room alive after hunting him for over four years.

Defaulting from your clan on either side is punishable by death. You are blood-bound. Breaking that bond should not be taken lightly. Most people do not break it, but Danny didn't even think twice about it when given a chance.

A sword hangs at Carnegie's side in an ornate sheath. I glance at Danny in fear. His curly light brown hair falls in his face as he glares at Carnegie, and the sunlight sets his eyes ablaze behind the curtain of hair.

"Well, well, well," Carnegie says with a chuckle; there is an all too excited gleam in his ice-blue eyes for my liking. "This is my lucky day," he says to no one in particular.

The arrogance in his tone makes me want to slap him, but Danny and I stay silent behind the gags over our mouths.

Carnegie studies me, undressing me with his cold eyes as they roam over my body. I feel like a piece of meat on display for sale. His eyes pierce my soul as he drags them upward to meet my own, and the hairs on my neck stand up straight.

The angular black marks around Carnegie's eyes are endearing, and his eyes almost glow in contrast. His white-blond hair is shaved on the sides, the long middle section braided down his back, revealing angular black tattoos on the side of his head that match the ones around his eyes.

Carnegie Lysander would be a handsome man if his countenance were not so terrifying.

"How about we have a chat?" Carnegie asks as he continues to stare at me. He pulls away the cloth over my mouth much slower than needed and strokes my hair where it has fallen over my face.

I shrug away from him, and he lets his hand fall with a glance at Danny, who growls through his gag in protest. Carnegie shifts to stand in front of him, looking Danny hard in the eyes. Carnegie rears back, punching him in the gut with one swift movement.

Danny gasps for the breath forced from his lungs as I cry out. "Leave him alone!" I yell, straining against my chains again, despite the futility of my actions.

Carnegie smiles, turning his attention back to me. His gloved hand reaches out, stroking the side of my face gently. The kiss of the cold black leather makes me shiver, and I jerk away from him. He roughly grabs my chin, forcing me to look at him.

He points to both of us with an accusing finger as he speaks. "There is only one thing each of you is here for. *Danny Boy* is going to die for his treachery, and you are going to watch. It is only right since you are the reason he broke the Blood Covenant in the first place," he says matter-of-factly.

I watch in abject horror as Carnegie turns his attention to Danny, at a loss for words.

"I've been waiting a long time for this day." Carnegie happily rocks back and forth on the balls of his feet as he speaks. "Our dishonorable defector. All for a good lay, right? I can see why." Carnegie stares at me again, taking in my form with a hungry look in his eyes.

He continues, ignoring the scathing glare on Danny's face. "Did you know that your face has been plastered on every Wanted board for four years? 'Wanted: Dead or Alive,' by the very Chief himself," he tells Danny, speaking of himself in the third person with a flourish of his hand. "Now, that is quite some time to manage to stay off of my radar, not to mention completely undetected," Carnegie says, pausing to smile wolfishly at me. "My patience has finally been rewarded, and I managed to kill two birds with one stone."

Danny tenses next to me, gripping his chains in anger.

Carnegie turns to me, grinning like the Cheshire Cat with nearly perfect, well-kept teeth. "You ever question if your husband is as loyal as you think?" he asks.

"No," I say bitterly as butterflies flit around my stomach at his question.

"Maybe you should have." My eyes widen at his unspoken accusation, and his grin grows.

"What do you mean?" I ask, voice shaking as dread bubbles in the pit of my stomach.

In Carnegie's silence, I turn my gaze, searching Danny for answers. He shakes his head at Carnegie, refusing to look at me. His garbled speech is unintelligible through his gag, and I cannot tell if he is trying to deny Carnegie's claim or not.

"Let him speak for himself!" I try not to yell, but my emotions get the better of me. Tears threaten me as the belief that my husband might have betrayed Blackthorn starts to grab hold.

"He will only try to deny it. He didn't want you to know he thought he made a mistake in defecting. He thought I would let him come home if he got me inside Blackthorn's gates. I may have failed to mention that I do not make deals with traitors," Carnegie says, directing the last bit at Danny, who stares quietly at our captor while avoiding my gaze.

My world starts to crumble before my eyes. “Please tell me there is something we can do. It doesn’t have to be this way,” I plead, afraid for Danny’s life.

Even as the bitterness of my husband’s now very possible betrayal encases my heart, my love for him never falters. I do not want him to die. I want to know if Carnegie is telling the truth, and if he is, I want a chance to work through this.

“No, there isn’t. He broke the Blood Covenant. You know what that means,” Carnegie says darkly. “I want to watch him bleed for his betrayal. You should too.”

I stare at Danny, opened-mouthed but silent, as I watch on in horror. I am unable to process what I am witnessing properly.

Carnegie pulls his sword from its sheath with a metallic ring, and the shimmer of metal sends me into a panic.

“No, please!” I cry out in fear for the man I love, unable to stop myself.

Danny catches my eyes, silencing me as Carnegie stands stoically in front of him. There is defeat, and something like guilt, in the amber orbs looking longingly at me.

“I’m sorry,” he mumbles through the cloth gag, and my breath hitches.

“You *did* do it?” My voice is barely above a whisper.

Never would I have genuinely believed it, and I won’t without his actual admission. Surely I am misunderstanding him.

Carnegie shoves the sword's blade upward under Danny’s rib cage before he can answer, piercing his heart as he hangs helplessly beside me. A single huff of pain escapes his lips through the gag. Carnegie pulls the blade out, and Danny begins to choke on blood.

Time stops, and I cannot breathe.

Blood stains the cloth gag, seeping from the corners of his mouth as he tries to gasp for air. His eyes never leave mine as I stare back in horror, mouth agape in a silent scream of anguish. A red stain grows over the front of Danny’s white tunic, getting larger by the second.

A wretched sob breaks from my throat as Danny’s head drops to his chest, and the life leaves him. His body slumps against the chains holding him upright as a single tear rolls down his face.

"NO!" I scream, finding my voice as I kick out, unable to make contact with Carnegie's face like I want.

He laughs at me as he dances away from my kicking feet. It makes me angry as well as distraught. "You son-of-a—" I curse, my voice breaking off in a sob.

"Now, now, don't insult my mother. She was no saint, but that's just rude," Carnegie says with a wicked smile.

I cry out again at the sight of Danny's lifeless body. A painful yearning burns through my chest, and my vision turns red.

I will never get to set things right or learn the truth. Treason will be his legacy.

My ears start to ring, louder and louder, until it consumes me, tears clouding my vision. I want to rip Carnegie apart for taking that from me.

Carnegie has to pay. He cannot get away with this.

I don't have time to plan my revenge. Carnegie pulls a syringe from a pocket inside his vest and pops the cap off. I am unsure if he means to knock me out or kill me with it.

He strikes quick as a rattlesnake before I can twist away, impaling my thigh with the needle before pushing down on the plunger. The contents are cold in my veins, chilling me to the bone, and my vision starts to fade.

"See you soon, my love," Carnegie whispers.

"No—" My voice trails off as the stupor sets over me.

The serum is potent, but the feeling is unlike the dart, and unconsciousness creeps in rather than rushing over me. I cannot fight it and succumb to the darkness as my world completely shatters around me.

I know only one thing as everything fades away. *Nothing will ever be the same.*

***

I surface from a dark dream world to find my mouth gagged again, but I am no longer chained against a wall. Instead, I am strapped to something cold and hard that rests on an incline—a table, maybe. I attempt to lift my pounding head to look through the darkness but quickly give up.

There is nothing to see in the pitch-black encompassing me, and my head is too heavy to lift in my lethargy. Or maybe it is strapped down, too—I cannot tell.

Tears burn my eyes as memories come rushing back through the drug-induced fog, crashing down on me like a tidal wave. The breathlessness of grief has me gasping for air in seconds, and the sound of rustling leather escapes me as I try to claw my way out of the recesses of my mind.

My prison door is forced up, and late afternoon sunlight filters in as the door rolls open with a clatter. I jerk at the sound, and my head flops to the side.

Not strapped down, then.

My gag absorbs most of the tears streaming from my eyes, but I try to wipe away the remnant on my shoulder as someone appears beside me. A familiar gloved hand grabs my chin, preventing me from ridding myself of the evidence of my weakness. My vision starts to clear in the light, and Carnegie's face comes into focus faster than I would like him to.

His infuriating smirk appears as our eyes meet. "Rise and shine, my love."

Carnegie carefully pushes the gag down around my neck, freeing my mouth. "I was starting to think I put you through too much."

I'm not sure what he is talking about, but with my mouth free, a surge of energy goes through me, and I use it to curse him again. "You're a son-of—"

The back of his hand connects with my jaw, cutting me off mid-sentence. My head snaps to the other side, blood filling my mouth with the taste of iron, but the pain clears my head. Before I can spit the mouthful of blood at him, he grabs me by the throat, pushing me against the hard surface of the table I lay on.

"Is that the only insult you have? Watch it," he threatens, his fingers tensing around my throat in warning.

I find my voice in the pressure of his fingers. "You killed him!" I rasp out, tears cutting fresh rivers down my face.

Like a film reel playing before my eyes, I relive the red stain spreading across Danny's chest. I am entranced by the ruby red drops of blood that run down his chin as the viscous liquid soaks his gag and drips from the corners of his lips—lips I will never feel pressed against my own in passion again.

"Yeah, well, I don't take lightly to my men disgracing Charon and running off with some Blackthorn whore. He deserted his clan, becoming enemies with his fellow brothers-in-arms—his *family*," Carnegie spits out angrily.

I close my eyes, wishing I were anywhere else.

Anyone else.

The heavy weight of grief on my chest will surely kill me if I have to stay in this reality any longer. I would give anything to turn back time, but this is my life now. I will regret everything I never said—and all the things I should never have let pass my lips for the rest of my life.

Carnegie loosens his grip on my throat, stroking my bottom lip with his gloved thumb in thought. I open my eyes out of distrust of his motives, glaring at him with all the vehemence I can manage.

Curiosity softens the anger in his eyes as he mulls a thought over. "You must be something special to make a man do that," he says, voice soft as he smells my hair.

My skin crawls, but I only give him the truth, my voice becoming stronger with each word. "Danny didn't leave Charon because of me. He hated you before he met me. I just gave him a reason to finally leave," I hiss.

Anger flashes back across Carnegie's face. My jaw clenches, readying myself for another hit. It does not come, so I continue to goad him. "You disgusted him with your barbarism and blatant disregard for your men's life. He got out before you sent him on some fool's suicide run," I say in a stronger voice than I thought I could muster past the lump in my throat.

The blood I have yet to spit out pools in my mouth, coating my bottom lip as my confidence builds with each second. I clench my fists as the adrenaline begins coursing through me, leaning forward as much as the table straps allow. Carnegie does not pull back, glaring at me studiously. Malice is evident in his eyes, but I know he wants to hear what I have to say.

"You can't take us down," I growl between clenched teeth. I spit the blood onto his face in disrespect. "The blood you've lost to us has been in vain. You can't overcome us. No matter how hard you try. It was for *naught*," I say with a snarl. I do not know *who* came out on top in the attack on my village, but it doesn't matter. Even if Blackthorn lost, I am willing to bet that we took most of the Charon that made it through the gate down with us. The thought fills me with pride.

I want Carnegie to lose his composure, but he must know this as he calmly wipes his face clean of blood. He merely responds with that infuriating smirk and a chuckle. With his foot, he nudges something at the base of the table. A clicking sound coaxes his mouth into a wide grin.

My stomach drops as his hand tips the table backward, dunking me into a barrel of cold water behind me. I scream out involuntarily, losing most of my oxygen supply in one fell swoop. Unable to fight against my restraints, I stare up through the water, captivated by Carnegie's icy eyes distorted by the water, quickly drowning me. I use what air I have left to keep it out of my nose, and my lungs start to burn.

Carnegie tilts the table upright, saving me from a watery grave as my vision starts to darken. Spitting and sputtering, I gasp for air. Despite my tenacity, I cannot manage a glare at the man in front of me now—I can barely manage to hold back the threat of tears.

Standing over me with his arms crossed, he watches me gluttonously suck in air before speaking in a calculated voice. "So *you* think," he says, making my spine tingle. "You don't know who else I have." He gently brushes wet hair out of my eyes.

Damian's face flashes in my mind, and a bitter sickness rises in my stomach.

How could I have forgotten?

My breathing becomes shallow as I try to control my panic. With my increasing distress, Carnegie's toothy grin grows, and he lets out a solitary whistle. Two guards drag a limp body through the open door at the sound.

"Damian?" I ask in a small voice, rivulets of water blurring my vision as they drip into my eyes.

A groan comes from the man, and Carnegie grabs a fist full of his hair, lifting his head. Blood runs from his hairline, and his eyes are unfocused, but it is my brother—the direct heir to the Blackthorn throne in the hands of our enemy.

Oh God, no.

"Your brother is off to hang next to your dear *husband*," Carnegie says happily, his words sending my heart into the pit of my stomach.

Carnegie releases Damian's hair and saunters back over to me, lowering his voice to a seductive whisper to speak into my ear. "By the way, lover boy makes a nice scarecrow."

The color drains from my face as he chuckles in my ear, but no tears threaten this time. I can only feel pure, unadulterated hatred for the man standing next to me.

I look past Carnegie to lay eyes once more on my brother. "Fight, Damian!"

"He can't do that. He got whacked upside the head pretty hard," Carnegie says, smiling happily at Damian over his shoulder. "Take him away," he orders, ignoring my angry protests.

My anger turns to panic as they pull my brother's limp body from the room. "Wait, please! What do you want?" I cry out, still holding on to the hope that I can say or do something to save my brother's life despite failing to save Danny's.

Carnegie ignores me.

The two men drag my brother off without a fight, and Carnegie's voice drops an octave. The monotone way in which he speaks unsettles something deep inside of me. I want to lash out, but I am paralyzed. "I want you to continue on, and sooner or later, you will do exactly what I want you to do, whether you want to or not." He tucks a piece of hair behind my ear as he continues to speak in the same wearisome tone. "Your people won't accept your leadership when your father is gone. Not after Danny. When they find out your husband is a traitor, they won't trust you as they should and will look for someone else to lead them. You will do what you feel you must do to protect your people.

"Your clan is forged by blood, my dear. Blood rules, and you will be the only one left who can fill that order when they need it most. No one other than you will do with Damian gone, but unfortunately, you won't do either."

Soft music fills the atmosphere, and my heart pounds against my rib cage. An anxiety attack surfaces from the pit of my stomach. My entire body shakes uncontrollably, and I glance at Carnegie, confounded and fearful. A small wooden box plays a song I have never heard before in the palm of his hand.

The tremors rolling through my body are not from a normal anxiety attack, the likes of which I have had years to learn to control. I am powerless against this. This is different from anything I have ever experienced, and it is terrifying—uncontrollable.

My vision shimmers like sunlight on ice. "What did you do to me?" I ask breathlessly through chattering teeth, barely holding on to the last vestiges of consciousness.

"It won't do me any good to try and explain it to you right now. You will only remember what I want you to, and that wouldn't be one of those things. You won't even remember most of *this* for a while," Carnegie says. His voice is soft and reassuring. "Don't worry," he continues, "everything will be as it should be."

The music pierces my eardrums with a low hum. The straps over my arms and legs strain against my limbs as convulsions rip through my body, and my eyes roll into the back of my head. My back arches off the table and I yell out once as a shock-like jolt runs from my head to my toes.

It only lasts a moment, but I fall back against the table, drained and weak, as if it has lasted a lifetime.

"It is not too painful, I hope?" Carnegie asks, almost as if he cares.

"W-what was that?" I ask, voice shaking as the music fades. Tears slowly leak from my eyes, cascading over my cheeks one after another.

He disregards my question, a faint smile gracing his thin lips before he speaks. "*Despierta, mi amor.*"

Like the flip of a switch, everything goes black, and I see and hear no more.

Three

A familiar, hard cot, a foot and a half off the cold, hard-packed earth floor, is not where I wanted to wake up. But I will take it because it means I am back behind the tall oak wood fence surrounding the Blackthorn compound.

I would rather be buried under the layer of furs on my dense bedroll, insulated well against the cold earth by a thick layer of pine needles. They do the job of holding warmth much better than the cloth cot under me. The dingy white blanket covering me now barely keeps out the worst of the chill in the air, far less superior than my collection of furs.

No one knows how I got home, including me. All anyone has been able to tell me is that I walked right up to what is left of the South Gate and collapsed at the feet of Warren Payne, the Captain of the Guard who was on duty at the time.

The sensation of having lost time and the pounding headache have left me disoriented. I've been trying to focus on the pale hand-woven curtains hanging around my bed from a wooden pole frame and hammered iron rings. They shade my quaint space, shielding my eyes from most of the light from the hallway. But it blocks out neither the voices, which float lazily over the barrier from the space to my right, nor my thoughts, which have wandered back to Danny with the sight of the iron rings.

Danny made them, along with many other seemingly insignificant things like them. My husband was not the best blacksmith, but he was good enough for the master smith to entrust him with village necessities—no easy feat. He became entrenched in this place more than I believe most people realize. It is one reason I still cannot believe Danny would betray everything he has put his heart and soul into over the past four years.

But he was never accepted as Blackthorn. Surely a man can snap without the feeling of belonging to keep him grounded.

The thought leaves me feeling insignificant and alone. Maybe even a little unwanted, if I am honest with myself.

The lowly flicker of a small pine pitch candle on my bedside table casts the room in a soft yellow glow. I watch the shadows delicately dance across my lap until a familiar voice rouses me from my stupor.

My Father's Right Hand, Jai Norris, has a distinct assertiveness that breaks through the atmosphere with authority, despite his age. He is no more than a year or two younger than Damian, but he has more clout than some senior clan members around here. Hell, even my father listens to his opinions over his son's most of the time.

"Is Chief Vance here?" Jai asks.

"No, sir, Mr. Vance said he had a family issue to attend to. He didn't explain, but he said he wouldn't be back until later," Carika, the head nurse, says in her upbeat tone. I would recognize her chipper voice anywhere. It grates on my nerves even on the best of days.

"Oh, well, is Ms. Iylara awake yet?" he asks her hastily as if it is what he wanted to ask to begin with. I picture Jai looking over the short brunette woman's head to see if he can get a glimpse inside my room.

"She was a few minutes ago," Carika says.

I grimace, not caring to speak to anybody at the moment, especially someone so good at making me talk. Not that I mind most of the time. Jai is one of my closest friends, basically a brother after having grown up together, but I am not sure I am ready to talk—or if I even can.

There is a shuffling sound and footsteps. I look up to find Jai's cropped blond hair peeking through the curtain a few moments later, followed by his over-observant lapis-blue eyes.

I watch him dazedly. Upon seeing me awake, he slips quietly between the curtains. "Ray," Jai says with a sigh, relief written clearly on his sharp features. The candlelight casts dense shadows on his angular jaw and in the hollow of his eyes as he walks over, sitting on the edge of the wooden chair next to my bed. "How are you?"

I stay silent for a moment, trying to find a truthful answer to his question. He will know if I am lying. Reading people is his specialty.

I clear my sandpaper-like throat painfully. "I don't k-know, I—" I stop, not sure how to explain it with my brain working in a fog.

Too many thoughts bounce around the forefront of my mind, and I cannot focus on any particular one without my head pounding. Tears start to well up in my eyes as I search for the words to say, but I cannot keep the waterworks at bay. I sniffle, looking down at my hands lying limply on the quilted blanket.

I try to process the flood of emotions, but my sniffles turn to sobs as they hit me like a ton of bricks. I utterly fail at gathering my thoughts to speak, and the weight of my husband's death lands in an unseen heap on my chest, suffocating me.

I take a shuddering breath, forcing myself to speak. "There is this weight on my chest, and I don't know how to deal with it," I say, tears streaming down my face.

I have to tell him about Danny, but I do not know if I can speak the truth about what has happened. Someone else needs to know, though. I cannot pretend that Carnegie did not finally get what he wanted most.

"Argh!" I groan. I throw my hands up to my face, pressing on my eyes to try and make the pounding in my head stop. It intensifies as a display of fireworks erupts behind my eyelids under the pressure of my hands.

"My head hurts," I whimper, overcome by everything. I look up from my hands at Jai, my face crinkled in distress. "This isn't all some bad nightmare, right? This is reality?"

Jai's brow furrows, and I turn my eyes away from him, not wanting his answer, but needing to hear it regardless. He will not lie to me. It is not in his nature. Jai will tell me the truth, no matter how much it hurts.

"Yes."

I cannot fully comprehend the simple little word, but I watch him nod as he says it, and it breaks something inside of me. I bury my face again, crying into my hands.

"Dan—" I cannot even say his name without reliving his death over again in my mind. My heart twists in my chest as I grit my teeth and clench my fists in frustration.

"I can't *unsee* it," I say, a lump lodging in my throat.

"What can't you unsee?"

I swallow. "Carnegie killing Danny." The very thing plays over in my head yet again, despite my desperate attempts to ignore it, but it is the only thing I can remember.

I would give the world for this to be a bad dream, and to wake up now, wrapped in Danny's warm embrace like nothing ever happened.

"Do you know where you were?" Jai asks, voice quiet.

"N-no. It looked like an old s-storage facility if I had to guess. I don't remember a-anything else, though," I stammer out through tears.

Jai's eyes glisten darkly in the light from the low-burning candle flame. Even with the expert mask, he cannot hide his grief, not from me. I know him too well.

Jai was one of the few who treated Danny like he was any other Blackthorn, not a Charon defector. Not best friends, but somewhere close to it. My gut wrenches. I am not the only one who lost someone close to me today.

Or was it yesterday? The day before?

I do not even know what day it is anymore.

I sit up and swing my legs over the side of the cot. I cannot continue to lay here drowning in my thoughts.

"Whoa, wait," Jai says, realizing what I am doing. He grabs my arm, gently pushing me back down on the pillow. "You need to rest. Doc said you have a concussion."

My memory may be fuzzy and missing time, but I do *not* have a concussion. At least, that is the story I am sticking with. I have no idea what could have happened with the missing time in my memory.

Maybe I am dying.

The thought brings more comfort than any other bouncing around inside my mind. I grit my teeth, unwilling to be given a reason to stay in this bed any longer. "I don't have a concussion. I need to go for a walk. It's suffocating me in here."

I can already sense his next question, 'What happened?' floating around in the air like something tangible. The anxiety building in the pit of my stomach cannot be ignored. The fear of explaining what happened has me on the verge of a full-blown panic attack, so I must escape—or at least put some space between Jai's questioning gaze and myself.

My body protests with aches and pains that refuse to go away, my head being the worst. Still, I push past it, determination overriding the protest from my body with a vigor that shocks me. I am in control on the outside but manic on the inside as I try to control the shaking of my hands.

Jai awkwardly clears his throat as I throw my legs over the edge of the cot. "If you aren't going to stay, I will wait outside." He slides out between the curtains without a second glance.

His quick action confuses me until I look down to find myself in one of those ridiculous gowns without a back. I manage a snort of humor as I put two and two together, but it is half-hearted at best.

A rickety two-drawer dresser sits in the corner. A clean set of clothes waits for me on top, along with my weapons belt. My swords are gone, though, undoubtedly taken from me when I was captured. My pair of light boots sits on the ground beside the aging dresser.

As I slip out of the gown, I shiver in the cool air, and goose flesh creeps up my arms. I look around and find my long, dark green coat hanging on a hook behind the chair Jai vacated; I am relieved to know I will not have to be cold for long. Rabbit fur lines the inside, beckoning me to sink into its warmth.

I slip into the pair of worn leather leggings someone raided from my house, and it irks me. I am grateful to wear my clothes, but someone has been digging around my dresser in our home.

My home, I correct myself. Only one soul lives in the quaint little cabin behind my father's house now, if I can ever step foot inside it again.

And just like that, it no longer feels like home.

I may be overreacting because it would not have been anyone other than my father. But the issue remains on my heart. Home is where the heart is, but my heart is not there—it is dead.

I have no home.

There is a part of me that wants to be angry at Danny's betrayal, if I truly believe it, but the other part of me is too weary with grief to feel or deal with anything at all. I mentally shake away the depressing thoughts as my countenance falters under the threat of new tears and pull the shirt over my head.

I tighten my belt around my waist to hold down the flowing ends of the oversized linen shirt. I doubt my father meant to grab one of Danny's, only wishing to help, but the woody smell embedded in the cotton cuts another pain of longing straight through my heart. It takes my breath away.

I reach out, steadying myself against the dresser as the world tilts. I inhale a shaky but steadying breath and continue getting dressed in a daze. I yank open the dresser's top drawer packed full of socks harder than necessary. I fumble, trying to stop the drawer from falling out onto my toes, wincing as the dresser bangs against the wall.

Jai's voice immediately follows the sound. "You okay?"

"Y-yeah," I stutter out unconvincingly.

"You sure?" I can hear the concern in his voice plain as day, but he withholds himself from entering in case I am still underdressed.

"Yeah." My voice is steadier this time around. "The dresser drawer was stuck," I add, less than truthfully, but if he catches the fib, he leaves it alone.

Jai doesn't say anything else, and I grab a pair of socks out of the drawer along with my leather boots from the floor before sitting down on the edge of the cot again. The socks are thick wool and feel like heaven on my feet. I sigh with pleasure and pull on the mid-calf boots, followed by my coat. I shrug on the fur with another sigh as it envelopes me with warmth, and step out of the secluded room somewhere close to contentment despite everything.

The candle chandeliers strung up along the ceiling are not bright in their own right, but they are much brighter than the single candle in my room. I close my eyes, blocking the harsh light with a hissing through my teeth.

"You sure you don't want to go lay back down?" Jai asks from his place by my room entrance, waiting for me.

I squint through my eyelashes, adjusting my eyes to the light while still managing to cast him a dirty look. "I'm sure," I say shortly, heading off for the exit before he can push the matter.

I get about ten feet down the hallway before Dr. Matthews comes out of the maze of adjoining halls to intervene in my escape.

"Where do you think you are going?" she asks with a motherly yet scathing tone to her voice.

Dr. Lorelie Matthews is a stubby middle-aged woman. Her shoulder-length black curls, graying severely on the right side of her head, bounce with each antagonizing step toward me.

My eyes narrow. I am prepared to be brash to escape this damned infirmary. "I'm going to see my father. Are you going to try and stop me?" I ask her defiantly. Dr. Matthews knows that she cannot stop me from leaving or make me do much of anything; however, it does not stop her from trying to block the small hallway with her wide hips.

"You know I can't do that, but I do have to strongly suggest that you go back to your room and wait for him, ma'am." Dr. Matthews puts her hands on her hips for emphasis, and I huff with impatience as she continues to speak. "You have a severe concussion. If I had it my way, you would be bedridden for at least 48 hours and quarantined in a dark room," she chides.

I am starting to feel like a caged animal. The hall begins closing on me, and anger rises in my chest. "I do *not* have a concussion!" I say for what I hope is the last time. "I'm not staying locked up for days. Not happening. *Goodbye,*" I say a little more harshly than I mean to, but it makes her move out of my way, allowing me to push past her.

"Come see me later, please," she calls after me, a timid tone to her voice now.

I give her a thumb up over my shoulder and make a beeline for the exit. I shove a chair roughly aside in my haste to get out of the building. The anxiety attack building within me becomes more prominent the longer I stay inside. Everything is closing in on me, trapping me under the rubble of my broken world.

Out of earshot of Dr. Matthews, Jai asks, "Did you have to be like that?" He strides ahead, opening the wooden door leading outside for me.

"Thank you," I say as I sigh in relief once we are outside.

Bright sunlight blasts through the wispy clouds drifting along in the unseasonably cold breeze. I hold my hand up to shield my eyes from the light before answering Jai's question.

"And no, I didn't." I frown a little at the thought before taking a deep breath of cold, fresh air. Being rude is not in my nature. That is more of my brother's forte. "I didn't mean for it to sound like that. It just did," I admit.

Jai gives me a look, and I huff at him, guilty at my tone. "I will apologize later. I need to be there for that issue I heard Carika tell you about."

Jai's eyes widen. "You could hear that?" he asks, surprised.

"Yeah, noise carries in that place. I can never get any rest there," I say, looking around at the modest shacks surrounding the village's infirmary.

Charred forest litter lay mere feet from some—a reminder that things could have turned out worse than they did. White stone pathways usually connect every structure to the main path winding its way around the village, but now, ash stains them all an ugly blackish-gray.

There are only two ways to the Chief's Courtyard. Unfortunately, the least populated way is also the longest. Jai leads me toward the South Gate, and the burned remnants of buildings and trees in the entrance square come into view before I can prepare myself.

My heart drops at the sight of the charred rubble where the Apothecary my mother's mother had built. Keena runs it now, or did, because I am usually too busy to hang around all day, but it holds a special place in my heart. I spent many days in my childhood hunting down plants to help fill the shelves. And now it's all gone.

Jai seems unfazed by the destruction. I am sure he witnessed it burning, though, so this would be nothing compared to a raging inferno. I cannot emotionally deal with the wreckage at the moment. There is enough destruction inside of me, and I do not need to add to it. I walk faster, trying to get past the worst part quickly.

"You've only had to spend the night there like twice," Jai says incredulously, oblivious to my internal struggle. "And I was upfront. How could you hear that?"

I head down the path to the Chief's Courtyard, brow creasing at his words, but I do not respond.

I shouldn't have been able to hear him from up front.

Jai's hand reaches out to steady me as I trip over my foot, distracted. He is about to protest my walking about before I shrug him away.

"I'm fine," I assure him weakly.

The world begins to spin around me slowly. I may be lying to both of us. "You have a very distinct, and might I add *loud*, voice," I say lightly, trying to continue like Jai's words have not struck something as off to me.

"Not *that* loud," he mumbles more to himself than me.

I shake off the uneasy feeling threatening to prod the lingering shadow of another anxiety attack back to the forefront of my mind and push on. "I figure everyone will be at the cabin. Let's go."

***

The garden in front of my father's cabin has fallen far from its glory days under my mother's loving care. However, its self-sown and overgrown state still holds a natural beauty. Give it a few more weeks, and nature will prune itself once the frost comes. Everything but the hardiest plants will die out, leaving a skeleton until spring, when the cycle will start again.

The ground my mother cared for carries her memory in the self-sustaining habitat she created for it like the metal curtain rings Danny made. It fascinates me how the little things a person does in life can impact others once they are gone.

Why do we not give those things any thought while their makers are still around?

My eyes wander past the garden, and I freeze in my tracks, wrenched from my thoughts. Beyond the garden to my right, the cabin I shared with Danny stands in all of its glory—the home we made together with our own hands, as tradition dictates.

My heart lurches into my throat, and the earlier anxiety attack starts coming back with force. Jai does not notice and keeps walking. I take a wavering breath and force myself to follow him with a heavy sigh. Having to answer questions would surely be worse than shoving the nauseating feeling aside.

I rip my eyes away from the cabin, focusing on my father's home. It may reside behind a secondary gate, unlike much of the rest of the village here, but it is modest in size. My great-grandfather built it and erected the fence around it right after the Desolation, or Great War as some would call it, as a means to start over. The rest of the village sprung up around the fence over the years as Blackthorn grew and got stronger. The border fence was built about fifty years ago.

After all this time, even my great-grandfather's memory remains, if only within the sawn logs of a cabin in the middle of the woods. Before today, I had never given any of this a thought, but I will not be able to forget it now.

Raised voices cut through the peaceful garden atmosphere before we get to the cabin door. It sounds like my father's deep voice trying to cut through Keena's incessant high-pitch tweeting. Jai moves to knock, but I shove past him. I throw the door open roughly with ever-shaking hands.

Keena stands in the middle of the living room on my father's patchwork rug, tears raging as my father towers over her petite form. Ysabel sits on the couch near the fire, silent tears rolling down her face as she listens to the bickering.

The noise of my entrance draws all three pairs of eyes. My father stares at me for a moment before turning his gaze back on his daughter-in-law. "Enough," he says tersely, looking back at me as Keena sinks into the couch.

Ysabel melts against Keena's side as her mother wraps her arm around her shoulders, pulling her close.

"Iylara," my father says with relief in his gruff voice.

At the sound of my name, I run into his arms, tears streaming down my face again. He holds me as I cry, the furs around his shoulders engulfing my face and absorbing my tears as he comforts me—or tries to. My father is not a compassionate man, but he does his best, rubbing soft circles on my back with his thumbs as he holds me close. It is enough to be held, if only for a moment.

Keena releases a dramatized sigh behind me. I let my father go, turning to her. I am not in the mood for her attitude. "Do you have something else to say?" I ask scathingly, wiping tears from my face with the back of my hand.

Keena raises a dark eyebrow, her chocolate brown eyes filled with frustration. She has no desire to understand why I am so upset. "Only that we are wasting time. We need to find Damian!" she croons.

"He is missing?" I ask, fear feeding the anxiety still swirling in my belly. There is something, a memory, maybe? It scratches at the edge of my mind, but I cannot grab hold of it.

"You didn't know? He disappeared when you did!" Keena retorts.

I look back at my father, searching his age-weary face for answers, but he has none. The last time I saw Damian was when—

"The people who took me were surrounding him when I blacked out," I say, trying hard to remember *anything*. I am on the verge of remembering *something*, but the harder I try to recall it, the more my head hurts, so I stop. I glance over at Jai, who seems to be about to speak but remains quiet.

"We need to send out a search party," Keena demands, looking at my father as he sits down in his chair, a forlorn look darkening his face. "We have to find him."

My father nods solemnly. "We will broaden the search. Get more feet on the ground." He chews on the inside of his beard-covered lip as he stares off into the crackling fire in thought.

"What about Danny?" I ask. I want to put my husband to rest with a proper funeral and try to forget that he might have caused all this.

Keena bristles at the mention of my husband, cutting off my father's next words. "The traitor, you mean? He is missing too."

I turn on her, but Jai grabs my arm, pulling me back.

"Don't you say a *word* against him," I snarl, but I let Jai pull me toward the door.

"I will say what I please. Can you guess how many people are dead because of him?" Keena demands. She already believes wholeheartedly that he is guilty but has no proof that I am aware of.

What will that mean for everyone else?

"He's dead!" I yell at her, unable to find anything else to say. I wrench my arm out of Jai's grasp, leaving the cabin in a swirling of cloth as the anxiety begins to mount once more, nearing full-blown panic.

Keena follows us out of the cottage, unwilling to let it go. My proclamation has not fazed her. I am sure she will silently celebrate later.

"Our people's blood is on your hands. If you hadn't gone off and seduced Danny away from his clan, we wouldn't be in this mess." Poison drips from her voice, and my anger rises to meet it.

"Excuse me?" I turn on her, failing to keep my emotions in check.

Ysabel appears on the porch to see what is happening, but my father pulls her back inside the cabin. I am grateful. She should not have to witness us fight—again.

"You heard me," Keena says, trying to spur me on.

"Walk away," I warn through clenched teeth, trying to control myself. Everything in me wants to lash out.

I stare into her eyes, watching the rage and grief swimming in her misty eyes that mirror mine. I know Keena wants to hurt me, if only to lessen the intensity of emotions raging inside her. I let her have the first hit, merely to have a reason to put my hands on her. Keena does not have much strength, but her fury-filled fist still stings. I shake off the hit and shove Keena roughly with both hands, sending her stumbling back a few steps.

The shove tames her momentarily as she stands there seething, unable to speak or act. She looks appalled that I would even try to touch her. "You get one more chance to walk away. I'm warning you," I say.

Keena disregards my words, finally finding her voice. She does not hesitate to blame me for everything. "This is entirely your fault! Admit it. My husband might be dead because you couldn't keep your legs closed!" she screams at me, tears running down her face.

"Keena!" my father's voice warns from the cabin door. He knows I will only take so much from her.

I hold up a hand in his direction. "I want to hear what she has to say."

My eyes never leave hers as she starts spewing at the mouth. "You couldn't just do what you were supposed to and marry a strong Blackthorn soldier. You had to cross enemy lines and bring a world of hell on us. Your selfishness has brought destruction to our home and death to our people!" she yells.

I react in ill-contained anger. "Are you *kidding* me?" I shout at her, taking a step forward. I want to respond rashly, maybe grab her by the throat and choke the life out of her, but I force myself to stop with what little restraint I have left. Keena is right, but I do not want to admit that my past choices have brought this on.

She strikes as the guilt settles on me. I am distracted, and she strikes my face with a clawed hand before I can block. I hiss as her nails draw blood. I clench my fist, landing one hit to her jaw that sends her sprawling on her back before she can rear back to hit me again. I stand over her, waiting for her to make her next move.

Keena lay there huffing and holding her jaw, but she does not move to get off the ground. Wanting to believe that she is done, I turn to leave her, wishing to escape the guilt beginning to weigh me down.

"Iylara!" My father's voice alerts me to danger.

I spin around as Keena picks herself off the ground with a small dagger in her hand. It is a pretty little thing Damian gave her as a wedding gift. She usually keeps it in an intricately tooled leather sheath on her belt, never removing it until now.

Keena lunges at me, the blade extended toward my abdomen. I catch her wrist as the tip pierces the fabric of my shirt. A sharp sting emanates from my belly as she manages to force the blade into my skin before I restrain her completely, but the wound is shallow.

I push her arm out and away from me; at the same time, I grab her by the throat, pulling her back against my chest. Holding her in a choke-hold, I lean back, lifting her off her feet.

She struggles against me, feet kicking wildly. I cannot feel the impact of her heels against my shins over the adrenaline pumping through my veins. I twist her arm back until it pops, forcing her to let go of the knife. It lands tip down in the dirt at our feet, and Keena screeches in pain as her shoulder dislocates.

Jai grabs me by the arms. He tries to get me to loosen my hold on Keena as my father hobbles across the yard toward us, but I am not done with her. She has crossed the line attacking me like that.

I growl in her ear, grip tightening on her throat to get my point across. "Come at me one more time, especially with my mother's blade, and I swear, I will kill you with it."

Without another word, I let her go, throwing her to the ground. She collapses in a heap, gasping in pain while she holds her shoulder, arm hanging limply at her side. She gazes up at me in a dazed shock. My father kneels beside Keena, assessing the damage I did.

Jaw clenched, I say nothing and stalk past Jai. Heading out of the courtyard gate, I make the mistake of glancing up to meet my niece's wide eyes as she stares at me in fear from the cottage door.

The girl has enough issues as it is, and I keep adding to them.

Four

I find myself standing under the Willow tree outside the village in a small meadow—my thoughtful place. It's been quite a while since I've been here. The state of the area only adds to the sadness inside of me.

The once lusciously green grass crunches underfoot as I approach the tree. Its leaves hang yellow and fading—dying after weeks upon weeks of no rain, and the creek that runs by it is bone dry. Yellows and browns have taken over my once vibrant green forest meadow. Even the familiar blue sky has turned dark as if changing along with my mood. A drizzle of water begins to fall on the earth around me, but the miracle of long-needed rain is lost on me.

Keena's screams of pain still echo in my ears, but all I can see is the fear in Ysabel's eyes. Keena and I have fought before, but this time was different. Keena was the one to pull a blade on me, but the fear I saw in my niece's eyes was fear *of* me, not *for* me.

I stifle a sob as crisp grass crunches behind me. Wiping my eyes, I grimace as the rough fabric of my coat scrapes the claw marks on my cheek from Keena's fingernails.

I look up as Jai steps through the trees. "I shouldn't have done that," I say solemnly before he can speak.

All of my anger has ebbed away, leaving me distraught and exhausted. I cannot even fathom the unknown eternity I currently stand at the edge of. I grip my upper arms, trying to hold myself together before I fall apart.

"Why is this happening?" I ask pitifully, unsure if I want an answer or not.

Jai watches me for a moment, mulling over my question. "Life doesn't generally go how we want it to," he says. "Shit happens," he adds, placing a comforting hand on my shoulder.

"Seriously?" I ask. I expected some kind of poetic answer, not brutal honesty. After all, he is my father's adviser, regardless of our friendship. Tactful life advice is his thing. My anger rears its head, and I pull away from his hand. "And I guess everything happens for a reason?"

Pain flashes in Jai's eyes, but he shoves it aside, being patient with me, as always. "I am, actually, and yes. I would like to believe that everything does happen for a reason."

I let out a mocking laugh, and Jai's nostrils flare as his patience begins to wear thin. "You expect me to believe that? You sound like my father."

"Believe what you want," he says with a frown, "but when you realize why something has happened a certain way, you will know I am right."

Jai is ever-wise—it sickens me.

"Whatever," I say, shoving past him for the village. I can no longer find solace in my thoughtful place with him here.

Jai grabs my arm, forcing me to turn and look at him. "Don't do that. Don't shut down," he says.

I shrug away from him again. "Too late."

Lightning strikes with a bang on the other side of the creek, making me jump. With a huff, I take off back home as the rain starts pouring down around us. Jai follows closely behind me as

I sprint for cover, but our efforts are futile. We are soaked before we reach the South Gate.

The rain has cleared the streets, except for the handful of children dancing around in the rain with mouths open wide toward the heavens.

"You want a drink?" Jai calls out through the deluge, shielding his eyes with his hand from the rain pelting our faces.

"Sure, why not?" I grumble, none too happy to be drenched in the rain. The effort of running home has doused my anger, but I am holding on to my foul mood. I see no reason not to.

"Well, don't get so excited about it," Jai says lightly, trying to break the tension radiating off me. "Come on. Eddie opened shop in the cafeteria." I ignore Jai, stomping off down the path for the cafeteria with water squishing in my boots. No use in running anymore. The rain has now softened to a dense mist, sticking to our wet skin and hair like dew.

The bar may have burnt to the ground, but the wine cellar was untouched. Good thing, too, because tensions are already high enough. Or maybe that is just me. Without liquor to ease it, I am not sure what would happen.

The cafeteria is a large dome building made from felled pine trees and scavenged metal with a large skylight in the center. The cloudy sky gives no amount of decent light, and torches have already been lit, lighting the room with a soft orange glow.

Eddie stands behind a makeshift bar drying a glass on the far side of the cafeteria. I make a beeline for him, ignoring the people who stop eating or talking to watch me walk across the cavernous room. I focus on Eddie, trying not to let my ears settle on the whispers that start up. I do not want to know what people have to say. I plop down on a stool at the end of the bar. Eddie migrates over to us as Jai sits down next to me.

"What can I get you, dear?" Eddie asks, slinging his dirty dishtowel over his shoulder.

"Whiskey," I say brusquely.

Eddie glances at Jai, eyebrow raised. Jai shakes his head once, and Eddie turns to grab the whiskey bottle on the counter behind him.

"Same for you?" he asks Jai over his shoulder.

"Sure," Jai says, observing me from the corner of his eye. I ignore him, staring at the whiskey bottle in Eddie's wrinkled hand.

Eddie slides two shots of whiskey our way, and I inhale both before Jai can even reach for his. With a pinched face, Eddie refills both glasses without asking. I slide one toward Jai and toss the other back as he does the same. I give Eddie a dark, narrow gaze, and he refills the glasses once more without a word.

"Thank you, Eddie," I say apathetically before dismissing him with a wave of my hand. I may be slightly more rash than usual, but I can't help it. After everything, the depression settles over me, blocking out anything good from my mind. I do not see how it can get any better than this.

Not now.

We have had nearly a decade of relative peace. Sure, things get tense occasionally, but it usually comes down to minor disputes that are quickly taken care of with one-on-one fights to the death and so on. Never anything major.

After a deliberate attack on Blackthorn's center of power, there can be nothing but a war in our future. I have always liked fighting but never wanted to see war again. As a little girl, I witnessed enough horrors of war to last a lifetime. And I was shielded from the worst, for the most part.

"Life went to hell pretty quick, huh?" I ask Jai flatly, downing my fourth shot.

He sighs deeply. "Yeah, it did." Jai gulps down his shot, wincing at the amber fire going down his throat.

"You know what makes it so hard?" I ask him, voice already tinged with whiskey fuel anger.

"What?"

"My father will try to stop me from fighting when the time comes. After everything, I know he will not allow me the chance to get my revenge," I say, a sour downturn to my thin lips.

"If something happens to you, there isn't an heir if Damian is dead," Jai says.

I frown in confusion, and regret shadows Jai's face. "Do you know something about Damian?" I ask, worried.

Jai hesitates for a moment, but he is not one to lie or withhold information when asked directly. "Zeke Rekkon sent me a message. He said rumors were swirling around that Carnegie had Damian killed, but he couldn't be sure who the man hanging in the square was."

"Danny's brother?" I ask, shaking my head in denial. "No. My brother is alive," I say defiantly. I will not believe anything else.

"I hope he is wrong," Jai says, avoiding the possibility that I would be a fool to ignore. Maybe I am a fool, but I do not believe I could handle accepting such a thing right now.

"Ysabel will lead when we are gone," I say, trying to lessen the blow Jai's words strike.

"Ysabel is *eleven*," Jai says, making me frown. "She has quite a few years until she is anywhere near ready to lead. A lot can happen between now and then. You would allow Keena to lead your people if your father, brother, or you were not here?"

I huff. Jai is correct, but I do not want to accept it.

He continues, ignoring me as I have done him very recently. I grit my teeth. "Without you, Blackthorn will fall."

I freeze, something clicking into place inside of my brain. Again, that nagging sense of having forgotten something important comes back. Jai keeps talking, and I have to focus on his lips to keep from losing myself in my mind. "Keena will run this place into the ground. You can have your revenge in other ways."

I tap my shot glass on the bar, alerting Eddie as my frown deepens. "And how would I do that if I can't kill the bastard behind all of this?"

"You're smart. I am sure you can find a way. Death is not always the worst thing in the world," he says.

"No?" I ask in a scoffing tone.

"No, it isn't. It is the easy way out if you ask me." Jai pauses, letting me take the shot Eddie pours. "Do you want to talk about something?" he asks gently.

I slam the empty glass on the bar, making both men jump. Eddie scurries off to serve a couple at the other end of the bar.

"Talk about what?" I hiss. "About the fact that my husband was murdered in front of me and is now hanging to rot somewhere as a trophy? Or that my brother's fate may be the same?" I turn to him, my voice dropping to a desperate whisper.

"Or do I want to talk about how my husband most likely did exactly what Keena has accused him of?"

I sit back, regretful and wide-eyed. I should not have said anything, but the whiskey loosened my tongue.

Jai looks shocked, as he should. "He *did* do it?" he asks quietly, knowing that no one else needs to know about this. The people likely already have their theories because if Keena is anything, she is a gossip.

I grit my teeth, looking Jai hard in the eye. "You cannot tell anyone." My voice is pleading, but I do not hide the unspoken warning in my tone. There will be consequences and repercussions if he speaks a word of this to anyone. "Please," I add because he is like a brother to me. I should not be threatening him into silence.

"I won't tell anyone. I know what they would do," he says, holding my gaze.

"Thank you," I say, looking down at my hands in shame. "Keena was right," I admit. "This is entirely my fault—even more so than Danny if he did betray us. I still refuse to believe it, but damn it, it sure looks like he is guilty. I cannot deny that. If he did open the gate, or whatever else I am sure people believe, he was betrayed too. Carnegie lied to him to get him to do it, if he did it." I am grasping at straws, and Jai does not answer. He will not lie to me, not on this. But silence is worse.

Jai finally speaks, but his words are not comforting. I did not expect them to be, but they still sting. "Nothing can make his actions okay if he did do it. You know that, right?" Jai always speaks the truth, even when I do not want him to. It is one reason my father values his opinion so much.

"Yes, but I love him. I still believe he loved me. He made a bad choice, and he died for it. Isn't that penance enough?"

Jai holds his tongue, but he wants to say something, anything, I am sure. But I believe what I said, and there is not a single thing he can say or do to change my mind.

"I would like to be alone now," I say quietly, looking down at the counter in disdain.

"Okay," he says, getting up to leave. "Don't drink too much," he adds. I do not miss the sideways glance he gives Eddie, who nods in understanding.

"Sure," I say before swallowing another shot in one rebellious gulp.

Jai knows Eddie cannot deny me, and he heads off with one last glance back at me, worry written all over his face.

His concern will not move me. "Another round, Eddie," I say with a pointed look, offering him both of the shot glasses to refill.

Eddie sighs before conceding. "Yes, ma'am."

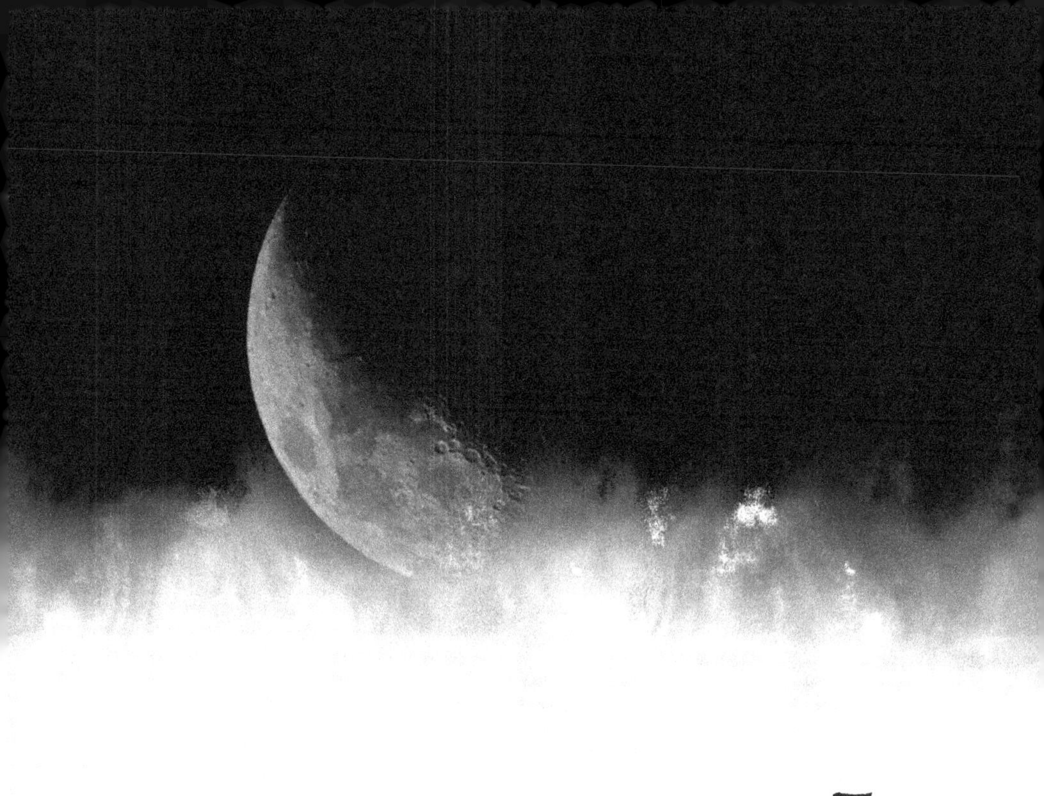

Five

I am out of control, and my life is spiraling into chaos as it falls apart around me. I have never felt turmoil swirling in the pit of my stomach as I have of late, and I am beginning to believe I am not wholly in control of myself.

But that could be the whiskey.

This jarring sensation inside me is far beyond the usual anxiety I am so attuned to, nearly overwhelming me.

I tap out after two more shots and leave without a word to Eddie. I will pay him later. The old man's gaze weighs heavy on my back as I unsteadily make my way out of the cafeteria. But I am always in control of myself—in front of the masses.

As a part of the ruling family of Blackthorn, I've been conditioned to hold it together under the scrutinizing gaze of our people. 'Never show your weakness to the public' is my life motto. We are the manifestation of the people's strength. If we fall apart, so do they.

It is a heavy burden to bear, but it is one I've been trained to carry on my shoulders. But even now, I can feel my feet digging into the ground beneath me, dragging me into a suffocating pit under its weight. I do not think I can muster the strength to climb out alone, but I cannot bear the company of anyone right now.

I slog my way back home, numb from the alcohol in my bloodstream. I do not falter at seeing the cabin I shared with Danny. Not this time. My blurred vision is a filter against the reality of my world, and I am unaffected.

The numbness spreads outwards from my chest, making its way down to my fingertips and toes. As though on autopilot, I shamble inside and roll up a few furs. I tie the bundle to Danny's leather rucksack, identical to the one I left at the safe house.

I should get that one day, I think dismissively.

I shove a change of clothes into the bag with a package of dried fruit and jerky. I take a dagger and short sword from the weapon rack and slide them into the sheathes on my belt before turning to fill up my canteen. I cannot feel the cold water from the well-pump sink as it splashes over the sides of the container and my fingers. I should acknowledge that this is not normal, but I don't. I can't.

My mind is blank as my hands move of their own volition. I watch, but I can't feel it. I can't stop. My fingers lithely wrap around the two bottles of corn liquor under the kitchen sink. I uncork them with my teeth and turn the bottles upside down. Then I begin to twirl.

Liquor splashes around me, grasping at everything it touches. It rolls in rivulets down the walls and soaks into the blankets and rugs. The pungent smell of alcohol permeates the air, taking my breath away, but I don't stop until they are empty. I let go, and the bottles hit the walls with a shatter. A dark part of me rejoices as the broken pieces rain down to the ground as shattered as I am.

From inside the bedside table, I grab a pack of hand-rolled cigarettes I keep for a rainy day. Heading for the door, I pull one out and place it between my lips. Despite my lack of touch-sensory, the taste of delicate mint leaves envelops my mouth as

I breathe in through my mouth. I can feel the heady high before I even light the tobacco.

I inhale deeply as the end of the cigarette ignites in the small flame of a match and take one last look around the room. The earthen tones are drab, and the sand floor is only made bearable by the fur rugs, but it is home—*was* home.

Now it is a dark cell of painful memories.

Standing outside the door, I drop the flaming match at my feet. It lands in a puddle of liquor and ignites with a whoosh, quickly spreading across every surface unlucky enough to have come in contact with the alcohol. I languidly step away, never taking my eyes off the fire engulfing the structure. Flames pop, sending burning debris into the air as the thatched roof catches fire. Within seconds the entire thing is consumed in a raging inferno.

I take a deep drag off the cigarette and flick it into the flames as the first of the shouting starts. I dart into the dark toward the back exit and away from the chorus of voices converging on the blaze.

"Iylara!" a voice cries out desperately.

I am afraid my father has spotted me, but no. There is too much fear in his voice to have seen me. He must assume I am inside, but it doesn't matter. I still can't feel anything, not the cool night air on my skin or the light mist swirling through the air. My body acts and reacts as though in control of itself, with no input from me. My feet take off in a sprint carrying me away into the forest.

***

I don't know how long I run, but weariness finally overcomes my body. Every ache and pain that has so far been numb to me as my feet have carried me further and further away from the village finally catches up to me, forcing me to stop.

I brace myself against a large pine tree, gasping for breath. It only takes a moment, and my knees give out. I crumple to the ground, choking sobs ripping at my parched throat.

How did I get here?

Blinking, I glance around at the trees, and my vision clears brilliantly. The noise of the woods around me grows louder, like I am coming out of a tunnel. My senses are heightened as the fog clears in my mind. The forest animals around me scurry about, sounding like men tramping through the woods. The rustle of leaves in the wind is like a heavy breath in my ears. I can almost taste the dirt of the earth around me, and the breeze washes over me like crashing waves.

"What in the world?" I wince, my voice sounding as if I were screaming in my own ears.

My hands start shaking. I *did not* choose to come out here. It was like my body was taken over, and I went with it in a daze.

I didn't even think twice about it.

It felt right then, but now I am horrified at what I have done.

Why would I burn it down?

I stare down at my hands, sticky with corn liquor I could not feel spilling onto my hands.

You snapped. It happens.

"What?" I ask, frightened at the proximity of a man's voice. The familiarity screams at me, but I cannot put my finger on how I know it.

Looking around, I find no one there.

I am in your head, my love.

"Danny?" I ask in a hopeful whisper, but Danny never called me 'my love.' I stand with weak knees, eyes sweeping the trees for any signs of movement.

No.

I am rooted to the spot, a million thoughts running through my mind, and I cannot settle on one.

It is shocking, I know, but you don't need to be scared.

"I'm not scared," I say, "only crazy. I can't do this." I turn and walk away, but I cannot escape my mind.

You can try to run, but you cannot hide.

Anger rises in my chest, but another voice stops me dead in my tracks before I can retort back.

"Can't do what, sweetheart?" The voice is rough and unfamiliar but very much real and nothing like the voice in my head.

I turn to face the voice's owner as he steps out from the brush behind me. I unsheathe the dagger and sword, holding them out in front of me defensively. My eyes narrow in distrust.

A second, larger man follows the first, and adrenaline rushes through my veins. Both men are filthy and bare the signs of a hard nomadic life.

The voice speaks again, catching me off guard, but I do not let it show. *Forest rats,* it says, as if I need to be told.

"Anything we can help you with, sweetheart?" the first, smaller man asks.

"No, I'm fine," I say stiffly.

The man ignores my blades, speaking cordially. "Well, that's not what it sounded like, did it, Bill?" he asks the bulkier yet younger man next to him.

Bill shakes his head. "Sure didn't, Frank. What do you say we help each other out? How does that sound, doll?" The man named Bill speaks in a greasy voice. They smile at me with blackened, rotting teeth, and I cannot contain the disgusted grimace that spreads across my face.

Bill takes a step forward as Frank speaks. "What's wrong? Cat got your tongue?"

I take a step back, the grip on my blades tightening. "Oh, don't be like that. You're such a pretty thing, ain't she?" Bill asks Frank, beady black eyes never leaving my face.

"Mmmhmm," Frank purrs, licking his cracked lips. He steps forward to stand next to Bill, but I hold my ground this time.

"Stay away from me. I'm only going to warn you once," I say, fight quickly taking over flight in my brain. An unfamiliar blood lust bubbles up inside of me, emboldening me.

Bill raises his hands in surrender, but Frank draws a short, rusting sword from a sheath on his belt. "If she ain't gonna put out willingly, maybe we should just take what we want," Frank says darkly, caressing the ill-kept blade lovingly.

"I don't think so," I say with finality.

"You should make it easier on yourself. I don't take too kindly to 'No,'" Frank says, holding his blade out to touch my own as Bill draws two rusting daggers from under his jacket.

Fear of being outnumbered rises in my throat, but it is quickly doused by anger under Frank's hungry gaze. I run my sword down the length of Frank's, testing the waters as resolve settles in my belly.

"You sure you want to do that, doll?" Bill asks. "I don't think you know who you are up against."

I narrow my eyes as I stare at him. "I don't think you know who *you're* messing with, and I'm positive," I spit out.

I strike before either man has time to react.

Twisting my sword around Frank's, I push up and out. Frank's wrist bends with it until he lets go. He stumbles back with a yelp, blocking my dagger from coming at his face with his bare hand. He cries out in pain as the blade slices through his palm like butter.

With a growl, Bill brings his daggers down toward my chest. I thrust my blades out in front of me to block, staggering backward as he bears down on me. I dig my heels into the dirt to keep him at bay, but he is much too large to hold back for long.

Our faces inches apart, I gag at the smell of his putrid breath. Holding back bile, I push him away with everything in me. The force sends me, rather than him, stumbling and I struggle to maintain my footing.

I turn at the sharp sound of Frank stepping on a twig behind me. I sidestep his fist rushing through the night air, barely missing my face. I slash out at him across the abdomen. He withdraws with a hiss of pain as I duck and spin back to face Bill. I deflect his blade with my sword to slash him across the ribs with my dagger.

"Bitch!" Bill doubles over with a growl of pain, protecting his midsection.

"And you thought this was going to be easy," I taunt. "You should have thought twice before messing around with a Vance," I say arrogantly.

There is recognition in the men's eyes because they know the name—clan-less or not.

Frank retreats to pick up his sword before turning back to me. "I don't care who you are. You are just some bitch we are gonna gut," he says before lunging at me.

I knock his blade away with my sword, but my foot catches on a tree root as I shuffle backward. Frank's fist lands a right hook on my jaw in my desperate attempt to stay on my feet. The impact spins me around a full one hundred eighty degrees, and I fall to my hands and knees.

Frank kicks my sword away, leaving me with only my dagger to contend with. He towers over me, and I kick, knocking his feet out from under him. Frank hits the ground with a grunt, and Bills rushes at me. I roll to avoid being pounced on by the hulking man.

A meaty fist grabs hold of my rucksack, yanking me back and throwing me to the ground. I hiss in pain as the buckles of the pack cut into my shoulder. I try to scurry backward, but Bill grabs my boot, pulling me to him like I weigh nothing. I swing my dagger at his head, but he deflects it with a metal arm guard, knocking the blade from my hand. Bill pins me to the ground with his legs and wraps his fingers around my throat. I yank and claw at his hands, but I cannot break his vice-like grip. Even in an injured and weakened state, the man is much stronger than I could ever hope to fight off from this position.

"I love watching the light fade from their eyes," he says as Frank stands to his feet.

My vision begins to blur as my body starts to struggle for oxygen.

This is not your end.

The voice would be comforting if I believed it, but I can no longer fight against the brute of a man hell-bent on choking the life out of me. The little bit of hope that I have left begins to fade.

The ringing in my ears muffles Frank's voice. "Don't kill her, Bill. I can't get my jollies off if you kill her. Dead bodies make me soft."

Bill lets go with a sigh a moment before I lose consciousness. He gets up, leaving me gasping for air on the ground. I roll over and push myself up on my knees.

Frank pants in anticipation. "Hold her still."

Bill grabs me from behind, pulling me from the ground as he pins my arms back against his body. I throw my head around weakly, trying to make contact with his face, but the back of my head hits his collarbone. As Frank starts tugging at my belt, I let out a pained, desperate cry.

"Hey now, sweet thing, don't make this so hard. You might like it," Frank says through a hungry grin.

My ears begin ringing again, and my vision turns red as he kisses sloppily down my neck. My belt hits the ground with a thump, and time slows down as he lifts his head to look at me with lust in his spirit-less eyes, his fingers working at the clasp of my pants.

I smile sweetly despite it all. How I can manage such a thing is beyond me, but it has nothing to do with submitting to this man's will—that's for damn sure.

Frank smiles devilishly, believing that the smile on my face is a good thing, but he is wrong.

Oh, so wrong.

Frank leans forward, and I strike, my teeth sinking into the side of his throat. He screams out and tries to pull away, but a predatory growl rumbles in my chest. I bite down harder and yank my head back, taking a chunk of Frank's neck with me. Blood gushes from the wound. Frank screams in agony, grabbing at his neck as he tries to stop the torrent of blood cascading down his chest.

Stunned, Bill lets me go out of pure shock. I turn, head-butting him before he can retreat. I don't feel the pain through the adrenaline driving me as my forehead connects with his face. Bill cries out, holding his broken and bleeding nose. He looks at me in terror, and I smirk with satisfaction at the sight of his fear.

I yank a small dagger from his belt, unhindered by the man in his hesitation. I ram it into the side of his head, straight through his temple. I pull the blade out, staring blankly into the black pits of Bill's eyes, the light of life gone from them. He crumples to the ground dead as Frank collapses behind me with a gurgling sound. Frank twitches once and moves no more.

As reality sets in, I drop the dagger and stagger away from the two dead men, spitting out the chunk of flesh still held tightly between my teeth.

Violent shaking starts in my hands, making its way up my arms, and before even a moment has passed, my entire body begins shaking in shock. I violently vomit, bracing myself with my hands on my knees until nothing is left in my stomach. It is mostly whiskey and leaves a bitter taste in my mouth, but I welcome it over the caustic bite of iron.

I collapse to the ground once more, still shaking. I desperately try to wipe the blood from the lower half of my face, but I only succeed in smearing it around.

"What have I done?" I ask no one, my voice coming out in a low rasp. Bill's hands have damaged my throat, and even the simple task of swallowing is nearly unbearable.

But the pain is overshadowed by something else.

Taking drastic measures to preserve my life and dignity is not that astonishing. What *is* astonishing is the ecstasy swirling around in my belly like a gusty wind. It would make me sick again if I had anything left to throw up.

I look to the heavens as if the sky will answer me, but my vision begins to blur and spin. I rub my eyes, trying to clear the haze clouding my vision, but the trees turn to mush around me as I try to focus. I blink, and everything goes black, snuffing out the sound of my heart hammering away in my ears along with my vision.

It would be utterly silent if not for the faint chuckle that sends a shiver down my spine. I cannot place the familiar voice through the crackle of what sounds like an antique record player or understand the language, but the words are plain as day. "*Tu seras mia, mi amor.*"

Six

How long have I been gone? When will this hell end? Is anyone even looking for me?

These are all questions I have asked myself for only God knows how long—if there is a God. I'm not getting an answer.

I cannot even get an answer from that strange voice in my head. It is there, telling me to keep going and not to give up whenever I believe I have nothing left, but it never answers my questions.

Ice water rushes down my throat, suffocating me as I inhale out of pure shock, caught off guard by the strong hands of the man behind me. Coughing and gagging, I try to calm myself, despite the fire in my lungs overcoming the icy water, making me wish for it to return. I will take the ice over fire any day, but my wants are laughable.

I am the fire.

My handler, the owner of the strong hand gripped tight in my matted hair, pulls me out of the water before I can embrace the peace of darkness. I violently spit up the water that continues to choke me, and my ears ring from the lack of oxygen. I gasp covetously at the damp, stagnant air around me. Water streams from my hair into my eyes as I search for the light I know all too well. It hangs in the center of my hell, a literal and figurative light in the dark.

The edges of my vision darken, and sparkles shimmer in the harsh white light, but they fade with a decent breath of air. I completely ignore the well-dressed man watching on quietly with his hands clasped behind him, his face hidden in the shadows.

The hand in my hair forces my head down again, back into the barrel of ice water. I suppress the gasp that threatens to inhale another lungful of water and go still. But he knows what I am doing and doesn't let me up. My lungs ignite from a lack of oxygen, even without the deluge of water. Against my self-control, I begin to struggle, desperate to make the pain stop and so very desperate to breathe.

My movements weaken, and only then am I lifted from the water and thrown unceremoniously to the floor in a limp heap. My head hits the concrete, and I cry out in agony. Tears mix with the water dripping off of me onto the floor. I roll onto my back, searching for my light, and savor each wretched breath that slowly puts out the fire in my lungs.

Part of me believes that this is all some sort of horrible nightmare that I can't wake up from, but it is far too real for me to believe that wholeheartedly. The light is the only thing that allows me to hold on to reality. Without it, I sink inside myself, and someone other than me takes over as a now all too familiar song plays in the background. I don't know who she is, but she isn't nice. Not that I was ever considered nice, but she is something else—a whirlwind of fury and anger finely tuned into an obedient and blood-thirsty wolf.

And when the man in the shadows says jump, she asks how high.

She asks with *my* mouth, *my* voice. She controls *my* eyes that travel around the bare room to find her Master's eyes when he finally steps out of the shadows. His gray-blue eyes stare at her, at *me,* in adoration. The man only shows himself to her, and I forget his face as soon as she sinks back inside me again.

She is me, and I am she. We are one, and I have no say in the control of what she proudly calls her meat suit.

My body.

And the worst part of it all?

I can't look away when she does terrible things with *my* hands, and I don't even know her name. I can't do anything as *my* hands wrap around the stranger lady's throat. I can't pull away as *my* fingers choke the life out of her. And I can't look away as the light leaves her eyes.

I cannot stop the satisfied smirk that spreads across my lips as I sit back and study the lifeless woman from my spot on top of her, where I pounced on her like a starving lion. The pride within me when the man says, "Good job, my dear," sickens me, but *she* is delighted.

When the light is gone, I have no control. I might as well not even exist anymore—until she sleeps. As she slumbers, her control fades, and I am brought back in control of myself. I come back to stare at the hands that have become a terrible weapon to kill without question.

I am brought back to fear *myself.*

I no longer sleep. Not when every time I close my eyes, the only thing I see is the light being extinguished in nearly a dozen people.

Over and over again.

No one can overtake her. No one can overtake *me*—not even the biggest man.

He falls the hardest.

I don't know any of them, but I do not doubt that it wouldn't matter. If the man in the shadows says kill, I kill.

We kill.

I can't escape it. I can't escape *her* because she is me, and I am she.

My masked handler offers his tattooed hand, an intricate star prominently inked on the back and unfamiliar runes on his fingers. Every single one is different, and if I were anywhere else, I would wonder what they mean.

But I can't care. Not here.

I take his hand time and time again. His skin is soft and warm to the touch—soothing despite what that hand has done to me. He pulls me to my feet, only for me to kneel before my Master—to let his praises sink into my very being.

When my Master's hand cups my face, I smile brilliantly at him in adoration. My life purpose is to serve him—to do his bidding. I understand this within my spirit as the terrible guilt that haunts me subsides, and peace washes over me. It frees me of my tormented mind so that I can embrace this *other*.

I forget all the pain and shove it inside the dark, overflowing corners of my mind to be recalled later—to torment me when I least expect it.

Seven

I bolt upright in a cold sweat. Disoriented, I look through the darkness around me. A mass of trees surrounds me, but nothing is familiar. I do not recognize the forest, and I do not know how I got here.

These are not my woods.

The waxing moon shines down on me, dimly illuminating the expansive and unknown pine forest. Still, I can make out every twig and leaf as if it were daylight. The area was cleared recently by fire, and sparse new growth has already sprung up with the absence of the pine straw floor of the forest.

Ash coats my backside from being on the ground, staining the tattered leather of my pants black as I attempt to brush it off. My hands go still, and I stare down at my torn shirt and pants, trying fitfully to remember something.

What happened? These clothes were in good condition when I put them on. And where is my coat?

Confused, I run my hand over my loose hair. It is dreadfully knotted and greasy, hanging loose from my usual braid.

What the hell happened?

The forest sounds grow louder around me as if the volume of the world is slowly being turned up. With it comes the sound of purposeful footsteps striding toward me, growing ever closer. I reach for my blades, but my belt is missing, along with my sword and dagger. No rucksack in sight either.

The bare forest floor offers me no concealment other than the pine trees. I scamper behind a relatively large tree, trying to determine from which direction the sound comes. The noise bounces off of and around the trees, melding together with seemingly no particular point of origin.

What am I doing here?

I do not expect an answer and jump involuntarily as that same voice from before speaks again.

For your piece of the puzzle—the key.

Well, that is not comforting, only confusing. Not to mention crazy. *Puzzle? Key?* I cannot help but question this seemingly free-thinking voice in my head.

The key to your progression.

What progression? I get no answer in response.

The footsteps approach, and I have no place to run. I lean up against the tree I try to hide behind, fear bubbling in the pit of my stomach. I grasp desperately at the hope that maybe it is dark enough for me to be overlooked, but it is a feeble hope—the growing light of the moon is bright enough tonight to illuminate my face, even filtering through the tree canopy as it does.

I pause as the realization hits me. That moon was beginning to wane the last time I looked up at the sky. Now it looks to be only a few days away from being full again. It takes around three weeks for that.

Three weeks.

What the hell?

Carnegie Lysander steps through the trees, nearly dragging me screaming from my mind. His vibrant eyes bore into my own as he pockets a black box. I feint right, making a break for it, but Carnegie is fast—impossibly fast. His leather-clad fingers close around my arm before I can even get ten steps away. He yanks me backward, slinging me to the ground.

I grunt on impact more out of frustration and fear than pain. The soft ground pads my fall, and I quickly push myself up. My fingers grope for anything I can use as a weapon on the charred forest floor. They close around a blackened but pointed pine branch. I hold it out in front of me defensively, as if it could do that much damage.

Desperation makes fools.

Drop it, the voice in my head says softly.

No. I can kill him now and be done with all of this. I am talking to a voice in my head. This is crazy.

I am crazy.

"You won't need that," Carnegie says, motioning at the stick.

I glare at Carnegie, ready to shove the stick in his eye. "Why are you here?" I demand, matching his smug demeanor with malice.

Carnegie feigns hurt at my words. "What, I can't check in on you? See how you are doing after everything?" He speaks as though we are old friends.

"No," I growl, actively searching for the opportune time to strike with the meager stick in my hand. The charred thing will surely snap after the first strike. I have to make it count.

Carnegie ignores my hostility. "It's time to go home."

"Really?" I ask with a sneer, trying to keep my emotions under control. "Why?" If looks could kill, my revenge would be made so much easier.

Carnegie holds out a large silver signet ring in the palm of his hand. He speaks three simple words, freezing me in place and rendering me unable to process the thought of trying to kill him.

"Damian is dead."

My eyes lock on Damian's ring in Carnegie's palm, engraved with the Blackthorn crest. The metal shines dully in the moonlight against the backdrop of Carnegie's black glove, entrancing me.

I have never seen my brother without it, not once since he passed the initiation into manhood and received it as his prize at the age of twelve. The coyote is engraved with such precision as not to miss a detail, including the snarling teeth.

Unshed tears pool in my eyes as Carnegie reaches over to grab my hand, ignoring the stick still in the other. I do not strike out, but I weakly attempt to jerk away from his touch unconsciously, captivated by the ring as I am.

Carnegie holds fast until I stop resisting him and places the ring in my palm. He closes my fingers over the cold metal, and I stare wide-eyed at him. His ice-blue eyes keep me frozen in place, like a mouse mesmerized by the cat cornering it.

"This is merely a piece of the puzzle—the key to your progression. It's all a part of the bigger plan," Carnegie says innocently.

My heart skips a beat. "What?" I ask, astounded at his word choice. I must have heard him wrong.

Carnegie's grin widens, but he ignores my question. *"Drop the stick, Iylara,"* he says, a strange quirk to his voice.

My hand moves of its own volition, and I drop the stick without hesitation at his command.

"Good girl," he says with a genuine smile.

I jerk as if prodded with red-hot metal, coming back to myself. The same sensation that led me out here in the first place fades, and tears well up in my eyes.

"Why did I—" I ask, looking at the stick lying at my feet, then back at Carnegie with wonder—and complete terror.

"Because in the end, you will always do what I want," he says, leaning close to me as if it is our little secret.

Something clicks in my brain almost audibly, and words once forgotten come rushing back to me. *Sooner or later, you will do exactly what I want you to do, whether you want to or not.*

I choke back a frantic sob as the visage of Damian, beaten bloody and dragged off to his death, flashes before my eyes. I sink to my knees with a moan, clasping my hands in front of me with my brother's ring between them. Carnegie stands back, watching me patiently as forgotten memories play in my mind, paralyzing me. Agonizing seconds pass before there is a finality with the feeling of cold water covering my face. I jerk with a gasp, the familiar sensation of suffocation taking my breath away.

Despite how horrible they are, I should be glad to have my memories back. But knowing the truth is worse than living in blissful ignorance because it solidifies Carnegie's claim.

My brother is dead.

My grief once again clouds my mind, but the burden of forgetting something eases. And yet it does not disappear completely, and I now have more questions than answers.

"It will all make sense soon, but until then, know that if you ever need me, just holler," Carnegie says with a devilish grin. The quirk in his voice comes back as he adds, *"Go home."*

I am incapable of speaking, as if I have lost the ability to form words completely. I nod my head, unable to control myself. I will do exactly as he says, and I have no idea why.

What is happening?

That single question is the only one I can form in my tormented mind.

Carnegie turns to walk away but stops mid-step to glance at me over his shoulder as if stopping to answer my unspoken question. *"Tu seras mia, mi amor,"* he says in a velvety voice with a sideways smirk.

He turns on his heel, disappearing into the woods with a swirling of black coat-tails, leaving me in shock.

"Oh my God." My voice comes out in a whisper as that now familiar voice floods my mind. The voice that called out to me from the dark in a language I did not understand.

I have been listening to the same voice since I ran off without question. Uneasily, yes, but that is beside the point.

Now, uncannily, I understand what the words mean before he speaks them in my mind, his voice now all too familiar. How I never recognized him before is beyond me.

You will be mine, my love.

***

It takes the rest of the night and half the morning, but I step foot through the newly repaired South Gate at around ten o'clock. There is barely any recollection of the journey home, and I have no idea how long it has been since I ran off into the woods.

Three weeks. No, that can't be right.

I stop mid-step, looking back at the progression of the repairs in the South Gate Courtyard. Nearly complete buildings have been erected in the place of what was lost in the fire.

That isn't something that can be done in a few days. But, if possible, more pressing matters distract me from that troubling thought. For one, Damian's ring bounces against my leg in my pocket, never letting me forget Carnegie's words.

"Damian is dead."

With those words, my grief has resurfaced, becoming a constant companion trailing after me. But it cannot hold a candle to the torment raging inside me over the voice in my mind. Not to mention my inability to do anything other than drop the stick and walk home after Carnegie told me to do so.

I never stopped walking—merely continued like it was the very thing I wanted, but I did not want to return. I also did not personally know the way home, but my feet sure did.

Damian's ring triggered something inside of me. I can remember all too clearly what happened when I was taken, but the pain of Danny's death is somehow muted inside of me now. The loss of Damian is fresh. I do not want to face my father and tell him his son is dead, but I must because he deserves to know.

Remembering what happened is much more than seeing Damian to solidify Carnegie's claim. It is also the realization that he *did something to me*, and I have no idea what. All I know is that the one person I want to kill is also the same person invading my mind—who can *control* me. None of it makes sense.

Whispers and pointed looks follow me as I walk the path toward my father's home, and I am all too aware of how I must appear. I pick up the pace, nearly running for my father's cabin.

"Ma'am?" the gate guard asks, surprised to see me as I skid to a halt outside the closed gate. "Where have you been?"

"Around," I say with a wave of my hand. The guard raises an eyebrow but does not question me further. "I must speak with my father," I say, pushing through the gate without waiting for him to open it.

"Chief Vance is in the War Room, ma'am."

I slowly turn at his words. "Why?" I ask, dread flitting around like butterflies in my stomach.

"Some men showed up before dinner last night asking for a meeting with him. He has been entertaining them all night," he says.

My brow furrows. "Charon?" I ask.

I am afraid of meeting Carnegie again, but I know it will not be him. This is something else.

"No, ma'am. They go by Vesper," he says.

"Thank you," I say. Turning around, I head for the War Room on the northwest side of the village, near the creek, trying my hardest to ignore every confused look that comes my way.

***

I hurry down the carved dirt steps overlaid with wooden planks but stop at the bunker door, my hand outstretched to touch it, but only just. With a deep breath to prepare me for the inevitable, I place my hand upon the stone door, much like the one leading into the safe house. The stone pricks my fingertips, and the heavy door swings open on silent hinges after absorbing the droplets of blood.

The narrow hallway opens up to a domed room. Roots hang from the ceiling, and the walls are lined with hardwood bookshelves. The smell of damp earth permeates the air in a thick haze, and a slight water leak trickles down the back wall. The water collects in the sunken dirt floor that restrains the muddy puddle on the floor underneath.

Large leather-bound volumes fill the shelves, with even more stacked on top. Most books were destroyed during the Great War, making my father's collection one of the largest in the region, or the world for all we know. But nobody is keeping tabs on that sort of thing these days.

Charts and maps cover a large oak table in the middle of the room, and the space glows in the yellow light of wall sconces made from goat horns. My father stands huddled around the table with three men, deep in conversation.

My father looks up at the sound of my echoing footsteps. His eyes widen as they land on my silhouette in the mouth of the hallway. "Iylara, where the hell have you been?" he asks, disregarding the other men.

"That doesn't matter right now," I say, causing him to raise an eyebrow questioningly. "Can we speak in private?" I glance between the men, and the oldest stands straight with pursed lips as if aggravated that I interrupted.

My father grits his teeth, failing to restrain the frustration in his voice as he speaks. "Gentlemen, will you please wait outside for a moment?"

"Sure," the oldest says. "Don't be too long," he adds coldly.

I openly glare at the men as they walk by. The disrespect in the older man's voice sparks a disdain in me for him immediately. His is peculiar in more ways than one, including his choice of dress.

The man's attire matches what I imagine a suit to look like from before the Great War. I have only ever seen such a thing in picture books my mother once read to me as a child. Seeing one in person solidifies my impression that they are stiff and uncomfortable.

The dark gray of his suit brings out the silver in his gray-blue eyes and perfectly styled chocolate hair. As he walks by, my glare fades into a frown as his eyes land on me. Something is familiar about them, and that nagging pull to recall something I have forgotten scratches at the edges of my mind again.

Once the door shuts, my father looks hard at me, and the feeling vanishes. Amid the disappointment and frustration, there is relief in his eyes. "Then what does?" he asks, voice softer than before but still rough and hardened with exhaustion.

I cannot find the words to speak and reach silently into my pocket instead. I pull out Damian's ring and lay it on the table.

"Oh God, no!" His voice is barely audible, but I can hear the pain he cannot contain at the sight of his son's ring. He knows the chunk of silver well, having been the one to put it on Damian's finger.

Tears spring up in my eyes at the torment in his voice. My father carefully takes the ring, holding it in his palm as he gazes mournfully at it. "I knew it," he says, shaking his head, "but I didn't want to believe it."

"I'm sorry, father." It is hard to speak through the lump in my throat.

I never believed Damian was dead until I did, but somehow my father already knew. I merely brought the evidence. I feel wretched inside. If I had stayed in the safe house when he told me to, my brother would still be alive.

My father stares at the ring for a few silent moments before speaking. "We will grieve properly in due time." He swallows hard and takes a shaky breath, forcefully replacing the sorrow on his face with determination.

I do not understand how he does it. Maybe he has already cried all the tears he will shed for his only son in private. It is the only reasonable answer.

"We have to look at what lay in front of us, and those men are from a group called Vesper. They are not part of any war clan like we are. They prefer diplomacy over fighting and want to speak with us, Blackthorn and Charon alike, on neutral ground."

Through the sadness threatening to overwhelm me, fury rises at the thought of diplomacy with Charon. The world would be much better off without the lot of them. "You mean to say you will just sit down and talk peace with those bastards? Like nothing has happened? Like no one has died? Like—" I close my mouth before I say something I cannot explain. Something I cannot tell my father.

Carnegie needs to die, and now for more reasons than mere revenge. If he is dead, he cannot invade my mind. There is no way in hell that we could live peaceably together now. But my father can never learn about this. I don't know what he would do if he found out I have been compromised.

If I were not the only surviving child of my father with a duty to uphold, I would disappear into the woods again and off myself—save everyone the trouble that may come upon us because of me. Since I cannot do that, I must not let Carnegie get the chance to use me against my people—while keeping the truth of our strange connection to myself.

Under normal circumstances, my tone would anger my father. But now, his voice is softer, almost pleading. "If Charon agrees, we need to go and listen to what they have to say." The lack of backlash stuns me. He steps around the large table, hugging me before I can protest. "We will need to talk about where you have been later. When the cabin first caught fire, I thought you were in it."

I stiffen under his touch but relent to wrap my arms around his broad back. I will try to avoid that conversation, but it won't be easy.

"How long was I gone?" I ask into his shoulder, barely audible.

He pushes me away to study my face. "Three weeks," he says after a moment. His eyes have a questioning look, but I watch it fade as he replaces his concern with the business before him. "I need to talk to these men some more. Vesper wants to end the fighting before it begins, bring us all together." My father heads for the chair next to the table, sitting down with a grunt.

"What did they offer you?" I ask, knowing there must be something in it for him. He has never been eager to drop arms against anyone before, especially Charon.

My father looks at me thoughtfully, mulling over his words. He averts his gaze, taking a deep breath. "Peace of mind," he says after a moment.

Something about how he refuses to look at me now sends a nervous tremor down my spine. It is a pretty evasive answer, and I cannot help questioning him.

"Don't you think the people should have a say in whether we fight or not?" I ask. "You can't decide this without presenting it to them first."

My father nods, still avoiding my gaze. "Yes, but first, I need to talk to Luther and his advisers some more. What the people want may not be what is best for them." The tone in his voice all but screams, 'No more questions.'

There is no point in arguing with him over this at the moment, but he is crazy if he thinks I will drop the subject entirely.

"I will see you later then," I say, saving my argument for later.

"Alright, sweetheart," he says gruffly. My father's eyes meet mine once more, but it is like he is looking through me rather than at me. "Send the men back in, please." He smirks at me, but his grin doesn't meet his eyes. "And go take a bath. You stink," he adds with a wrinkle of his nose.

I sniff my armpit with a huff. "Sure thing." He isn't lying.

I hesitate, realizing something. I turn back to face my father. "Where is Jai?" He should be here for peace talks—or any kind of talks.

My father falters, and my heart starts to beat faster. "Luther didn't want him here."

My eyebrows nearly disappear into my disheveled hairline. Jai has never been absent for something as important as this.

"It's okay," my father assures me—or tries to. I am not assured in the slightest. This all feels very wrong. Jai is a voice of reason—*the* voice of reason—against my father's own very unreasonable voice.

I withhold my question under the heavy dismissal in my father's stern eyes. He will not give me a straight answer. Not yet.

Stepping outside, I turn to the formal-looking man waiting on the left side of the door, assuming he is Luther.

"You can go back in now," I say snidely.

"Finally," he says, disappearing inside once again. The other two men remain silent as they follow him.

Jerk.

The door shuts behind the men, and I shuffle off with a swirling storm of anxiety in my belly.

I hope my father knows what he is doing.

Eight

The current of the icy river gently glides around my bare feet as I walk back to the bank. I almost feel like a new woman, free of the dirt and grime caked up in all the wrong places. It took longer than I would have liked to scrub and untangle my hair in the swirling river current, but I could not bring myself to chop it all off.

I flex my toes, squishing sand between them while watching the pine trees lining the opposite riverbank sway in the gentle evening breeze. The trees block out the harshest mid-afternoon sunlight, but the abundance of goldenrod lining the bank brightens the shade-dappled river.

Shivering in the cool breeze, I slip my coat over my damp shoulders and crawl onto a large stone jutting out of the sandbank. Turning my eyes to the swathes of goldenrod, I watch it sway hypnotically while running my fingers through my hair, not nearly as absentmindedly as I would like.

If I cannot keep my mind from replaying my newfound memories, I will surely lose my mind, but if it goes silent, another voice will be there to fill the void. I am not sure what I would prefer: Bloody images of my brother and the sensation of ice water flooding my lungs or his killer's voice in my head.

You are stronger than you think you are. Carnegie's voice is soft, something I do not associate with the vile man.

I scoff but do not reply. That is a lie. I am more fragile than I have ever been. I do not miss the compliment, but I cannot bear to agree with Carnegie, of all people, on *anything.*

He does not let my silence deter him. *You think I am lying. You have already bought the lie that you cannot continue. It will destroy you if you let it.*

I bang my forehead against my knee with a groan.

Just shut up, I plead.

My fingers find my hair and roughly pull it into a braid over my shoulder.

If you could remember everything you have forgotten, you wouldn't push me away like this.

My fingers freeze in their braiding, and my eyes widen as fear courses through my body like electricity. I look up from my hair, staring blankly out over the water. "What else have I forgotten?" My voice is faint, and my heart starts racing. There is an instinctual knowing deep inside of me that I cannot explain. All my anger toward Carnegie twists into an ugly knot of terror, constricting my throat.

My father said I was gone for three weeks. Weeks! Carnegie is *not* lying. I *have* lost time and forgotten who knows what, but to be told it is real? That is something else entirely.

Everything he doesn't want you to remember—not yet.

His words sink into my being as though he has screamed them, silencing the chorus of thoughts in my mind. "Who's he?" I sit upright, ignoring how crazy I must appear talking to myself—not that anyone is around to see me.

There is no answer.

"Why even bring it up if you aren't going to say anything?" I ask, my anger returning to uncoil the knot that constricts my voice.

You will understand soon enough, he says after a moment.

I growl out in frustration, abandoning my hair. I stand up hurriedly on the stone like it will prove my point to someone who cannot see me. "I am done with cryptic answers!" My distraught voice echoes across the water, but Carnegie does not answer, leaving me with a silence that only makes me angrier. "So much for being helpful," I spit out, staring at the sky with narrowed eyes.

It is almost too easy to forget who I am talking to when it is only a voice in my head. It should affect me more than it does, but some part of me has already accepted that this is how it will be—for a little while at least.

I hope.

I have *completely* lost my mind.

Letting out a heavy sigh, I hop off of the rock, landing with a grunt as my feet sink into the sand. My body is sore, but I cannot recall why—one of the many mysteries ruling over my now complicated life.

I shove my soiled clothes into my bag before slinging it over my shoulder. I do not even bother putting my boots on before heading home. I opt to swing them childishly at my side if only to distract myself with the rhythmic beat they pound out against my leg with each footstep. When that does not work, I try to revel in the softness of the pine needles covering the worn path under my bare feet, desperately trying to ignore the words repeatedly playing in my head.

If you could remember everything you have forgotten...

But what have I forgotten?

***

"This running off thing is becoming a habit I do not like, Iylara," my father says as soon as I step through his cabin door. I feel like a teenager being chastised for staying out past curfew again.

I bow my head, knowing I was gone longer than I should have been. "I was bathing in the river. I'm sorry. I should have told someone where I was going—" My eyes fall on the half-empty whiskey bottle sitting on my father's chair-side table. "When did you start drinking?" I ask, trying to change the subject as I grab a glass from the cupboard.

"Not too long ago," he says, pouring me a glass as I hold the cup out to him.

I sink into the soft leather couch cushions with a sigh and tuck my feet under me, warming my chilled toes under my bottom. I cradle the glass of whiskey like a steaming mug of tea. The amber liquid glows in the light of the roaring fireplace that warms the room a little more than necessary.

My father sits quietly in his recliner, staring at his glass. "How did the meeting go?" I ask, taking a sip of my whiskey.

He clears his throat, looking up at me. "We got word that Chief Lysander has agreed to meet with Vesper and ourselves before Luther and his advisers left.

"We leave for the Market in three days. Luther is supplying food and music. A way to show the people he means well. We have a supply wagon with some things we can trade to make a good impression with him. I suggest you take notes," my father says. He takes a long drink of whiskey, downing the rest of the glass. "I'm not arguing about it either."

I clench my teeth, biting back a futile argument. "What has you drinking?" I ask.

Most would miss the slight slur in my father's words or how his eyes droop, but I can see it. He has been hitting the bottle hard. The last time he drank this heavily was when my mother and sister died. Otherwise, he usually stays away from the stuff.

My father looks at me with sorrowful eyes but doesn't say anything.

Damian.

That is why, of course. I still feel as though I am dreaming, and none of this is real. To honestly acknowledge that my brother is dead will surely break me past the point of ever being mended again. Not just because it is my brother, but because of the repercussions it brings. My mind will not process it all, and my nightmares become my reality when I think about them too long. It is all I can do to not buckle under their weight.

I slipped out to the river while my father relayed the news of Damian's death to Keena. She was hysterical, of course. I could hear her wailing as I escaped out of the North Gate. Even though my father would not let me go with him and hear it for myself, I know she blames me. She practically shrieked that very thing at the top of her lungs for the entire village to hear.

I take another sip of whiskey, bracing myself to ask the one question rattling around in my head that stands out amidst the chaos. “Are you so gung-ho about Vesper’s promise of peace for the sake of peace or because you don’t trust me to lead our people when you are gone?”

My father looks up at me too fast for comfort, and my stomach drops. Sure, Luther showed up while I was gone, but my father only agreed once I was back and clearly in line for the throne after him.

My father doesn’t trust me, but if I am honest, I don’t trust myself either. “I might not have raised you to lead, but you are smart. I know you picked up a thing or two over the years.” He tries to deny what I already know, but I shake my head.

My father’s gaze falters, and he turns away. Something has him seriously unsettled, and it is more than his son’s death. The man before me never falters and averts his eyes from those he speaks to. Yet that is all he can do when talking to me now.

“Don’t lie to me,” I say quietly, tears filling my eyes.

My father gnaws on the inside of his cheek, his eyes darkening as he looks up at me. “There are things you do not understand—things I cannot tell you, Iylara. Please trust me when I say that I am doing what I am doing for the good of our people.” His voice is unsteady, and he appears decades older than sixty. “And for God’s sake, don’t make me answer that question.”

A tear rolls down my cheek as I stand. I swallow the rest of the whiskey in one gulp and nod. “Yes, sir.”

I set the empty glass down on the counter and flee the cabin. I don’t know where I am going, but I refuse to sob like a child in front of my father. He already doesn’t believe I can lead Blackthorn, regardless of what he does or does not say. I will not give him any more reason to think I am weak.

The only thing worse than my father’s unbelief is my knowing that anyone else would be better suited to the job than I am—even an eleven-year-old girl.

Nine

The wagon trundles up to the side door of the Market. I cannot overcome the creeping and constricting anxiety that has had my foot tapping the entire ride here. My father has not said anything, but the sour look on his face and his tense jaw tell me it is driving him crazy. Jai stays silent next to me, and I try to ignore the concerned look on his face.

I hop down from the wagon before it comes to a complete stop, but I halt in my tracks at the sight of a checkpoint at the entrance door. Jai mutters something to my father as he helps him out of the wagon, but I'm too preoccupied with my thoughts to hear his words.

Today you cannot get inside the Market without a pat-down—a weapon-free zone. I have an issue with the entire thing, which I voiced to my father when he told me about it. He then reprimanded me, telling me to trust him, which I do, but he is not the problem. My trust issues are with everyone else.

A blonde-haired woman in black stands guard at the checkpoint and motions for me to stop as we approach. My heart rate increases as she begins to pat me down.

Don't look in my boot. Please don't look in my boot.

The small knife I keep in my boot weighs heavy on my conscience. Despite my father's warning, it felt wrong to go without it. My trust only goes so far. I couldn't bring myself to enter the unknown without some form of protection.

The thought of using it on Carnegie when I have the chance still dances around in my mind. We can have peace without him—even more so if you ask me.

I sigh with relief as the woman finishes her search, allowing me through without inspecting my boots. For a moment, I felt regret at undermining my father's orders, but now that I am inside the Market, the feeling fades away.

Today, the Market barely resembles the old dirty warehouse that it is. Bright lights have been strung along the walls, giving the place a more welcome feeling than the torches have ever achieved. Tables full of finger food and drinks sit on one side of the room, and black curtains hang along another wall as a backdrop for a group of musicians. They play a twangy upbeat song on beautifully crafted instruments, the likes of which I have never seen before.

I glance around the room to find X-marked Charon talking civilly to tear-drop-marked Blackthorn for the first time. Something like this has not happened in years, if not decades, and the people somehow manage to put their differences aside and act cordially with one another. This is what the people want. The Market may be neutral ground, but each clan usually tries to avoid the other on a day-to-day basis. To witness anyone conversing amicably like this is beyond strange to me.

We are purposefully brought together, but the hope that it brings cannot squelch the anxiety mounting within me. It grew stronger the closer we got to the Market, and now it has me biting my nails, which are quickly becoming nubs. I will draw blood soon if I don't stop, but something is brewing under the surface of the civility around me. I cannot explain how I know it, but it's there.

Leaving my father and Jai to converse with a man at the door, I creep to the closest food table, trying to avoid human interaction. Glasses of a bubbly pink liquid catch my attention, and I head for the table they sit on.

I pick up a glass and inspect its contents. Brow furrowed in curiosity, I bring the glass to my nose and sniff—my nose wrinkles at the overly sweet smell of flowers and some vaguely familiar fruit.

"It's champagne," a voice says from behind me.

I turn in haste, trying my best to keep the surprise off my face as memories flood my mind from nearly six years ago—back to the first day I met Danny and the man standing before me.

***

"Are we gonna gut this bitch or not?" the lanky black-haired teen asks. His voice is almost as dark as his almond-shaped eyes.

"No," the honey-haired teen next to him says, voice low. His amber eyes glow with a light the first is missing as we stare at each other.

I am arrested in the grip of a rather large woman pinning my arms none too gently behind my back. Something about the man freezes me, rooting me to the spot. The spark in his eyes captivates me, warming something inside of me that I have never felt before.

"What?" the dark-eyed teen asks, bewildered.

Amber-eyes shakes his head slowly. "I said no." His voice is languid, silky.

The dark-haired teen darts his eyes between us, eyebrow raised in question. "So you want to keep her?"

His amber eyes never leave mine. "I didn't say that. You know how I feel about slavery, Max." He speaks as if they could get away with keeping me as a pet.

Over my dead body.

"Well then, what do you want to do with her?" Max asks.

"Let her go."

"Let her go? Have you lost your mind, Danny?"

Danny turns his eyes from mine to glare at Max. "Did I stutter?"

The woman behind me remains quiet, the two of us watching the duo arguing in silence. However, I do not miss her fingers tightening around my wrists. My captor waits for instructions, and I wait for an opportunity.

"Let her go," Danny says again, and the woman's grip disappears from my arms.

I stand silently, still frozen in place. "Run," Danny says, leaning toward me slightly. "Don't stop until you get home."

So I run, knowing deep inside that it is not the last time I will see those amber eyes. I cannot help the smile that pulls at my lips.

***

"You good?" Max Parker's voice breaks me out of my memories.

I stare at the dark-haired and well-muscled man, caught like a deer in headlights with the shock of seeing him again. The gangly teenager is nothing but a memory to me now. He has grown into his own, that's for sure. But regardless of his cordial smile, he is not someone I care to act peacefully with.

That can happen when a person wants to kill you for the fun of it.

I restrain the urge to blow everything and draw the knife in my boot meant for Carnegie, but it is not worth it. Killing Max where he stands would bring on a world of trouble no one needs, so I take a wildly different route from the scene playing out in my mind's eye.

I force a smile across my face. It comes out more like a grimace, but my voice is more in line with my act. "Champagne? Never heard of it," I reply conversationally. I take a small sip while praying it isn't poisoned. I smack my lips at the sweetness of the drink. "It tastes almost like—"

"Rose and blackberry," Max says, smoothly cutting me off. "Or so he says."

"He?" I ask, annoyed with his interruption.

"Luther Cain. He is Vesper's Chief, but they call him Commander or something. He supplied all the food and drinks as gifts of hospitality. Even brought solar panels for the lights—big ones," he says, eyes flashing as he grins. "And that isn't all they got," he continues, taking a step toward me.

Every part of me wants to lean away from Max, but I hold my ground as he speaks softly. "This meeting could be very beneficial to all of us. Wouldn't you say?" he asks, tilting his head quizzically. "I can put our differences aside. Can you?"

Max extends a hand in peace, bridging the short distance between us. It takes everything I have to force my hand out to shake his. Turning him down would not bode well for the image my father is trying to portray, but that does not make my skin crawl any less as our hands grasp each other in a tense handshake. His skin is cool and calloused.

"Well, that was nice of them," I say with a more grateful tone than I thought I could manage. I jerk my hand back too quickly, and Max smirks.

"Very much so," Max says, downing a glass of champagne in two gulps. He discards the glass on the table and takes another step forward, lowering his voice as he speaks in my ear. "Meet Carnegie on the rooftop in five minutes."

My heart drops, and nausea swells in my belly. I cannot come face-to-face with Carnegie. I am afraid of what he may make me do. I did bring the dagger to kill him with, but my plan never got further than that.

Don't even think of running. Carnegie's voice is soft, a mere whisper in my mind, but he means business.

I glance around, surveying the area. Dotted around the room are pairs of eyes watching me—waiting for me to make a move. Someone will drag me to stand before him if he cannot compel me through our connection.

That thought is terrifying, to say the least.

Maybe it will be easier to meet him without causing a ruckus or forcing his hand to reveal if he can indeed control me at a distance—easier on my mental health, anyway. I could end up dead.

Max steps away with a subtle grin on his face. He turns and walks away without another word. I stare after him in a daze. It takes a few moments to gather myself before I can move my feet. I finally take the first step, and my feet take over. They lead me to the dilapidated staircase on the other side of the room like they already know where to go.

***

The second floor creates the ceiling for half of the first, and the balcony opens the way to the cathedral-style roof over the central area of the warehouse. Unused storage rooms line the wall across from the balcony, only interrupted by a small hallway at the end.

I head for the hallway, my feet guiding me until I stop in front of the last door on the left. *Roof Access* is neatly hand-painted on a sign nailed to the door. I reach out, slowly turning the rusting knob as my heart thunders away in my chest.

I shouldn't be doing this.

The door creaks open, and I step into an empty, sunlit room with a narrow set of metal stairs on the opposite side. I cross the room, my footsteps echoing off the walls, the sound pounding in my ears like drums.

I place a foot on the first stair, testing it. Not even a creak of metal as I carefully put all my weight on it. The stairs are sturdy despite the rusting edges, but I take them one breath at a time. My sweating palms leave the railing damp. I take deep breaths that shudder past my lips on release and reach for the doorknob with my bottom lip held painfully captive between my teeth. It takes a little effort to get open, but it swings on quiet hinges with some persuasion and cursing under my breath.

Pebbles litter the roof, crunching underfoot as I step out from under the alcove around the door. Carnegie stands near the roof's edge with his back to me, gazing out over the meadow surrounding the Market. His long black coat billows behind him, caught in the persistent breeze.

"It's about time you found me. I thought you were going to stand me up," he says without looking at me. "I should have known Max would strike up a conversation, though. He talks too much."

"I wasn't aware we had a date," I say, as my olive green coat-tails flap in the soft breeze wafting across the roof in almost perfect unison with Carnegie's. I watch for a moment, caught by the peculiarity.

"It's okay. You aren't aware of much." Carnegie turns to face me. I don't miss the jab, but I remain silent. I turn my attention away from our coat-tails to be frozen again in the iciness of his gaze.

My hand itches for the blade in my boot, longing to lodge it in his eye like I failed to do with the pine branch in the woods—

or I could shove him off the roof. I only have to wait for the right moment.

Carnegie speaks with a resigned smirk on his face. *"Come here."*

The compulsion to comply with the quirk in his tone is too strong for me to deny. I immediately regret coming up here. I walk to stand directly in front of him, teeth clenched, but I am grateful for the opportunity to get closer to him so I can strike.

Carnegie studies me while I stand there rigidly, trying to coerce my body into shoving him, but I cannot even raise a hand to him. A horrible thought occurs to me.

He could probably make me throw myself off.

He looks me over once as he speaks. "What if a person could be changed completely on the inside but remain nearly untouched on the outside?" he asks me softly.

"I don't know what you mean," I say, not much louder, surprised I can even speak.

A sideways smirk appears on his lips. "I mean, what if everything *you are* could be turned off at a moment's notice and turned into something else?" he asks, trailing a fingertip down my pointed nose.

"I still don't understand," I say, peeved at his games. I am growing weary with his words, unable to rid my face of his hand, much less end his life.

"Our mind connection is only the beginning." His words bring fear like they so often do now. It grips me at my core, and I struggle to catch a breath.

Carnegie removes a glove. His hand is covered in tattoos, but I am too entranced to recognize the symbols marked on his skin. He reaches out to cup my cheek with his bare hand. I try to flinch away from his cold touch, but I still cannot move, no matter how hard I try.

My cheek starts to tingle where his fingertips touch me. "You feel it?" he asks.

"Yes," I whisper.

Trailing his thumb over my lips, he lowers his hand to hover above the skin of my throat. Static pops at his fingertips. The sensation increases in strength, and I hiss in pain as he withdraws his hand.

With a pushing motion, he sends me stumbling back without touching me. I catch myself before I fall and bend over with my hands on my knees, groaning at the lingering effects of the shock that ripples through my body.

"As you evolve, you should be able to do the same thing, with greater effect," he says with a friendly smile.

"Evolve?" I stand up straight, refusing to cower before him.

He ignores me. "You are one of a kind, you know that?" he asks.

"Don't try to flatter me," I say, anger boiling alongside horror.

What was that?

"I'm not. Only speaking the truth," Carnegie says, walking by me calmly as he heads for the door. "The power you will be able to possess has the potential to surpass my own. Sound—"

Pulling the knife from my boot, I lunge, aiming for his neck.

He turns, quick as a whip, bringing his arm down as if to strike me. He does not touch me, but the knife is knocked out of my hand, sending it skidding over the edge of the roof. It disappears out of sight, wholly out of my reach.

"You cannot kill me, Iylara. I know you want to, but you are no match for me," he says, disappointment in his voice. "And I thought we were making progress."

I stare at him, speechlessly holding my hand in pain, eyes wide. As if the first time he used that trick was not shocking enough.

Carnegie does not give me a chance to ask questions before he continues, like I have not tried to kill him. "*Walk with me.* We have something to attend to," he says with a full-on grin, the quirk back in his tone.

He opens the door, motioning for me to go first. I step through and fall into step behind him against my will, like a scorned dog who tried to bite its master. We descend the stairs in silence.

Impending finality washes over me, and I cannot withhold my following words as we cross the room. "My father is willing to work toward peace. Are you going to turn that away?" I ask.

He opens the door for me again. "I am here, aren't I?" he asks evasively.

I scowl at him as I walk through the door. “My father is willing to forgive you for what you have done and let you live—even after you killed his son. You wouldn’t try and do anything to hurt that, would you? You know how easily we can take you out,” I passively threaten while prodding for confirmation of my gut feeling.

Carnegie chuckles but otherwise remains silent. I follow him to the balcony overlooking the mass of bodies below us before he finally speaks. “Some things have to happen for others to come to pass,” he says, stopping to look at me, his hands casually gripping the railing in front of us.

“What things?” I do not miss the fact that he has failed to answer my question.

“Just watch. Don’t move. Don’t speak,” Carnegie compels me.

I grit my teeth, my eyes skimming across the mass of bodies carrying on with their business. They are all oblivious to the two of us standing above them in the shadows.

I find my father standing by the food table I stopped at earlier, talking to a rather large Charon man with a bald head completely covered in tattoos. He stands at almost six and a half feet tall. Even my father has to look up to speak to him.

Jai appears, pushing his way through the crowd opposite the room of another Charon man who makes a beeline for the food table. As the man gets closer, he pulls a pistol out from under his jacket. I try to scream out, to alert someone, but I am compelled to follow orders of silence. Jai calls out something unintelligible, and my father glances around.

The bald Charon man grabs Jai in a headlock, keeping him from pouncing on the gunman. Jai says something else as he struggles against him, but I cannot read his lips. My father turns as the other man stops within feet of him, gun raised. The man’s lips move as he speaks to my father, who stands his ground with a dignified look. He stares down the barrel of the gun without flinching.

The people nearby look around, confused for a moment before a blast reverberates off the metal walls of the building. The crack of the gun cuts off the band and shuts down the idle chatter bouncing around the room. My father’s head snaps backward. Jai looks on in shock, limp in his arrestor's grasp, with my father's blood splattered across his face.

Leeland Vance crumples at his killer's feet, eyes staring up at me in death, where I stand next to Carnegie on the balcony. A scream sticks in my throat as blood trickles from a hole in the middle of his forehead. His eyes are accusing.

"Go do what you must," Carnegie says, releasing me from his hold. The smugness is gone from his voice, but the quirk is back.

Shaking like a leaf, I rush for the staircase as the room erupts into chaos with gunfire. At the foot of the stairs, the crowd swallows me. Panicked bodies toss me to and fro, jostling me back toward the door, away from my father's body. I cannot bear the thought of leaving him, so I push against the crowd.

Gunfire rips through the air with an endless ammo supply, and unarmed civilians scurry for the exit. I stand my ground for a second before the wave of bodies is too much for me, urging me to the door. Bullets miss me as people fall dead all around me, unable to escape quickly enough through the checkpoint barricade.

Guns have appeared in the hands of Charon that they smuggled in somehow, and they are making easy work of the helpless Blackthorn inside the warehouse who followed the rules of the meeting. Charon begins to fall as Vesper joins in a firefight against them. The echoing dissonance of gunfire pierces my ears painfully. I have never heard such noise. Charon somehow managed to get a hold of bullets, lots of bullets.

And Vesper, for all of their 'no fighting' nonsense, has the bullets to match them, despite their no-weapons rule.

Jai appears out of the crowd with a snarl on his bloody face as he grabs my arm, steering me toward the door. A sharp gun blast distinguishes itself, louder than the rest, and Jai stumbles. He regains his footing with a groan and forces me out of the warehouse, staying close behind me.

I glance over my shoulder, catching sight of Carnegie on the balcony. He lowers a large revolver in our direction with a fiery look. Jai drags me outside, pulling me none too gently to our wagon. The people who make it through the door scatter in all directions, running across the field, unable to fight back against the barrage of bullets.

"We gotta go." Jai's words come out strained. He roughly pushes me onto the wagon bench with a grunt of pain.

I am in shock. "But my father!" I cry out desperately, about to hop down from my perch. "I can't leave him!"

Stricken with grief, tears pour down my face as Jai shakes his head, grabbing my shoulder. "We can't help him. I have to get you out of here. We can't lose you too," he pleads with me.

Unable to deny his urgency, I nod my head. Jai pulls himself roughly onto the seat next to me. He grabs the reigns, awkwardly holding his left arm, and pushes the horses to follow the path toward home.

My eyes do not leave the warehouse until we take a sharp curve, and it disappears behind the trees.

Ten

"Take the reins."

"What?" I ask in a daze.

"Take the reins," Jai repeats through gritted teeth.

I look at him, and worry settles in the pit of my stomach. His tanned skin has gone pale. He shoves the reins into my hands before I can respond. My fingers grasp the worn leather, and Jai clumsily climbs over the backrest of the wagon bench.

He collapses into the back of the wagon with a grunt of pain. "Get home," he says, barely loud enough for me to hear over the thudding of horse hooves, and then he is out cold.

"Jai?" I yelp, frightened at seeing him like this.

A Y-bend approaches, pulling my attention to the horses. We only have a few miles left, but not knowing whether Jai is alive or dead makes it feel like a hundred.

I stand as the South Gate finally comes into view, waving at the guards on duty.

"Open the gate!" one guard shouts upon spotting me.

I lead the horses through the gate and up the path to the infirmary. Stopping at the open front door, I jump in the back to check on Jai, with a "Get Dr. Matthews!" to Carika, who comes outside to see what is going on. With two fingers on Jai's throat, I find a faint pulse. At my touch, he opens his eyes and looks up at me blearily, coming back from unconsciousness for the moment.

"Asshole was going to take you out the same way they did your—" Jai inhales as a shudder runs through his body.

I strip off the fur covering his shoulders and back to find that blood has completely stained the back of his beige undershirt. A single bullet wound rests off-center between his shoulder blades.

"Dammit," I breathe. "He wasn't shooting at me." Jai doesn't answer if he can even hear me.

I look up as heavy footsteps pound toward us. "Alec, help me get him inside!" I yell out in panic, recognizing the burly, red-haired man headed for us in a sprint.

With a nod, Alec leaps into the back of the wagon, grabbing Jai's head and shoulders while I grab his feet. We carefully lower him down and walk awkwardly toward the door with him between us.

Dr. Matthews meets us at the door with a rolling cot for us to lay Jai down on. "What's happened?" she asks frantically.

"Bullet wound." My voice quivers at the ramifications of those two words.

Dr. Matthews nods, rolling Jai into an open room without another word. Alec follows behind us, brows furrowed in confusion.

Bending over Jai's prone form, Dr. Matthews checks his vitals while I hover over her shoulder. "Roll him onto his side, gently," she says to Alec.

He carefully rolls Jai onto his side, revealing his bloodstained back. Dr. Matthews turns to the shelves, pulling a few jars of herbs and liquids down before mixing up an unknown concoction in a bowl. She sits it on a rolling tray next to Jai's cot, along with scissors, tongs, bandages, and a scalpel.

With the scissors, she cuts Jai's shirt, revealing his back. Dr. Matthews dabs around the wound, cleaning the blood away to assess the damage, and I start pacing.

Too much blood.

"Stop and come here," Dr. Matthews tells me sternly. I raise an eyebrow at her tone but say nothing. I am not helping Jai with my pacing.

I approach with apprehension, not knowing what to do. Helplessness nearly overwhelms me as I stand next to Jai's head, watching blood continue to ooze from the hole in his back slowly.

She hands me a clean strip of cloth from her tray. "Clean his face."

I do not understand what cleaning his face will do for him, but I withhold my question, dipping the cloth in the bowl to find the liquid lukewarm. It smells strongly of mint and basil. Squeezing the excess out, I dab at the side of Jai's face, wiping away the blood with shaking hands.

"Whose blood is that?" Alec asks warily. "Can't be his."

I stare at him, trying to restrain the tears that threaten to spill forth. "My father's," I manage to say loud enough for them to hear. Dr. Matthews glances at me in surprise, and Alec nods solemnly, but neither of them asks any more questions.

Without warning, Dr. Matthews grabs a set of forceps from the tray and starts digging the bullet out. Jai yells out in pain, his eyes opening in alarm. I grab his shoulder in an attempt to hold him still.

"It's okay. Stop moving," I say firmly, trying to be calm for Jai's sake as he attempts to arch away from Dr. Matthews' probing tongs. I don't hide my aggravation from her. "A little warning next time would be nice."

She does not respond, as if I have not spoken, and focuses on her work. I sigh in annoyance and turn my attention back to Jai, who has stopped fighting me. His muscles are tight under my fingertips. He is still conscious.

In record time, Dr. Matthews lifts the forceps gripping a rather large, twisted bullet covered in blood. Jai goes limp, and I look at her with worry in my eyes. "He is out again."

Dr. Matthews nods. "He has lost a lot of blood. We need to find a match for him." She gets up to rummage through a stack of drawers under the shelves on the wall. "Luckily, I already have you all on file. I will be right back," she says, darting out of the room.

"What does she mean?" I ask Alec. "I thought blood was blood."

"You have to have the right blood type to give a person, or their body will reject it, killing them," Alec answers. I stare at him questioningly. "I'm trained as a field medic," he adds.

"Oh, so what will happen without it?" I ask, looking at Jai with fresh tears in my eyes. I already know the answer, but I need to hear it.

Alec frowns, blue eyes glistening. "Without it, Jai dies."

I force tears away, but it is not easy.

I can't lose anyone else.

"But there is bound to be a match somewhere, if not one of us," he adds to reassure me, seeing the distress on my face. "But the match has to be willing to donate."

No, they don't. I will force it from them if I have to.

Dr. Matthews appears with a black box in her hands, her eyes on me. "You're a match. Take your coat off." I unclasp my jacket and slide out of it without question. I sit on the chair Dr. Matthews offers me. She yanks my right arm out straight on the tray. "Don't move," she orders.

I glance up at Alec, unsure of what is about to happen. He nods in reassurance, and I try to steady my racing heart. I turn my eyes to the older woman's fingers delicately cleaning the area of skin in the bend of my elbow. I take slow, deep breaths, my foot tapping with anticipation.

Dr. Matthews looks up at Alec, motioning to the black box she brought in. "Open that."

Alec opens the box to reveal a glass bottle with a strange-looking stopper on the top with hoses coming out of it. Dr. Matthews produces two needles from a bowl filled with some solution from the cupboard and attaches them to the ends of the hoses Alec hands her. She ties an elastic band around my upper arm tightly, thumping the crease of my elbow with her middle finger. In one practiced motion, she steadies my arm and pushes the pointed end of the needle into my skin. I hiss at the sharp pinching sensation but hold steady against the discomfort.

Blood gushes inside the tube, and Dr. Matthews places a piece of tape over the needle to hold it in place. "Stay like that," she says, releasing the elastic band. My arm goes tingly for a moment as blood rushes back to the area, only to be siphoned into the jar. I watch in amazement as my blood fills it before flowing through the other tube. When all the air is out, Dr. Matthews sticks Jai with the needle connected to the other hose, and my blood disappears into Jai's arm.

I lose track of time, entranced by the procedure. I start getting lightheaded as Dr. Matthews hobbles back to me. She removes the needle from my arm and wraps a piece of gauze around my elbow to staunch the bleeding. "You are good to go," she says. "Fresh air may do you some good. You're pale."

I stand up, and Alec has to steady me as the room starts to spin. "Never gone without that much blood, huh?" he asks me, trying to lighten the situation.

I take a deep breath, trying to ease the room's spinning. "Is it that obvious?" I ask in a strained voice. "I might puke," I say, hands clenched around my jacket like a lifeline.

"Jai is going to be fine," Dr. Matthews says.

Jai's pallor is not as drastic as earlier, and his breathing has steadied. I will have to be content with that as Alec leads me outside. The cool air of evening causes goose flesh to rise on the exposed skin of my arms, wet with sweat. It helps the nausea, though, so I cannot complain about being cold for once.

"Would you like me to walk you home?" Alec asks. "You should rest now."

"I can't leave him," I say earnestly, eyes filling with tears. "They killed my father. I can't lose Jai too. I need to be near in case he needs me."

Alec looks at me sadly. "There is nothing else you can do for him. Trust the doc's skills. She knows what she is doing."

He is right, of course. I have seen that woman work miracles. "Fine," I say, taking a slow step forward. "I can do this," I assure myself under my breath.

My knees start to get wobbly after a few feet. Before I can protest, Alec scoops me up carefully in his arms and carries me home as if I weigh nothing.

"Thanks," I mumble, breathing deeply as my ears start to ring. It takes a moment to recede.

"You're welcome, uh—" Alec's brow furrows. "I guess I call you Chief now, huh?"

My breath shudders, and I unconsciously grip the front of his coat. "I suppose so," I say drearily, the cause of my sudden promotion searing my heart like a hot knife.

At the courtyard, the guard hurries over to open the gate to let us through. Seeing his worried face, I force myself to tell him everything is okay, but I am lying. Nothing is okay.

I focus on the buttons on Alec's coat, ignoring the empty place where my cabin once stood. Mother Nature has already begun to cover the patch of dirt with weeds despite the coming of winter.

Alec takes me up the stairs and stops, unsure what to do. "I will be fine. Sit me down on the porch. I'm not ready to go in yet," I say, saving Alec from the awkwardness.

"Yes, ma'am," he says, sitting me down on the edge of the porch. My feet dangle, booted toes brushing the grass underneath.

"Will you stay with him?" I hope it is not too much to ask, but he will do it either way.

"Of course," Alec says with a gentle smile on his rugged face. "I will let you know as soon as he wakes up."

"Thank you," I say again. I don't know what else to say.

"Anytime, Chief," he says, leaving me alone on the porch to silently tremble at my new title.

I'm not prepared for what comes next, but I have no choice but to face it. It is all up to me now to do whatever it is that we are doing.

But what are we doing?

I remember Carnegie's words as if he were speaking to me now. Maybe he is. They pierce my mind, affirming my fears regardless of being past or present.

Blood rules, and you will be the only one left who can fill that order when they need it most. No one other than you will do with Damian gone, but unfortunately, you won't do either.

Eleven

Warren Payne stands in the middle of the living room of what is now *my* cabin, balding head glowing in the flickering light of the fireplace. His voice is somber as he recalls the scout report. "Despite favoring diplomacy over fighting, Vesper could not look past what Charon did, ma'am."

He sounds as tired as I feel. His one good eye droops with exhaustion, and the eyelid of his blind eye has fallen shut, hiding its milky white color. His salt and pepper beard is looking saltier as well. No one has slept in days, worried we may be attacked again as we lick our wounds.

"I would hope not. There isn't anything much lower than one who takes advantage of peace talks to slaughter the competition when they are defenseless. It is dishonorable," I say, sinking into the end of the couch closest to the fireplace. "All anyone has these days is their word. What did Vesper do about it?"

"Report is they took control of the Market after subduing Charon, but they didn't put them down as I would have done, ma'am. Some whispers speak of cages and torture, but it sounds like wild speculation over something none of us know anything about."

I take a sip of the whiskey from the glass in my hand, staring into the low-burning fire in thought. "All I know is that Vesper sent wagons loaded down with ammo, guns, medicine, and our dead—" *including my father's body.*

"I heard, ma'am. How will you respond?" I turn my eyes to Warren, chewing on my lower lip. Curiosity gleams dully in his olive green eye.

"I haven't decided yet," I say with a slight shrug. "I will figure it out once we have dealt with the funerals. They need to be put to rest—all of them. I don't care how long it takes. The morale is low enough without tossing corpses in a mass grave."

"Yes, ma'am. I will keep the Watch on guard."

I nod my head. "Good. Dismissed."

Warren beats his closed right fist over his heart once with a bow of his head. He leaves the cabin, and I turn my attention to the fire, downing the rest of the whiskey in one gulp.

***

Thanks to Vesper, we can give our people a proper send-off before they start rotting. Funeral pyres have lit up the riverbank for days, and nearly every Blackthorn from the outer villages has made the pilgrimage here. Our village was not the only one that lost people.

On either side of my father's unlit pyre, memorial flames already burn for Damian and Danny. As the next Chief, no one questioned me when I commissioned Danny's pyre next to the others, but many still whisper.

Whether I could ever prove Danny's innocence or not, some believe he is guilty. I will be hard-pressed to change their mind when I am not sure of his innocence myself. So, for now, I will ignore it. The fact that I do not have the bodies of my brother or husband to close this chapter of my life has not fully hit me, but I am grateful to be able to put my father to rest. There is something to a proper funeral, and whatever happened to the two men's corpses is too morbid to ponder.

The pyres are built on the river's edge, overlooking the white sand bar meeting the water a half-mile from the village. Rose petals litter the ground around the wooden structures where some of the children took it upon themselves to help decorate for the send-off—spearheaded by my niece. The red petals glisten like blood in the torchlight surrounding the meeting area. Who could tell a little girl that she should not pick the last of the year's roses for her grandfather's funeral, much less her father's memorial? A shortage of rose petals in the newly rebuilt Apothecary is nothing compared to the importance of this single night.

Small ceremonies have been ongoing for days, but tonight will be different. Tonight we are sending off a Chief. Our Warlord. My father. His coyote pelt mantel rests on my shoulders, shielding me from the bitterly cold wind that whips my wool skirts around my ankles. The cold of winter is approaching fast, nearly two months ahead of schedule.

The Matron of Death, a white-haired woman who tends to our dead, appears from the shadows. She ignites the torch in her hand by the flame of Damian's pyre, and the riverbank goes silent. She slowly lowers the flame, resting it in the cavern underneath my father's body in silence. Tongues of fire crackle to life and spread out from the point of contact with the mother flame, sputtering around the base of the pyre before fully engulfing the shrouded figure on top.

The Matron speaks, but I cannot focus on her words as I watch the flames dance across the latticework of tattoos on her wrinkled face. Her milky eyes glow orange in the fire as she turns to meet my gaze. She motions for me to step forward, and I kneel at her feet.

The Matron lays a short ceremonial dagger into the flames of my father's pyre, heating it to red-hot. She speaks with her low, ambient voice ebbing and flowing in unknown tongues. The sound sends shivers down my spine. She slips the coyote fur from my shoulders, brushing the thin straps of my shirt away to expose the skin beneath, and withdraws the dagger from the fire. She holds it in front of my face, and I peer into the yellow-orange heat pulsing through the metal. I should fear the pain it will bring as it scars my skin, but I almost welcome it.

With one side, she presses it into the skin on my right shoulder. I grit my teeth, withholding the hiss of pain I wish to exude, but I must go through with this in silence. To show pain is to show weakness. The leader of Blackthorn cannot be weak.

My nostrils flare, and I close my eyes as the putrid smell of cooking flesh fills my nose. The Matron pulls the blade away, placing it back in the fire while repeating her words. She withdraws it and places the other side of the dagger on my left shoulder. I almost cry out, but I refuse to make a noise. I take a deep breath, embracing the pain, and she withdraws the dagger from my burning flesh for the second time. I open my eyes to meet the Matron's gaze. She holds her hand out for mine. I try not to hesitate in giving it to her, but I know what comes next.

She places the still-hot razor edge of the blade against my palm and slowly drags it along my skin. I flinch but do not pull away. Blood wells up in my hand, and the Matron pulls a small stone bowl from her robes. I turn my hand over the bowl, allowing my blood to run freely into it until she pulls it away. I wrap my hand with the bandage she hands to me. She smiles a toothless smile with a short nod, holding the bloody dagger above her head and the bowl at her breast.

Her voice is raspy but full of pride as she speaks words we can all understand. "Bear witness to the transition of power!"

I stand, and the Matron hands me the bowl of blood. I take a steadying breath and turn to face the mass of bodies watching the ceremony quietly. I shiver as cold glares from some of the crowd penetrate me like blades, shuddering out an uneven breath under their scrutiny. All eyes are on me, but Keena's gaze from the front row burns more than the blistering wounds on my shoulders. Ysabel's eyes are wide with fear as she glances between us.

Why is she fearful?

Keena looks down at Ysabel, a single eyebrow raised in question, but her daughter shakes her head quickly in disbelief. Keena bears her teeth in anger. She rears back and slaps Ysabel across the cheek. The smacking sound echoes down the river, and Keena turns on her heel, cutting through the crowd to leave without looking back. Ysabel watches her go with a hand over her cheek, tears glistening in her eyes.

Keena will not swear fealty to me. I can accept that. I never dreamed that she would kneel in front of me and kiss the Blackthorn ring on my finger, must less allow me to mark her with my blood. The ring should be her husband's, on his hand, with his blood on her forehead.

What hurts is a third of the crowd that turns to follow her without a second of hesitation. My breath hitches as I watch Blackthorn fracture before my eyes—because of me.

Your people won't accept your leadership when your father is gone. Not after Danny. When they find out your husband is a traitor, they won't trust you as they should and will look for someone else to lead them.

Carnegie's words will haunt me forever.

Some people nervously glance around, unsure of what they should do. Only a fraction of the group is unwavering in their loyalty, staring daggers at the backs of those who dare turn on our clan.

I cannot discern the tone of the Matron's voice, but the pride so evident in it before is gone now. "Line up to swear fealty to your new Chief!"

Ysabel steps forward, leading the remaining group to line up in front of me as if nothing has happened. Her mother's handprint is already red against her olive-toned cheek, shining brightly in the firelight.

My niece kneels first and delicately kisses my father's large Blackthorn signet ring on my outstretched hand. I dip my thumb into the blood, and she lifts her head. With a gentle dab, I mark her forehead. Tears well up in my eyes as she stands, kissing me on the cheek before stepping away to allow the next person to kneel.

She doesn't leave, merely stands off to the side while the remaining members of our clan kneel before me. Not because she wants anything, but because she wants to be here; otherwise, she would not have turned her back on her mother.

I cannot let her sacrifice be in vain.

***

Everything is off-kilter with fewer people. The jobs others would be doing fall on those already burdened with keeping our village up and running.

We have not been attacked, but war looms on the horizon with Charon nipping at the heels of the outer villages. With an impending war comes more work on top of everyday chores. Even the children hasten to work twice as hard. Ysabel has stepped up wondrously, rallying the pack to complete the workloads handed down at a near-impossible rate.

The weapons and ammo that Vesper sent take some of the burdens off our shoulders in the weapons department. But the Blacksmith has been working overtime sharpening and making new swords, daggers, and axes. Without Danny's help, the work is slow going. The blacksmith apprentices have never had to work under the pressure that they are currently experiencing. Unfortunately, not all can withstand the test, painstakingly slowing down the process when they crack.

I feel useless, unable to put my hand to anything, but too many questions and things happening at once require my attention. I walk through the streets as I tighten the furs around my bandaged shoulders, shielding them against the brisk breeze. I have to make sure everyone is breaking their backs and getting things done, but it does not sit well with me. Not to mention, it is way more mentally exhausting than I thought it would be.

Answering questions is becoming tiresome, and I long for the monotony of following orders without thought. It may not give my weary body a break, but it would at least give my overworked brain a much-needed reprieve. I sigh as someone calls my name once again and turn to face yet another onslaught of problems I have to figure out how to fix.

Would it be worth it to pray for a bit of rain? If it rains hard enough, we will have no choice but to retreat inside.

Ask, and you shall receive—my mother's voice echoes in my mind, a faint memory. I fear I will soon forget what she sounded like, but she had to have told me that saying at least once a week, if not more, while she was alive. My mother was a woman of faith who believed in the impossible being possible, but my selfishness will not do us any good. So I refrain from trying to will thunder clouds into existence with my mind.

We don't need any more setbacks, and I don't believe in that mess anyway.

Twelve

Whiskey slides down my throat in an amber stream of lava, settling in my belly with the only lasting warmth I can attain these days.

My father's funeral pyre flashes before my eyes more frequently than I would like, followed by the desertion of a third of our fighting force.

The fact that they found the idea of my leadership so appalling that they chose to leave the safety of our clan hurts worse than their actual disapproval. I had problems with swearing fealty to my father because I felt it took away a part of *me*, but when given the only other option of fending for myself in the wilderness, I gladly knelt and kissed the ring. I can't fathom why they would risk it on the brink of war.

But I was never meant to be in this position. Leadership was meant for my oldest sister, Nadia, the epitome of a humble leader. Then, the future role fell upon my brother's shoulders, who embraced it with an overbearing pride, frequently trying to push his agenda before his time. Then in one sweeping pull of a trigger, the responsibility landed on my unready shoulders in a smoldering heap.

As the youngest, I learned things like tattooing clan marks and helping to train fighters, not leading the people. I have picked up a thing or two, but I am wholly unqualified for this position.

A log falls into the fire with a spray of sparks, startling me from my alcohol-fueled rumination. Ysabel wakes with a gasp from her place on the couch and lifts her head, glancing around the room. She finds me watching her and settles back into the couch cushions. She is asleep again in seconds.

I wish I could sleep.

The decisions I must make soon weigh heavy on my mind, and I am now forever restless. I gaze blearily into the fire. Flames roar in the fireplace, warming the cabin against the chilly rain that has halted all work in the village. I didn't need to pray for rain for it to show up with a vengeance, completely unannounced within the following hour after thinking about it.

Now, all the rain we have needed for months decided to show up at one time. We will be lucky if the river does not flood at this rate. We have had a torrential downpour for a day and a half already. The creek is overflowing, creating a small lake at the back of the village—the likes of which I have never seen before.

Lightning cracks in the distance, followed by a violent strike of thunder that makes the cabin's foundation rattle. Ysabel cries out, bolting upright.

"It's just thunder," I say tiredly.

Her light brown eyes are wild, but after a moment, she relaxes. Ysabel leans back against the couch, rubbing the sleep from her eyes. She looks around, finding the open letter at my elbow. "Did you read it yet?" she asks.

With heavy eyes, I stare down at the letter sitting on the table next to my father's recliner in which I have taken up residence. Luther Cain's handwriting runs across the page in an elegant slant. And yet, the letter's contents are nowhere near as lovely as the writing.

"Yeah," I say sluggishly. I am acutely aware that I have had more whiskey than I should, even as I take another drink.

To put the conversation off, I light a cigarette in the candle flame. I take a long drag as I glare at the letter, and Ysabel waits patiently for me to gather my thoughts. It took me days to read it. Not out of fear necessarily, but more out of putting off added responsibility. I wish I could ignore it, and everything still turn out okay in the end.

"He apologized for what happened at the Market," I say cautiously. I am not sure how much a young girl should be burdened with, but she is next in line to lead. I do not see myself having an heir of my own because I will never be able to replace Danny.

If only I were a worthy mentor.

Blackthorn's only saving grace is that Ysabel is wise beyond her years. Damian undoubtedly trained her for the role in some aspects. Maybe I *should* let her lead, but that would be frowned upon.

Join, or risk annihilation is the gist of the contents of Luther's letter, although he did not use those exact words—nor was he threatening. I cannot tell her that, though. I don't want to frighten her. Ysabel watches me expectantly with those wise eyes, and part of me cannot help but feel that she already knows everything. She just wants me to speak it out.

I sigh, picking at my fingers. "Luther gave me the same offer he gave your grandfather. He insists that we would all be better off if we joined together."

Luther believes our way of life is unsustainable. Still, he overlooks the fact that we have survived for a century the way we are. I can almost hear the pompousness in his voice through the overly stylistic script on the page. The man has superiority issues, and my first impression of him in the War Room was not flattering.

"And you believe grandpa was wrong in going along with it?" she asks conversationally, despite me withholding most of my thoughts from her.

My father may have thought it was a good idea to join, but I am convinced that it isn't in the best interest of our people. I know how many want to fight, and the majority rules. I have already pushed enough of them away. "Not necessarily, but—"

"Then why don't you follow through with what he was going to do?" She catches me off guard with her statement, and I cannot even reprimand her for interrupting me. Her eyes glitter in the firelight with curiosity.

She reminds me of me.

I stare at her open-mouthed for a moment before I can form coherent speech again. "Because I cannot join forces with someone I know nothing about when we can finish this mess ourselves," I say defensively. "Luther didn't want Jai in the meeting, so I have no way of knowing what was discussed. Luther didn't exactly lay it all out on paper either."

"You don't think grandpa wrote anything down?"

I shake my head. "No, Jai was his scribe. He never wrote anything down himself, not within the last five years. His arthritis was getting too bad."

Ysabel shrugs and stands, stretching like a cat. "It wouldn't hurt to search through the War Room and see if he left anything that could help you," she says.

"Yeah, I guess not," I say softly as I watch her flit around the kitchen, hunting for food.

"You don't have any food?" she asks after a futile search for anything edible.

I look down at my glass of liquor sheepishly. I have been sustaining on whiskey and cigarettes for the most part. "I've been eating in the cafeteria lately."

Ysabel opens her mouth to say something but snaps it shut with a sigh. I have not left the house since it started raining. Food has been the last thing on my mind for more than a few days now. My skin-tight pants hang looser than they should, and my wrists are bonier than usual. I try not to look in the mirror at the sunken pits that have become my eyes. I'm not looking too hot between the excessive alcohol and lack of food.

Ysabel stares out the window with disdain as her stomach growls audibly across the living room. "I'm gonna go get food. You want anything?"

I shake my head. "No, I'm good."

She purses her lips, looking more like my mother than I thought possible. She bites back whatever words she wants to say and answers with a simple, "Okay," before slipping into her boots. "I'm going home to find something to eat. I'm not making a trip across the village. My socks are still damp from the walk over here."

I nod, guilty about her having to get back out in the weather. "You don't have to come back tonight if you don't want to. You should get some rest in your own bed." I know how empty her home must feel, but Ysabel does not seem to be taking the current turn of events as hard as I thought she would.

"You sure?" she asks.

"I will be fine," I say with a nonchalant hand wave. I am not very convincing, but she takes the hint. I want to be alone, but I have not had the heart to push away my niece—not after what she has done for me.

Ysabel leaves me in silence. I should follow her out into the rain and head for the War Room to sift through every journal and bound book in the place. But I cannot bring myself to do so. I don't want to know more details because I don't want a good enough reason to join Vesper. I don't want anything other than to fight—to steal the last breath of as many Charon as possible and ultimately put a bullet between Carnegie's eyes. I want to watch the light of his existence fade to nothing, knowing he will never be able to make me do anything or harm anyone I love ever again.

Before the wagon loaded with supplies, we could not match Carnegie's firepower, forcing us into Vesper's bosom for protection. Now we are equipped to take his army on headfirst with a genuine chance of finally putting an end to this thing before it ever truly starts—*without* selling out to Vesper.

So why does Luther still insist that Blackthorn may not survive unless we join forces? He could know something I do not, but he will not tell me anything like that through a letter. I'm not too fond of the idea of having to speak with the man face-to-face.

There are a few terms for joining that Luther managed to fit in the letter that caught my eye, but nowhere near lovely enough for me to drop arms by themselves. I cannot work out why my father jumped on board with the peace talks so fast. If we join Luther, there may be some useful perks, like food security and better medicine, but at what cost? It could be to sell out everything I believe in, destroying everything my family has built in the last hundred years.

I growl in frustration. Unable to sit any longer, I stand, pacing the rug in the middle of the living room. Much more of this, and I will wear a path through the aged fabric.

"What am I supposed to do?" I ask no one with a stressed tug of the shawl around my shoulders. Tears burn my eyes, and in my frustration, I chuck the glass of whiskey into the fireplace with a distressed cry of outrage. The glass explodes in a hail of crystal, and the remnant of alcohol causes the fire to swell dangerously past the hearth before dying back down.

I sink to my knees, head in my hands, as I finally break down after days of ignoring the raging storm inside my mind.

Damn this rain.

If I weren't cooped up, I might be able to continue to ignore it all with menial tasks, but no. All I have now are my thoughts for company, and they are far from hospitable.

"What do I do?" I ask again with a sob.

Join me.

Carnegie's voice is not what I want to hear, but I have no control over it.

I laugh out loud, nearing hysterics. "You've got to be kidding me," I say into my hands. The last thing I want is to have a conversation with Carnegie, of all people.

We can take the fight to Vesper. Who are they to show up out of nowhere? They want to take our land and enslave our people. Once we take them out, we can get back to you trying to kill me if you want.

"I would never join you for anything," I hiss, staring at the wall as though he were standing in front of me. I can almost envision the smarmy grin on his face.

Or we could make something new.

"Destroying everything in the process," I say through clenched teeth.

Nothing lasts forever.

I shake my head violently, trying to will away his voice in my head. "I will never join the likes of you. You will die by my hand, and I will bathe in your blood." My threat sounds hollow, even in my ears, but I mean what I say. I can already picture that glorious day, currently and distressingly out of my reach for the moment.

At least, I *want* to mean what I say, but part of me doesn't believe that I can beat Carnegie. Not after what I witnessed on the roof of the Market. He wields some unnatural power that I fear nothing, not even my need for revenge, can overpower.

I am the lesser of two evils, my love. Don't forget that.

I do not have the energy to yell at him. "You're a liar. Go away," I whisper, but it is enough.

Have it your way, then. But don't say I never offered. Carnegie's weighty presence in my mind disappears, and resolve settles on me.

A gentle knock sounds on the cabin door, and I freeze, my heart pounding. I take a deep breath, composing myself as I wipe away a stray tear that manages to escape. I stand, smoothing down my shirt.

"Come in," I say breathlessly.

I turn as the door opens, and Jai steps in. Every problem fades upon finding him in the doorway, and I dart toward him, wrapping him in a desperate hug.

He is real. He is alive. He is okay.

Jai grunts in discomfort, and I let him go, stepping away to look at him with wide, tear-filled eyes. I lost myself in the ocean of responsibility thrust onto me, and I never got a chance to visit. I came to rely on Alec's updates to keep me afloat.

But to *see* him—*God, I missed seeing his smiling face.*

Jai's meek smile fades to a frown upon seeing my frazzled face and the dark circles under my gaunt eyes. Fear darts through me that he might have overheard my side of the conversation with Carnegie. I really should have kept it all in my head.

"You okay?" he asks before I can speak.

I swallow the torrent of things I want to say and shake my head, hoping he heard nothing. "No, I'm not," I answer honestly. I turn and walk into the kitchen to grab another glass. "You want a drink?" I ask.

Jai shakes his head, sinking into the couch with a sigh. "Not a good idea. Doc has me on some fancy pain pills Vesper sent. She explicitly warned against booze."

I shrug and pull out a double-shot glass, filling it to the brim. I gulp it down in two swallows and slam the glass down on the bar, refilling it before returning to my chair.

"How much whiskey have you had?" Jai asks with a glance at the glass in my hand.

I pause, looking at the fifth of whiskey on the counter with pursed lips. "That bottle might have been full last night," I say, wincing at the nearly empty bottle. Trying to divert attention away from the severity of my drinking, I add, "Did you hear about the desertion?" as if it justifies my behavior.

Jai nods quietly, watching me with concern on his usually stoic face. "What are you going to do now?"

I tuck my legs under me and peer over the rim of the glass at him. "*We* are going to fight. Blackthorn doesn't back down," I say with determination. "Vesper sent guns, and I intend to use them to solve our Charon problem without selling out to Vesper."

"Do you believe going to war is the wisest decision?" Jai asks quietly, falling into the adviser role he fulfilled for my father out of habit. He is not technically an adviser anymore unless I formally offer him the position, but he cannot help himself. It is all he knows, besides acting as my shrink over the years. I would be an idiot to deny him to continue in his position, but now is not the time to talk about such things. Not when I have had this much to drink. It seems unprofessional.

I look at him with a raised eyebrow. "Carnegie has to die for what he has done. You cannot deny that." Doubt clouds my expression and waters down my resolve. Jai can surely pick up on the slight uncertainty in my voice.

"Maybe not, but throwing ourselves into all-out war will probably kill more of us than not."

I grit my teeth. "It's either that or bow down to a strange power I do not wish to serve. There are no strings attached to what Vesper has already sent. I do not intend to ask for more that will carry a price. We have to finish this *now.*"

Jai picks at his thumbnail. "That may be so." He turns his gaze to the window in thought.

I watch him quietly, but he makes no move to continue speaking. "That's all you have to say? You aren't going to argue with me?" I ask, astounded by his surface-level acceptance despite his brief questioning.

"Why would I argue with you when I know you have already made up your mind?" he asks.

I let out a genuine chuckle. "It's what you do," I say, but the slight grin that appears does not reach my eyes.

His eyes meet mine. "Is it?"

I hold his gaze, making my decision. "If you want." A small smile appears on his lips. "Will you fill the same position for me as you did for my father?" I ask, almost shy about it.

Jai holds my gaze for a moment longer, trying to read me in his offhand way. He must find something he can agree with because he nods his head. "I would be honored to advise you." He pauses with a smirk. "Not that I expect you to listen."

Thirteen

Propped up on my elbows, I lay prone on a moth-eaten mattress, looking down the scope of my rifle at what is left of the incoming army of Charon. The gun in my hands was one of the many gifts sent on that fateful Vesper supply wagon, literally with my name on it, and I am smitten with the thing.

After shooting arrows and muzzle-loaded single shots my entire life, the power I now wield has me buzzing with excitement. It unlocks a particular blood lust within me that I cannot quite explain. But now that I am finally getting to kill Charon indiscriminately, I'm not going to ask too many questions. There may only be one I truly seek to riddle with bullet holes, but I will take any that come my way. They are all fair game.

X marks the spot, I think wryly to myself, unable to suppress a small giggle at my joke.

There will be peace when Carnegie has nothing left to play games with—when he lay lifeless at my feet. He cannot compel me through our mind connection that I am aware of, so I need to stay away from him. Kill him from a distance.

I can do that. I gaze at my rifle like a mother looking upon her first child.

"Incoming explosives! Over," a voice crackles through the hand-held radio beside me. It is a small but helpful gift from Vesper. I am not sure what we will do once the batteries die, but they are an invaluable tool for the moment.

Glancing in the direction of the voice on the other end of the radio, I can barely see Connolly's silhouette hidden in the shadows of a covered roof patio. A deafening explosion rocks downtown of the decrepit city that is our current battleground. The second-floor windows of the crumbling brick building I have made my sniper's nest rattle violently.

Positioned on the outer edge of a square grouping of antique buildings, I watch the cloud of smoke billow into the sky as the old bank, already crumbling from decay, finally meets its end in an explosion. Red brick and concrete fly in every direction.

Fortunately, I had the foresight to keep my fighters out of the old building. I knew Charon would destroy it if they made it this far, but that's what I was counting on. If they didn't take it down, we would have eventually.

As the dust clears, the absence of the large building opens up my range of sight considerably, allowing me to see another quarter-mile down the dirt road beyond it. With the high-powered scope, I watch a new wave of Charon coming around the bend, marching over the pitted road straight for us. I start strategically picking the outsiders off, and they have no idea from which direction the shots come. The weariness on Charon faces is plain as day as their comrades' bodies drop around them like flies. And yet they hold their position.

It did not take me long to get warmed up to this new weapon—it came naturally. Almost too easy, actually, but I can't complain. We had less than a week to prepare with our new weapons before Charon burned an outer Blackthorn village to the ground, pushing their way into our territory.

Charon's firepower has encouraged them, and Blackthorn numbers are far from what they should be after the desertion. And yet I am confident that my plan here today will succeed.

Charon should soon be running scared, and it won't matter that we are outnumbered; however, even one slip-up could cost us everything. If we can make a show out of today, I am hoping we can at least put a dent in their morale, if not completely end this by putting a bullet between Carnegie's eyes. But I have yet to find any sign of the man. Reports are clear that Carnegie somehow made it out of the Market, the slippery demon. Unless he is a coward, he should be here today.

I catch a glimpse of a cannon being wheeled slowly down the rough road. I line up the cross-hairs of my scope over the chest of the man holding the torch and release the man's death sentence with a delicate pull of the trigger. A split-second later, the chunk of lead hits him in the chest, sending him stumbling back before falling to the ground, dead. The men around him hunker down behind the cannon, but not before I take out the guy going for the torch in the same fashion. I sit back in the shadow of my nest, relishing in watching them scramble.

"Fire in the hole!" sounds out from the right side of the square. An artillery shell strikes the middle of the first group of Charon to make it within a hundred yards of the bank's remains. They scatter, running for their lives as gunfire erupts from the building across from the bank.

I turn my attention to the cannon across the way, picking off another soldier who dares to run for the torch. The last three guys manning the cannon get it into position for a shot at the building across from the demolished bank, but the torch lay on the ground, feet away, useless. The fear on their faces is evident as they hesitate to make a move for it.

Reaching for the radio, I hold the button down before speaking. "Take out the cannon—over."

"10-4—over," a voice responds.

I count five seconds before I watch another shell fly from behind the buildings on my right, hitting the cannon head-on. It kills one soldier who doesn't see it in time to move. The other two take off, running for a cove of trees. They line up almost too good to be true, and I take my shot. One, then the other, stops mid-step with the same bullet to the head.

"Nice one—or two," I say with a chuckle to myself, caught up in the thrill of the chaos swirling in the atmosphere. That will be worth talking about later.

"WEST SIDE BREACHED! WEST SIDE—"

My heart drops with the terror in the voice and the abruptness with which it is cut off. I turn my scope in time to find a small black disk-shaped thing I have no name for appearing under the awning with Connolly. It catches the woman off guard, and she stares at it for a moment before something moves on the bottom of the flying object.

"What the—"

Reality dawns on me a second too late. I watch Connolly's head snap back through my scope as the thing shoots her in the face.

"Shit—" I go silent as the thing spins around in my direction as if it heard me. I aim for the red light blinking from the center of it, and my bullet shatters it to bits.

This isn't good.

I hastily grab the radio, depressing the talk button. I speak frantically into the speaker. "Connolly is down! Get reinforcements to the west side—over!" I throw the radio down beside me, looking back into the scope to scan the area. My heart thuds violently against my chest, and my hands begin to shake.

A group of Blackthorn exits the mouth of the alley from the right, heading for the west side. I blindly grasp for the radio again, finding the button without taking my eye away from the scope. "West side, speak to me! Over."

No response.

"Dammit," I mutter, nearly chucking the radio across the room. I shake myself, trying to eliminate the lurking dread that black disk brings.

What was that?

"Watch out for flying black disks. I don't know what they are, but they are deadly—over." I warn through the radio.

I have only just spoken when almost a dozen little flying things burst into the middle of the square from the west. My blood runs cold, and I only have enough time to take one out in a hail of debris. The disks dart into the buildings around me where my men and women are posted up, waiting to ambush the Charon who make it to the square.

"No, no, no," I say, fumbling for the radio again. My fingers wrap around the plastic box, my finger depressing the button. "Breach in the square!" I nearly scream through my rising panic.

My plan is falling apart.

Gunfire erupts around me but cuts off abruptly. I wait for a disk to enter the building I am in through the open window, but I am overlooked while every other building is infiltrated. Moments later, the disks come flying back out, and a shiver runs down my spine.

My voice is weak as I ask, "Anybody in the square read me? Over." But again, I get no response.

Taken out, just like that.

I do not have the luxury of letting myself feel the pain of the loss as I manage to take out another disk. The third one *dodges* my bullet. A second disk dodges my shot, but it catches the edge of the one to its left, and they both crash into a wall, disintegrating on impact. The rest disappear around the corner to wreak havoc elsewhere.

"Watch out for the flying disks!" I frantically warn anyone who can hear me.

In the short time I have been preoccupied with the new threat, Charon has advanced much farther than is okay. My front defenses against them are no longer firing back, and I have a horrible feeling that they have also felt the onslaught of the flying disks.

We are not equipped to fight *this*.

"Chief!" Alec shouts as he runs into the square, dodging behind an old blue mailbox for cover. "My radio died. We are being overrun, ma'am!"

"Withdraw!" I shout into the radio, hoping someone is left to hear me. "Go! I'm coming!" I shout down to Alec. He hesitates, about to wait for me, but I will not be the reason for his death.

"That's an order!" I shout.

I take one last glimpse down my scope as soldiers make it to the bank rubble, and Alec darts down the cracking sidewalk in front of the long row of buildings. I take one more shot, hitting the guy who spots Alec in the chest.

"Light the other cannon!" rings out from the street where the Charon soldiers are starting to advance on the square, unhindered by the dead Blackthorn in the buildings around them.

I cannot find the other cannon they speak of.

Get out now! Carnegie's voice yells in my head.

I do not question him as I grasp tightly to my rifle and scramble off the old bed where I have been for hours in the shadows. I can ask myself why he would be helping me later if I survive.

A cannonball rips through the window, landing in the wall directly behind where I was posted up at. It throws glass, brick, and mortar straight for me. A stray piece of glass from the edge of the window catches me on the side of my right thigh, sending me stumbling into the hallway with a grunt of pain.

"Throwing Molotov!" The voice comes from directly below the hole in the wall.

A glass bottle comes hurling inside my nest with a flaming tongue. The glass vessel shatters on the hardwood floor, unleashing a fury as the fuel inside ignites. Dust and smoke fill the air as the flammable contents of the room catch fire.

I hiss as a sickening sting radiates from my left thigh. I grab my leg reflexively, finding a rip in my pants. I jerk my hand away, my fingers touching the edge of a fairly deep wound. I force myself not to look at it. I have much bigger problems.

A whirring sound sends a bolt of panic through my chest as I picture one of those flying disks coming for me. The smoke starts whipping around me as the body of a large black mechanical bird-like contraption appears in the window from above the building.

Much worse than a *little* flying disk.

A man sits behind the glass window where he controls the thing encasing him, and a large headpiece covers his ears, making him appear larger than life.

I stare wide-eyed and lift my rifle. I fire one shot that ricochets off the glass, leaving no damage behind. I stare at the man in shock for a moment from around the door frame, unable to move. I have never seen such a thing, but I am pretty sure it is called a helicopter, from what I can recall in the few history books I have read. It takes fuel to power one of those things, something no one has had in fifty years or more, so how is this possible?

Of course, I know what guns are, and those are two massive guns moving to point in my direction that are mounted on the bottom side of the helicopter.

With a yelp, I throw myself out of sight of the two guns as they start spinning. I trip over rotting floorboards, dropping my rifle as I catch myself. Rapid gunfire fills the atmosphere. I reach out to grab the gun, and a bullet shatters the scope. I jerk back with a cry, shielding my face from the debris. Bullets force me to scurry along the long hallway, unable to retrieve my newfound love. But I am severely hindered by my injured leg.

The man guiding the guns cannot see me, but he knows my direction. He does not hesitate to follow, and I cannot move fast enough. Closer and closer, the holes forming in the drywall behind me become. I stagger along, unsteady on my injured leg, but I cannot stop. I will not go out like this.

The stairs are within reach.

I grab the railing and throw myself down the stairs as a bullet pierces through my shoulder. I tumble gracelessly down the stairs with a cry of pain, slamming into the wall at the bottom where the stairs turn. The impact knocks the wind out of me in a rush. Adrenaline numbs the pain, but my rapid heartbeat only amplifies the amount of warm blood running down my arm and leg.

Don't think about it.

The gunfire continues along the second floor, blowing out windows and throwing debris and dust around, making it nearly impossible to breathe as I gasp for air. I need to get out of this building. Charon moves around out front, and smoke begins to billow from upstairs as the fire spreads. The metal cage covering the front door and windows slows Charon down, but it will not keep them out forever if they want inside bad enough. There is only one way out from here.

I roll over and slide down the last few remaining steps, landing with a huff as I hit the hard-tiled floor at the bottom. I stand on shaking legs and hobble to the back exit. Blood smears the wall as I stumble into it. I groan in pain, pushing myself closer and closer to the door.

The back door is stuck. Desperately, I throw myself into it, once, then twice, bruising my previously uninjured shoulder. The impact on the old building from the explosion must have upset the foundation because it opened without a fuss when I arrived earlier.

The door gives way, sending me stumbling outside and falling to my hands and knees with a shock of pain from my injuries. Blood seeps down my arm and across my chest under my jacket where it appears, coating my fingers in blood.

Alec appears in the mouth of the alley. "We have to go, ma'am!" he yells, quickly closing the distance between us.

He pulls me to my feet. "Yeah," I say with a huff and a nod.

I let Alec pull me along as I fight through the pain in my leg with each step, but I am beginning to get light-headed. "Wait, please," I say breathlessly.

Alec turns, looking at me in confusion. "Are you okay?" he asks, eyes roving over my body with concern. His eyes go wide as they find the blood.

I am clammy, and a cold sweat is starting on my brow. I am losing a lot of blood. I cannot lie to him. "No—" My knees buckle, and I collapse into him.

"No, don't do that. Hold on," Alec says, turning to try and pull me along as he gets me back on my feet. "I can fix you up when we get out of sight."

A single, eerily familiar gunshot rings out, and Alec gasps in shock. He halts, and I stumble mid-step. I turn to face him, and he clutches at the front of my jacket.

Alec stares down at me, his eyes wide, lips parted. Blood coats his teeth, running out of the corner of his mouth.

"No!" I gasp.

I reach around him, feeling his back, and find a single bullet hole straight through to his heart. Alec exhales as his eyes roll back, and he falls into me. I would not have the strength to hold him up on a good day, and we both collapse. Alec falls to the side, and I stare at him dumbfounded. He stares back lifelessly with an all too familiar death gaze, and I turn my head, unable to meet his eyes again.

"Goodbye," I say weakly, closing his eyes without looking.

I glance back at his face, shielded from his gaze by pale eyelids. He could almost be sleeping—if not for the blood trickling from the corners of his mouth.

Footsteps alert me to a small group of Charon headed straight for me from the alley Alec appeared out of. My adrenaline spikes, and I stagger to my feet as they surround me. I pull my short sword from my belt, daring them to come any closer—despite the guns pointed at me, the severe blood loss from my leg, and the throbbing ache in my shoulder.

"It's her. She has the mark on her chin!" a woman with a gun pointed at me calls over her shoulder.

"Disarm her," a familiar voice answers from the mouth of the alley—the owner of the bullet in Alec's back.

"You can try," I say to the men around me in defiance of the tingle of fear that Carnegie's voice instills in me.

The soldiers look at each other once in decision. Three of them lower their guns and withdraw swords, challenging me.

"Why don't we have a little fun?" I tease, trying to sound stronger than I feel. Pure adrenaline is all that is keeping me upright.

I need to feed it.

The first man attacks, and I dodge his swing, hopping backward on my good leg. A second man meets me face-to-face, and I plant my sword in his neck with a deft swing, knocking his sword away with my forearm. The reinforced leather of my jacket deflects most of the damage, but the blade bites my skin where it manages to cut through. I cry out as my injured shoulder protests at the impact, but the pain does not fully register. I shove the man away from me roughly, stumbling backward.

"Stop!" Carnegie commands.

I fall to my knees, unable to stand any longer and utterly helpless against the quirk in his voice. The third person, a woman about my size, stands behind me, her sword at my neck.

Sucking in a steadying breath, I stare into the face of the man trotting toward me with purpose. His buckled boots fall heavy against the packed earth. The grip on my sword tightens. All I want is to end this, but I do not have the strength to raise the steel blade nor the energy to strike fast enough before the woman slices into my neck.

I drop my gaze from Carnegie to my injured leg, breathing deeply to calm myself. An inch-deep gash mars my thigh. It oozes blood freely, coating my leg and turning my leather pants black with crimson fluid. I close my eyes as ringing starts in my ears.

That doesn't look good. Carnegie's voice is light and airy—almost joyful.

I bare my teeth at him, eyes still closed. *I will plant this sword in your skull when you get close enough.*

You can't, and you won't.

Watch me, I mentally retort, trying to gather enough willpower to strike regardless of my current predicament.

"It's so good to see you," Carnegie greets me cordially for everyone to hear. He carefully closes the distance between us, disregarding the body of the man lying dead next to me.

"I disagree," I say, weaker than anticipated. I open my eyes to glare at him, but my vision is blurry.

"Oh, not feeling too well, huh?" he asks with feigned concern, accompanied by that infuriating sideways smirk. "Let me help."

Carnegie walks right up to me and kneels. He removes a roll of gauze from the inside of his jacket and presses it against the gash in my leg. I shudder in pain at his touch and drop my sword. I unconsciously put my bloodstained hand over his, where they stay like that for a moment.

An electric current flows from his hand, leaving a tingling sensation in place of the worst throbbing in my leg. It is reminiscent of his hand on my cheek on the Market's roof, but I am not sure what is happening.

Carnegie gently pulls his hand away, and I am left holding the gauze in place in confusion. I gaze up at him in wonder. The pain recedes along with the lightheaded sensation and ringing ears, but not the weakness—or maybe it is not weakness. It is as though I have completely lost the will to fight. I at least had thoughts of retaliation before, but now there is nothing.

"Better?" he asks soothingly. Stars sparkle around him for a moment, and I have to blink them away, unable to answer.

Music.

That's what the soft hum in my ears is. It is vaguely familiar, and the melody seeps into me, even as it plays, barely audible. The two of us are probably the only two that can even hear it.

I focus on Carnegie, and my vision clears. My eyes drift down to an obsidian stone encased in a delicately carved iron enclosure. It hangs around his neck by a leather band, resting below his tanned collarbone, glowing faintly. The music softly emanates from it.

The thing begins to pulse with energy to the beat. A strange sensation pierces my abdomen, and I double over with a surprised gasp, my hand going to my belly. Not knowing what is happening to me, I shakily breathe in and out, trying to maintain control. A current runs through my body, and I tremble involuntarily. It is nothing like the anxiety attacks I have become accustomed to in the wee hours of the morning, but not wholly unlike them either.

"Incredible," he mutters, looking down at the stone around his neck. "This is good," he says, placing a hand over the bullet wound in my shoulder.

"Mmm," I groan, unable to control myself. I close my eyes and lean into his hand as an ethereal sensation pierces my chest. The tingling starts again, and then the pain fades, like before. Carnegie takes his hand away, and I lean forward, hands on my knees as I try to get a grip on reality.

"Head back," Carnegie orders the group standing around us.

"Yes, sir," one man says. The sound of footsteps heads away from us, and we are alone.

My wounds no longer hurt, but nothing seems real. I cannot comprehend what is going on, but I have a curious feeling that the necklace has something to do with it—or at the very least, the music does.

"What happened to the music box?" I ask.

Carnegie chuckles. "You broke it."

I shake my head. "No, I didn't."

Carnegie shrugs. "Well, not you, technically."

I don't know what he means, but I can't care now. I breathe in and out slowly, trying to gather myself. I watch the stars shimmering behind my eyelids, my heart hammering away at the implications of his words. I know there are more things I do not remember, and it tears me apart.

The touch of a hand appears under my chin, lifting my face. I slowly open my eyes to look at the man I hate, but at this moment, I am entranced by a sea of blue as our eyes meet.

Staring intently at me, he whispers, *"Despierta, mi amor,"* in an elegant accent. I do not understand the language he speaks, but it does not matter.

I groan as a pulse of energy radiates from my belly again, stronger this time. It sends me forward into Carnegie's arms. There he holds me still as I start to seize up, my body racked by uncontrollable spasms. I clench my teeth, trying to hold on to myself. Inky blackness takes over my vision, and my body goes limp in my enemy's arms.

Fourteen

Sparkling gray. The low hum of music. But it isn't soothing. It unsettles a part of me. Angers me.

"Despierta mi amor." And everything goes black.

Blinding pain awakens me, electricity shooting through my veins. A hand strikes me as I cry out, and I quickly learn silence will lead me down a road of much less pain. Sometimes there is even bliss.

The drug injected into my arm brings on ecstasy I have never felt, not even in the throes of passion. I crave it, but to partake, I must break—scream out in pain for it to stop. Kill a part of myself.

It becomes too easy to give in, in such a short amount of time. I broke the first chance I got, like I never had a choice at all.

"Tu eres mi, mi amor."

You are mine, my love.

Fifteen

I jerk awake from nightmares of electricity coursing through my body. I sit up, and the world spins, blurring reality around me, before the sensation of being shot jolts through my shoulder. I yelp, reflexively reaching up, searching for a wound, but I find nothing. I frown in confusion, sure that I witnessed seeing a helicopter and that it shot me. But that is crazy. Nobody has helicopters—none that work anyway.

My head throbs painfully, and I press my face into the soft forest floor, breathing in the smell of damp pine needles. After a moment of deep breathing, the pain recedes to a dull ache, and I make myself stand, taking in my surroundings. The world tilts and spins, and it takes me a minute to realize where I am. I recognize the trees from the outskirts of my village with a sigh of relief. Still, the familiarity does nothing for the fog clouding my mind.

I do not know why I am out here, but I am no more than five hundred yards from the South Gate, with only a thick border of trees separating me from home. I start trudging along, delirious.

Why can I not remember?

I stop for a moment, a thought nudging my brain. With it is another twinge of pain that flashes behind my eyes.

Did I get knocked in the head?

Sighing deeply, I continue walking, lithely sliding between trees in the faint light of dawn. Within minutes the gate comes into sight. The guards at the gate spot me as soon as I step out of the trees. The two on the ground meet me halfway with shiny new guns drawn before I get close enough for them to recognize me in the dim light.

A man with a balding head and graying beard rushes toward me with a worried look. “Chief?” he asks.

I stare dumbly at him, unable to form words.

“What happened?” he asks when I do not respond.

A light green eye stares at me, filled with concern. I blink, recognizing the face of Warren. This isn’t his usual time on duty, even with our work spread thin, but I don’t question it as flashes of memory make the world topsy-turvy.

A memory of black flying discs flickers back in pieces. With a jolt, I remember the helicopter in all its furious glory with a force that makes me cry out. I stagger a step to the side, hands over my eyes.

“Are you okay, ma’am?” Warren asks. He gently shakes me, trying to get me to respond.

I glance down at my leg to find a rip in my pants and dried blood coating the area, but no injury. I gaze thoughtfully at the tear for a moment before another pain jabs behind my eyes. It sends me to my knees.

Warren yells out as I collapse to the ground, but I cannot hear the words he speaks.

What happened?

I cannot begin to explain that one, but I must tell him. I have to tell someone.

“E-everyone is—they’re all d-dead,” I mumble into my hands. I start to rock back and forth, knowing it to be true, even if I cannot recall precisely what happened.

The other guard, an ebony-skinned Amazonian woman named Beatrice Sartor, scans the trees around us for enemies. Her grip is tight on her rifle, and her stout arm muscles are tense. "Are you hurt, ma'am?" she asks. I look up to find her pointing at the dried blood on my hands. I glance down at the rust color in question.

Warren looks back at his comrade. "Go get Jai." Beatrice nods, taking off at a run toward the gate. She whistles a simple three-note tone and slips through the gate as it opens for her.

"Your blood?" Warren asks. I nod numbly as my hands fall to my sides and look up at him.

"Dr. Matthews," I say, bobbing out of consciousness.

Warren catches me before I hit the ground. My eyelids flutter. I can still hear clearly, but my head is foggy, my eyes unseeing. He picks me up bridal style, hauling me off to the infirmary without hesitation.

"Stay with me, ma'am," he says as my head rolls to the side. "You say *everyone*. Do you mean that, literally? Like nobody will show up later? Talk to me," he prods, carrying me down the winding side path toward the infirmary at a jog. The trees above me come and go as my vision fades in and out.

I chuckle darkly from somewhere between light and darkness. "I guess we can always hope, but—"

A coughing fit takes over, and I cannot speak. I can barely breathe, for that matter. Warren rushes me through the door into the lobby of the infirmary.

"I need Dr. Matthews!" he nearly shouts at Carika, seated behind the front desk again.

Startled, she jumps up, motioning for us to follow her. My vision wavers, and I watch the world around me go by in a blur of color as I fight for air. I cough fitfully, and warm blood trickles down my chin.

"Miss Vance!" Dr. Matthews exclaims upon seeing my disheveled body in Warren's arms.

"She started coughing up blood. I think she has some other injuries. There is dried blood all over her. She said it's hers," Warren elaborates hastily.

Dr. Matthews holds open a curtain, revealing a cot inside the nearest empty room. "Lay her there," she says, pointing at the cot.

Warren carefully lowers me down as the coughing subsides. I lean back into the pillow with a groan.

"I've got it from here," Dr. Matthews says, waving him off.

I grab his arm, stopping him before he can leave. "Thank you," I say before letting his arm go.

"You're welcome, ma'am," he says with a slight bow, taking his leave.

Dr. Matthews starts prodding me. Her face is a blur above me, and sparkles float around her head. At least the coughing has stopped.

"Where are you hurt?" Dr. Matthews asks.

"I don't know." I shake my head from side to side, but it makes the room start spinning, so I stop. "I remember getting shot, but there isn't anything there now. Only blood," I say, still somewhat breathless from the coughing fit. I wipe the blood from my chin with the back of my hand.

"What do you mean? Show me," she says. I weakly point to my shoulder, where the bullet hole mars my jacket and the shirt underneath. She frowns. "Anywhere else?" she asks.

"My leg." I motion at the torn leather of my pants, where my leg is coated with dried blood.

"Mmmm," she hums thoughtfully.

"What?"

"I'm not sure. Anywhere else?" Her tone is vague.

I shake my head. "Not that I know of, but I keep getting these sharp pains behind my eyes," I say slowly, trying to assess any other ailments lurking about. The headaches are the only actual pain I feel. Every other part of me is fine, minus the exhaustion, but I could be dead, I guess.

"You get hit on the head?" she asks as she shines a light in my eyes, making me follow her finger.

"I don't feel like I got hit, so no?" I end in question, unsure. "Wait. I fell down a flight of stairs—" I am cut off by another round of hacking, followed by more blood.

"Oh dear," Dr. Matthews says, rushing to prepare a soothing-smelling liquid that she dips a rag in to clean my face. The coughing only lasts thirty seconds, but it saps my energy reserve.

"That only happens when I try to remember something," I say, my voice faint. I cannot tell her that there are other things I have forgotten, only to remember later, but it does not seem to matter.

Dr. Matthews' eyes widen as if something clicks, and she drops the rag. She turns back to a cupboard. "I'm going to have to sedate you," she says, turning back with a syringe in her hand.

"What? Why?" I ask in surprise. I turn defensive as she comes at me with the needle glinting maliciously. "I don't want it," I say, but she disregards my words.

"Your body needs to rest, my dear. I will if you don't let it," she says softly.

The woman is small but armed with a syringe which I do not know the contents of, she is terrifying. I cry out feebly as I try to knock her hand away, but I am weak, and she is faster than I expect. She stabs me in the neck with the needle, pushing down on the plunger. I yell out in surprise, anger, and pain.

"I said no, woman!" I say harshly, trying to stand. Instantly I feel woozy and stumble backward, landing roughly on the cot.

"It's for your own good, ma'am," she says sweetly, directing my head onto the pillow.

Within seconds everything goes black.

***

My eyes flutter open, and the familiar infirmary ceiling greets my eyes. I groan, blinking back the haziness clouding my vision.

"Aunt Ray?" a small voice asks. I turn my head, looking for the source.

Ysabel sits in the chair next to me, knitting what appears to be a burgundy scarf or shawl. "Welcome back," she says, her lips turning up at the corners in a strained smile of relief. She sets her project aside and leans forward.

"H-how long have I been out?" I ask, voice croaking from disuse. I clear my throat with a wince. My vocal cords are once again like sandpaper rubbing against one another. I'm not too fond of the feeling.

Ysabel stares at me for a moment before answering. "A week."

I bolt upright, wincing as the movement tugs at the IV lines pumping fluids into both of my arms. "What?" My face flushes with anger at Dr. Matthews. The woman will be lucky if I do not kill her the next time I see her.

“Before that, you were missing for three days,” she says quietly. “I thought you were dead like everyone else, but we couldn’t find your body. I-I thought I lost you like I did my dad—never to be seen again.” The pain in her voice pricks my heart, but I don’t feel anything anymore concerning grief—for any of my lost family or my people. I am empty.

“We’ve lost so much time,” I mutter in disbelief. I drag my hand down my face and bite down on my thumb. The pain helps me focus. “What’s happened?” I attempt to rub the sleep out of my eyes, but the room starts to spin when I close my eyes for more than a few seconds, and I stop.

“Jai took over your rounds. He was with Grandpa enough to pick up on the day-to-day operations,” she says, voice quiet.

“Oh,” I say with downcast eyes. I start picking at the blanket over my legs, unsettled by the flurry of emotions creeping into the void where my grief should be. I am relieved that Jai could take up the slack, but at the same time, it makes me feel unneeded.

All I wanted was a chance to rest my mind, and I got my wish—even if it was against my will. I shove aside Carnegie’s words trying to replay themselves again in my mind, but I fail for the most part. I cannot make out the words anymore, but the sound of his voice takes over my mind with an incessant hum.

Ysabel speaks, silencing the tormenting sound of the bastard’s voice in my mind. “I went to look through Grandpa’s stuff in the War Room,” Ysabel says slowly.

A spark of hope ignites in my chest. “Did you find anything?”

“Well—” she pauses, and my heart starts pounding away.

Something bad has happened.

She takes a deep breath, unsettled. “No.”

My niece is keeping something from me. I can see it in her eyes that there is something that she does not want to say. It must be bad.

“What’s wrong?”

She looks at me, eyes sad. “All the rain-soaked through the back wall. Washed it out and completely flooded the place. Nothing is salvageable.”

I stare at her, mouth agape. "You're kidding me."

She shakes her head. "I wish I were, but I'm not. You should go see for yourself when Dr. Matthews releases you."

At the sound of the doctor's name, anger flares up once more, overshadowing everything else. "I'm not waiting for shit from her."

I sling my legs over the side of the cot. I am stiff, but nothing hurts except the uncomfortable tugging from the IV tubes. I rip them out of my arm with a frustrated growl. Ysabel stands as I do, but she does not try to stop me.

"Please don't do anything stupid," she pleads.

I turn on her, throwing the last IV needle on the cot. "What could I possibly do?" I ask. There is more bite to my tone than I would like. Ysabel recoils, and I instantly regret speaking to her that way.

"I don't know," she says meekly. "But I don't want to lose anyone else." Tears well up in her eyes, but she does not let them fall.

I falter, and my lips move wordlessly as she sniffles. I am unable to find words. I sink onto the edge of my cot with another groan. I tug at my hair with both hands, willing the anxiety and otherwise chaotic emotions overwhelming me once again to go away. The pain of hair separating from my scalp does not do much to lessen the conflict within me.

I can't take much more of this.

"Can I do anything?" Ysabel asks. Her small hand reaches out, gently clasping my shoulder.

Against my better judgment, I shrug away from her touch. "Please leave," I say, covering my face with my hands.

"O-okay," she says, taken aback by my response.

The pressure of her hand leaves my shoulder, and a second later, the sound of the curtain falling into place tells me she is gone.

There is that regret again.

I shouldn't push her away. She is the only family I have left.

Tears escape, leaking from the corners of my eyes. With a sniffle and furious rubbing of my face, I push them back. I stand, searching for clothes much like the last time I was here, but there are none.

I frown, looking around once, twice, then three times. Nothing. The room is bare, like my backside. I rip the blanket off of the bed and wrap it around myself.

I storm out of my room in a much better physical state than I was the last time I made a break for it from the infirmary. But like last time, Dr. Matthews appears out of nowhere, blocking my way before I can escape.

"Get out of the way, woman," I say, voice low and dangerous. My fingers twitch, and I repress the urge to wrap them around her throat.

"You can't leave yet," she says frantically, hands held out in front of her chest as if to stop me.

"Bullshit, *move*. You should be happy I haven't snapped your neck yet." My words shock me, but I do not back down.

Dr. Matthews stares at me wide-eyed and steps aside, bowing her head as I pass. "I was only helping you, ma'am."

My tone is bitter. "I don't need your help," I say irrationally. I *was* the one who asked to be taken to her, but that is beside the point.

I slip out of the infirmary, still clothed in my backless gown, and shrouded in the thin blanket. I look both ways before slinking off in the direction of home, taking the long way. Even from here, I can see the flurry of activity at the South Gate square.

I already did one walk of shame through the village. I don't need a second, but damn, it is cold. A young laughing couple turns the corner ahead of me. Before I am spotted, I slip behind a hedgerow, waiting for them to pass. Their voices fade, and I creep out of my hiding place. A gust of wind breaks through the trees, and I pull the blanket tighter around myself. Making a beeline for home, I dart between cabins vacated for a day of work. At the courtyard gate, I pause, glancing around. The guard is nowhere to be seen.

Once inside, I head straight for the antique armoire in the corner without a second thought. I hastily dig through the clothes inside, pulling out a pair of dark gray pants and a mid-calf length overdress split up the sides to the hips to match. I rip a brush through my greasy hair and braid it down my back to get it out of the way. I am overdue for a bath, but it will have to wait.

Diving back into the armoire, I shove aside my father's jackets before settling on a hooded cowl of my mother's, knitted with a deep indigo-colored thread. I put on boots and throw on my mother's old coyote-fur-lined duster coat.

My eye catches sight of my reflection in the glare of the living room window. I pause to stare at the half-starved woman looking back at me with obsidian eyes. My pupils are blown out, and my cheekbones are hollow, with dark circles ringing my eyes. The rings are almost dark enough to pass for purposefully placed charcoal, but none of that is what disturbs me.

What disturbs me is the lifeless gaze staring back at me. No spark of life shimmers within it, and I frightfully turn away from my reflection. I leave in haste for the War Room. I have to see it for myself, as Ysabel said. I won't believe her until I do.

The wind has dried up a lot of the water saturating the ground, but my feet still sink half an inch into the mud that has washed over the footpath the closer I get to the creek. I carefully trod down the slippery steps. On the bottom step, I slip, and my hand meets the cold stone of the War Room door to catch myself, but it cannot tell the difference. It pricks my fingers, drinking in the key before I can prepare myself. I hiss in aggravation and pain as the door silently slides open.

Water rushes out around my feet, washing away the caked mud on my boots. The door must have been holding in two or three feet worth of water inside. I slosh through the remaining water and stop dead in my tracks at the end of the entrance hall.

Ink-stained water still submerges the room in multiple inches of water that cannot escape through the open door. Bookshelves lay on their sides where someone flipped them over while trying to find something that might be untouched by the water. A three-foot-wide hole at the back of the room still leaks water from the swollen creek.

I take a hesitant step forward, staring at the books floating around my feet. All of the ink is smudged and completely unreadable. One of my father's journals catches my eye on the oak desk. I reach for it, hoping against hope that I will find something I can still read.

Every page is a swirling of black ink. I cannot make out a single word. I drop the journal on the desk with a whimper. I never expected to find anything, but seeing the place in its current state breaks something inside me.

All that history.

"It's bad, huh?" Jai's voice makes me jump. Startled, I turn to face him.

He holds up his hands in surrender. "My bad. Ysabel said you woke up." He raises an eyebrow. "And ran off."

I ignore the last part. "Unfortunately," I mutter.

"What do you mean by that?" Jai steps toward me with a sloshing of water around his feet.

"You are doing pretty well for our people, from what I gather. Might have made it easier if I never made it back."

Jai frowns, shaking his head. "I still don't understand you, Ray," he says as he steps forward to stand in front of me.

"I screwed up bad," I say. "We shouldn't have gone off to fight Charon. You were right. Maybe *you* should be the one making the decisions around here."

Jai stares at me in disbelief. "We need you around here."

I scoff. "Yeah, right."

Jai shakes his head angrily. "I'm telling the truth. Without you here, the rest of the clan falls apart."

"Everything seems to be in one piece, and I haven't been conscious."

"For now, but you haven't been able to see what's been going on around here. We wouldn't have been in one piece much longer if you hadn't woken up."

"And how is that? I don't know what the hell I am doing!" I say, trying not to yell.

Jai sighs. "You're so worried about being a good leader that you don't realize the people who never faltered in their loyalty to this clan look up to you. Idolize you. You give them hope. Without you, hope has been slipping away."

I stare at him, dumbfounded. "I'm useless," I say quietly.

Jai shakes his head once more. "You may feel that way, but that isn't how the people see you. They always liked you better than Damian anyway, even—well, even if they disagreed with your life choices," he admits.

I grit my teeth. I am not blind to the fact that most people disagreed with my marriage to Danny, but I disregarded it. I regretted bringing him into our family with his death because it got him killed. It surprises me that people can overlook everything and still find something in me that is worth having around.

Your people won't accept your leadership when your father is gone. Not after Danny. When they find out your husband is a traitor, they won't trust you as they should and will look for someone else to lead them.

"What is it?" Jai asks, pulling me from my mind with the gentle touch of a hand on my arm.

"Mmm?" I ask, looking up to meet his eyes.

Jai leans in. "Whatever is going through your head," he says softly.

My heart skips a beat. "N-nothing."

Jai takes a step back. "You are a terrible liar," he says with a sad smile.

I hesitate. Of all the people I have left, I should be able to talk to Jai, but I can't. Not about this. "It's nothing."

Jai sighs. "I know you're lying, but I won't ask again. Just remember, I'm here to listen when you are ready to talk." He turns and walks out, leaving me speechless as tears begin to stream down my face with abandon.

Sixteen

"What are you doing?" Jai asks, walking up to me where I am seated on the cafeteria bench.

"I'm eating lunch," I say.

Jai shifts behind me. "Don't play dumb. You know what I mean."

Of course I know. I could not ignore Jai's questioning glare this morning when I had a meeting with what is left of Blackthorn's fighting force—without running any of it by him first.

Word came of a Charon attack at the border, and I rallied what fighters I could spare to send them off to defend the border. No other choice felt like the right one. He only has a problem with it because I am going with them.

He leans down next to me, glowering, but I do not take my eyes off the bowl of sweet potato chili in front of me. "Did you consult with anyone before making this decision?"

I chew my food slowly, savoring the salty sweetness. Jai sighs with impatience. "I didn't know I had to," I say after a moment more.

Jai's voice is disapproving in my ear. "You don't *have* to, but most people expect it anyway. It's a show of good faith. You may be within the realm of what you *can* do, but it doesn't mean you should."

My nostrils flare in annoyance. "I never said I would do things the way my father did."

"I never said you did," Jai says with a groan. "But at this rate, you are going to get us all killed," he mutters into my ear.

I place my spoon down with a snap and stand up angrily. "Shut your mouth." I face Jai head-on, vaguely aware of the chatter of the rooming dying away around us.

Jai takes a step back, shocked at my response. His eyes flick around the room once before returning to my gaze. He lowers his voice so only I can hear. "You don't want to listen to me? Fine, but when it all goes to hell because you wouldn't stop for one minute of rational thought, don't think I won't tell you I told you so."

"Would you go away?" I hiss through my teeth.

Jai shakes his head in disappointment. "You can't keep pushing people away. You aren't the same since you've been back. You're starting to scare me," he admits.

"What?" I ask. "I'm fine," I say, a little too fast.

You're not fine, Carnegie whispers in my mind.

Jai huffs in disbelief, oblivious to the voice in my head. "Forget it. You won't listen anyway." He turns on his heel, leaving me to stare after him as he crosses the cafeteria with long strides, eager to escape the room.

Afraid to tell him anything that could lead to me? Like your revenge fantasy? Or why you jump at any chance to kill me that you can get your hands on?

Shut up.

I already told you that you can't kill me, but you are afraid to admit that you aren't in complete control of your actions.

I said shut up!

Carnegie's chuckle reverberates inside my skull, and he disappears from my mind. I plop back down on the bench and pick up my spoon, staring daggers at my bowl of chili. Nausea rolls through my belly, and I wrinkle my nose with disdain. I *was* set on finishing my food, but now I can't. I slam my spoon back down onto the table, no longer hungry.

If the people sitting in my general vicinity were not already staring at me with questioning eyes, I would bang my head on the table and scream. But I can't do that. Not here.

With a groan, I stand back up and saunter out of the cafeteria with all of the arrogance Damian could ever come up with—if only to hide my discomfort at Carnegie's parting words.

They only add more credence to Jai's concern.

***

"You should think twice about this," Ysabel says quietly.

I shove a change of clothes and food rations into my pack, readying myself for the trek to the border.

"I'm getting sick of being told that I should 'think twice,'" I mutter, more to myself than to my niece.

"Maybe that is your sign that you should listen," she says.

My nostrils flare, and I grit my teeth, but I withhold the harsh words I want to say. Ysabel does not deserve the brunt of my aggravation, but I will not agree with her.

"I won't be gone long. I need to ensure we have a firm perimeter set up with the resources we have left. Charon has been darting around, causing mayhem where they can, but we cannot let them get across the river. It will only be downhill from there if we start losing ground like that."

"I agree," Ysabel says.

"But what?" I ask, knowing there is a 'but' coming.

"But maybe you should take it easy. Send Jai to check on the border. We need you here, and you need to get some sleep."

"My sleep is fine," I lie with a shake of my head. "I need to get out and do something, or I will completely lose my mind. All the questions are driving me mad."

Ysabel sighs. "Okay." She pauses. "My mom sent me a letter."

I swing around in shock with a bag of rations forgotten in my hand. "Oh really? What did she have to say?"

"She apologized to me and said that if I have a change of heart, she will gladly take me away from here if I thought I made a mistake."

My jaw drops. "Are you trying to guilt me into not doing what I am doing?"

Ysabel stands up straighter, and I raise an eyebrow at her. "You are being irrational, Aunt Ray. I don't believe you are making the right decisions. I am willing to give my life for this clan for many reasons, but not because you made stupid choices."

She might as well of slapped me. Tears burn behind my eyes, but rather than let them surface, I turn them into anger—something that is becoming a habit. "Well, carry your ass if you don't believe in what I am doing! I am doing my best with what I have, which isn't a lot! Or better yet, if you think you can do a better job, go for it!"

Ysabel back-steps away from me, shaking her head. She opens her mouth and shuts it, unable to speak. Tears well up in her eyes, and she darts out of the cabin before I can call after her.

I shudder out a breath. "Dammit." I sink onto the bed, dropping the package of dried food to the floor. My head falls into my hands, and I press my palms against my eyes, blocking the waterworks that threaten to overtake me.

I am so sick of crying.

Shame, anger, grief, and every incapacitating emotion flit through me until a resolve settles on me.

Maybe she is *better off away from here—and away from me.*

***

It does not take long for all hell to break loose once I show up at the border. I wouldn't be surprised if Carnegie waited for me to show up before launching the attack. I expected it, though. He already knew I was coming.

Gunfire and explosions surround the large field we converge in, and in the center of it all, the clashing of swords rings out in the fading evening light. Even with the help of Vesper weapons, we do not stray far from what we know this time—barbaric bloodshed by steel.

The chaos surrounding me fades from my mind as I catch sight of a stark blond head darting into the trees. I duck under a sword and impale the man wielding it in the gut with my sword. I push him off the blade and dart for the tree line.

Artillery rains down around the battling mass of bodies. Dirt explodes into the air as the shells make contact with the earth, and I have to shield my face or be blinded by it. I run through the tree line, down the large game trail where Carnegie disappeared.

Blue eyes find mine over his shoulder before he disappears around a bend, taking off in a sprint. He runs, so I chase.

"Stop running from me!" I yell out breathlessly in the direction he goes. "Turn and face me like a man, Carnegie. And none of your tricks!"

"Then stop chasing me," he calls back, further ahead of me than I thought.

I come to a stop, listening for his footsteps. They come to a halt before walking back toward me. Moments later, Carnegie appears around the bend, and my hand tightens around the leather-wrapped hilt of my sword. Blood lust overcomes me, and I charge at him, bringing the blade up and around with a flourish.

He deflects the strike with a short sword he pulls from his belt, pushing me backward with a brute force that makes me stumble. "I don't want to fight you," he says calmly.

"Then you will die on your knees!" With a cry, I whip the sword around, gaining momentum as I strike again. Carnegie deftly blocks, and our blades lock with a shower of sparks, bringing us nose to nose.

"I want to talk to you, Iylara," he says, still calm.

I bare my teeth at him. "As if I would listen to what you have to say after everything!" I am deranged, shaking from head to toe with the sudden need to end this. It will all be over if I run him through with my sword.

I know I cannot keep going down this spiraling path of revenge that I am currently on. It will drive me insane, but I cannot help myself. I shove away from him, another ray of sparks flying as steel scrapes steel.

I bring the sword up offensively, ready to attack again.

I'm not backing down from this! Do you hear me? I scream at him mentally, hoping my raging emotions will bridge the gap in our minds.

"Dammit, woman," he growls, and I charge.

Carnegie brings his other hand up, palm facing me. I freeze, caught by whatever force he directs at me. Mixed with my rapid heartbeat in my ears is that soft music I have only now noticed. Its effect is instant. The fight leaves me, and I fall to my knees, my sword forgotten on the ground where I drop it.

"I said no tricks!" My words fall weakly on uncaring ears. With his hand still outstretched, Carnegie bends his fingers slightly as if squeezing something.

"Argh!" I cry out, leaning forward with my head in my hands.

"And I said I just wanted to talk," he says patiently.

"Okay! Stop, please!" Tears escape the corners of my eyes, shut tight against the pain.

"I didn't want to have to do that, but you wouldn't listen to me," Carnegie says gravely.

The onslaught to my head stops, and I glare at Carnegie with hatred in my eyes, but my anger is fading away, replaced by something else—curiosity. He once said that I might be capable of more than him. Maybe it will explain the tingling in my fingers that happens sporadically. I've dismissed it as nerve damage, but now I am not so sure. It is like electricity crackling through me, without the pain. I've ignored it for the most part, but now—

I slowly shake my head. "How can you do that?" I ask.

Carnegie looks at me with a sly smile. "The nanite receptors in my program manipulate the energy around me at the atomic level, when and where I focus it." Carnegie takes a step forward, looking at me with bright eyes. "You will be able to do the same, maybe even more," he says, almost excited that I asked. "You only need to be taught how to use it."

I frown at him. "Your program?" I ask, confused.

He takes another step forward, bringing him within arm's reach. "We are the same, but you haven't become one with your own yet."

"What program?" I repeat.

Carnegie shakes his head. "You wouldn't understand," he says simply.

"Try me," I challenge.

Carnegie quirks an eyebrow up at me skeptically. "Can you comprehend anything of science past the molecular composition of water?" he asks in a doubting tone.

"Excuse me?" I ask, woefully ignorant to whatever it is he speaks of. Water I know of, but molecular composition? I'm not sure. I definitely don't know what a nanite receptor is.

"That's what I thought." He pauses, looking sideways at me. "You remember what I told you on the Market roof. You were curious then, despite trying to kill me, and you are curious now." Carnegie offers me his hand as he speaks. "You can stand," he adds.

I scowl, realizing that I am still on my knees. I quickly stand to my feet, refusing his hand. Taking a step back, I glare at him with narrowed eyes. "What did you want to talk about so bad?" I ask, trying to avoid admitting that he is right because I am indeed curious—extremely curious.

Carnegie grins. "We can subdue these people ourselves," he says. "Bring peace to the region together. We are already on the same side—you just don't know it yet." I open my mouth to interrupt him, but he holds up a finger, silencing me. "Those people we left fighting are just pawns, and you are their puppeteer out here on the battlefield." Carnegie takes an unconscious step toward me, bringing us face-to-face. I do not move. "It's all to better your skills. But you are just dangling your feet at the edge of the rabbit hole, my love." I frown at his term of endearment, but he continues. "If you don't jump, you will be pushed in. Remember that when the time comes to make a decision." He pauses to smirk at me with that sideways grin of his. "You will know which one it is."

"We are not on the same side," I say through clenched teeth, disregarding everything he says out of spite.

Carnegie chuckles. "Keep telling yourself that if it lets you sleep better at night, but the ground under your feet will give way eventually."

Seventeen

I want to say that it has been about four days since that last battle, but my days are blurring together. Between the mess of responsibilities knocking at my door every five minutes and the whiskey I use to keep Carnegie's voice away, it has been chaos in my head. Having a moment to sit down and drink with Jai eases some tension, but not all.

Jai sits on the couch across from me as I sip on yet another glass of whiskey. I should drink something else, like water, but without it, every terrible memory comes flooding back, which in turn brings Carnegie's nose into my business. Then I am left a mess on the living room floor, unable to escape his taunting voice—without the company, of course. I cannot let myself break in front of anyone, not even Jai.

No one can know how messed up I am.

"Ysabel left this morning," I say, unfeeling when I should be sad. I have been running on autopilot, and none of it feels real.

"Do you know where she went?" Jai asks.

"To her mother, because Keena isn't off the rails crazy like I am apparently—even if she is the world's biggest bitch." I manage a smirk, but it does nothing to reduce the tension settling on Jai's shoulders. "She was meeting her down by the river."

"Why didn't Keena come to the gate?"

"Because I can be a bitch too. Keena isn't allowed anywhere near the walls. Only those loyal to us are allowed here."

"Isn't that a little harsh?" Jai asks.

I shake my head. "No, it isn't. They forfeited their right to be here. We needed them, and they turned their back on us. Their own people!"

"At this point, we are probably going to need their help. It isn't wise to antagonize them when we should be talking to them," Jai says with a sip from his glass.

I scoff at him. "They want nothing to do with us. They made that clear when they left." I pause. *I've got to tell him.* "I am going to meet with Luther. I want you to watch things at the Eastern border while I'm gone. Charon has been trying to work their way up and around our boundaries, picking fights here and there."

Jai bites the inside of his bottom lip, eyeing the glass of whiskey in his lap. "Is that a good idea?" He looks up at me. "Going alone, I mean."

I sip my whiskey, looking over the rim of the glass at him. "If it isn't, I refuse to put more people in danger. We have lost enough people already."

Seeing the uncertainty on his face, I sigh, gritting my teeth. "Please don't try to talk me out of it. My mind is made up. Are you in or not?"

Jai glances away, weighing my words before he nods. "I'm in," he says, capturing my eyes in his azure gaze.

A genuine smile crosses my face. "Thank you."

Jai nods as he stands and walks to the window. He stares out at the oak trees in the backyard before speaking. "This is the only way you foresee the defeat of Charon? You won't even try to speak with the defectors?"

"Yes and no," I say, trying to convince myself as much as I am Jai. "Luther has promised more supplies and support if we join with Vesper. At this point, we don't have a choice. I won't go groveling to Keena's little band of rebels."

"What makes you so sure that we don't have a choice? A week ago, you were all gung-ho about finishing this ourselves."

Jai is right to question me, but I am afraid he will believe I am genuinely crazy if I tell him why I must meet with Luther. But I can't keep silent about it either. I inhale the last bit of whiskey, finding my resolve to tell him the truth. "I had a dream."

Jai turns to look at me, his face contorting in confusion. "What?"

"I had a dream about why we need to join Vesper," I repeat.

Jai stares at me, mouth agape. "You don't make those kinds of decisions based on figments of your imagination, Ray. Have you lost your mind?" he asks.

His words hurt, piercing the small part of me that doesn't believe I am going crazy. I have to protect it. "I know what I saw. I know what I felt. I don't want to be the destruction of my family's legacy. We *don't* have a choice."

Jai isn't convinced. "You keep saying that, but when it's done, what will we have left if we have given up ourselves to win? Won't that destroy the legacy you say you want to protect?"

I look down at my lap, eyes downcast. "You make it sound like life could change that much. I know what it will look like if I don't follow through with my decision. It is more than I can stand."

Jai gazes at me with a deep frown. "What makes you so sure this won't be what causes this destruction you fear?"

I hesitate before speaking, the truth weighing heavy on my shoulders. "Nothing."

***

It takes longer to get to the Vesper compound than I thought it would. The two horses pulling the wagon, Gynn and Mynn, are weary, and my backside is sore from the rough road.

Dusk settles as I approach a vast fenced-in facility with guard towers dotted around the perimeter. The towers have to be at least seventy feet tall. A rusting sign with faded letters is hard to read, but I can make out *Federal Prison* through the century worth of grime, weathering, and lack of light—a remnant of a time past, before the Great War.

A newer and larger sign has been erected on the fence, emblazoned with a strangely shaped star. I stare at it, unable to push away the strange familiarity I get from it. A flash of bright light illuminates the moonless night, blinding me. I throw my hands up to shield my face as my eyes adjust. The wagon stops, and I look up at the woman standing between the horses and the gate.

She has shiny blonde hair pulled tightly away from her face and is dressed in black fatigues. After a moment, I realize she is the woman from the checkpoint at the Market. "You are Iylara Vance," she says with a smooth yet clipped tone.

"Yes," I reply with a curt nod. "I am here to meet with Luther Cain."

"Do you have a summons?" she asks.

The thought of needing an invitation never crossed my mind, but I brought Luther's letter, thankfully. "I got a letter from him. Does that count?"

"Depends. Let me see it," she says briskly.

I sigh and pull out the now wrinkled letter Luther sent to me. The woman steps around the horses, gently petting Mynn before reaching for the letter I extend to her.

She snatches it from my hand and scans the letter with her eyes. The severity of her pursed lips softens. "Yeah, that works," she says, putting on a friendly smile. "Your horses look exhausted. I can take them to the stables for you. Get them some water and food. That okay?"

I can see through her feigned cheeriness like glass, but I meet her demeanor for show. "That would be great, thanks," I say with a smile of my own.

She makes a hand sign up toward the guard tower on the left side of the gate, and it swings open immediately. "My name is Pippa. The man at the door can take you to meet Mr. Cain. The doorman's name is Yates. I will take the horses from here. Knock three times at the front door." She points down the path that ends with a heavy metal door.

"Okay, thanks." I hop down, giving Mynn a gentle stroke. "Be good," I tell the horse, and Pippa laughs.

"You talk to them too?"

"Oh yeah, and sometimes I swear they want to talk back," I joke. "Take care of them," I say with a thinly veiled warning behind my words.

Pippa hops up in my spot on the wagon bench and delicately takes the reins in her hands with a nod. "That they do, but don't worry. They will be well taken care of," she says, the clipped tone back in her voice at my words. She clicks her tongue with a flick of the reigns, and the horses comply. They turn the wagon around and disappear into the darkness, where the floodlight cannot reach.

I step through the gate, and it shuts behind me. I hesitate a moment before heading for the door at the end of the walkway. I stop in front of it and knock three times. It swings open immediately, bathing me in the artificial light inside. I wince at the brightness and look around for the person who opened the door. I see no one and step inside. The door snaps shut, and I jump at the sound. Turning around, I find a small-built man releasing the door handle, dressed in a suit, much like Luther was the first time I saw him.

"You Yates?" I ask, glancing around.

"I am," he says with a terse nod. "Please follow me."

He turns on his heel, heading for a desk in the middle of the large entry room with a slight limp. Arched metallic contraptions are positioned in a row on either side, cutting the room in half.

"What are those?" I ask.

"Metal detectors," he replies curtly, with the same clipped tone that Pippa had. "We must get you signed in before you go through."

"What do they do?"

Yates purses his lips. "They detect metal, ma'am."

I grit my teeth. "I get that, but what are they used for?"

"Keep people from entering with weapons."

"Mmm," I say, eyes dancing over the devices suspiciously. Those might have been useful at the Market.

Yates ignores me, stepping through the metal detector closest to the desk, and lights flash green above his head. He takes a seat, looking up at me expectantly, before motioning for me to take my place in front of him. "Please fill these out," he says, handing me a small bundle of papers and a pen. "I assume you can read and write?"

"Yeah, I can. What are these for?" I ask, glancing over the paperwork.

"Our records." He does not care to elaborate, and I resign to turning my full attention to the papers in front of me to fill out.

Name, birthday, tribal affiliation—blah, blah, blah.

The following page has two large boxes but no instructions. "What do I do with this?"

Yates pushes a black rectangle the size of my hand toward me. "Handprints. Dip your hand in the ink and place it on the paper. The next page will be individual fingerprints."

"What do you need all that for? I'm just here for a meeting," I say, exasperated.

"Our records," he says again.

I huff in aggravation. "Whatever."

I put my prints down as fast as I can. Anxiety is beginning to stir inside of me. I want to get this over with. When I am done, I push the pages back to Yates, and he hands me a wet cloth to wipe the ink from my hands.

He reviews the pages quietly before setting them aside and looking at me. "Any weapons?"

"Yeah, you think I trekked all the way here unarmed?" I ask snidely.

Yates purses his lips again. "Please put them on the desk. You cannot take them in."

I unbuckle my weapons belt and set it on the desk with a heavy thud.

"Any more?"

I pull my jacket back, revealing a pistol in the leather shoulder holster hanging under my arm.

"Unload it, please."

I withdraw the pistol slowly and release the magazine, sitting it on the desk. I empty the chamber before placing the single bullet and gun next to my belt and magazine.

"Are you wearing anything metal?"

I stare down at myself. "A few things, yeah."

"Please remove them. Put them in here." He sits a small container on top of the desk. "Then step through the metal detector."

I oblige him by removing the hammered metal cuffs around my wrists and the half-dozen metal rings in each ear. I hesitate to take off my father's ring. "Do I get this stuff back before I go in? I'm not leaving this here," I say, staring pointedly at the ring.

"Of course, but not the weapons."

"Okay," I say with a nod. I put everything in the container and look up expectantly.

"Anything else?"

I shake my head. "Nope."

"Step through, please," he says, motioning at the metal arches.

I walk through the same detector Yates did and almost scream in surprise as a loud alarm starts blaring. Red instead of green lights flash across the top of the metal detector, and Yates is on his feet instantly with a small handgun pointed at my chest.

I take a step back. "Whoa, whoa!" I say with my hands up in surrender. The alarms fade, but the lights continue flashing over my head.

"Don't move," he says threateningly. "What are you hiding?"

"N-nothing, I—" Then I remember. "Oh."

"What?" he demands.

"There is a small knife in my boot," I say sheepishly.

Yates' eyes widen. "And you thought you could get through with it?"

"No, no. I forgot about it." I am not lying. Jai gave it to me in place of the one I lost on the Market roof, and old habits die hard.

"How do you forget about a knife?" he asks skeptically.

"I don't ever take it out. It stays in my boot." My reply is honest, assuaging his hostile protectiveness for the most part.

Yates flicks a button. "Step back through and put it on the desk. And anything *else* you may have forgotten about. I would hate to have to shoot you."

"Okay, chill." I do as I am told and stand in front of the detector.

"Step through."

I hold my breath, hoping nothing else will set off the metal detector. I release my breath when no alarms sound and find green lights flashing instead of red ones. Satisfied that I will not try and kill anyone, Yates puts the gun away under the desk in a holster attached to the side of the drawers. He hits another button, and a heavy glass door slides open at the back of the room.

"You will go straight after the doors. Take a left when you get to the crossway, then a right at the next one. Mr. Cain's office will be at the end of the hallway. You can't miss it. It has a large oak door with engravings on it. Only one like it."

"After all this, you're gonna let me go by myself?"

Yates shrugs. "It isn't like you could do anything, and you came after hours. There isn't anyone else available."

"Well, alrighty then." I guess it will remain to be seen whether my miscalculated arrival time will work to my benefit.

I take my things and head for the open door. I am met with a closed door on the opposite end, but as soon as I step inside the small room, the open door starts sliding shut. I put my things back on, trying to steady my breathing as I am encased inside. I do not like enclosed spaces in unknown places. A moment before I start freaking out, the second door opens. I stumble out gratefully.

I spot the crossway further down and make haste for it.

Rounding the corner into a sterile white hallway, a strong hand grabs my upper arm, tugging me against my captor's chest. I gasp out in surprise, but I am shut up by a large, gloved hand covering my lower face. I struggle in vain to get loose, grunting in frustration as the hand arresting me pulls me into an empty room on the left. Soft, warm lips brush my ear.

"Please don't scream. I'm not going to hurt you," a masculine voice breathes into my ear. Something about the way the man speaks is familiar, and his breath on my neck sends a shiver down my spine.

He eases his grip on my arm as I go still, and his hand slowly falls away from my mouth. I spin around to find the eyes of my captor gleaming in the light shining into the room from the hallway. They freeze me to the spot.

Danny? But, of course, it is not him.

"Zeke?" I whisper, heart thudding loud enough that if anyone were to walk by, they would surely hear it. I have only ever seen a faded charcoal portrait of the man in front of me, but the familial Rekkon resemblance is striking. There is no one else it could be, but this close to him, lost in his eyes, I could believe it is Danny and not his older brother.

Zeke nods in answer to my breathless question.

"What are you doing here?" A thought crosses my mind, and I try to tug my arm out of his grasp. "Were you at the Market that day?" It would explain why he is here if he were taken with the others.

Zeke is still very much Charon, despite his baby brother's choices. I do not know what kind of person he is, and the thought of him killing my people disgusts me. He may look like his brother, but they cannot be the same on the inside, no matter how closely they resemble each other in appearance.

Zeke nods again, eyes sad. "I didn't want to be," he says quietly, "but I couldn't say no." He drops his arms, freeing me to step away to look at him thoroughly.

Zeke is taller than Danny was, if only by a few inches, with broad shoulders where his brother's were more narrow. His black shirt hugs the lean muscles of his arms down to his wrists. Swirling Charon tattoos appear from the v-neck of his shirt, reaching for his ears on either side of his neck.

I may want to believe he is telling the truth, what with my heart still screaming *Danny* with painful longing, but I am not stupid. I take a step backward. "You expect me to believe that?"

"No, I don't." Zeke glances out the door to ensure no one is coming down the hallway. "You shouldn't be here," he says, voice low.

"And why is that?"

"Luther isn't what he seems," he whispers.

The hairs on the back of my neck stand up. "I figured that much, but I don't have much choice, thanks to ya'll."

Zeke shakes his head, distraught. "That's how he wants it. It's how he gets you." Zeke bares his teeth in frustration as if holding back what he wants to say.

"Please, spit it out. Luther is expecting me any moment. You keep me too long, and he will know something is up."

"It isn't what it seems," he says, shaking his head.

"What isn't?"

"The deal," he says simply.

My eyebrow quirks at his words, and my heart rate spikes as a seed of doubt is planted. "I don't want to hear this." I turn to leave, but Zeke's hand grasps my upper arm again, holding me in place.

"Don't agree to whatever bullshit he tells you." His tone is pleading.

"Why?"

"It destroyed my clan. Killed—" Zeke pauses, shaking his head, eyes closed. "Just be careful."

I narrow my eyes at him. "Okay."

"I mean it. Be careful. You don't know what that man is capable of or the power he holds."

I chew on my upper lip. Looking at him makes my heart ache at his very appearance, but I cannot lose sight of why I am here. He is still the enemy. "Yeah. Sure. I will be," I say, nodding unconvincingly.

Zeke grits his teeth. "I'm serious."

I nod again, quickly turning myself into a bobblehead. "Of course you are. Now I have a meeting to get to. Will you excuse me, or are we going to continue to go 'round and 'round?"

Zeke shakes his head. "No. Go on."

I can tell he is defeated, but I cannot bring myself to care. I cannot let *anything* get in the way of my decision, especially not a pretty face. I have made up my mind, and some dead-husband-look-a-like will not deter me—even if a part of me pleads to the other to listen to the man.

"Thanks," I say, heavy on the sarcasm. Zeke looks out the door again and motions for me to leave. I brush past him into the hallway, trying not to touch him.

Before I turn right at the end, I glance over my shoulder. Zeke still stands in the doorway where I left him, and for a moment, I find Danny staring back at me. My heart somersaults in my chest, and I cannot help the small smile that tugs at my lips—then my brain catches up, and I almost throw myself around the corner out of embarrassment.

Zeke is not *Danny. He isn't.*

My heart doesn't seem to care.

***

I stop in front of Luther's door, hesitating out of anxiety as much as I do out of admiration. The door is beautiful. Sigils and tribal filigree surround an ornately carved owl. Its eyes are so intricately detailed that it looks like they are staring at me—boring holes into my soul. It is beautiful and unnerving at the same time.

I rip my eyes away, heart racing in anticipation, and knock three times. There is a split second of silence before a voice says, "Come in."

I push the lever knob down, and the heavy door swings open easily. The room is bathed in orange light from lamps that resemble stones placed around the room on the hardwood tables and shelves. A large desk sits in front of a wall made of windows, covered by elegantly embroidered black and gold curtains that fall to the floor.

The man behind the desk appears no different than when I first saw him, except his tie is loosened. There is a relaxed air about him rather than the stiff and standoffish persona he exuded in the War Room. Luther stands as I enter with a welcoming smile on his face. "Ms. Vance, I am so glad to see you!" His upbeat tone differs greatly from the arrogant and standoffish one I first encountered.

I cannot find words and simply nod with a forced smile. My nerves are on edge, and my hands shake. Luther quirks an eyebrow ever so slightly, and I force myself to speak as I fidget with my hands. "Thank you for having me at such a late hour. I tried to get here earlier, but the roads were worse than I planned for."

Luther smiles to reveal a mouthful of well-kept teeth. "Ah, yes. Fixing the roads is at the top of my to-do list, but the locals aren't cooperating at the moment. Maybe we can remedy that. Please, sit." He motions toward the two chairs sitting in front of his desk.

I sit in the closest one, and Luther follows suit, sinking back into his high-back chair. His aura is much more welcoming than the first time I met him, and I slowly begin to relax.

"To be honest, I have never been this far north," I say, unsure of where my want to be honest with him comes from.

"Oh really?" he asks, surprised.

I shrug. "Not that I can remember anyway."

He smiles knowingly. “You must be hungry after such a trip. I will have the kitchens prepare you something if you would like.”

My stomach growls audibly, and I smile shyly. “That would be great,” I say as Luther chuckles.

He reaches over and presses a button on a fancy-looking phone on his desk. No one uses them these days, but I have seen a few in my time—not quite as elaborate as his, though.

“Yes, sir?” The woman’s voice coming from the phone is crisp and clear, unlike the crackling of a radio. I raise my eyebrows in surprise—and a little envy.

“Would you please have a dinner plate made for our guest?”

“Of course, sir. Anything in particular?” the woman asks.

Luther looks at me in question, and I shake my head. “I’m not picky.”

Luther nods. “The chef’s special, please.”

“Right away, sir.”

“Thank you,” he says with a smile in my direction.

“You’re welcome, sir.” The woman’s voice disappears with a click, leaving us in silence.

“You are here to discuss joining us?” Luther asks me.

Right to the point, then. It makes it easier on me, I suppose. I am not sure what I am supposed to say. I am out of my element if we are going to be negotiating anything.

I try to loosen up as I speak, but there is a stiffness that I cannot soften. “Yes. I have to protect my people. We have absolved all the resources we had to take Charon out on our own without significant loss of life,” I say, repeating my side of a made-up conversation I had in my head on the way here.

Luther nods. “The people of this region have suffered greatly. I am very sorry about what Charon did. I intended to help people, not hurt them when I arranged that meeting at the Market.”

“They have,” I say quietly, looking down at my fingers clasped tightly in my lap to keep the shaking at bay. “If I am honest, I should have taken your offer sooner, but pride permits me to try and do it my way until I have no other choice,” I say to my surprise. I can’t help but kick myself internally.

Not tactful.

Luther chuckles. "Don't we all?" He stands and walks over to a small table. On top is a variety of bottles filled with what I assume is liquor. I recognize the whiskey, but he has others I am unfamiliar with. "Would you like a drink? Vodka? Whiskey? Gin?"

I try to restrain my impulsive need for a drink to calm my nerves. "Whiskey is good," I say.

"Ah, a whiskey woman. I will have to keep my eye on you," he says with a hearty chuckle.

I grin and laugh politely with him, but his words make me uneasy. Luther pours a generous glass and hands it to me. I hold on to it as he pours himself a glass of clear liquor. The bottle says Gin, but I have never heard of it before. Whiskey and near undrinkable moonshine are the only libations you can generally find around these parts.

Luther turns to me, holding out his glass. I stand, mirroring him. "To a brighter future," he says.

"To a brighter future," I echo robotically.

Our glasses clink together, and I down half the glass. The whiskey takes my breath away, stronger than I am used to, but I hold back the sputtering and smile in appreciation.

"So," Luther begins, sitting back down in his chair. I follow his lead. "I am sure that you have questions."

I bite my bottom lip. "It's more of just one question," I say honestly.

Luther smiles at me. "Ah. Well, I will do my best to answer. What is it?"

I take another sip of whiskey, the effects of the first taste already warming my cheeks. We don't make it this strong in Blackthorn. "If we join, how much of our lives will change? I understand the perks, but I don't believe that it doesn't come at a cost."

"Well, of course, there *is* a cost. Nothing is free, my dear." My heart drops, but Luther smiles sweetly, quelling my rising panic. "But you aren't selling away everything you believe in if you join us. We merely ask for cooperation. We want to bring the region together—make life more abundant and profitable for all."

"But what exactly does that entail?" I ask skeptically.

Luther shrugs. "It's as simple as helping out when needed. We want to share our provisions with you, but we need to know that if, say, a tornado takes out something important, your people are willing to help rebuild, regardless of who it belongs to." Luther takes a sip of Gin, his gray-blue eyes shining.

I stare at him blankly, not entirely grasping what he means. It is as if the man can read my mind, however, and he answers my unspoken question. "All I ask is that we can depend on you if we need you."

That sounds simple enough, but— "You want to unite the region, and yet you are willing to help us defeat Charon. Why?"

Luther does not hesitate to answer. "What Charon did was wrong. They will either submit, or they will all die. It's as simple as life or death. I do not tolerate those who rescind their word."

What are you doing?

Despite the whiskey buzz, Carnegie's voice appears in my mind, freezing me in place. I nod my head for Luther's benefit, but I am immediately lost in my head.

What I have to. I can't let you win.

A soft chuckle fills my mind, and I shiver. The following silence makes my adrenaline spike, and I am not sure if I am doing the right thing or not.

"Or if some outside force attacks, or Charon gets unruly again, we help you take them out?" I ask, ignoring the feeling of impending doom.

"Precisely."

"We treat you as our own?"

"Yes." He smiles kindly.

I sigh deeply and drain my glass without a second thought. "Then okay. Let's do this."

Eighteen

"Chief!" a frantic voice calls out. I turn on the barstool I sit on in the pub to find Warren running toward me.

"What?" I ask, already weary from the tone in his voice.

"We have a problem," he mutters in my ear.

"Again?" I ask. For once, I would like to have a relaxed day and pass out drunk for a dreamless night's sleep, but no. There is always something going on that needs my attention.

"There has been another attack."

I sit up, immediately on alert. "What happened?" I ask, my glass of whiskey forgotten for the moment.

"You know that convoy of Vesper soldiers that Luther was sending?" he asks.

"Yeah," I say slowly, already weary of what news he brings.

"Part of the group that abandoned us attacked them on the road."

I stare at him, speechless, for a moment before I can find words. "What does that have to do with us? They aren't my problem anymore."

"Defectors retreated, leaving only a few Vesper dead. It was near Jai's outpost. Luther's troops took the group you had stationed there, believing they are the ones who attacked them."

My eyes widen. "And Jai?"

Warren looks forlorn. "Taken."

"Shit!" I curse, standing up from my stool in haste, nearly knocking it over.

"There's more," he says hesitantly.

"Seriously?" I ask.

"Luther sent a message. He wants you to meet him as soon as possible. He is pissed."

My heart drops into my stomach. If Luther thinks we turned, he will surely retaliate, knowing how weak we are. I told him so myself. I already know how he feels about people going against their word.

"Get me a horse ready. No wagon. I need to get there as fast as I can."

Warren nods. "Yes, ma'am."

I hurry home to gather the few things I may need on the road, trying my damnedest to keep the panic building in my chest at bay.

***

I can't believe this!

My panic and aggravation come out as shaking hands and fumbling fingers. I throw a change of clothes into a bag with some rations.

You thought this was going to go so easy? Join Vesper, and your problems end? I told you to join me. You will regret this. Carnegie's voice is soft, but it ignites a fury in me.

The only thing I am going to regret is not killing you sooner. SHUT UP!

He chuckles, and I bare my teeth at the wall.

Have it your way, then. Don't say I didn't warn you.

I scream out in frustration, kicking the table next to me. The candle on top is unlit, but the bottle of whiskey is uncorked and spills across the floor. "Son of a bitch," I growl, swiping the bottle up before I can lose too much. I'm angrier at the waste than the mess as I take a swig from the salvaged bottle.

"Ms. Vance?" a voice says timidly from the doorway.

"What?" I turn, voice bitter and biting, whiskey bottle held tightly in my grasp.

The young messenger boy takes a step backward. "Your horse is ready, missus."

I try to soften the anger on my face, but it comes across as more of a grimace. "Thank you."

"Y-you're welcome, ma'am." His nervous stutter softens the sharp edges of my emotions, but he is gone before I can apologize.

I growl, taking two more large swigs from the whiskey bottle before pushing it aside. I hiss as it goes down my throat and shove the rest of my supplies into my bag before darting out of the cabin door.

Warren waits with Gynn, saddled and ready to go. "Do you need someone to come with you?" he asks.

"No." I grab on to the saddle and sling myself up into place with ease. "Lock down the gate, and don't let anyone in unless they are with Jai or me."

Warren salutes with a nod and steps away as I turn Gynn around to face the gate. "Yes, ma'am. Godspeed to you."

I nod in acknowledgment and nudge Gynn in the side. She takes off at a trot. Once we pass through the gate, I urge her on, and she takes off in a gallop. I hold on to the reins tightly, praying I make it before Luther does something crazy.

***

"I sent reinforcements, and what do your people do? Attack them! They would have all been executed on the spot had they not fled like cowards!" Luther says scathingly. "I'm not sure I still don't need to do that very thing. They clearly cannot follow orders. What use is a group of AWOL soldiers?"

My heart pounds against my rib cage painfully as I listen to him speak from behind his desk. His demeanor is completely changed from the last time I was here. I may stand in the middle of his office like a scolded child, but my rising fear does not come from my own misbehaving. I have to stand my ground.

"Those were deserters—not my people." Luther is already shaking his head before I finish speaking. "You're men took the wrong people!" I say desperately.

Luther glares at me venomously. "Do not lie to me. They were marked. The lot of them were Blackthorn. You never mentioned having deserters before this. That is a convenient excuse, Iylara." He says my name in a way that makes me shrink back as if reprimanded by my father.

I should have known withholding that information from him would bite me in the ass. But I didn't think it would happen this fast.

"You should know Blackthorn will do whatever they think is necessary to survive. It's all we know how to do, and when a foreign army strolled up and made camp at their doorstep, they felt the need to defend themselves!" I say, containing the urge to scream.

"So you admit they were your people?"

I sputter, caught by my own words. "N-no! Not anymore."

"That's not what you just said," Luther says with a sneer.

I shake my head, defeated. "You know what I mean."

"Do I?" he scoffs. "It sounded like a confession to me."

With each passing second, Luther is getting more impatient, so I try a different tactic—pleading. Something I don't do lightly. "Please don't take this out on them. The people you have are not the ones who attacked your men. There has to be something I can do to smooth this entire thing over. This is all a horrible misunderstanding. I'm sorry that lives were lost."

Luther sits stoically in his chair, elbows propped up on the arms with his fingers entwined in front of him. He stares at his thumbs, twiddling them in circles as he thinks. An idea seems to occur to him after a drawn-out moment, and he looks up at me knowingly before he speaks. "Have you heard the story of Jesus?"

I raise an eyebrow at his ridiculous question. Jesus is not someone you hear of much, but I know who he is. My mother used to read to me about him before bed. "Yeah," I say bluntly. I go silent, waiting for Luther to speak as he works out the words in his head before beginning whatever tale he is about to spin.

"Then you understand that God gave his only son to save humanity from their failure and grave mistakes caused by the fall of mankind in the Garden at the beginning of our history. A sacrifice for all so we may have a more abundant life." Luther watches me closely as he tells his story. "God gave him because every life is precious, redeemable, regardless of the choices a person may have made in the past—because of one." His voice is smooth, never stumbling over his words as if he has the entire thing memorized by heart.

I do not like where this is going, and I cannot control the slight downturn of my brow as a thought dawns on me. I turn my gaze away from Luther's piercing stare and down at my dusty boots. I try to keep my breathing steady as what I assume he is proposing settles on my shoulders.

"What do I need to do?" I ask quietly in defeat.

Luther does not hesitate to answer, a grin spreading across his face. "Don't fight it," is all he says.

Two Vesper soldiers converge on either side of me, grabbing me firmly by my upper arms. Luther smiles mischievously. "Let's go for a walk."

The men on either side of me have much longer legs than I do, and I struggle to keep stride with them. They end up half dragging me out the door to the area in front of the courtyard fence where they have my people imprisoned. We are noticed immediately by the people closest to us. I watch one by one as every Blackthorn member turns their attention toward us with varying degrees of concern.

The two men leave me standing some ten feet from the fence as Luther approaches behind me. His overly-shined shoe kicks me in the back of the knee, dropping me to the ground at his feet. A collective gasp and shudder pulses through the crowd. Everyone has been disarmed, so even if they wanted to try and help me, they don't have much going for them.

From where I sit, I can see over a dozen guard towers encircling the courtyard. They are manned with two snipers each, prepared to start picking people off one by one if the need arises. There are surely more guns in the shadows, but they are unnecessary.

No bonds hold me captive as I sit propped up on my knees in submission. Only the omnipresent fear for my people's lives should I try to save my own skin keeps me contained. Everything in me wants to flee and preserve myself because I now believe Luther might be cruel enough to kill me to make a point. The feigned niceties during our last meeting melt away, and I can see what kind of man he is. My first impression of him was correct, but I lost sight of that in my desperation.

If my sacrifice will save them, I must do what is best for my people—even if it is a dishonorable handful that got us here in the first place. They will have to be shown the magnitude of the seriousness of our situation in a way that they will understand. If I die, the ones responsible for this mess will surely hear about it.

We are no longer playing by our own rules. I knew this when I signed the dotted line, but Luther made it sound so easy—so simple. I was a fool. It didn't take long for everything to fall apart, and the others will understand shortly. I can only hope I somehow come out of this alive because dying was not what I had planned for the day.

My hands lay limply on my lap, and I stare down at the sandy ground in front of me, trying to steady my breathing. I finally look up at the people closest to the fence, and from the look on their faces, they know this will not end well. It is too late to take back what was done. Men died. Someone must atone for their lives.

Terror courses through me as I scan the crowd for Jai, but he is nowhere to be seen.

Maybe it is for the best.

Luther begins to speak, addressing the crowd, and there is arrogance in his voice that I overlooked before—he has been hiding it. "Before you all get yourselves worked up into a tizzy, I'm going to have to shut you down."

I peek over my shoulder and find a grin gracing Luther's face that makes me cringe. I am seriously starting to second guess my life choices.

"You see, I need you—all of you. So I would hate to have to mow you all down in a hail of bullets. But you have already killed some of my men. I don't care how or why. Vesper died at the hands of Blackthorn. It's as simple as that," he says, holding a hand up to silence the few naysayers who dare to say anything.

This is all completely unfair.

"Your loving Chief here has given herself up as a sacrifice for you people so that I may forgive your trespasses, even after you failed to heed her orders. How glorious is that?" He says it as if he is God himself, and I cringe. I know when the Word is being twisted, even if I cannot call myself a religious or Godly woman like my mother. I can feel it in the pit of my stomach instinctively, and I have to fight my rising anger.

Snake.

Looks of abject horror dawn on the faces of the people in front who can hear him, and they begin to pass the message backward. Jai steps up to the fence as the crowd parts for him. Concern and worry are evident on his face. His knees go weak at the sight of my predicament, and he grabs the fence for support. He is helpless to defend me. I find his gaze and hold on to it for dear life. Only Jai can see the terror and swirling sea of emotions behind my eyes. His brow creases starkly, and mist wells up in his eyes as he stares back at me.

"Anybody moves, and you all die, but here is the good news. As I said, I need all of you, so if your Chief here can manage to survive the bullet I am about to put in her, you can keep her, and I still have a Captain. Hopefully, it's a win-win for us all," he says cheerfully.

Jai's and many other sets of eyes widen at Luther's words, but I cannot hear their dissent. Their voices are overcome by the ringing that begins to fill my ears. My heart thuds in my chest as only the hammer click of a pistol cuts through the high pitch preening against my eardrums.

I don't want to die.

Luther pauses for a moment, and I cannot help but wonder if he is relishing the moment or just trying to hit the right spot.

Don't stop fighting. Please don't give up when the dark comes for you.

It is not Carnegie's voice but a familiar-sounding stranger that speaks in my mind.

Luther pulls the trigger with a loud bang, and I jump with a gasp as time slows. The intense force of the bullet hits its target, and my breath hitches as it exits the right side of my chest. The bullet strikes the ground at Jai's feet, but he does not move. An intense burning sensation radiates outward from the bullet wound, and warm blood fills my mouth.

I shudder, trying to inhale, but I choke on the blood filling my throat. Life drips from the corners of my mouth, and I groan before falling to my side.

"NO!" Jai and many others scream out. I close my eyes, trying to focus on catching a breath.

Jai's voice is lost in the screams around me, but no one moves, per Luther's orders, because he means business. He never said they could not scream and, in some cases, cry, which he must enjoy.

My right lung fills up with blood, choking me, and an awful gasping sound escapes my throat as I make every effort to get air into my good lung. I am only inhaling blood, drowning myself faster.

So this is how it ends?

Don't give in to it.

I am grasping at straws to do as the familiar voice says. My strength is quickly leaving me.

Luther speaks, as if from far away, even though he still stands over me. "Remember this the next time you want to go against direct orders from your superior. Your fearless leader might have given her life for you today. I do not recommend making it a choice in vain. You are dismissed."

To the guards, Luther says, "Take them to Receiving, gentlemen. And Lydia," he adds, "see what you can do for her." I open my eyes to find the compound's doctor nodding before she kneels next to me.

With that, Luther strolls back to his office without a second glance at me writhing on the ground. I catch a blurry glimpse of Jai and the others being hurried away through a door on the right side of the courtyard. For a second, our eyes meet again.

I lose consciousness, knowing that my decision saved his life, and I do not regret it. It is more than I could ever do for Danny.

Nineteen

"Let me out!" I demand angrily, yanking on the strap around my left wrist. The damage to my right side was extensive, and even after two weeks is still quite tender. But it will not keep me from pitching a fit.

I have been bedridden for far too long with tubes and hoses coming out of me from places I would prefer them not to. I am at my wit's end, and not knowing what is going on outside of my room is driving me insane.

Carika frantically shakes her head. "I'm sorry. I'm under orders. You have been deemed a threat risk until Mr. Cain says otherwise."

I was surprised to see Carika's face when I woke up, but she has fallen into submission under Luther without hesitation. Nothing I say will make her listen to me or do what I want, not as it would have before. She is trapped as much as I am—because of me.

"I'm not going to hurt anyone! I just want to scratch my damn nose by myself!" I say, trying not to yell. I resort to begging her. "Please!"

Carika nods her head nervously. "Okay, I will go get him. Maybe he will decide you are safe to untie. I can't do anything without his say, ma'am."

I have been pretty out of it, for the most part, between relative unconsciousness and painkillers, and I have missed a lot. Luther made his point when he shot me. He strikes fear in everyone, and I wish I could have seen his true self sooner. I would have run as fast as I could in the other direction. Nothing good can come from a man so full of himself.

The man who put me in this hospital bed is the last person I want to see, but if he is the only way to being untied, then so be it. Thankfully, he has not felt inclined to visit, but nobody else has been allowed to see me either, not since a brief visit with Jai a few days after the incident. I barely remember it, but the fact that everyone is okay has stuck with me.

My nurses have been my only company. Carika is the only one I know, and most of them are not very nice. I like Lydia, the head doctor, though. She could come around more often, but she is the equivalent to Dr. Matthews around here. She is rarely seen for more than a few minutes at a time.

As much as I wanted to hurt Dr. Matthews the last time I saw her, the fact that she is not here like Carika worries me. I don't know what has become of her, and I haven't wanted to ask.

It does not take Carika long to come back with Luther. She holds the door open for him before closing it behind him, leaving us alone.

"What is it that I am being bothered for?" Luther asks, a bored tone to his voice. He is dressed to the nine like always, but his hair does appear a little more salt than pepper since the last time I saw him.

"I just want out of the handcuffs," I say politely, even though I could spit in his face. "I didn't do anything other than what you wanted."

"But why would I let you out before I can make sure you aren't going to renege on our deal? You must have *some* resentment for me after I put a bullet in you," he says with a smile.

"Because I'm so dangerous? Please. I just want to scratch my nose," I reiterate. "If you haven't noticed, I'm still pretty messed up. I'm not going to hurt anybody," I add defiantly. He steps forward to study me.

"And how do I know you aren't playing me for a fool?" Luther reaches out and brushes the top of my gown out of the way, tracing the edge of the bandage covering the mending hole his bullet pierced through me. My breath hitches as his cold fingers splay out over the bandage, the tips of his fingers caressing the bare skin of my chest.

I look up at him, nervous at what his intention could be. His eyes go hard as he raises his other hand to my mouth. He presses down on the bandage, and I howl in pain, his hand muffling my shrieks of agony considerably.

He removes his hand a moment later from my wound. He draws a knife with a flash of metal, holding me at its edge. The kiss of the razor-sharp steel against my throat stings, and I dare not move. My wretched breathing rasps in my chest as the silver pommel shines menacingly in the glow of the light bulb hanging over my bed.

Shoving my head back, hand still over my mouth, he exposes my neck, and I am at his mercy again. Luther leans forward, lips an inch from my ear. "I need you to remember this. Remember why it all happened. Remember my mercy for your people." His voice drips with poisonous honey as he whispers in my ear. "You are mine, you understand?" he growls lowly.

I do not respond to his question but rather stay defiantly quiet. Nothing I want to say to him will help my cause.

"Everyone will know whether you want to speak or not." His hand slowly slides down my mouth, resting under my chin over my clan mark. He wraps his fingers around the top of my throat, holding me still. He brings the blade to my face, placing the tip under my left nostril. The edge bites into my skin from the delicate pressure he applies. With an agonizingly slow stroke of the blade, he drags the tip diagonally down through my lips, nicking my chin for good measure. I moan pitifully in pain as I fight the urge to flail about, but that would only make the stinging pain hurt worse.

Luther lowers his head back down to whisper in my ear. "Go against me, and people will die. I don't care whose idea it is. I will have obedience," he says threateningly.

His hand around my throat goes even lower, and he squeezes. Blood oozes down my chin, into my mouth, and down my neck, leaving the bottom portion of my face coated in blood as I start to gasp for breath, unable to fight off his hands.

Everything in me wants to fight, but I cannot breathe or move. I must listen to him speak while black spots flicker across my vision. "If you have a problem with how something is done, all you have to do is give up one man. One man per issue, and you can have it your way—one life for one say. Otherwise, keep your mouth shut, and do what I tell you to do. Do you understand, Iylara?" I try to nod my head, and he lets me go.

"I want to hear you say it," he says, voice as smooth as velvet. He is unsatisfied with my silence. "Do you understand, Iylara?" he repeats.

I glare at him. What he proposes is obscene.

In an innocently sweet voice, he says, "All you have to say is, 'I understand, Master.'" The sneer on his face says he is enjoying himself a little too much.

I grit my teeth, taking as deep of a breath as I can manage, all dignity squashed. "I understand, *Master*," I say stiffly.

Luther sneers at me. "Good. We will need to work on that tone of voice, though." With a quick whistle, Luther summons a nurse as he leans away from me. One of the Vesper nurses enters, not even twitching at the sight of the bloody mess. This must happen more often than not.

The nurse grabs a tray and starts putting supplies on it. I can only wonder where Carika went. "Get well soon, my dear," Luther says, looking down at me. "Nothing much would have changed for you had these recent events never occurred," he says solemnly. "But now everything is going to change. Just wait and see."

Without another word, he leans down, grabbing my chin delicately at first until I try to turn away. Then his lips come crashing against mine. I groan as the pressure agitates the cut in my lips, and Luther pulls back, satisfied. He walks away with my blood smeared on his chin with a grin only the devil can muster. With one last glance at me, he licks his lips clean. He leaves with a flourish, and I shiver.

I told you to join me.

Carnegie's voice physically makes me sick.

I turn my head and vomit, but tied to the bed as I am, it coats my arm in warm stomach bile. I whimper as the nurse cleans up the mess, silent in the wake of what has transpired.

I shut my eyes and wish for the simplicity of death.

***

The guard's voice is faint from outside my door. "Why are you doing this, sir?"

I can hear the smile in Luther's voice as he answers. "I need to break and remake her, that's why."

Stringy hair hangs over my eyes, obscuring my vision in one eye, but from where I lay on the concrete floor, I can see Luther staring at me through the small glass window in the door to my cell. In the faint light, he watches me, and I can barely keep my eyes open as I stare back at him. Small convulsions make my body twitch sporadically every few seconds.

"I'm close," he tells the guard with relish.

I cannot fully comprehend his words, not with the sharp bolts of what feels like electricity shooting through me with each convulsion—the painful after-effects of whatever drug he has been pumping me with.

"But, sir," the man says timidly. "You are torturing her. It isn't right—"

"Isn't right?" Luther asks him, disappearing from the window. "How long do you think it would be into our mission before she became a turncoat and tried to destroy everything we have worked so hard for? These people's loyalties are extremely hard to break, so the safest bet is to reset her. The others will follow. They are already starting to. They just need another little push to fall in line completely."

"Understood, sir—sorry, sir," the man mumbles quickly in shame.

Luther appears in the window again, opening the door to my prison. He throws it open, none too gently, watching me with a sadistic smirk as I involuntarily jump at the sound of the metal door banging against the wall. I jump again as he slams it shut.

"No," I say with a groan. I press my forehead against the cool concrete floor, wishing him away.

"Oh yes," he says through a smile.

Grinding my teeth painfully, I hit my forehead on the floor once with a quiet, distraught sob. "Please, no more." My voice is so weak that I can barely understand myself. Another convulsion jolts my body as he kneels beside me.

"What was that?" Luther asks, grabbing me by my shoulder. He roughly rolls me onto my back. A pained exhale of breath leaves me as the tense muscles in my body pull tight at the movement. "I want to hear you say it again." His voice is soft and reassuring. "Then I will stop."

My silence does not deter him. Luther stares at me, studying my face. "Such a delicate touch of artwork I did on you," he says, a finger tracing the edge of the nearly healed cut that will surely scar my lips. "Most whose faces I scar are not spared deformity, but then I wouldn't get the primal satisfaction of looking at you."

Through my pain, his words strike a nerve in me, bringing me back from the edge. I know what he is doing, so how could it work? For a moment, I can defy him again. "Go to hell," I manage to muster up enough willpower to say. I weakly spit in his face for good measure.

With a sigh, he swings out, hitting me across the face with the back of his hand. The impact slings my head to the side with a pop of my neck. A yelp of pain escapes me, and I roll over on my side, holding my face.

He does not give me time to recover. Grabbing me by the hair, he forces my head to the side, exposing my neck while I struggle weakly against him. Luther pulls a syringe from his jacket pocket, the same as each one before it, and uncaps it with his teeth. He jams the needle into my neck, pushing down on the plunger.

Within seconds of the liquid entering my bloodstream, violent, painful convulsions cause me to seize up on the floor at Luther's feet. He stands with a smile while wiping away my saliva on his cheek.

Luther slowly backs up, only taking his eyes off me to recap the syringe and place it back in his pocket. He grabs the chair by the door before making himself comfortable. He watches the effects of the serum with an expectant glimmer in his cold eyes.

My silent screams are all too real in my head as I jerk around on the floor, unable to control the muscle spasms. Intermittently, a shriek escapes me, bouncing off the walls and through the gap at the bottom of the door to terrorize the guard outside.

After an eternity, something in my resolve snaps as one convulsion sends my head to the floor, breaking my restraint. "Master! Please, no more!" I cry out in agony, my voice rough and cracking.

Luther's laughter bounces off the walls of my cell as he stands. "Finally!" he says, kneeling next to me.

"Please. Make it stop," I whimper. "Please." Tears stream down my face as I curl into the fetal position, my pride damaged by the involuntary use of the word "Master" more so than anything else.

"No, dear," he says as he caresses my cheek with the back of his hand. "You shouldn't have spit at me. Remember that."

I scream out in pain and anger as he stands and walks away, leaving me alone to writhe on the floor with my shame.

***

It has been hours, and I still lay twitching on the floor, tears streaming down my face. The evil of whatever Luther has been injecting me with keeps me from blessed unconsciousness.

I lost track of time, but I am sure it has been days since I slept or ate. I don't recall being given water, so it can be no more than three, but it feels like an endless eternity of hell.

Broken—that is what I am. Something I thought I would never allow. Another sob racks my sore body, followed by a groan of pain as I finally try with what strength I have to sit up. I lean against the stone wall, hissing as the cold stone meets my burning skin. Even the faintest movements are painful, but after the convulsions, I can bear it. Another round with the syringe and my heart might have given out.

A shadow passes the door, and a second later, it swings open with a bang, never failing to make me jump. My body still twitches sporadically, and I brace myself against the wall for whatever Luther has in store now. I can only hope he holds to his word, and I am done with whatever he pumped into my veins.

Nothing could be worse than that, right?

Luther struts into the room, stopping in front of me. "Glad to see you off of the floor after all that. It means I might make something out of you yet." His head blocks the light from the bulb, appearing like a halo. As if he could ever have such a thing.

"So," he says with a wolfish grin. "Your people have been homed here, where all needs are being met. They have food, clean water, plentiful medicine, and clean clothes. The able-bodied have already been training with my soldiers and, after six weeks, will be evaluated. From there, the ones who pass the final test will be sorted into one of our branches of power. Some will stay close to home; others may be sent far away, for what could be a very long time, but only because they are needed elsewhere. Our influence is not contained in your region. The people not up to par with training were put to work around the compound to earn their keep.

"You will go through strenuous training, and a portion of your men will be sent to you after evaluation. You will lead one of three companies integrated with my soldiers. Sound good?" He does not wait for an answer. "Remember, all you have to do is say *'Yes, Master.'*"

He holds that devilish grin once he finishes speaking. Instead of anger, like I thought I would feel at such terms, all I want to do is cry like the broken and scared little girl I am.

"What about the ones who don't pass their test?" I dare to ask weakly.

"To fail is to die. Don't worry about them," he says dismissively.

I do not want any of this, but here it is right in front of me, and I have no choice. It is either 'submit and obey,' or more people will die. All my father ever did was try to protect our people, so against my better judgment, I force out a "Yes, Master" while still holding back tears.

Luther grins, pleased. "I am so glad to hear that, Captain. I will send someone to take you to get cleaned up." He turns to leave but stops at the door, peeking over his shoulder at me. "Welcome to the winning side." He leaves, shutting the door behind him gently for once.

I catch the guard's sad eyes looking at me through the window and turn away. Unable to hold back my tears, I bury my face in my hands and sob until I have nothing left, leaving a hollow shell of who I once was on the stone floor.

***

END PART 1

PART 2
The Beginning of the End

Twenty
IYLARA

SEVEN MONTHS LATER

The courier stands silently in his black fatigues, the Vesper star prominently displayed in white stitching on the upper left arm. “You have got to be joking,” I mutter as I read the letter he delivered.

Things are not going well with this most recent battle—or any other conflict. This war was never supposed to last as long as it has. There shouldn’t have been enough bodies in Charon’s arsenal to *let* it continue as long as it has. If I didn’t know any better, I would say for each one we kill, two more take their place, and I have no idea where they are coming from.

We must break this currently forming cycle before Charon gets the upper hand, but I do not understand what we are doing wrong. Our strategies are fool-proof, yet Charon always seems one step ahead of us. We should have stomped them into submission weeks ago, if not months, with the help of Vesper's soldiers and firepower. None of it makes sense, striking an already sensitive nerve deep inside me.

I did not join Luther to fight a never-ending war. I joined him to finish it once and for all so we could get on with our lives. After everything I have been through, I should have known it would never be as easy as I wanted it to be. The only thing that makes it worthwhile is that Carnegie's voice has been silent in my mind. It seems a near-death experience might have disrupted whatever the hell he did to me.

I can only hope.

I turn my gaze away from the note and into the shadowed eyes of the tall yet squalid rat-like man standing before me. It is most befitting that his name is Rat—or his nickname, anyway. I never bothered to learn his real name. He is Blackthorn, albeit from a different village, but I never deemed him essential enough to get to know him, despite him being one of those to stay by my side.

His mousy brown hair peeks out from under his black issued cap with another white star stitched into the forehead, front and center. He is due a haircut, but I have more pressing matters to attend to than Vesper-sanctioned dress-code formalities. One of Luther's brainwashed Lieutenants ambling around will set him straight if they see him. I am still not sure why they even bother to enforce idiotic regulations like that.

"How many more reinforcements were deployed to the area, Private? Captain Malik should have enough to spare, so there must be more to the story. If you know anything, please, don't leave out the good stuff, for both of our sakes." My eyes bore into his dull grays, and the swirling black marks freshly inked around my charcoal-lined eyes reflect at me.

Rat shifts uncomfortably. The bill of his hat is pushed down lower than usual, casting most of his face in shadow—like he is hiding from my observant gaze. Of course, he should not have anything to hide from if he wishes to see the morning. But I am starting to believe that is not the case. It is a lingering feeling I have had for a while now, yet I have never had any proof to say

I am right. It is only a feeling, albeit a strong one, deep inside that I cannot wholly ignore.

"I am afraid there ain't any *good stuff* to tell, ma'am. Captain Malik hasn't received any reinforcements either. Mr. Cain, he, uh—" Rat trails off as he pulls his eyes away from mine. He looks despondently at his feet, effectively blocking my view of his face, to my great displeasure.

Anger flares within me at the mention of Luther. I put my hands on my hips with one knee bent in a chastising, motherly way, but there is no motherly love to quench the anger and stress that has been building for the last few months.

My tone comes out sharp as a razor. "He what? Spit it out. I can already tell that I'm not going to like what I hear, so you prolonging the inevitable will only piss me off." I bend forward, trying to get a better view of his face under the hat, but he refuses to look at me.

After months of delivering messages between camps, he has witnessed plenty of my angry outbursts over bad news, but even after all that, he has never acted this way. It solidifies my theory that something is going on.

Timidly, Rat answers, still looking at his feet. "Mr. Cain has—"

I cut him off as anger surges inside me like an uncontrollable wildfire caught up in the wind. "Look at me when you speak to me, Private," I hiss, my patience wearing thin.

Rat forces himself to look me in the eyes before continuing in one breath. "Mr. Cain has withheld reinforcements until you meet with him."

"Luther can send me a personal telegraph if he wants to meet with me," I say bitterly. "You send messages between camps."

Rat takes a deep breath before speaking, keeping eye contact in fear of being hit. It has happened before, and I apologized after, but he has not forgotten about it. "The other Captains have already left to meet with him. He believes one of you has been compromised, and he doesn't trust the telegraph lines at the moment."

Auburn red waves sway with the nodding of my head where they escape the long braid draped over my shoulder. "Mmm," I purr. I relax into a calmer demeanor, which is not the reaction Rat is expecting.

That's how I want it.

I turn on my heel and walk to the hardwood desk at the back of my tent. Sitting the letter aside among the scattered papers on my desk, I dig through the side drawer while Rat watches me uncertainly.

He is a liar—a traitor.

The voice that speaks is not Carnegie, nor the voice that told me to hold on when Luther put a bullet in me once upon a time. She sounds like me, but it is not my head-voice. Maybe I have finally lost my mind, talking to a part of myself that has fractured beyond recognition.

I *could* very well be crazy after Luther's torturous training and witnessing everything I held dear split up and scattered into the nether regions of an unknown forest. I may never know, but she is not wrong, nor has she been wrong the few times she has made an appearance in my mind before now. I am too worn out to care if I am honest with myself. I will take direction where I can get it.

Rather than pulling out a piece of parchment to write a reply as I normally would, I pull out an elaborately decorated dagger. Holding it in my hand, Rat stiffens as I ponder my next move.

This is it.

"Are you saying he does not trust you to deliver a letter if he does not trust in the telegraph line? He knows that I don't trust hearsay." Rat freezes at my words, and I know my hunch is correct.

"W-word of mouth delivery. H-he didn't want the message intercepted." Rat fumbles over his words in a vain attempt at saving himself. "The rebels have been causing m-more trouble than usual."

Rat. Vermin!

I chuckle darkly. "Okay, here is what we are going to do," I say, a fog coming over me as I slam the drawer shut.

Rat almost jumps out of his skin, and I march right up to his face, causing him to shake gently. I can give him credit for not backing away. I am a good five inches shorter and visibly smaller in every way, but I have learned how to instill fear. Size does not matter. Of course, the dagger in my hand helps as it glistens in the candlelight dangerously.

"First, you're gonna need to calm down. You look like a pansy right now. Secondly—get this, okay?" I pause, glancing up at Jai for the first time. He stands by, quietly guarding my tent. He raises an eyebrow in answer to my smirk in his direction.

I smile lovingly back at Rat, and my anger completely vanishes—on the outside. "Secondly, I am going to stab you in the heart with this dagger for being a filthy, lying traitor. All will see what happens to rats." My voice is as smooth as velvet, only my words conveying my actual animosity.

Fight-or-flight kicks in, and Rat strikes out at me, as I knew he would do. With a single deft deflection with my left forearm, I strike fast with my right, penetrating Rat's belly with the dagger before recoiling for another strike if necessary. Rat cries out in pain, falling to his knees with his hands holding the bleeding wound in his abdomen.

I catch Jai jumping in surprise out of the corner of my eye, but I focus on the man kneeling at my feet. "Then I am going to send your head back to Carnegie and let him know he can't lead me into a trap. I have no sympathy for traitors."

Rat squeaks in terror, and Jai steps inside the tent, dust puffing up around his booted feet. "You're going to send his head to Carnegie? How do you know he is working for him? He is Blackthorn, after all."

I frown, looking up at my Right Hand. Luther reluctantly let me keep him at my side as a Lieutenant after much pleading rather than shipping him off somewhere up north as he wanted. Unbeknown to Jai, it cost the life of one of our own, but in my depraved mind, it was worth it. And I don't regret it. I did not even know his name, much like the man at my feet now. Ignorance on both our parts makes it easier.

"My reasons are my own, Lieutenant Norris," I say briskly.

Jai's brow furrows as he glances at the man preening in pain on the floor. "But why would you kill him and send him back to Carnegie?" he pushes.

"Because killing the messenger sends a message, believe it or not, dear Jai," I say with a smile at my closest ally while combing through Rat's coat pockets. I find an undelivered letter, its seal still intact. I stuff it into the pocket of my burgundy overdress.

I grab Rat by the chin, forcing him to look at me. "I want you to use the last few minutes of your life to think about the choices that got you here. You understand?" I ask. "All you have to do is say 'Yes, ma'am,'" I coo, not missing the irony of my words. I don't even recognize myself sometimes anymore.

With a groan, Rat nods his head before a pained "Yes, ma'am" passes his lips.

Satisfied, I turn to Jai. "Please escort our friend here to the Pit, and ring the bell for a meeting. We are going to have ourselves an execution." Rat looks up at Jai in terror as if pleading with him to save him.

"Yes, ma'am," Jai responds with a stiff nod, ignoring the man's gaze as he hauls Rat to his feet. Jai pulls him along to carry out my command. The tent door falls closed behind them, cutting me off from the outside world.

I drag my hand over my mouth with a heavy sigh. Gritting my teeth, I gingerly pull the letter back out of my pocket. I carefully break the plain seal. No insignia, just a drop of wax. Unfolding the parchment, I find one word scribbled in a slanted script.

Dusk.

What lay below that single word catches my attention. A wax stamp of a snarling coyote replaces a signature, pricking my mind with its familiarity. I grab the leather cord around my neck, pulling the ring hanging on it from under my leather bodice. The coyote engraved on my father's signet ring perfectly matches the one on the page.

Only one other ring could make this mark, and my father gave it to Keena when he told her Damian was dead.

***

Anger and betrayal fight for the spot in my heart as I head for the Pit. I don't know what is going on, but I cannot help but believe that my sister-in-law and her little band of deserters have something to do with this rather than Charon. I have felt their betrayal before, but this is deeper.

Keena's merry band of rebels are generally quiet, ignoring us for the most part. But on occasion, Vesper troops get too close, and they strike, decimating entire platoons in an impressive show of strength while leaving Blackthorn alive. Then they fade into the shadows. We have not been able to find where their camp or village is, but our numbers are stretched thin against Charon as it is. It isn't feasible to send out a squad to hunt them down at the moment. It isn't like I actually want to see them dead; however, Luther is less than happy with them and has demanded they be killed on sight.

I walk by row upon row of canvas field tents in the middle of the dirt flat surrounded by trees that makes up what everyone here calls home. I spot the occasional Charon going about their upkeep and cleaning duties like the good little slaves they have become, but I ignore them and keep walking. I would have put them down for attacking the Market, but Luther found it better suiting to make them do the chores. The less we have to do, the better, so I can't complain.

The hot summer air is heavy with humidity. It clings to my bare skin, constantly making me feel dirty and irritated. No rain in weeks, plus living in a dust ring, plus sweat equals sand sticking in places you don't want sand in, and we have been stationed here since mid-April. If it weren't for the steady supply of liquor, I would have deserted weeks ago without a second thought. I am sure many others feel the same way.

The chiming of the meeting bell echoes around the camp, and I prepare to present the stark Captain persona I have perfected to the masses. Still, inside I am merely a broken girl, wishing for the comfort and peace of a father's embrace. I want to hear that everything is okay or that it will be eventually if it isn't right now. But the dead cannot comfort the living, and everything is *not* okay.

***

The crowd gathered in the Pit parts, allowing me to pass down the middle of them unhindered. A light breeze drifts around me, tossing the loose ends of my sleeveless overdress to and fro. For a moment, the air is cool against my sweaty skin as I mount the stairs to the raised platform with heavy footsteps—then I feel nothing.

Rat kneels, hugging himself. He appears to be near the edge of unconsciousness. Jai stands stoically behind him, watching me. I look back at him, but his eyes do not quite reach my own. I lick my lips, my tongue tracing the scars engraved in them. I kneel in front of Rat with the dagger I plunged into his belly firm in my grasp. The once shining blade is crusted over with drying blood.

"Have you had time to think about your life choices?" I ask quietly, loud enough for only the two men on the platform with me to hear.

Rat's bottom lip trembles as he nods his head but holds eye contact without hesitation. "Yes, ma'am," he forces out with a gasping breath. His impending death seems to have had a positive effect on him. Maybe he has seen the error of his ways, but it will not save him.

"Get him on his feet," I order Jai as I turn to address the crowd.

There is universal worry on the faces of the people standing before me. Something like this has not happened before. There have been disobedient soldiers on the whipping block, but there hasn't been an execution since the very beginning.

I silence the murmurs of the crowd with a wave of my hand. "The enemy has tried to make a move, but it isn't the enemy we think it is." My voice bounces off the makeshift metal buildings around the Pit, amplifying my voice without me having to shout.

Barely contained anger saturates my voice. "Rat here is actually a *rat* for our lovely local traitors. He has attempted to trick me into an ambush by getting me to leave camp but has failed miserably."

I glare at the crowd. I may not know for a fact that what I say is true, but it has the effect that I want. The emotions flitting across their faces let me know that some are in on something. Surprise, indifference, anger, guilt, and anxiety display themselves for me to take in.

"We exterminate rats," I say, meeting the eyes of those who appear guilty or anxious.

I spot Zeke at the edge of the crowd standing stoically, a rag still in his hand from his task of cleaning up in the nearby chow hall. Our eyes meet, and I shyly turn away from those amber eyes. He never ceases to leave me flustered, even at a distance. I tried my best to stay away from him, but Luther felt compelled to station him with me at Camp #3. I couldn't bring myself to give another life to keep him away, and part of me even rejoiced when I learned he would be with us.

I grit my teeth and turn, wedging the slender blade of my dagger between Rat's ribs, piercing his heart with an upward twist. Jai steps back, releasing Rat. "The penalty for treason is death," I whisper, watching the light fade from his eyes.

The dying man stares at me, mouth open in surprise as blood dribbles over his thin lips. The blood catches my attention, and the memory of Danny meeting the same fate surfaces. But I have become numb to his death—to everything. None of it seems real anymore, and I shake the memories away with ease. The nightmares will come later, but only if I manage to go to sleep—an unlikely scenario.

Rat collapses one last time, and I pull the crimson-coated blade from his chest as he falls. He lay unseeing in death at my feet. I look at Jai, and the thick silence of the Pit is almost a tangible thing.

A battle cry echoes through the Pit, and a woman breaks from the crowd—Rat's sister, if I am not mistaken. She holds a blade high as tears stream down her face. I grit my teeth and swiftly draw my gun as she leaps onto the stage, lunging at me. With practiced precision, I pull the trigger. She collapses with a bullet to the chest, tumbling backward down the stage steps like a rag-doll as the gunshot echoes around the Pit.

Shrieks dot the crowd, but it is nothing compared to the shrill wailing of a siren that comes on over the intercom. We cover our ears as the piercing sound blares painfully against our eardrums.

As suddenly as it starts, it stops.

"What the hell?" I look around in question as everyone composes themselves.

It is dusk.

In the blink of an eye, the Blackthorn mixed among the Vesper soldiers turn on the latter, and chaos ensues as the crowd erupts into an all-out mêlée. I turn to look wildly at Jai as an impact knocks me down painfully. The dagger and my gun fly out of my hands, lost to the fray closing around the stage. I kick out, my boot catching something hard, a leg that doesn't give way. The effort sends me over the edge, where I land on my back, gasping for the breath knocked out of me on impact.

"I loved you, you know?" Jai says, barely audible above the clashing of steel. He hops off of the stage to stand over me. His eyes meet mine as I gaze up at him in a daze.

My voice comes out strangled as I try to catch my breath. "I thought you loved me still." Of course, I knew, but I never felt the same, so I ignored it. I always hoped his feelings would keep him at my side in the darkest times.

Selfish.

My vision blurs, and I blink away the tears flooding my eyes as the reality of what is happening sets in. The droplets escape down my cheeks in hot streams. I force myself onto my hands and knees, half-expecting Jai to help me up, but he merely watches me with narrowed eyes as I stand.

"But you never felt the same way," Jai states, mirroring my thoughts. "You aren't the same person I fell in love with. Something happened to you, and I couldn't save you from it. For that, I am sorry."

Tears break forth at his apology, but anger, not sadness, drives them down my face. "And that gives you the right to betray me?" I ask as he draws his gun. Jai does not answer, and his lack of words feeds the fire of my rising anger. "The man I knew would never betray me like this!" I shout, pointing at the gun with an accusing finger. "And now you have chosen to destroy me!"

Jai's voice rises in response to my hostility. "You destroyed yourself!"

"I didn't ask for this!" I say with a sob as grief and anger battle it out for the dominant emotion raging inside my chest.

"But you didn't fight it either," Jai says, quieter this time. I barely hear him over the roar of battle around us.

"You have no idea what I have been through," I say, jabbing myself passionately in the chest with a finger. "What Luther put me through—" I pause, pushing painful memories down as they try to surface. "He *owns* me." The cracks in my voice give a small look at the pain I keep hidden. I *know* I messed up.

Jai's lips turn down in a scowl, making him appear years older as weariness takes over his sharp features. "And that is exactly why I have to do this. You rolled over and let the devil in, and now everything I knew and loved is gone, including Iylara Vance."

His words are like a knife blade cutting deep into my heart. "Don't say that to me, *please*. You think I can't feel the weight of my decisions?" I unconsciously take a step forward. I can barely resist the urge to reach out to him.

Jai does the same, putting only a foot between us. He cannot find words, and the gun shakes in his hand at his side, if only slightly. I look up into his storm cloud eyes, darkened by grief. I do not recognize the man glaring back at me.

"When we were younger, you said you would always be there for me." My words are not nearly as sad as I feel saying them. They come out bitter as I stare squarely at him, barely restraining the urge to poke him in the chest like a petulant child.

He looks down at the ground between us before speaking. "I can't do that. Not now," he breathes. His hand visibly tightens around the grip of his gun, and the shaking ceases.

"I won't go down easily," I warn, unsure if he can pull the trigger, but I cannot give him that chance. My will to live is strong.

"I know," he says with a nod, his eyes slowly coming back to look at me, finally meeting my eyes full on.

"Tell me one thing. None of this has anything to do with Charon, does it?" I ask. I need to make sense of it all in the little time we have left.

Jai's jaw tenses. "No. This is for *us*. You can fight and die, or you can run."

Adrenaline bubbles up in the pit of my stomach, and I ready myself to release the burst of energy fueled by it. I may have shunned the power that Carnegie tried to entice me with before I joined Vesper, but the primitive part of me demands a fight. I will not go down without one. I strike out, knocking the gun from Jai's hand, and sidestep around him. He thrusts his elbow back, hitting me in the ribs with brute force. I stumble as he spins, kicking my feet out from under me.

I hit the ground and am left gasping for air for a second time. The impact knocks the fight out of me, and my broken heart takes precedence. Jai is one of the last few people I genuinely care about, and he has turned on me.

I push myself onto my knees, trying to catch a breath. "H-how could you do this to me?" I ask as the noise around us starts to fade. "After e-everything?"

Jai approaches, kneeling in front of me. I stare at him with tear-stained eyes. "You feel it, don't you?" he asks quietly. "That hatred you feel right now under the pain. It's what has you so conflicted. The hatred formed out of love, no matter what kind of love, is the worst kind." Jai does not wait to let me answer his question. "It physically hurts you to look at me, doesn't it? *Right here.*" He hits his chest over his heart with his fist fervently. "I know because I loved you for so *long*," he gasps out, grabbing me by the face roughly to stare into my eyes as if his life depended on it.

There is a longing in his eyes, but he stops himself as he moves a fraction of an inch toward my lips. My slender fingers wrap around his hands, and I am unsure if I want to tear them away from my face or hold them there.

Jai speaks quietly at first, but with each word, his voice rises. "I did everything for *you*. But I was never good enough. It was always someone else. *Still is,*" he says in disgust as he shoves me away from him. "But Zeke isn't Danny. You should know that."

Jai stands, stalking away before turning back to me. I look up at him. The vehemence on his face leaves me speechless, his words like barbed wire around my heart, constricting tighter and tighter, slowly killing a part of me.

"You aren't fit to lead these people anymore," he says. "I will lead them out from under the thumb of our oppressors, to whom you have fully given yourself. Luther broke you, and now he is using you for a worthless fight you are losing! Charon isn't even the real enemy! Not anymore!" His voice echoes around the Pit.

I glance around as the fighting subsides. Blackthorn has easily defeated the unsuspecting Vesper soldiers in their midst. Charon stands by, not even perturbed at what has transpired as if they knew about it all along.

And now *I* am considered the enemy—the outsider.

My heart pounds in my throat, choking off my air supply. I'm not sure if I am angrier at Jai for trying to kill me or for being right. I cannot openly admit the latter, though.

I cannot believe that Charon could be anything but the enemy. Or that my people would willingly treat those who once rallied against us and killed my father and many others with enough respect to let them live when given a chance to end them. Yet I cannot deny that Vesper, or Luther more specifically, has been incredibly conniving.

"You believe you can take them on?" I ask. "Luther will decimate you. I have done everything I have done to *save* our people. Not get them killed!"

"You saved us to die in bondage, fighting a futile war! We are slaves, haven't you realized? Exactly like the Charon here!" Jai yells in my face. *"For the better* didn't take very long to turn into hell, did it?" he spits out, our exchange now witnessed by the survivors of the fight in deathly silence. "I would rather die than be a slave!" he cries out angrily. "You won't admit it, but you sold yourself to Luther, and it was for *nothing*. You should have let us *die."*

His words are biting and sharp, cutting at a part of me that I keep locked away. If he is correct, then I gave everything for nothing. I have to deny it, push it aside like everything else, and keep it under wraps down deep, or it will ruin me.

Instead of accepting the truth, a spiteful grin spreads across my face. An all too familiar fog clouds my mind. "And how long do you think it will take for you to end up exactly where I am?" I ask, slowly standing up.

"I won't make the same mistakes you did," Jai says, throwing salt in the wound.

I laugh out loud, despite my hurt, and he frowns at me. "What?" he asks.

I shake my head with a snort, glancing at the gun on the ground. The fog takes away some of the pain. "Are you brave enough to kill me?" I ask, challenging him against my better judgment. I know damn well I cannot win in a hand-to-hand fight against him. He could easily snap my neck with his bare hands if he wanted to, but something inside me won't let me back down.

"I'm gonna do what I have to, no matter what it takes," he says darkly.

My eyes narrow. "Then do your worst, Jai Norris. Kill me if you can."

We stare at each other for a breath before I kick out, landing a booted foot square in his chest. He staggers back a step before charging at me.

I spin out of the way, dodging his hand, but he is fast for his size. He grabs a fistful of my hair, swinging me around headfirst into the support beams under the platform.

"Argh!" I cry out on impact, my head bouncing off of the hardwood. My eyes dim before I can refocus.

Jai reaches out, grabbing me by the throat. Warm blood runs down my face as he pins me to the stage support.

That didn't go how I planned.

He pulls his dagger from its sheath on his belt and brings it down toward my chest with his free hand. Everything slows down again, and from the corner of my eye, I see everyone waiting with bated breath for the outcome of our conflict.

I grab hold of his wrist, slowing the descent of the blade toward my heart. The blade's tip cuts through the fabric between my collarbone and breast, but I can barely feel the bite through the adrenaline as it punctures my skin. It takes everything in me to hold out against Jai's brute strength bearing down on me. Even with both hands, he is overtaking me with one, and I cannot breathe.

Fear that he might succeed in killing me strikes as he pushes down. In a frozen moment, I look him in the eyes and see a manic glint clouding his vision—a man out of options and thrown into an impossible situation.

A cry of indignation escapes as I weaken, and I brace myself against the support beam, using every ounce of strength I have left. The tip of the knife starts to sink into my chest despite my efforts, and I hiss between gritted teeth in pain. Zeke appears, throwing himself into Jai, knocking him away before he can force the blade into my heart. My knees give out, and I sink to the ground.

"It doesn't have to be this way," Zeke pleads with Jai, who has regained his footing.

Jai stares at Zeke, a light dawning in his eyes as the manic glint fades. His hands start visibly shaking, but he stands his ground, unable to look at me. "Run, Ray. Don't come back," he says to the dusty ground between us.

Fresh tears escape, rolling down my cheeks. I glance around at the faces of the people I sacrificed everything for—people I would have died for. All I find is anger and bitterness as they glare at me.

Oh, how the mighty fall.

I dart out of the Pit with a sob, ashamed and betrayed. I cannot stop whatever Luther will do to them when he finds out what has happened. And he will find out. There is no doubt about that.

I can only hope Jai actually has a damn good plan, or we are all doomed.

***

My heart pounds fiercely against my rib cage, and I cannot control the shaking that courses through my body as I make haste for my tent. A throbbing starts in my head as the adrenaline fades, and a horrendous headache takes over my pain receptors. I cannot feel the shallow knife wound with all my attention on keeping my eyes open through my splitting headache. I'm probably concussed, but I cannot stop moving. Not yet. Not when I have watched everything I have fought so hard for finally crumble at my feet.

Jai betrayed me.

But I cannot blame him. I have seen the change in myself, as if from the outside, and have been unable to stop it. If anything, my want to change only fuels my descent further and further into the depths of darkness. Days passed before I realized they were gone, and the deeper I got inside my head, the faster I spiraled.

And now I'm here.

I shove my tent door aside and stumble into my home away from home. A small pool of Rat's blood stains the dirt floor, and I turn away from it, the sensation of my blade piercing through his flesh still very much in the forefront of my mind.

It had to be done.

Or maybe not, but it is too late to think about it now.

Trying to ignore the pain pounding through my head, I sporadically move around the room. I shove things like a water canteen and some odds and ends I have collected over the months that I deem essential into my field bag. Not much here is of use anywhere else, so why take it with me?

Satisfied with my packing, I grab the *Dusk* note parchment. In a hasty script, I write a note for Jai on the bottom half with a vague hope that he will find it.

With a flourish, I sign my name under the message out of habit. I place the pen on the desk with a snap and look up. The room is a mess. I did not realize I did that much damage, but every piece of dark-toned Vesper clothing I own is strewn across my bed and the floor.

Go to Luther. Everything will be okay.

That woman's voice is back. I shudder at her proposal, but I don't have anywhere else to go. I am an enemy to Charon, but now my own people are against me as well. So against my better judgment, I set off for the last place I want to go on earth.

Twenty-one
JAI

My ragged breath shakes on the way out, my heart thudding away erratically in my chest. The adrenaline fades, and my body begins to shake. I am left staring at the cloud of dirt Iylara's feet stirred up as she fled.

"Is this what you wanted?" Zeke asks calmly.

It would be better if he yelled.

I cannot speak, opening my mouth once, then twice before closing it with a snap. I shake my head, turning to face the people in the Pit. They silently watch me with wide eyes and expectant faces.

Vesper soldiers lay in pools of blood between Blackthorn feet, and Charon slaves stare on with rapt attention, unsure of how they should feel. Relieved? Scared? Justified? They shouldn't worry. I have no need or want to have them killed.

What they did in the past does not matter. Not anymore. If they join us, the help will be much appreciated.

As Iylara's Right Hand, with her and the Vesper Lieutenants gone, the leadership role falls to me. I'm unsure how to feel about that, but it does not deter the crowd standing before me. Starting in the front row, people start kneeling. A ripple effect occurs like a sigh of relief, and everyone in the Pit kneels, including the Charon—all but Zeke. He continues to stare at me accusingly. I can't hold it against him. I know how he feels about Iylara, as twisted as it is, but he will have to pick a side eventually.

He cannot toe the line forever.

I nod once at the mass of kneeling bodies before all but fleeing from the Pit in Iylara's footsteps.

I take a deep breath at her tent door before stepping inside, feeling very much like a trespasser.

It's probably because I didn't knock. Not that it matters.

The room is void of its occupant. Things are strewn about the living space, and Iylara's field pack is gone.

She works fast.

A white piece of parchment catches my eye from its spot on top of Iylara's desk. It beckons to me, and I know instinctively that it was left for me to find. I hesitantly approach the desk, still shaking.

I spot the Vance signet impressed into the wax under the word *Dusk*—the letter I never got. It doesn't matter. Iylara only caught one informant because he couldn't keep it together when the going got tough. If he had succeeded, I wouldn't have had to try and kill her—others received the same message, and the alarm was a clear sign.

Under the wax seal, Iylara's elegant script, though hastily scrawled, shines like gold against the page waiting to be read:

I hope you can do what I couldn't, for all our sakes.

A shuddering sob racks my body as I read her words, but I must hold it together. Now is not the time to break. There is still much to be done.

I look up at the sound of the tent flap opening to find Zeke. He stands silently in the doorway, watching me. The dagger Iylara used to kill Rat hangs loosely in his grasp.

I stare at him for a moment in silence. “Thank you,” I say, looking back at the note. “I don’t think I’d be able to live with myself if you hadn’t stopped me.”

“Glad to hear it.” Zeke steps forward, letting the tent flap fall shut behind him.

“We need to move soon before Luther learns what’s happened. He has eyes and ears everywhere. It won’t take long,” I say. I have no intentions of killing any Charon, so they need to know the plan. Zeke is the best person to get information to them. “Keena and some others will meet us at Camp #2, hopefully before we engage the Vesper there, but we will converge on Camp #1 together. We need to liberate as many of our people as we can.”

“And the Charon slaves?” Zeke asks. “What will you do with us?”

I scowl at him. “I’m not doing anything with you that you don’t want to do. And I won’t let anything happen to any of you. I believe you are more valuable alive and on our side than dead. We are in this together. Keena can’t turn down the help if she knows what is good for her,” I say diplomatically.

Zeke gives me a small smile. “That’s good to hear. When do we leave?”

“As soon as possible. No later than midnight. We should be able to make it to Camp #2 by morning. Possibly ambush it while it is still dark. I’ll let you rally your people. Tell Sartor to get everyone else ready. I need to see if there is anything important that we can use here.”

“Okay then. Anything else?” Zeke asks, glancing around the chaotic mess surrounding us.

“Nope. Just do what you need to get us out of here before reinforcements show up. If anyone has a problem keeping you guys around, tell them to see me about it.”

Zeke nods, silently placing the dagger on the desk in front of me. Rat’s drying blood coats the blade and pools in the engravings of the handle. A pang goes through my heart, and I must restrain the tears that threaten me again.

I wish I could have saved him, but he was already a dead man.

Zeke turns to leave but stops at the door, looking over his shoulder. “Where will she go?” he asks.

I scowl, looking down at the words Iylara scribbled once more. “Back to Luther,” I whisper.

“Why would she do that?” Zeke asks.

I look up sadly as the truth settles over me. “She has nowhere else to go.”

Zeke’s face falls. “Maybe I shouldn’t have stopped you then?”

I shrug. “Damned if you do, damned if you don’t,” I say with a sigh. “Now, please leave me alone.”

“Okay,” Zeke mumbles with a bob of his head, a downcast look on his face. He leaves without another word, and I am left alone—so completely alone.

A dark shadow crosses my psyche, pulling my lips down at the corners, and I cannot help but wonder if this is how Iylara felt before it all went to hell.

***

Dawn is near, but darkness conceals us as we creep over the ridge to Camp #2. It is silent as the camp sleeps, and I have high hopes that this will go smoother than I believed it could.

I give a soft bird call, and we converge on the camp, splitting into groups to enter the tents. We move swiftly, slitting Vesper's throats before they can cry out to alert their fellow soldiers, and I make my way to the Captain’s tent near the camp center.

Malik is already awake and stands as I enter with a questioning look. “You aren’t from my camp. Who are you?” he asks, hand inching toward the gun on his hip.

I hold my hands up in surrender. “Sorry to disturb you, sir. I’m from Captain Vance’s camp. Something has happened.”

His hand relaxes, but he doesn’t let his guard down. “You’re Lieutenant Norris, are you not?”

“Yes, sir,” I say, shocked that the man knows my name.

“What has happened?” he asks earnestly, his trust in me rising exponentially at those two simple words.

“There was an uprising,” I say, trying to find the right words. “I brought the culprits to you. We have them outside.”

“Why didn’t you kill them?” he asks.

Damn.

I falter for a moment. I've never been the greatest liar. "Because they are Vesper. I didn't think it would be appropriate for me to make that call."

Confusion flits across his face. "For *you* to make that call? Where is Captain Vance?"

"Dead, sir," I say without hesitation.

Genuine shock contorts his face, and he moves to exit the tent, his guard toward me completely down as he gives me his back. He reaches up to open the tent flap. I grab his head from behind and twist as hard as I can, snapping his neck with a grinding of bone that reverberates through my hands.

I shudder at the sensation as he collapses, shaking my hands free of it. With a sigh of relief, I glance around the tent. It is much more orderly and put together than Iylara's ever was. Not a stitch of clothing is out of place, and the desk is clean—no stacks of paper or anything other than a freshly lit candle.

Inside the drawers, I discover a different story. I can barely get the middle drawer open for the junk tossed inside. I shuffle through the mess, but nothing stands out as important. From another drawer, I shove the maps and other tactical things into the bag hanging at my side. On my way out, I kneel to retrieve Malik's weapons belt. I strap it next to my own and exit to find the sun breaking over the horizon.

Blackthorn and Charon alike exit the tents. The liberation on their faces warms my heart. Warren approaches me with a huge grin on his face.

I grab him, hugging him with enough force to break a rib. "Damn, it's good to see you," I say into his shoulder.

"Same to you, man. I was afraid this wouldn't work," he says.

"It did go smoother than I thought it would. The night was on your side," a familiar voice from behind me says. It startles me, and I turn in disbelief.

Familiar dark brown eyes watch me with a deep sadness. Dirt settles in the creases of the skin around the man's eyes, and the coyote pelt draped over his shoulders makes him appear larger than life compared to the people behind him. Blackthorn tattoos cover his bare arms, and the sword at his side gleams in the morning sun.

"I thought you were dead," I say in disbelief. *"You're* the leader of the rebels?"

Damian Vance nods. "I'm not, and I am."

"But—" I begin before closing my mouth for lack of words. A group of Blackthorn deserters stand behind him, watching patiently.

Zeke's voice cuts through my racing thoughts. "You were strung up in Charon square. I saw you."

"It was only a badly disfigured decoy, not me," Damian says. "Who are you? You look familiar."

"Zeke Rekkon, sir," Zeke says with a slight bow. I cringe inwardly, doubting that Damian will take a better liking to the man standing next to me than he did Danny.

Recognition crosses Damian's face. The name is a dead giveaway, but Zeke's appearance would surely give him away eventually. I cannot say that I notice it much, what with being around him almost every day, but looking at him now, I can easily see the Rekkon family resemblance.

No wonder Iylara is infatuated with him. He is like Danny's twin.

Damian looks at me. "What's Charon doing here?"

I knew this would happen, but Keena would be much easier to deal with. "They are all willing to help. And they did. Would you turn that away?"

Damian grinds his teeth, turning his gaze on Zeke for longer than I am comfortable with. "I'll allow it for now, but if they cause any trouble, I will have them put down."

They aren't animals! I want to scream at him, but I reside to nodding in acquiescence after a glance at Zeke standing stoically at my side. There is tension in his jaw as he surely withholds the words he would very much like to say to Damian. I'm grateful for his restraint. "Thank you," I say as Damian steps closer to me.

"Is it done?" he asks quietly.

Being here should mean his sister is dead if I had followed through with instructions—which I initially thought came from Keena. But it looks like Damian tried to have his own sister killed. It doesn't sit right with me. Keena, I can understand. Damian? Not so much.

I hesitate to answer. "No."

"And why is that?" Damian asks with pursed lips.

Zeke cuts me off. "I stopped him from killing her." I wince at his confession.

Damian's jaw clenches. "Jai, follow me." He turns to say something to a short, broad-shouldered man behind him, but I am not listening.

"It's okay," I say, placing a reassuring hand on Zeke's shoulder. "It's all gonna be okay."

"I'm gonna kick your ass if it ain't."

I chuckle humorlessly. "And I will let you."

I fall into step behind Damian, leaving the others behind. "Why didn't you let us know?" I ask once safely out of the hearing range of our group.

"That I was alive?" Damian asks.

"Well, yeah," I say, trying not to be sarcastic.

"I didn't ask to be spared execution. It *should* have been me hanging in Charon square. Thankfully, my father had spies stationed inside that could get to me without anyone in Charon knowing when they heard what was happening."

"So Carnegie believes you are dead?" I ask, amazed.

"Yes. I would like it to stay that way for as long as possible. But there are rumors that he is dead as well."

"What? Really? Any news on what happened?"

"No. He disappeared about a week ago. I won't believe he is dead until I see a body. Don't buy into it."

"Noted," I say, reeling at the possibility that the bastard is dead. It is probably too much to hope for, but a man has to have hope. "So you're using Keena as cover?"

Damian nods. "The fewer people that know I am still alive, the longer it stays a secret against those who haven't yet joined us. Keena didn't know I was alive when she walked out of Blackthorn, but it worked out for the best."

"For the best?" I stop walking. "Have you ever thought about how any of this has affected Iylara? 'For the best' sent her on a path I couldn't save her from." I take a deep breath, trying to calm myself. "I don't think we would be where we are if she had known you were alive!" My voice rises with each word, despite my restraint. I clamp my mouth shut before I say something regrettable. Damian is, by all rights, still an elder, the rightful Blackthorn Chief who demands respect, but I am having a hard time clinging to that in light of everything.

What I wouldn't give to wring the man's neck.

"We will talk about this later. We have to attend to more pressing issues. We are running out of time to get to Camp #1 before Luther retaliates."

So many things I would like to say right now.

But Damian is right. I sigh. "Fine, tell me what to do."

Twenty-two
IYLARA

It takes more than a day to make it to the Vesper compound while trying to avoid any possible ambushes. My horse is nearly dead on her feet when we step through the trees near the entrance.

The guards turn their attention to me as we enter the light of the buildings. Their weapons are ready to fire on anyone who means to harm the place. I raise my hands in surrender, holding myself upright on my horse with what little energy I have left.

"Identify yourself!" one of the guards shouts.

"Captain Vance, Camp #3," I call out weakly, breathless from my trip. My legs are weak and shaky, barely keeping me on the horse.

"Step forward to the gate," the guard orders.

I slide off the horse, collapsing to the ground. I groan as I pull myself up, dragging my feet to the entrance gate. I stick my arm out, revealing my forearm to the computer console inside one of the pillars. A beam of light scans my arm, and a Vesper star glows faintly under my skin among the swirling black tattoos that wrap around my arm before it fades away. Withdrawing my arm, I wait on unsteady legs for the gate to open completely before entering.

Yates opens the door when I knock, and we go through the same process that we go through every time I visit, minus the fingerprints. It is tiring. I thought they would have a little trust in me at this point, but no. The only difference this time is that he hands me a rag to wipe off the dried blood streaked down the side of my face. I do not miss the faint look of pity behind his eyes.

I could fall out now, but I push myself a little more. Luther surely already knows that I am here. He will not take kindly to me holding off meeting with him, no matter how bad I feel. I shuffle down the hallway, headed reluctantly to Luther's office as I scrub at my face, trying to make myself appear somewhat presentable. All the while, my head throbs dully, just enough to bring on a painful headache that I cannot ignore.

A sharp, exacerbated pain bolts through my head past the constant throbbing, and I stop, bracing myself against the wall with a hand. I breathe in deeply through my nose and out through my mouth until the intense pain subsides.

I look up at the dreary off-white hall and matching floor made of old cracking ceramic tile. It gives the place a cold melancholy feeling that does nothing to help the nausea swirling in the pit of my stomach. It could be from a concussion, the rising dread within me—or both.

My heart aches for the warm brown log walls in my father's cabin, softly glowing with the light of the fireplace. I have not seen it since everything changed, and I'm unsure if the village is even still standing. The people I left behind were rounded up soon after Luther put a bullet in me and brought here against their will. I've been too scared to go against Luther, who forbade me from returning. I can only hope to one day return to life as usual, but that seems a bit too much to hope for in my current situation.

I push away from the wall with a groan and focus on putting one foot in front of the other. My hands begin to shake, and my feet feel heavier by the second, but I do not stop walking. Luther's fancy door looms up in front of me, the owl watching me in its unnerving way. I take another deep breath and knock twice.

"Come in, my dear," Luther's velvety voice says from the other side. I turn the knob with bated breath, burying my dislike and fear for the voice's owner as deep as I can.

Luther stands as I enter, walking around the desk to greet me with a kiss on the forehead. I let him, but I inwardly cringe at his touch.

"Sit, my dear. We have much to discuss," Luther says, eyes glittering with something I cannot put my finger on. He either doesn't know what happened or is playing it cool. I almost hope I have to tell him. The latter is far scarier than the prior in my experience with Luther Cain.

"Thank you, sir," I say meekly, sinking into the chair and the submissive shell of a person I long ago figured out was less likely to be punished. It is my escape from the inner turmoil, and he eats it up every time.

His lips turn down at the corners in a concerned frown. "You look tired," he says, sitting back down in his high-back leather chair.

"I am, sir," I admit with a shaky sigh.

Luther nods. "Well then, I won't keep you long. Thank you for coming." His voice sounds sincere, but I am no fool.

"You're welcome, sir," I answer mechanically.

Luther sits back, gazing at me over the half-moon spectacles he wears while working. "So, I am told you discovered a—what was the word you used? Rat?" he asks curiously with a sideways glance.

My quickening heartbeat echoes inside of my head painfully. Of course, he knows. "Yes, sir," I say with a short nod.

"And then you executed him, correct?" he adds.

"Yes, sir," I repeat, trying to focus through my exhaustion and suppressed terror.

A grin spreads across his face. It is quite the opposite of the response I thought I would receive. "Wonderful," he says in a low voice. "You feel no remorse." He says it as a statement rather than a question.

"No, sir," I say, shaking my head. "Traitors must die."

He nods. "Yes, they must. Tell me about the woman you shot," he continues.

I'm unsure who his informant is, but they are speedy and precise with their Intel. It is one of the reasons I have always been so hesitant to do or say anything against him. He knows *everything*, and fear causes me to spill my guts whenever he asks a question.

"She was the traitor's brother. She tried to attack me with a knife, so I put her down." My memory of the entire thing is foggy, and even the pain of Jai's betrayal is almost non-existent. I either do not have the energy to feel anything or am more screwed up in the head than I thought.

Luther laces his fingers together. "But there is something else, yes?" he asks, voice turning dark. "Something that caused the blood on your face that you failed to wipe away?"

I nod, staring down at the floor in shame. "There was an uprising. I didn't catch wind of it until it was too late." I force myself to look at him. "I am so sorry, sir." My apology is laced with a pleading tone.

Luther's expression softens as my eyes meet his. "As unfortunate as this ordeal is, I had anticipated something like this would happen eventually. That Blackthorn flame is a hard one to douse." There is a flicker of pride in my belly at his words, but it is short-lived. "They will all die for their treachery, but we must find them first. They packed up and left sometime last night. They will have gone off to join your little band of rebels. They are becoming quite the nuisance."

"Do we have news of their whereabouts?" I ask. I cannot help but feel fear for them, even after they turned against me. To be honest, their actions do not surprise me. In their position, I would have done the same thing if I believed what Jai believes—which I guess I do, in a way. But I don't know what to do about it now.

Luther shakes his head. "No. I have men on the job, but they have turned up with nothing so far."

The fact that he does not know something leaves me speechless and slightly hopeful—unless he is lying.

"Since you are here, I could use your help to draw them out," he says with a smile.

Anxiety flutters in my stomach, and I shake my head almost too harshly for the situation, amplifying the painful pounding inside my skull. "I don't think I can be of any help in this, sir."

Luther laughs out loud, and I frown in confusion. "Oh, my dear, you would be surprised at what you can do. But for now, get cleaned up and rest. Come back this evening."

Despite questioning his meaning, I do not hesitate to accept the invitation to leave. If he wanted to elaborate, he would.

I stand with a slight bow. "Yes, sir."

"We will make things right in no time. Don't worry," Luther says.

His assurance only adds to my anxiety, and I leave his office with a heavy heart. I do not want to do *anything* for him, but deep inside, I know I will—maybe not out of willing obedience, but out of fear.

***

I *am* a mess.

The woman staring back at me in the shower room mirror is almost unrecognizable. I did manage to get most of the blood off, but traces were left behind in the corner of my eye. It's barely enough to notice, but bruising has already started over my temple. It mingles with the tattoos around my eye before disappearing in the smudged black charcoal on my eyelid.

My eyes fall to my lips every time I find myself in front of a mirror. The fine scar is carefully placed, and there is no deformity, but it is visible for all to see—Luther's mark of ownership. I have seen a few others marked the same way, but their marks have all been jagged, pulling their lips in strange directions. Some even have a permanent scowl that no smile can pull up. I guess I should be grateful.

I force my eyes away from the mirror and tug off my boots. They are caked with dust dried to the spatter of Rat's blood across the toes. It takes some pulling to un-stick my clothes from my sweat-soaked skin, and I rip my shirt from the dried blood on my chest before I remember that Jai may have failed at killing me, but he did indeed draw blood. The pain of his blade was forgettable after everything else.

With my shirt free, an irritating stinging starts as blood seeps freely from the half-inch deep wound once again. I grit my teeth at the thought of having to endure stitches and turn the shower on with unsteady hands. The pipes snarl and sputter, but clean water spews from the rusted showerhead after a few seconds.

I step into the shower, hissing as the scorching water nearly blisters my back. I adjust the heat and stick my head under the water, gingerly rinsing the coagulated blood from my hair. Pink swirls go down the drain, and I stand still, entranced.

I jump, almost losing my footing on the slick shower floor as a timid knock echoes around the room.

Without waiting for an answer, the person on the other side opens the door. "I brought clean clothes, ma'am," the petite woman says in a nervous voice. She is extraordinarily plain in a gray jumpsuit, and her skin lacks color. She averts her eyes from my naked form standing in the open shower as she steps inside the bathroom.

Greasy blond locks cover half of her face, but they are not long enough to hide her mouth. The woman's lips are deformed with thick scars, some of the worst ones I have seen. I want to feel something for her, but I can't. The Charon mark is much too prominent on her neck for me to see past my prejudices. I know what she did to get here.

My voice lacks the sincerity I feel at the thought of clean clothes. "Thank you," I manage to say, barely above a whisper.

The Charon woman sits the clothes on the counter and leaves with a bow of her head, never meeting my eyes. I watch her go, wishing I could feel some sort of pity for the battered woman, but it is too much to deal with right now.

I am too tired and weary to feel anything, much less put in the effort to scrub myself clean. I curl up on the shower floor and lay under the water until it runs cold.

***

After a quick meal and a long overdue nap, I head back to Luther's office as he commanded me, but I am conflicted.

Yes, I have done as he has said over the past several months, but it was only out of fear for my people. Now that they have started to rebel, it gives me hope—something I didn't realize I held so little of until now. It makes me want to rebel myself, but there are still Blackthorn stationed at the other camps. Luther would surely use them against me, or I against them if I were to try anything. I have no way of knowing if the other camps have done the same as #3 or not, and I cannot risk going against Luther and getting them killed. Not to mention those he shipped off elsewhere. But I will no longer blindly follow if I have any say in the matter. It's like the light of day is finally beginning to dawn through the black storm clouds hovering over my head.

"Good evening, my dear," Luther says as I enter his office, but he does not stand up this time. He sips on a steaming cup of tea, motioning for me to sit.

"Good evening, sir," I say, taking the seat offered.

"How are you feeling?" he asks, lacking any sincere concern.

"Much better, thank you," I say, nodding automatically as my fingers fiddle nervously with each other in my lap.

"Did Lydia get you tended to?"

I nod, making eye contact. "She did, sir. Only a few stitches and a slight concussion, but she said I will heal quickly."

Luther takes a sip of tea, watching me over the rim of his cup. "Indeed. Sleep well?" he asks cordially.

As much as I want to remain quiet, I learned months ago to indulge Luther in small talk. Despite my disdain for it, I have even become good at it. "I did. It's been a while since I got a good night's rest. The pillows were heaven."

I did not have much choice, but I am not lying about the feather-stuffed pillows. They were delightfully soft, but with the pain medicine from Lydia and exhaustion, I passed out as soon as my head hit the pillow. I only briefly enjoyed the comfort when I woke up to a banging on my door before being roused from bed to eat.

Smiling, he says, "That is good to hear," before taking another sip of tea. "It is time for you to jump down the rabbit hole, my dear," he continues in his silky voice, sitting his cup to the side. "You will need your energy."

I freeze at his words, a memory clawing at my mind. "What did you say?" I ask faintly, forgetting all manner of politeness, but he only chuckles.

Luther stands with a polite smile and comes around the side of the desk. "I said it is time to jump down the rabbit hole." He reaches out, and I flinch, but I cannot move away from him in my chair. He touches my forehead, and I come to the edge of a forgotten memory as electricity pulses from his fingertips against my skin.

My eyes close involuntarily, and there is another world behind my eyelids. The memory of the battle before everything changed flashes across my mind, and the last bit of my conversation with Carnegie rings in my ears.

"Those people we left fighting are just pawns, and you are their puppeteer out here on the battlefield. It's all to better your skills. But you are just dangling your feet at the edge of the rabbit hole, my love. If you don't jump, you will be pushed in. Remember that when the time comes to make a decision. You will know which one it is."

The memory ends, and I open my eyes, looking up at the ceiling from my place on the floor. I don't remember falling out of my chair. Luther clears his throat, and I turn my head to look at him, but he is staring at the door, not me. Dread weighs heavy in my chest. I wince as I sit up, positive that I have popped a stitch.

A knock sounds on the door. I already know who is on the other side of the door, but I do not want to believe it. I *can't* believe it.

The door swings open, and Carnegie glides into the room, coat-tails sweeping in behind him with the clink of the many buckles on his mid-calf boots. He looks like an angel of death sweeping into the room, his blond hair gleaming in the evening sunshine streaming through the large windows of Luther's office. His blue eyes blaze as ice and fire coexisting in the same vessel in contrast to the tattoos around his eyes, so very similar to my own, but all sharp edges compared to my rounded swirls.

"What—" I start to ask, but Carnegie's voice in my head shuts me up, shattering every hope I had that something disrupted our connection.

Shh, my love. Have some patience.

Patience? The very reason I teamed up with Luther in the first place was to bring this man down.

I will not have patience.

"What is going on?" I demand, anger rising in my chest as I direct my question to Luther.

I realize a second too late that my tone is disrespectful. Luther strikes out, backhanding me across the face before grabbing my chin and forcing me to look at him. "I let your tone slide once. I suggest you refrain from speaking unless you are going to show me the respect that I am due," Luther growls, glaring at me with narrowed eyes.

I know what he could do if I let my tongue get the best of me a third time. "Yes, sir," I whisper. He lets me go with a caress of his thumb across the scars he carved.

"To answer your question," Luther says with a grin, "you are ready for a promotion."

My eyebrows shoot skyward. Rather than the joy one would typically experience when hearing those words, fear rises in my heart. "Sir?" I ask, glancing at Carnegie, who stands quietly by, watching me with a stoic look on his face.

"This conflict is not yours. Although I know you have a personal attachment to it, nothing you know is as it seems," Luther says as he walks back to his chair.

I stand up, lamely waiting for an explanation while watching Carnegie watch me in my peripheral vision. My fear of Luther overrides the anger Carnegie evokes in me, or I might attempt to kill him right now with my bare hands.

I wish I had not come here. I should have fled into the woods, never to be seen again, but something inside me drove me here. I followed blindly. At the time, I saw no other options, but now I see that whatever is going on cannot be good for my people or me. And it all has to do *with* me. I've been played and taken advantage of—by my own mind, no less.

"The man, Chief Lysander, that you love to hate belongs to me. He does my bidding, as you do, nothing more, nothing less. I chose the two of you to bring this region to its knees in submission to the Vesper Republic. The events of your past have merely been part of your training and conditioning, and you are now ready to fulfill the role I have so delicately groomed you for. The mental connection between the two of you will allow for full disclosure of your missions, regardless of the situations in which you may find yourselves. Your energy manipulation must be honed and mastered, but that comes with the next training phase."

I stare open-mouthed at Luther. He is telling the truth because no one except Carnegie and I know of the mind-thing, or so I thought.

"What do you mean the *events of my past?"* I ask with a trembling voice. I quickly tack on a 'sir' as Luther raises an eyebrow.

His smile is sinister. "Nothing Mr. Lysander has ever done to you has happened without my say, my dear." He says it as if it should be obvious. "I admit you were never supposed to marry that turncoat husband, but Carnegie remedied that. Put me a few years behind schedule, though, I admit. And that doctor of yours didn't have it in her to do what I needed to be done. I think you frightened her. She was easily taken out of the picture for her failures."

Tears well up in my eyes. "And my family?" I ask as memories flit across my mind—horrible memories full of pain I thought I had become numb to. Too much has happened to feel anything for Dr. Matthews, but if Carnegie is the reason my family are dead, and he only does as Luther says—

This is not happening. It can't be.

Luther's grin reminds me of the day he came to see me in my infirmary bed, and bile rises in my throat. "The people you loved would have hindered your progress, so they needed to be removed. If they wouldn't leave by choice, I had to take matters into my own hands. It just so happens that trauma is easy to orchestrate, and the effects are long-lasting." Luther chuckles, and I shiver in horror. "Lucky me."

***

Staring at the brick wall of my cell, I cannot help but allow my thoughts to run rampant. With the revelation of what Luther has done comes a flood of emotions that I cannot deal with. I try to shove it deep down into that dark place within me, pretending that everything I have done has *not* been for nothing—that I was not deceived.

But I am lying to myself. I have been doing that a lot lately. It cannot be good for me, but what else am I supposed to do? Accept the mess I have allowed myself to fall into, and drown in the despair that will inevitably follow? It will not do any good if I can't do a damn thing about it.

I don't know what my so-called promotion will entail. Luther never got the chance to elaborate before I completely lost it as the meaning of his words hit me full force. He had Danny, Damian, and my father killed so that I would be unhindered by their influence as he turned me into whatever I have become. I am now grateful that Ysabel left when she did. I could not bear it if she were dead because of me too. And thankfully, Jai pulled through after Carnegie shot him, thanks to Dr. Matthews. Luther's reluctance to let me keep him is now painfully obvious, but I was willing to make the sacrifice to change his mind.

Luther's words regarding the connection between Carnegie and me have simultaneously left me terrified and intrigued. My intrigue disgusts me, but I cannot help it. I was always curious about it. Maybe I can finally get some answers if I play my cards right.

Unable to stand being alone with my thoughts any longer, I embrace the anomaly against my better judgment, doing something I never imagined I would resort to. Eyes closed, I breathe deeply, trying to calm myself. I have never tried to start a conversation with Carnegie. I did scream at him that one time within our connection, but I'm not entirely sure if he actually heard me or if he merely assumed my intentions.

He has always manifested when I least expected it. But a few times, he answered my screaming into the void like he was always there. And yet I know he can't hear my thoughts—for the most part. Raging emotions seem to trigger my end, if nothing else. Grief or anger was present in all instances, to my recollection, whether I was trying to talk to him or not.

Carnegie?

I'm unsure what I am feeling now, and there is no answer to my hesitant head-voice. A mixture of emotions fights for my attention, so I try to calm the raging sea and focus on one as silence surrounds me.

I plead into the void as loneliness wraps me in a cold embrace. *Please answer me.*

Did you beckon?

I guess that singular, intense emotions bridge the gap between us.

How did I end up here? I ask, unable to stop the new tears streaming down my face.

The same way I did. His words bring about a flurry of questions, but I already know not to overwhelm him with them. He will only answer what he wants to answer.

Did you ask for this? I ask the one question I would know the answer to if I was asked. He does not disappoint.

No.

Who were you?

Remorse floods my being. I don't understand it, but I know one thing—my most hated enemy is no different than myself. Does that make him my ally? Or am I just desperate for someone to confide in?

My mother was one of Luther's servants; he took me when I was very young. He groomed me to make the decisions he wanted me to make. Then he completely took over my mind.

A pang goes through me at the thought of never having had a childhood—being forever in the grasp of Luther. Even riddled with war early in childhood, I had a decent life. What he proposes is a living hell. I cannot say that I wish he were not being honest with me, but the honesty only makes me feel worse—more out of control of my own life.

Why are you telling me this? I ask.

You asked, and within our connection, Luther has not figured out a way to tap into it against our will. Our thoughts, if not our lives, are our own.

A long moment of silence passes between us.

Does this make you the only true ally I have? I finally ask. *Everyone else has turned against me.*

A moment passes, and his voice is soft in my mind. *I suppose so.*

You never wanted this life. It is a statement rather than a question.

I can almost see Carnegie shaking his head. *I never wanted to lose control of my life, but when the guilt caused by the things he made me do became too much to bear, I gave in.*

Guilt?

He has not even begun to use you how he wants. You are a weapon in the making that he plans to use to bring this region to its knees like he has so many others. I have been unable to stop him, or I would never have done what I have done.

An unfathomable idea occurs to me. *Maybe together we can?*

I would like to believe so, but just because I can talk freely to you like this doesn't mean that I won't do whatever Luther asks of me. The same goes for you, and you would not believe the horror he plans to instill in the people you sacrificed yourself for if they continue to rebel.

Should I have let them die? The moment of silence that follows is almost too long to bear.

No. Even in the darkest hour, there is still hope. Just do what he says, and some of your people still have a chance of making it out of this alive.

And if I don't?

Death is not so bad when weighed against Luther's plans for their little rebellion.

***

The door of my cell opens, waking me from my fitful sleep on the hard floor. Luther steps inside, followed by Carnegie. I want nothing more than to attack Luther and rip his throat out with my teeth, but I haven't forgotten Carnegie's words from earlier.

"Are you better now, my dear?" Luther asks. His voice is soft and calming—like he has not admitted to ruining my life and taking nearly everything I cared for from me. The audacity of this man knows no bounds.

I nod my head, staring at his over-shined shoes. I find my wretched self in them staring back at me. "It is time to see how Ms. Aella is doing," he says, turning to Carnegie.

I slowly stand up from my position on the floor, hands against the wall to steady myself. I glance from Luther to Carnegie cautiously. I am helpless against Carnegie and his tricks. Luther may own me, but I will bow down to Carnegie's will whether I want to or not. I have no choice when pitted against his compulsion and tricks, and I can't help but think he is here for precisely that purpose. I have nowhere to run with the two of them blocking the door.

"What does he mean?" I ask, pushing the fear bubbling inside me down, my question directed at Carnegie. I attempt to control my breathing but only manage to stave off the hyperventilation, my chest heaving.

"It won't be permanent," Carnegie assures me, avoiding my question. The man I talked to earlier is deep in his icy eyes, but he cannot help me.

I swallow nervously. "What won't be?" I ask.

"The Switch. We need to see how Aella is progressing. It has been quite a while since I last checked on her," Carnegie answers calmly. The stranger in the depths of his gaze disappears with a twinkling of an eye.

"Who the hell is Aella?" I question, with no idea as to where this is going.

"Your shadow," he says. Luther watches on with relish.

"My *what?*" I demand, turning my attention to Luther for an explanation.

"She is the brain of your program," Luther answers, only bringing up more questions. He graciously overlooks my tone of voice, despite his previous warning. "But there will be a time to explain all of that later. I caught wind of Lieutenant Norris and the rest of your traitorous band of misfits. You two have some work to do." Mischief shines in Luther's eyes, capturing me in his gaze and imprisoning me in their magnetic hold.

Carnegie nods his head mechanically and steps toward me. I try to move away, but Carnegie freezes me to the spot with a wave of his hand.

"Please don't," I plead with him.

I'm sorry. Carnegie's voice is apologetic in my mind, but the eyes looking at me are hard and unreadable.

"Despierta, mi amor," Carnegie purrs, and darkness consumes me.

Twenty-three
JAI

I stare at the smoking desolation in front of me, lost for words. Field tents are nothing more than smoldering ruins. Badly burned support posts are the only things still standing, except for the metal chow hall in the middle of the camp. But even that has caved in, rendering it useless.

Damian should have stayed.

I don't want to be bitter about him leaving me in charge to angrily retreat to wherever the hell the rebels are hiding out, but it isn't easy. He said something about needing to make contingency plans, but who the hell knows?

The rolling hills on which Camp #1 is built hide the full extent of the damage from my low vantage point, but what lay before me is bad enough. The entirety would surely be too much to handle all at once.

I steel myself against the visage of charred bones and soot that mars the red clay dirt, staining the ground black. Footsteps crunch behind me in approach, but I cannot turn my attention away from the destruction as Warren appears in my peripheral vision at my side. He places a large hand on my shoulder, but there is no comfort in his touch. Not for this devastation.

"We were too late," I whisper.

Warren merely nods. His voice is thick with tears of frustration. "We knew this could happen when we chose this path. And Vesper moves fast. We should be thankful you made it to Camp #2 in time."

Desperation weighs heavy on my heart, and my breath stutters as I try to keep angry tears at bay. "We need as many people as we can get if we are going to survive this."

"I know," Warren says, sad eyes scanning the horizon.

"Spread out and search for survivors. Turn this place upside down. There has to be *something* left. It can't all be gone," I say, but I am not sure how accurate my words are. From what I can see, *nothing* is left—nothing alive or usable anyway. "Be on guard. I'm not sure what could cause this kind of damage."

"Yes, sir," Warren says with a slight bow. I watch him over my shoulder as he walks away, sharing a few words with Zeke. With a nod, Zeke approaches carefully, like I am a wounded animal in need of saving. Maybe I am.

"Firebombs," Zeke says as he stops beside me.

I grimace at the term. "What?" It is unfamiliar, but I know it can't be good.

"Firebombs," Zeke repeats. "That's what did this." He motions around us as he speaks. "Explosives dropped from the sky."

I stare at him in horror. "How the hell did they manage that?" I ask while gazing up at the cloudless sky. Rising smoke stains the blue of it, casting an eerie gray haze over us.

"I saw Vesper trying to get helicopters up and running after they took us from the Market. I didn't think they ever succeeded, though. They are the only thing capable of bringing them. The fighter jets were beyond repair." He says it so casually, but his words are horrifying.

"That is troublesome," I say under my breath. "Did Vesper know we would liberate this camp next? Or did they drop bombs out of spite?" I ask.

Zeke shrugs. "Hard to tell, but I wouldn't put it past Luther to bomb the place out of sheer spite. It could also be punishment for our uprising—for the disobedience of Camp #2 and #3."

"I thought people were his most important resource? Why would he kill so many?" I am desperate to understand the mind of Luther Cain. If he is depraved enough to cause this kind of destruction out of spite, it's no wonder Iylara bowed down so fast.

"We *are* his most valuable resource, but what good are we if we are going to do what we have done? I would bet money it is only Blackthorn remains here, and maybe some of my people. He would have pulled his soldiers out before dropping bombs. A few people are a cost he is willing to pay. I saw some horrendous things when we were first brought to the Vesper compound. I don't put anything past the man."

"A few?" I ask incredulously. "There had to have been almost a hundred Blackthorn stationed here—" My voice trails off, my eyes catching sight of a charred body, partially exposed under the smoldering canvas of a tent.

The body is unrecognizable, but a metal amulet around the corpse's neck has survived the intense heat of flames. I step forward, kneeling next to the body. The familiar Blackthorn coyote snarls at me from the amulet accusingly.

I reach out, pulling the necklace off of its deceased owner, holding it tightly to my chest as I grit my teeth, nostrils flaring. I take a deep breath and put it in my pocket before standing to face Zeke, my expression bleak.

"Iylara mentioned that Luther threatened her with killing her people if she disagreed with what he said. But I never thought of what would happen if *we* got out of line against *her*. We always followed her without question, especially after Luther put a bullet in her for us, until now." I shake my head, trying to fathom the mess that Iylara dealt with secretly. "I know she didn't tell me everything, but I never thought it could be *that* bad. I should have known better. She always had a rough time talking about the hard stuff. She had to be drunk off her ass before she would talk about any of it."

"We can't turn back now. We have already started this fight. We have to finish it, or these people's deaths will be in vain. We can't walk away now," Zeke says.

I hold his gaze, so similar to his brother's that it is eerie. But I nod, knowing he is right.

Shouting echoes over the hill in front of us, near the outskirts of the far side of the camp. "What the hell?" I growl, taking off in a sprint toward the sounds of distress without a second thought. I leap over burned bodies and charred debris, Zeke hot on my trail.

I crest the hilltop, and Zeke almost runs into my back as I skid to a stop at the sight in front of me.

Vesper soldiers hold about a dozen people at gunpoint. I lock eyes with Warren kneeling in the middle of the row, a rifle barrel to the back of his head. His eyes are livid with anger that pierces my soul before he breaks eye contact. His attention is drawn to the larger-than-life figure at the end of the row of prisoners. A few Charon cower in the line of Blackthorn, second-guessing the side they have chosen if I had to guess.

At first glance, it appears to be a terror-invoking creature from a long-lost legend, but no. A feminine figure sits atop a large black Clydesdale horse, seated in the black leather saddle like a Dark Queen. The woman is dressed in all black cloth and leather with a long overdress split heavily up both sides, revealing tattoed legs, allowing her to ride comfortably astride the massive horse. The boots in the stirrups are heavily buckled, and the long black cowl wrapped around her neck and shoulders looks unseasonably warm while concealing her face. An ornate sword and scabbard hang from one hip, with a dangerous-looking large-caliber revolver on the other.

The hooded figure turns her attention to me, guiding the horse smoothly to face me head-on as if the creature is an extension of herself. My breath hitches at the sight of familiar black tattoos wrapping around her bare arms. They are barely visible under the dark gunmetal of the hammered braces protecting her forearms and the cowl hanging from her shoulders, but I would know them anywhere.

"No," I whisper in disbelief.

That is not Iylara.

She brushes away the hood covering her face, and anxiety swells in the pit of my stomach. Auburn red waves cascade over the black cloth, turning to blood in the afternoon sunlight.

But it is.

"Captain Norris," she says derisively. I would not personally label myself that, but I guess that's precisely what I am—in her mind, anyway.

Her voice has no recognition, as if she does not even know me. She ignores Zeke altogether. The cadence she speaks with is cold and sharp, coated with malice, and woefully unlike what I am used to. I am unaware of ever having heard her speak in such a way, but it's her eyes that set my heart racing.

Those aren't her eyes. Ice-blue crystals shine where emeralds should be. *Something is wrong.*

"Ray—"

"Iylara is no longer in control. *I am,"* she says, an oppressive aura almost visibly pulsating around her. "I'm here to make a deal," she says. "That is if you want to make things easy. Otherwise, I will gladly make a point instead."

I stare at the woman, clearly Iylara Vance, but somehow not. "What kind of deal?" I ask carefully.

"Tell me where your little rebel camp is at, and I let them all go," she says with a brandish of her hand toward the people on their knees.

"Or what?" I ask.

A darkness falls over her face, and I fight the urge to shrink away from her. "Or I kill them all," she says, voice low and serious.

I cannot call her bluff. Something in her tone sets my nerves on edge. "You can't kill them all," I say before I can stop myself. "These are *your* people."

"Don't be so sure about that. I'm not who you think I am," she warns, eyes narrowing as she stares daggers at me. They glow ominously against the black tattoos around her eyes that take away from the stark Blackthorn mark on her chin.

I take a step closer to get a better look at her eyes. I've only seen that bright blue on one other person.

But that doesn't make sense.

"Then who are you?" I ask.

"General West," she says shortly.

I frown at the unfamiliar name. I grit my teeth and force out the truth she does not want to hear. "I don't know where they are," I say.

"You don't think I believe that do you?" she asks with a condescending brow raise.

I shake my head. "No, but it's true."

She sighs and draws the large revolver from its holster on her hip. "So that you understand I'm not screwing around," she says in a sultry tone.

She points the gun and pulls the trigger in one fluid movement. A booming crack reverberates through the atmosphere before I can even blink. My eyes flick toward Warren as his head snaps back. He falls backward at an odd angle, dead.

I repress a yell as my stomach lurches. Iylara would never kill Warren. Of all the people in the lineup, she would have picked a Charon—not the man that raised her in the training pit.

I now entirely refuse to believe that the woman on the horse is Iylara. But she does not give me time to dwell on it. "Do you have anything you would like to tell me?" she asks sweetly. I see no remorse for the man she just murdered in cold blood on her face. It's inconceivable.

I scan the Vesper soldiers, the faint idea of trying to fight flitting across my mind, but it is futile. I try my best to keep the tremble from my voice, but it lurks beneath the surface. "I'm telling the truth. I don't kno—"

General West twirls a finger in the air. Hammers click, and fear flashes across the captives' faces.

"Wait!" I plead.

"Then tell me where they are!" she shouts.

"Lie to her," Zeke whispers nervously from behind me.

"Don't even think about it," she says, her gaze falling on Zeke for the first time.

How could she hear that?

"Please, maybe we can work something out. I don't know where they are. None of us do. We have only been getting orders through letters." That is a lie, of course. Some here know, but they won't give up the rebel camp's position either. They would die or sacrifice others first.

General West huffs in exasperation. “I don’t believe you.” She lifts a hand and closes it with a twist. Gunshots echo through the camp, and the captives fall forward, motionless.

I stare at their bodies, mouth agape.

“I applaud your sense of honor, *Captain*. Although, I must say, blood for honor is a slippery slope indeed.” She sneers as our eyes meet. “Until next time. I hope you remember what happened here today.” She gives an unsettling smirk and pulls the cowl up to cover her face. She turns the horse around, lazily walking along the line of bodies.

“How is that possible?” I ask under my breath.

“What?” Zeke asks flatly as he stares at the retreating Vesper soldiers.

“That’s not Ray,” I say lamely.

“And you thought she was too far gone before. What do we do with this?” Zeke asks.

I let out a shaky breath. “I don’t know.”

Twenty-four
IYLARA

"Why won't anyone tell me anything?" I ask Carnegie angrily. "I want to know what happened!" I strike out with the dull training sword in my hand. He deftly blocks my strikes before going on the offense, and I step back on the defensive.

"Luther has ordered everyone's silence. You don't need to know what happened. Not yet," Carnegie says, bringing his training sword down at my head. I bring my sword up, parallel to the floor in front of my face, and shove him back with my foot as our swords make contact. "If you keep asking, he is going to punish you. He has already told you to stop," Carnegie warns.

With an angry shout, I strike out of order, but he anticipates my move, deflecting my sword before popping me in the ribs with the side of his dull metal blade.

I stumble to the side with a grunt of pain, staying my hand for the moment. "Anger makes you careless, and your body language gives you away when you are not in control," he says evenly, not even a bit out of breath.

I huff, tired of hearing him speak. I still hate the man. Just because I have stopped trying to kill him every time I see him doesn't mean much.

Sometimes I wish you would shut up, I say easily through our mind connection.

Something changed once I woke up from whatever escapades are being kept hidden from me. It no longer takes much effort to communicate with Carnegie now. The mere thought of intent is enough.

Well, too bad. Let's run it once more. Control yourself, and we can move on to something else.

I gnash my teeth at his words but position my feet shoulder-width apart, my left foot forward, knees bent. I draw the sword up in front of me, pointing it toward Carnegie. He mirrors me, our blades touching.

I start the offensive sequence with a calming breath, and Carnegie blocks with the defensive. On the last strike, I gracefully pirouette away from him, blocking his offensive strike behind my back, before striking at his leg as I dance out of range of his sword. On the last strike of the sequence, rather than pushing away, I lock his blade with the hilt of my training sword, staring into his wintry eyes.

"I will never stop," I whisper over our locked swords, and he bears his teeth. His voice is no more than a breath in my mind.

Good.

***

Not a soul lives in this part of the forest, let alone rebels. It's a dead end. Wherever Luther got his Intel from is garbage. There is *something* out here, though.

My grip on my walking staff tightens as I scan the darkness around me, my ears pricking at the slightest sounds heightened by my evolving program. I still do not understand it, but I can sense the changes in my body daily. Swords aren't as heavy and are much easier to swing, I don't need as much sleep, and my reflexes surprise me. I barely even eat these days, and it doesn't even phase me.

A low growling purr breaks the silence of the night before I spot the cougar lurking in the shadows. My eyes easily pick up the faint light from the full moon partially hidden by the trees. I draw my gun slowly, not wanting to discover how a hand-to-hand fight with a cat twice my size will go. I brace myself for a killing shot.

The beast's eyes glisten in the moonlight, and I gently pull the hammer back, waiting. The cougar steps forward slowly in a hunting crouch. I pull the trigger as the cat lunges without warning, my bullet hitting it in the chest, but it keeps coming. I shriek in surprise, dodging the feline with a pirouette I have perfected during practice, but against human adversaries, not animals. Animals are much faster, even with my improved reflexes. Its paw catches me under the shoulder blade, claws ripping at my side, knocking my gun from my grasp.

I grit my teeth through the pain that wraps from my shoulder blade and down my side. With a battle cry, I swing the staff, hitting the cat in the shoulder as it charges. The cougar backs up with a growl, not expecting the strike. It circles me, waiting for its moment. The cat lunges again, and I barrel roll over it. It looks around in confusion.

I whip the staff around my hip as it turns to find me, striking it in the side of the face. It flails with a horrific shriek, sounding too much like a woman screaming for my liking. I take the chance to dart for the gun on the ground, aiming once more at the cougar as it turns to attack again. The bullet lodges in the cat's eye, dropping it immediately. Damaged nerves send the cougar floundering on the ground, blood flying in all directions before it goes still.

I let out a shaky sigh of relief and reach up, finding three long gashes ripped clean through my light leather armor and the shirt underneath. I cannot see where the wound starts, further up on my back, but it is bad. Very bad. I step forward, but my legs give out as adrenaline fades. I fall hard to the ground with a groan of pain.

"Carnegie," I say into the now calm night air, staring at the cougar's face, slowly seeping blood from its eye socket. No answer. "Carnegie," I say again, half expecting the cat to lung at me again amidst the rising fear in my chest.

Carnegie! I shout mentally when again, there is no answer.

Finally, he answers. *What is it?* His tone is rigid, as if I interrupted something.

I've been attacked by a cougar. I groan in pain as I try to put pressure on the profusely bleeding gashes. *I'm in a bad way.*

Where are you? His voice is questioning but not concerned. I doubt he could be genuinely concerned for anything but himself.

Off the quarry, about a half-mile east. Spots start to shimmer against my vision. *There isn't anything out here.* Another groan escapes my lips as I lean back against a tree for support. *Don't let me die like this.*

Your programming should have evolved enough by now to allow you to heal yourself.

"Oh yeah?" I ask in disbelief, the echo of my voice eerily soothing in the pressing weight of the forest's silence.

You have to concentrate. Imagine the tissue healing, coming back together. The nanites in the program should respond to your focus, manifesting the healing.

I stare at my blood-soaked hand. "There is so much blood," I say weakly.

Focus, Iylara.

Okay, okay.

Taking a centering breath, I direct all my focus on visualizing the gashes in my side closing up. The hand pressed over the lower portion of my wounds starts to tingle, and I cannot believe something is actually happening, but I cannot stop. I will not die like this.

I keep focusing the consciousness I have left on healing my wounds, and the spots start to disappear from my vision. In my mind, I am healed. I gaze down at my side. The image burned into the back of my eyelids is reality. Only the blood staining my skin and clothes remain.

"It worked," I say breathlessly, and the world goes black.

***

Early morning sunlight breaks through the trees, falling across my face. I groan, turning my face away from the light.

“Iylara?” Carnegie’s voice breaks through the peaceful morning air like a knife. “Iylara!” he says, louder when I do not answer. He sighs, kneeling next to me. Carnegie rolls me over roughly, and I grunt, finally opening my eyes.

“Oh, my head,” I mutter, rubbing my temples. Carnegie sits me up against the tree, poking around my side, but there is no pain other than the discomfort from his fiercely prodding fingers.

“You healed perfectly, but it seems to have completely wiped out your energy. We need to work on that,” Carnegie says calmly.

I frown at him. “You didn’t send me out here just for this, did you?”

I want to smack him as he shrugs. “I wouldn’t put it past Luther, but it turned out to be a great learning experience, even if we didn’t find anything,” he says with a sideways smirk.

“Lovely,” I groan again, trying to stand. Carnegie offers me his hand, but I knock it aside. “I don’t need your help,” I say venomously.

“That wasn’t the case earlier,” he says arrogantly, unfazed by my attitude.

I grimace at him but ignore his comment as I plead with my body to rise from the ground. I get to my feet without his help and almost stick my tongue out at him childishly; however, my need to brace myself against the tree stops me.

“Can I ask you something?” I ask, unable to stop myself. I told him I would not stop trying to find out what Aella did, and I will keep asking until he gets tired of hearing it or Luther beats me into silence. I can’t ignore that something happened—something terrible. I can feel it in my bones.

“You just did,” he says with a sneer.

I want to slap him. “You know what I mean.”

Carnegie’s eyes narrow. He already knows what I am going to ask. “Sure, why not? I can’t promise I will answer it, though, but maybe I am feeling amicable at the moment—if you ask correctly.”

I pause, mulling over his words before deciding how I will go about this. I *need* answers.

What did you and Aella do? I ask, remembering what Carnegie said about our thoughts being our own. I did not think about it the last few times I asked him the same question. Maybe this is what he means about asking correctly.

He grits his teeth, annoyed that I am still asking the same question, but his response is different this time. *I didn't do anything except sit back and watch. No one even knew I was there. But you don't want to know what Aella did. It's easier if you don't.*

Getting more of an answer than I have in a week, bizarre anticipation flashes through me. I cannot stop pushing for more information.

Maybe so, but I need to know.

Carnegie takes a deep breath, his gaze unwavering from my eyes, and I know the answer will not be pretty. *The tide is turning in the war. Most of Charon are defecting and joining your rebels. The clans are joining together to fight Vesper. Camp #2 succumbed to a mutiny as yours did, but Luther dropped firebombs on Camp #1. The only people evacuated beforehand were Vesper soldiers.*

"W-wh—" My eyes fill with tears, and my heart wrenches inside my chest. My lungs deflate as my worst nightmares unfold. My people are dying, punished for their uprising, and I cannot stop it.

Aella had a dozen rebels executed after Jai refused to tell her where the rebel camp was. She shot one herself. His name was Warren.

I gasp for air as I sink back to the ground on my knees, holding myself as I begin to shake involuntarily. I can't bring myself to ask if Jai is dead or alive. I don't want to know. I couldn't handle it if he died. "I've got to be dreaming," I mumble, refusing to believe this is my life. "I can't do this."

"Yes, you can. And if you won't, you will be made to," he says stonily with a morose look.

I look up at him in distress. "Excuse me?" I ask bitterly through my tears, his words still sinking in.

Carnegie raises an eyebrow at my ignorance as he towers over me. "I told you, our lives are not our own. We were made to serve without question or hesitation—made to follow orders. You don't have permission to give up."

I stare down at the ground dejectedly, remembering what he told me before. It takes on a different meaning now that blood is on my hands, and I don't even really know what happened. Something living inside me brought my hand against my people. "I don't want this life."

"Well, too damn bad. It's the one you got. Deal with it," Carnegie says harshly, making me go rigid.

"I don't have to deal with it if I am dead," I say, finding a resolve I never thought I would have as I stand to face Carnegie.

I reach out, palm toward my pistol on the ground, and to my surprise, I can move it. It flies into my hand. Carnegie stands there, watching silently, with a trace of awe in his eyes. I have never seen *him* bring objects to himself.

I put the gun barrel to my head, but he makes no move to stop me. I try to pull the trigger, but my finger will not depress it. Confused, I aim at the ground and effortlessly pull the trigger. The gunshot rings through the trees, but I barely hear it over the roaring sound of blood rushing in my ears. I put it back to my head, and again, the trigger will not pull.

I cry out in indignation, my hand dropping limply to my side, but I still hold on to the gun.

Carnegie sighs. "Are you done?" I simply nod my head, trying to wrap my brain around not being able to pull the trigger. I have the will to, but still, I cannot.

"Do you think Luther doesn't have safeguards to keep us from killing ourselves?" he asks me. "Do you really think I never tried?"

My mind is too stuck trying to absorb my reality to realize what he is saying. "What?" I finally ask after a moment of silence.

"You can't kill yourself. The program won't allow it," Carnegie says, leaning against a tree casually with his arms crossed.

"I can still die, though, right?" I ask, getting desperate.

"Sure," he says with a shrug.

I point the gun at him. "So I make you kill me."

Carnegie chuckles. "You forget who I am, love."

My hands begin to shake. "Don't call me that," I protest. Desperation consumes me, and I try to will myself into pulling the trigger, but I can't.

Carnegie smiles sadly. "I never lied to you. I've already told you that you couldn't kill me if you wanted to. You should start listening when I speak."

I thought for a moment that my little plan would work before I remember *exactly* who he is.

Carnegie's voice is silky as he speaks. *"Despierta, mi amor."*

***

This is the stupidest thing you could think of, isn't it? Carnegie asks, perturbed, as I sneak down the hallway, hell-bent on my rebellion.

Probably, I admit.

I am still bitter about him waking Aella to get me back here without a fight. He could have used other ways but chose to wake the beast rather than compel me into action. I'm not sure if they went on any escapades before returning. All I recall is waking up to Carnegie's smug face holding out a cup of broth for me to drink.

I imagine him grinding his teeth now. *There is still time to turn back.*

I can't. There is something I need to find in there. I will not ignore this feeling.

He does not respond, his presence fading from my mind as I stop in front of Luther's door. Looking both ways to ensure I am alone, I pull a bent piece of wire and a small torque rod from my pocket, inserting them into the door's lock. My hands shake from nerves, and I have to force myself to calm down, steadying my heartbeat and, in turn, my hands. The tumblers are on the bottom rather than the top, and it throws me for a second, but I manage to bypass the lock after a few breathless moments.

The door creaks open, and I slide into the office, quietly shutting it behind me with a soft *snick*. I lock it back for good measure. The full moon's light coming through the office window is still bright but insufficient for an ordinary person to see by. *My* eyes pick up the faint glow like a cat's, and I quickly reach Luther's desk. I start rifling through the desk drawers, ears pricking for the faintest sound from the hallway. Files with names call to me, but I resist, knowing I do not have the time to read them.

Finally, in the bottom drawer, I find maps from different areas I have never heard of. A red X on a small area map with the title "Rebel Camp" scribbled in a hasty script jumps out at me, and I know it is what I am searching for.

The son-of-a-bitch already knows.

I study the map, memorizing the area. It is out of the way, but I could make it in a few hours on foot. I place the map back and shut the desk drawer. I have to go, no matter the cost. They need to know they aren't safe, even if they choose to kill me. All I need to do is get out of this place.

The named files still call to me, even from the closed desk drawer, but footsteps echo down the hall as I reach out to open it. My heart jumps up in my throat, and I frantically look around the office, spotting the wardrobe in the corner where Luther keeps his traveling coat and things. I scamper over to it, yanking the door open. There is barely enough room to squeeze into, but for once, being on the underfed side is a plus.

A key turns in the lock, and I am barely settled snugly inside before the office door swings open. The light flicks on, rays of light coming through the cracks around the wardrobe doors. I wait with bated breath, praying I am not found. I hope I left everything as it was in Luther's desk. He will notice if not.

There is a creak of Luther's chair and the rustling of papers. It is only a few minutes before he slams a desk drawer shut, and I jump, barely withholding an involuntary gasp as my heart goes into overdrive. It would not surprise me if he can hear it as it thuds away painfully in my chest, but the light flicks off, and the office door opens and closes. The lock turns, and I am alone.

Shaking from head to toe, I wait a few moments before leaving my hiding spot. Creeping to the door, I put my ear to it, listening for any sounds. I unlock the door and stick my head out, looking left then right. I freeze as Luther's eye bore down on me in anger from the right side of the door. He was waiting for me.

Footsteps! I should have listened for his footsteps again. How could I be so careless?

Luther does not say a word as I cower away from him. He advances toward me, backing me into the dark office, momentarily blinding me with a flick of the lights. He backhands me while I am distracted, and my head snaps to the side. I stumble, my head hitting the arm of a chair before I can catch myself. With a painful sting, the skin at the corner of my eye splits on contact.

Still, Luther is silent—deathly silent. Holding the side of my face, I stare up at him with wide eyes. His eyes are livid, boring into my soul, striking fear in my heart as blood runs down my face between my fingers.

"Please, Master," I beg, trying to stem the blood flow with my long sleeve. The cloth is too thin to do much.

"Did you believe hiding would work?" he growls, advancing on me. The edge of the desk stops me from retreating further, but he continues to bear down on me.

"I'm sorry, sir," I whimper, tears budding in my eyes. I am a fighter until it comes to Luther. The man terrifies me beyond measure. He evokes an irrational fear in me that I cannot overcome.

"Anyone else would die for such an act, but I have put too much work into you," he says darkly. He grabs me by the hair and drags me out of the office.

I yelp in pain, grabbing his wrist to prevent him from ripping my hair out. Strands are already coming loose at my scalp. He pulls me along the hallway as I struggle helplessly, barely able to keep my feet under me. He is strong for a man his age.

"Carnegie!" he yells as we stop outside a door at the end of the hall.

Carnegie opens the door to the training room, sweat shining on his face and the exposed skin of his arms not hidden by the black tank top he wears. I have never seen him in anything other than long sleeves, even during our dual training. I am startled at the multitude of tattoos reaching from fingertips to shoulders. Runes cover his knuckles, and tribal lines swirl delicately up his muscled arms.

"Yes, sir?" he asks, looking sideways at me where I kneel next to Luther, his fist still tight in my hair.

Please help me, I beg Carnegie, not knowing what else to do. He narrows his eyes at me before turning them back to Luther.

"She was snooping around in my office. She needs to be taught a lesson, but I have a meeting to attend. Take her to

Alastair. See that she learns her lesson," he commands, and I whimper at the mention of Alastair's name.

"Please, I'm sorry. I won't do it again," I beg, wanting anything other than to see the brutal man in charge of training and reconditioning again.

"Alastair will see to it that you don't," Luther says, livid. He finally lets me go, roughly shoving me forward. Luther leaves me on hands and knees in front of Carnegie as he stalks off to the meeting room.

I stare at the floor in desperation. *I can't go back to him,* I plead to Carnegie, but he has no reason to help me.

Carnegie sighs. *I told you not to do that, but you couldn't help yourself, could you? Did you at least find what you were looking for?*

I stay silent, staring at his booted feet. "Come on," he says, incensed with me. He grabs me by the arm to haul me to my feet. His hands are warm yet smooth, protected by gloves most of the time as they are.

"Don't take me to Alastair," I continue to plead as he pulls me down the hall, not nearly as rough as Luther for once.

"I have to," is all he says.

We pass by the entrance doors, and I take my chance. I sideswipe at Carnegie, hitting him in the neck with the side of my hand. He chokes, releasing me as his hands go to his throat. I kick low, knocking him off his feet, and dart for the open door and through the metal detectors. The alarms blare, but nothing can stop me. Carnegie could most days, but he can't speak. I burst through the front door, running as fast as I can for the gate, disregarding the shouts from both Carnegie and Yates.

Don't do this! Carnegie yells in my mind.

I have to, I say desperately.

A burst of gunfire comes from the guard tower as I reach out, palm forward, imagining the front gate blowing outward. My desperation fuels it, and the lock snaps as the gate bursts open. I run through it as bullets rain down around my feet. They are not allowed to kill me, so they will not shoot to kill, but I yelp in pain as a bullet grazes my leg. I keep running, breaking through the tree line, and still, I do not stop. I have to warn the rebels that Luther knows where they are. I have to do something—even if it is the last thing I ever do.

Twenty-five
JAI

Iylara is his most powerful weapon, even if she doesn't know it.

That's what Damian said, anyway. I was barely listening to his spill on why his sister must die once we made it to the rebel camp tucked away in the backwoods of the northwestern portion of Blackthorn territory. The shock hasn't completely worn off from what I witnessed at Camp #1, but Damian doesn't seem surprised.

She has to die before she kills us all.

Damian's words keep circulating through my mind as I pace back and forth on patrol. I'm afraid of the nightmares that will come if I go to sleep, so I pleaded for the job of the night watch to keep my mind off of things. Otherwise, I may start drinking myself to death. I never thought a bottle would make me feel better until now, but I didn't realize patrol would leave more time for my mind to wander. I am starting to regret my choice.

Were her eyes blue?

Yeah, but does that matter?

More than you know.

I can't get past the anger of being left in the dark for so long. Everything that Damian has told me lacks the effect that it should have. If he had let *someone* on the inside know he wasn't dead, things might be different. But now, a part of me can't trust him.

What does it mean? I had asked.

It lets you know who is in control.

Control? Like split personalities?

The thought horrifies me. The fact that I watched Iylara's body put a bullet in Warren's skull was and is too much. It would be much easier to deal with a clone or something, as crazy as it sounds. It would also make it much easier to follow through with the demand for her life if it wasn't actually her.

Yes and no.

Damian's answers are beginning to drive me crazy.

Have I ever done anything but serve Blackthorn? I ask myself now.

Damian should give me better answers than he has. It's like he doesn't trust *me,* either.

A snapping of a twig catches my attention, and I stop pacing. I look around, rifle raised. A shadow catches my eye in the pale moonlight, pulling me from my thoughts.

My finger is ready on the trigger as a hooded figure steps out of the trees, and a relieved voice cuts through the air. "Jai? It's me—Ray." She approaches from the shadows, slowly raising her hands in surrender under the scrutiny of my gun.

I take a step back in surprise but hold my form, sights steady on her heart. "Wait," she pleads. "Please, I need to talk to you." She steps out of the shadows, my nearby lantern light falling on her shrouded form. She lifts her hooded head enough for the light to catch her eyes.

They are green.

"You shouldn't be here," I say, tightening my grip on my rifle. Damian wants me to pull the trigger, but I cannot bring myself to do it. It is Iylara standing before me, not General West.

"I had no other choice. Please hear me out." I have never heard such desperation in her voice, and the tip of my rifle lowers a few inches unconsciously.

"I have the information you need to keep our people safe," she continues. Her eyes are frantic, and she speaks faster than usual. The cold tone I last heard come from her lips is gone. General West is *not* here, but I can't take my finger off the trigger. I'm not sure how easy it would be for her to reappear.

Iylara's bottom lip quivers as she speaks. "Luther knows where your rebel village is. He has been rallying soldiers and sending me on random training missions, making me think he still didn't know where to strike. *Please.* You have to listen to me," she begs, wringing her hands in apprehension.

After a moment of my silent staring, Iylara brushes the hood covering her head away, fully revealing herself. My eyes widen. There is a deep purple bruise on the left side of her face surrounding a relatively fresh gash that runs vertically at the corner of her eye. Dried blood stains the side of her face as if she tried to wipe it away and failed.

I grind my teeth together as I lower my rifle. "How would Luther know that?" I ask with a bite to my tone that I cannot help. I can't stand seeing her injured, but I also can't trust her, and it twists my heart painfully. I am starting to think that I can't trust anyone.

"I don't know, but I found a map marked 'Rebel Camp' inside Luther's desk. It is how I made it here," she explains. "He found me in his office, but I'm not sure he knows what I saw. Not that it matters."

"Is that where the shiner came from?" I ask, unable to stop myself—Iylara, in pain or injured, sparks fury in me that I cannot help, even after everything.

She simply nods.

"Is this the first time he has hit you?" I ask, righteous anger rising in me against my will.

Iylara chuckles darkly. "I wish," she whispers before trudging on with what she came to say with a clearing of her throat. "I am almost positive that you have a spy. I don't know how else Luther could know what he does. He insists that nothing has come of his patrols."

"You mean a *rat?"* I ask mockingly.

Iylara smirks with contempt before pausing. "Yeah, a rat," she says with withheld tears. The sound pierces me in the heart, and guilt settles on me instantly.

She bites her lower lip, turning away from me in shame. "Luther is rallying troops to attack. He was on his way to a meeting when he found me in his office."

"And what would you propose we do about it?" I ask skeptically. "How do I know that he didn't send you here? I'm sorry, but I can't trust you." A glint of pain flashes across Iylara's face that matches the pain in my chest at the truth of my words.

I don't know her anymore.

Iylara groans in frustrated agony as she looks at me desperately. "I can't make you believe me, but I can't sit by and do nothing with what I've learned. Please don't ignore what I am telling you. You have time to prepare before he attacks if you do." She is still talking too fast for my liking, but it would be ignorant to ignore any kind of warning—especially one that in all ways seems heartfelt rather than manipulated. Iylara was never one for acting.

I shift uneasily from one foot to the other. "If you are telling the truth and are here of your own volition, *why* are you here?"

Iylara bows her head sadly, a tear escaping down her cheek. "My time is coming to a close. I want to try and fix some of the many wrongs that have resulted from my choices."

I step toward her, letting my rifle swing from the strap as I let go of it, but I refrain from touching her. "What do you mean?" I ask. I cannot act like I feel nothing for her when she stands before me in such a way. Nothing else matters. Seeing her as herself, though disturbed, makes it nigh impossible to imagine killing her, ever.

"Aella—the woman with my face? Aella West?" she asks, sending a jolt through me at the name.

"Yeah," I respond sullenly. I didn't know the woman's first name, but *West* is forever etched in my memory.

Iylara's eyes sweep from side to side as if checking to see that we are alone. "She is the program that sleeps inside of me, quiet for the most part, but I cannot control when Carnegie wakes her."

I frown in confusion. "What are you talking about?"

She sighs deeply before speaking. "It's science. I don't understand it. I only understand the most basic explanation."

"No, I mean Carnegie," I demand. "What does he have to do with any of this? Everyone thinks he is dead, from what I can tell."

Iylara's face is void of emotion. "Carnegie works for Vesper, for Luther. This whole war with Charon is nothing but a game."

I stand there in shock. I'm still not sure that I can believe her, but I choose to humor her. Maybe I can get more information. "What about a program?" I ask, trying to ignore the pounding of my heart.

"I told you, I don't know how to explain it," she says timidly. I am not used to a timid Iylara Vance, and it only solidifies the severity of the situation in my mind.

"Well, I'm all ears," I say. "I need some kind of explanation for all that has happened."

Iylara steadies herself, forever fidgeting nervously with her hands, no matter how calm her eyes may or may not seem. "All I know is that there is a chip thing in my head. It's what caused the headaches after I was taken when we were attacked. It evolves with me and grows up in a way. Aella is its personality—its consciousness. The first time you met her was not the first time that Carnegie woke her up, but it was the first time that Luther used her against you."

I stare at her in shock. "When was the first time he woke her?" I *need* to understand, but this all seems way over my head.

"I think it was after the battle of Carthage—for the first legitimate time, anyway. I was injured, and Alec was trying to get me to safety. Carnegie shot him in the back the same way he did you. I managed to take out a few of his men before he subdued me. A-and then he healed my wounds." She closes her eyes, remembering a time past. "I should have died that day with everyone else."

Iylara opens her eyes. "The last thing I remember is Carnegie's voice. Then I woke up in the woods outside our village."

"Why didn't you tell me any of this before?" I ask. I can't process everything she is telling me through my hurt. Maybe I could have helped her before we got *here* if she had told me.

She shakes her head harshly with a wince. "I didn't remember what happened. Only bits and pieces even now. And I still don't remember the last time either," she admits, finally looking back at me.

I hurt at the memory of what recently transpired. *She doesn't know?*

"It's all part of whatever scheme Luther has laid out for me. Everything that has happened since Charon's invasion, if not before, has been his work. At this point, I wouldn't put it past him to have orchestrated that disease that killed my mother and sister, but that is only speculation on my part."

She pauses to take a shaky breath. "They put the chip in me when I was taken." Another pause echoes in the silence as she swallows back tears. "I'm pretty sure the trauma of Danny's death was a trigger or something, but no one has admitted to it. Most of what I know has been hearsay. Nobody really tells me anything."

Iylara takes a step toward me, desperation and grief shining in her eyes. "Luther had my family killed so they wouldn't get in the way. And all this fighting between Charon and Blackthorn is for nothing except my training." She shudders a sob, looking away from me to wipe her cheeks before turning back to me. "All of this is my fault. You were right to turn against Luther. *Against me.* I would say I forgive you, but there was never anything to forgive. You had our people's best interests at heart from the beginning. You always have."

I open my mouth to respond, but she cuts me off. "I want to join you, but Luther has other plans for me. I am in too deep. If I do not return to reap the consequences of my actions today, I'm not sure what he will do. He told me long ago that my people would die if I didn't cooperate." Iylara goes silent, looking at me sadly, her hands finally still. "One say for one life," she whispers, barely audible.

I look at her questioningly, and she obliges me to answer. "The only person I ever willingly sacrificed was the one who died to keep you at my side."

My jaw drops. "What?"

Iylara shakes with held-back tears, reaching out in desperation for the front of my shirt. "He was going to send you away. But he allowed me one say for one life." She drops her head, tears streaming down her cheeks as I step away. "I valued your life over one of our own, whose name I didn't even know. I can't say that I regret it, but I *feel* it."

I falter, trying to fathom what she is telling me. "That execution at the beginning?"

I don't have to elaborate. Iylara knows of whom I speak. I will never forget the fear and confusion in the man's eyes as she pulled the lever that ended his life, but I never knew it was for *me*.

Iylara only nods.

I step away from her, shaking my head. I'm not as affected as I should be by her words, but it still prods at me. So much has happened since then, but I will never forget that moment—and she did it for *me*. I can't find words as tears threaten to well up, so I change the subject. There is something else I want to know about. "You don't remember anything when Aella is awake?"

Iylara shakes her head, unperturbed by my change in subject. "No, it's like I am sleeping until Carnegie puts Aella back to sleep, and then I wake up. I'm not privy to what she does while I am out. But Carnegie told me what she did, and it goes against Luther trying to keep me in the dark," she says through fresh tears, pain flashing across her face. "Knowing makes me want to fight back, and Luther doesn't want that. It's why I am here now."

"Wait. Are you saying that Carnegie is helping you?" I ask incredulously.

She nods. "In a way. He is trying to keep me from becoming like him, but he only has so much control. I never know how he will act, but I think he found a way to fight the program," she says. She starts twiddling her thumbs mindlessly, but she is slowly calming down.

"Like him?" I ask, pushing for more information. I need to understand what is going on, if only a little.

Iylara gazes at me with sad eyes. "One with his program."

"His program?" I prod, even more confused.

Iylara's tone is dark as she speaks. "Carnegie and I are the same. We are experiments of Luther's. I said my time is coming to a close because when I get back, Luther will either kill me or finally force me to become one with Aella to keep me under control. I can only hope for death, but he has already told me he has put too much work into me to kill me."

My heart pounds rapidly in my chest as she speaks. The sadness in her is tangible, and it cuts through me like a knife. "Ray," I whisper, not knowing what else to say.

"Don't," she says, shaking her head. "I don't need your pity, and I don't want it. I made the choices that brought me here, and I killed Rat when I was myself. I am not blind to the irony of my last words to him. It is only befitting that I come to terms with the words from my own mouth, don't you think?" she asks with a sad half-smile.

"How can you be so sure Luther will know you left?" My voice is hopeful, but Iylara scoffs.

"He tried to have Carnegie take me to reconditioning after he caught me in his office. I throat-punched Carnegie and ran as we passed the entrance doors. Alarms blared, and guards shot at me." Iylara shakes her head, staring down at her feet. "It was a big deal. He knows."

"Did you get shot?" I ask, my concern for her well-being taking over.

"It's just a graze. It's fine," she says tiredly. "I can deal with it later. The pain keeps my mind clear," she adds absently with a wave of her hand. "I have a tracker as well. Something stops me every time I try to cut it out. Aella, I presume. Luther will know where I went. You guys should clear of here soon."

I take another step toward her, gently brushing the back of my fingers across the bruise on her face. "Stay here. Fight with us. Please don't go back," I say softly. "We can do this together."

Iylara leans into my touch for a moment before she shakes her head. She stares at her feet as she speaks but doesn't move away. "I can't risk Luther being able to use me against you. I don't know the full extent of his control. I don't want to find out if Carnegie can wake me up over a distance. Whether he has been helping me or not, he can't say no to Luther. He hasn't done it yet, but—" She stares into space past my shoulder with tear-stained eyes in thought.

"How could he do that?" I ask as my limited understanding goes down a notch.

Iylara looks at me with dark eyes. "Carnegie and I have a mind connection that allows us to speak telepathically at great distances. I don't want to find out if my trigger words work over it. I have my doubts, but I must return to protect you. He could be biding his time."

I stare at her, dumbfounded. "But aren't you already putting us in danger if Carnegie can trigger you mentally?" I ask, horrified at the thought. I do not want to be forced to kill her, but I will have no choice if Aella shows up and attacks.

"I had to take some risk. But that is also why I have to leave now. I wanted you to know that your camp is no longer a secret," she says. The nervous fidgeting is almost entirely gone, like the information she carried was tearing her apart until it was released.

"But what will he do to you?" I ask.

A single tear runs down her cheek. "Anything he wants. I have done all that I could. I will be at peace with that. You should be too. Please, let me go," she says quietly, staring at her hands as she picks at her thumbnail.

"No," I say as I take one last step forward to embrace her in a tearful hug. I bury my face in her hair. She smells of leather and pine, as she always has, as if nothing has changed. But that is a lie.

"I should never have given up on you," I say into her hair with a sniffle.

Iylara shakes her head, but her arms reach up to hug me back. "You can't help me. You were right to turn on me. Be the leader I failed to be," she whispers.

I cannot bring myself to tell her about Damian. It would surely only make things harder at this point. "There has to be something that I can do," I say, desperate to help her. I pull away to look her in the eyes.

She bites her lip, staring at me silently for a moment before answering. "Kill me. My program keeps me from doing it myself, or I would have already done you all a favor," she says with finality. Her voice is steadier now than it has been the entire conversation.

My lower lip trembles as I shake my head. "Don't ask that of me."

Her voice turns cold, and the change is jarring. "Then no, there isn't anything you can do." There is a bitter undercurrent to her tone, but I deserve it. I already tried to kill her once before, so why can I not do it when she asks it of me?

"I—" I stop, unable to find words. I lower my gaze to her lips, the thin scars across them only adding to her beauty. I unconsciously reach out, tracing her lips with a finger softly.

Iylara looks up at me with shimmering eyes. "I won't stop you," she breathes.

I frown in thought, longing pulling at me. "Just once."

Iylara nods, and I gently lower my lips to hers. They are colder than I imagined but as soft as in my dreams. She shudders, planting her palms on my chest, but she does not push away. Her fingers gently grip the front of my shirt.

I try to convey everything I have ever wanted to say with the pressure of my lips, not wanting to push my way through. The world stands still, and before I lose myself, I pull away, cupping her face in my hands. "Go. Do what you need to do," I say, voice husky with unspoken words.

"Thank you," she whispers, bowing her head into my chest.

I wrap my arms around her again, inhaling the scent of her hair. "I still love you, you know," I say before dropping my arms. "I could never hate you."

The faintest of smiles tugs at her lips. "I know."

***

Zeke desperately pleads Iylara's case with Damian once again. I stopped trying because I couldn't muster the energy to help him after seeing the look in Iylara's eyes when she asked me to kill her. The guilt from not being able to do what she asked weighs down on me. I cannot bear the torment I saw raging in her eyes, but I can never again think about pulling the trigger on her life. Death would set her free, but I am selfish enough to withhold that freedom from her.

I do not want to live with that pain.

Kicked back in one of the chairs by the empty fireplace in Damian's cabin, I watch Zeke pace the small living area. Damian watches on from his seat at the kitchen counter, annoyed.

"I don't care if she is trying to help. She still needs to die before Luther unleashes hell on all of us. What part of that do you not understand?" Damian asks. "She went back, for God's sake! What does that tell you!"

"I don't see how killing her could help! She just needs to get away from him. She is willing to talk to us! Who knows what else she wants to do!" Zeke shoots back ignorantly.

Even after watching Aella put a bullet in Warren's head, Zeke only remembers the woman I know he secretly loves, or at least lusts after, not the mess I encountered last night.

If only he could have seen the look in her eyes.

Damian bears his teeth. The unshaven salt and pepper beard on his chin makes him look more like his father than ever before. "These sleepers can't be reasoned with. Sure, there are glitches in the system, but I don't know how that works. If Luther unleashes Aella full force, we won't have time to try and figure out what works before she kills us all. She is a super-soldier. Heightened senses, quick reflexes, super-strength, blood-thirsty, and more! I have even heard of unnatural abilities that can manipulate the air around them, although nobody up north has any proof of that."

"And how do you know so much?" I ask, cutting Zeke off from another impassioned speech.

Damian turns his attention to me. "I have talked with a few of the old chiefs outside of our region, and they all had the same story. Vesper came in with grandiose plans to make life better. People in places of power and influence came under his control, and he destroyed their entire way of life. Carnegie and Iylara are not the only two experiments of Luther's, just the ones that he is using in our area."

"That doesn't mean we have to kill her!" Zeke says desperately.

Damian holds his hand up, staving off the rest of Zeke's tirade. "You love her, and you don't want her to die. I get it. She is my *sister*. But if you truly love her, you will let her go. Nobody has ever come away from Luther as they once were. He breaks them, rebuilds them, and ensures they can never return to the way they were. Do you think Iylara is the first one to try and fight back? Death is the easy way out for her."

My breath hitches. Iylara's words, *Let me go,* ring in my ears like a bad song.

"He's right," I say quietly.

Zeke turns on me in anger. "How can you side with him on this?" he asks. "You, of all people!"

My voice is not nearly as steady as I would like it to be as I answer. "I asked Iylara if there was anything that I could do for her. She told me to *kill* her. I couldn't do it. I will *never* be able to do it, but I can't go on while knowing of the torment that she is going through, either. Let Damian do what he is going to do," I say, ultimately giving up the fight to spare Iylara's life.

I may not be able to do it, but I won't stop it.

Damian turns to me, surprise and sadness clear on his face. "She wanted you to kill her?" he asks.

"She said she couldn't do it herself because whatever that program does prevents her," I explain, tiring of the conversation quickly.

Damian's brow furrows deeply, and he slowly nods his head. "That's interesting. So it has already started to take over."

"What do you mean?" Zeke asks, but I can only stare at Damian, waiting for him to explain. I can already see the words on his lips.

Damian ignores Zeke. "Since the attack on Blackthorn, you said she seemed to devolve." I nod in acknowledgment, a frown forming on my lips. "It was because of whatever conditioning she went through. The program has slowly been pushing through the entire time," Damian says.

The revelation sheds light on more than a few things, including the downward spiral I witnessed, even before Luther came into the picture. All the rash decisions I couldn't figure out make sense now, along with the times she went missing and returned worse.

"I don't want to talk about this anymore," Zeke says, clenching and unclenching his fists.

He can't handle the truth.

"Me, either," Damian says shortly. "It's time that you left—both of you."

"Sir, we have some stuff we need to discuss. Things have changed rapidly in a small amount of time," I say, sitting up straight in my chair. I need action to distract from the war raging in my mind.

"There is nothing to discuss. The entire population of Charon has decided to disavow their clan since Carnegie is missing in action. They believe he is dead, which we now know is not true. But without the threat of him around, they have finally begun to think for themselves, and even they are tired of fighting. As you said, Jai, we could use the help. I'm not going to deter them from joining us."

But you won't tell them the truth about their leader?

My mouth will get me in trouble if I can't control it. So far, I haven't spouted my thoughts for all to see. But Damian can sense them. He glares at me as if daring me to say anything else, but I know when to keep my mouth shut.

Damian gets up and walks over to the door. He holds it open expectantly. "Now, please, if you would leave me alone. Keena and Ysabel will be home soon, and I would like to spend the night in peace with my family."

Twenty-six
IYLARA

"What were you thinking?" Carnegie whispers menacingly, towering over me in the entrance corridor upon my arrival. I stay silent, looking up into his icy gaze in defiance.

"You understand what I have to do now?" he asks, and I could swear there is pain in his voice. The cruel Carnegie I knew has been few and far between as of late. Whatever he is doing to fight his program seems to be working until Luther has a say.

I try not to let the disdain show on my face, but I will not regret meeting with Jai. The relief at finding him alive was more than I could comprehend, and warning him was the right thing to do. I did what I could to finally help people rather than be their death. I will be okay with that, come what may now.

Carnegie bites his lip, forcing his anger down. There is a glimpse of remorse in his eyes to go with the pain I heard in his voice, and I scowl. "Just remember, I didn't want it to come to this," he says, voice thick with more emotion than I thought him capable of.

He grabs me by the arm, electricity crackling at his fingertips. I hiss at the sensation but do not fight him as he pushes me down the hall toward Luther's office. We walk in strained silence before stopping in front of Luther's door. Carnegie knocks twice.

"Come in," Luther's deep voice seethes through the oak door.

Carnegie throws the door open, shoving me inside. He pushes his foot into the back of my knee, forcing me down. Kneeling on the ground in the middle of the room, I stare at the hardwood floor. Luther stalks toward me, circling me like I am prey. I stare at the swirling wood patterns, avoiding his gaze as terror consumes me.

I am no longer as confident in my actions as Luther stares me down dangerously. I knew the consequences of my actions, but it did not prepare me for the fear this man still evokes in me.

Luther stops in front of me, and I turn my attention to his shiny black shoes. I can almost see my reflection in them—almost. Someone surely got beat for a half-ass job.

"After everything you have been through, why would you do something like this, Iylara? Have you not had enough of the pain? The torture? Your rebellion hurts not only you but those you care for as well. I will burn that rebel village to the ground and slaughter every last one in it for this. No prisoners. No questions asked," he says. "What's left of your clan that has not already betrayed us will believe that you left them for dead. A betrayal they will never forgive—if they live. I may still wipe every last Blackthorn off the map and have Aella slit your niece's throat herself for good measure."

His words shake me to my core, but Carnegie's fingers unleash a barrage of electricity from behind me, shutting down all thought. The nerve endings in my brain explode with unwanted activity, and I clench my teeth together, groaning with the effort to contain the scream building in my throat. It only lasts a few moments, but it is effective. I fall forward, face in my hands. My forehead rests against the cold floor, tears silently streaming from my eyes.

Selfishly, I do feel regret.

I didn't think this all the way through. I have killed to make the pain stop before. Why would now be any different?

"I am going to have to do something more drastic, clearly," Luther says with a sigh. He almost sounds happy, the bastard. "Scan her," he commands Carnegie.

Carnegie circles around me, grabbing me by the collar. He pulls me upright before pressing his hand against my forehead, invading my thoughts. I see everything he sees. My regrets. My pain. The overwhelming grief and guilt. The feeling of Jai's lips against mine. I do not doubt that Carnegie knows more about me than I knew of myself before this moment. So much for our thoughts being our own.

Carnegie lets me go, and I collapse to the floor. "Kill me," I plead, my tears pooling on the floor.

Luther shakes his head. "I can't do that. Like I said before, I have put too much work into you. What's the verdict?" He directs the last bit at Carnegie.

"She has given up," Carnegie says flatly, and more tears escape my eyes at his words.

I have.

And I said I would never stop fighting.

Luther kneels in front of me. He lifts my chin, forcing me to look at him. "You do not want this anymore," he says simply.

My chin quivers. "No, sir."

"Good." He stands, turning to Carnegie. "Take her to room 101. Alastair is occupied at the moment, but you know what to do."

"Yes, sir," Carnegie responds stiffly.

Room 101?

Carnegie's voice is silent for a moment before he answers. *The end of the line.*

Carnegie hooks his arm through mine, lifting me off of the floor. It takes everything in me to stand, but I do, allowing him to pull me from the office quietly and without a fight. He leads me to the basement, and I get colder the further down the stairs we go.

"How long will this take?" I ask, finally speaking.

"It could be hours or days. Depends on you," Carnegie says, his voice indifferent.

"What will happen?" I ask.

"Aella will wake, but you will not go to sleep. She will vie for control. The duration is based on how much you fight," Carnegie says slowly, letting his words grab hold of my mind.

"It won't be like sleeping, after?" I pray for that kind of relief.

He pauses for a moment longer than I like. "No. You will see through your eyes, but you will have no control over what Aella does. You will meld together, and who you are will disappear. But the pain will end."

I stop dead in my tracks. Carnegie tugs on my arm, but I stand my ground. "No," I say. There *is* a flame of fight still in me.

Anger rises in him quickly. "What do you mean, *'No'?* You don't have a say in this," he reminds me. "You made your choice."

I swing out at him. He is anticipating an attack this time, and I am weak in more ways than one. I have forgotten when the last time I ate anything was, and it is finally starting to affect me.

"I will not sit back and watch whatever hell she will bring. You are going to have to kill me," I say desperately.

"No, I'm not. Did you forget who I am again? The control I have over you?" he warns.

Despite his words, I strike out once more, and he blocks. Carnegie rushes me, pinning me to the wall with his forearm, his face inches from mine. "I don't like forcing you to obey. Please stop."

"No!" I cry, trying to fight him off. "I don't want to live like this. Don't do this," I plead, thrashing against his hold.

"I have no choice. *Stop.*" The quirk is back in his voice, and I immediately stop fighting.

"Please," I sob helplessly, going limp under his hold, and something behind Carnegie's eyes breaks. A single tear appears, escaping the corner of his eye to trail down his face slowly.

"I *can't,"* he says tearfully.

It finally sinks in. He *is* like me. Two people in one body. The real him watching while his shadow acts. Without a doubt, the man looking at me right now is the actual owner of the body pinning me to the wall, but he does not have control over his actions.

"Who are you?" I ask, and the pressure on my throat eases a little, but he does not let me go.

Something like a light switch flicks on and off behind his eyes, and the pressure intensifies, cutting off my air. He must be fighting within himself.

Who are you? I ask again, unable to speak out loud under the pressure against my throat, choking me.

He bears his teeth at me, eyes shining as he struggles with himself. *Gryndale.*

My breath hitches as a soft voice answers, nothing like the crassness I am used to.

Shut up. The snarling voice I *am* used to returns, but even though Carnegie is in my head, he is not speaking to me. He speaks to himself—to this *Gryndale.*

Breathing heavily, he steps away from me, looking frazzled. "What was that?" I ask, timidly bracing myself against the wall. Per his command, I do not fight, but he did not tell *me* to shut up. I do not know who I am talking to, but my guess is that Carnegie has taken back control.

He grinds his teeth and, without saying a word, grabs my arm to drag me along the dark corridor. Lanterns are spaced every ten feet, but they are dull and dusty and barely give off any light. They are not electric like everything else in the compound, either. Candles flicker in the orbs so low that the faintest wind could put them out.

Our footsteps echo off the concrete walls as we walk to the end of the corridor. The door at the very end is made of heavy steel, with the number 101 burned into the metal. Carnegie puts his hand on the door midway up. It glows, and I am reminded of the entrance to the Blackthorn safe house and War Room, but he doesn't appear to be bleeding when he pulls his hand away. The heavy door swings open silently, and two hulking black shadows appear on either side of the door. I gasp, trying to back away from them.

"What?" Carnegie asks at my sudden hesitancy as he tries to push me through the door. He either cannot see them or is unfazed. Beyond the door is darkness unmatched by anything I have ever seen, except for the two beasts guarding the entrance, unaffected by the dim light of the hallway. If anything, the light only makes them darker.

I push back, his compulsion not including this scenario. "What are those things?" I whisper in shock.

Carnegie stops, grip tightening on my arm to keep me from running. "You have the Sight?" he asks, astonished.

"The what? No. You can't see them?" I ask, petrified as the two shadows tower over us.

"No. Where are they?" he asks curiously, looking around.

On either side of the door. They aren't moving. They appeared when you put your hand on the door.

"They are Spectrals—our guardians. They keep watch and report back to Luther, but they can only do so much without corporeal bodies," he says, relaxing slightly.

I stare open-mouthed at him, not in the least bit relaxed. "How have I never seen them before?"

Carnegie shrugs his shoulders. "I don't know. I can't see them, but they belong to Luther."

I look at him, horrified. "Can they speak to him?"

"They see and tell him everything."

The Spectrals turn their shadowy heads to look at me, but they have no eyes. With renewed vigor, Carnegie ignores my hesitancy and pushes me through the door. The darkness envelops us until a light begins to glow under his shirt. He pulls it out, and I recognize the obsidian stone from so long ago glowing with a dark light. It only penetrates the darkness two feet in front of us. The light from the hallway is like the light at the end of a tunnel, leading the way back outside, getting smaller and smaller the further we walk away from it. The stone's light illuminates a set of shackles hanging from the ceiling. I stand solemnly under them as Carnegie locks them in place.

"Get on your knees," he says softly.

"Why?" I ask, but there is no fight in my curiosity. If he does not answer, oh well. I will obey. I'm just glad I don't have to deal with Alastair. That man is the worst.

He looks at me piteously. "It will hurt less," he says after a moment.

I am not sure what he means, but I do as he says. The shackles are barely long enough for me to kneel, my hands pulled up into the air. A lone rolling mayo table with a single syringe appears out of the darkness as Carnegie shifts to the left. He uncaps the needle, and I stare at it with wide eyes.

"What does it do?" There is no echo in the darkness around us as we speak, like there are no walls for the sound to bounce off of.

"Keeps you awake," he says.

He is gentle as he inserts the short needle into the side of my neck and presses the plunger down. The serum is cold, making me shake as it courses through my veins like ice.

Don't ever stop fighting. You did once, but I know it was only a moment of weakness, Gryndale's soft voice tells me.

I have heard his voice before—right before Luther shot me. I glance up at him, but before I can say anything, Carnegie says, *"Despierta, mi amor."*

My brain snaps like a rubber band being stretched and then released. I scream out in pain, knowing what Carnegie meant when he said it would hurt less to kneel. I would otherwise hit my knees on the concrete floor under the pain.

Finally, a sneering voice sounds in my mind.

Not you. I am shocked. I know that voice too.

She was the one helping me along—the one who spoke to me before I killed Rat and the one who only appeared with the fog in my mind. I feel it now, like an oppressive weight I cannot rid myself of.

"It's about time," Aella speaks aloud, my mouth moving of its own volition. The sensation is alien to me.

"Well, hello to you too, my love," Carnegie says with a playful frown.

"What's happening?" I ask, taking control of my mouth.

"That's my cue," Carnegie says. "I will be back later. The longer you fight it, the longer it will last." He walks back to the doorway, taking the light with him. When he shuts the door, the void devours me, but, for once, I do not lose consciousness.

***

"No, no," I mumble. A tingling sensation starts at the base of my neck again. Searing pain accompanies a flash of light behind my eyes. "NO!" I cry in agony, painful convulsions tightening already sore muscles—a sensation I never wanted to experience again.

I pull against the cuffs holding my limp body upright on my knees, trying to focus my eyes, but it is impossible in the utter black around me. The only sounds are my racing heart, labored breathing, the occasional jingle of my shackles, and *her.*

Give it up, Aella hisses in my mind. Unlike before, when her voice was muted and in the background, she is now in the forefront of my mind.

"NO!" I cry out again but now in anger.

Why are you still fighting? You already gave up. Let me do the work for you, Aella purrs. *It will make the pain go away.*

She pokes and prods, trying to coax me into handing over control with shocks of pain throughout my body. *You are only hurting yourself by fighting this.*

Before I can reply, the door opens, and a figure steps in, silhouetted by the dim light in the hall. In such inky blackness, the tiniest bit of light is blinding. As he approaches, I shrink from the light hanging around Carnegie's neck, squeezing my eyes shut with a groan.

"Look at me," he whispers, and I slowly open my eyes to find him kneeling in front of me. A grin lights up his face. "Good. You made it through the hardest part."

"Did I?" I ask, unimpressed by his observation. Nothing seems to have changed except the soreness in my body and the pain in my neck.

Carnegie pulls a small mirror from inside his jacket, holding it up for me to gaze into. Ice-blue eyes stare back at me from a gaunt face. I jerk away from my reflection, terrified of what I see.

"No, no, no," I start mumbling again, shaking my head harshly.

"It's a good thing. Some people die as the physical change becomes permanent. That's part of what makes you unconscious when I wake Aella," Carnegie says reassuringly.

But that's what I want. I grimly dream of the escape of nothingness.

Speak for yourself, Aella responds.

"It's been two days. How much longer are you going to fight this? It's not as bad as you think it is. What you are going through now is much worse," Carnegie says.

I glare at him with no intention of giving in. *"No,"* I say with finality.

He sighs deeply. *"Give it up,"* he compels me, and it is like another betrayal lodged deep in my heart.

That's it, Aella commends as I give up involuntarily. A ringing static fills my ears, and my eyes roll back in my head. I sink into my mind, numbness overtaking me. Aella steps forward, taking the reins from my relenting grasp.

Carnegie stands as Aella speaks. "Won't you let me out now?" she asks in a sweet voice.

"No, my love," Carnegie whispers, and anger flares up in Aella as if it is my own.

"Why not?" she shrieks—*we* shriek.

Carnegie traces my lips with a finger as Aella glares at him angrily. Gryndale is nowhere to be seen in the icy depths looking back at me. Carnegie has completely silenced him again. "That would be against my orders. Luther is on his way."

With Carnegie's words, Luther's form appears in the doorway. He steps into the circle of light Carnegie produces, and Aella bows her head.

"Master," Aella says reverently, and a genuine smile appears on Luther's face.

"My dear, it worked!" he exclaims, leaning forward to look at her—at *us*. All of his anger from before is absent.

"Will you let me out now, Master?" Aella asks innocently.

Luther nods his head enthusiastically. "Yes, yes. Carnegie, get her down. Take her to her room for some food and a hot bath. I will have someone bring the oils to soothe those tense muscles."

"Thank you, Master," Aella says, bowing again in reverence for the devil of a man before me. Unease stirs inside of me, apart from the emotions emanating from Aella, but her reverence slowly seeps into me, snuffing it out.

Luther's voice is as sweet as poisonous honey. "Anything for you, my dear."

***

After a steaming shower, I stare at my cold eyes in the bathroom mirror as Aella studies me with an arrogant smirk. It should disgust me, but her emotions are still seeping into me, suffocating my thoughts and negative feelings with her self-love and adoration. She is beyond excited to be free.

You are still holding on. Let go, Aella whispers in my mind—or our mind.

It is still my mind, right?

No. I have no control over anything anymore. With every moment, something seems to shift and fall into place within the program, taking a piece of me with it each time. With an inward sigh, I fall back into myself as Aella goes about her business. Her emotions cover me like a blanket, and for the moment, I am okay with it.

Striding confidently out of the bathroom, Aella halts at the sight of Carnegie kicked back on the bed, along with two trays of food sitting covered at his feet.

"You could at least let someone know you were staying. Spare us this awkward moment," Aella says conversationally. I motion to my naked body, revealing the twisting tribal tattoos along my ribs and hips normally concealed by clothing. Power resonates from Aella and washes over me like a wave of electrified water. She has no shame, and the look of momentary shock on Carnegie's face makes me inwardly giggle despite my embarrassment at being naked in front of the man.

Carnegie sits up, appearing uncomfortable as Aella makes no move to get dressed. She makes her way to the covered plates, lifting a lid with relish. "Mmm. Venison," she says, smacking my lips together. Taking the plate, she plops down crossed-legged and breathes in the delectable scent of steaming meat and vegetables on the plate in front of her.

"Aren't you going to get dressed?" Carnegie finally asks, shifting away a little. I have never seen him so out of sorts.

Aella smiles devilishly, picking up on the conflicting emotions on Carnegie's face. There is lust in his eyes, but also a knowing look. I cannot help but wonder if Gryndale is more in control now because surely Carnegie would not hesitate to make a move, but who am I to say? "You are the one who came in here uninvited. Now you have to deal with it," she says smugly, inching closer to him.

Carnegie stares, lips parted in speechlessness. His eyes glance down involuntarily before returning to look into my eyes. "Fine," he says shortly. "Eat alone." He gets up and grabs the other plate before leaving without a word.

Aella frowns after him, not getting the reaction she hoped for. "No fun," she pouts, digging into the plate as though she has never seen food before. Then it hits me—she has probably never actually eaten *anything*.

This is fantastic. I'm going to have the time of my life out here, she croons, taking a large bite of meat.

I do not even try to respond. Instead, I fall into the contentment radiating off of Aella and let it consume me as she eats her dinner. There is no point in fighting it anymore.

Twenty-seven
JAI

There is a promise of rain in the air, and warm wind whistles through the trees as the convoy of Charon pulls up. Horse-drawn wagons weighed down with people and supplies come to a stop within the boundary of the rebel village, and Damian steps forward.

"Welcome," Damian says stiffly, his hands spread wide in greeting. "We are glad you all decided to join us. Things will probably get worse in the next few days; I won't lie. But together, we can take what we are faced with."

The look I once had plastered on my face now shines back at me as the people put pieces together. Many would have believed they saw him strung up in Charon's square.

Charon glance warily between each other, uncertainty evident on all of their faces in one form or another. I never dreamed I would see the day Blackthorn and Charon would come together, but here we are despite everything that has happened.

Oh, the things we will do in the name of self-preservation.

I am still in disbelief at how unashamedly Damian took to the idea of accepting Charon's help. I don't doubt that he will try and stick them on the front lines, though. I would like to say that desperate times call for desperate measures, but I know there is still a lot more Damian has yet to tell me.

Damian motions behind him at one of the clusters of cabins in the rag-tag village surrounding us. "We have plenty of room if you don't mind sharing with a few of your brothers and sisters. When this is all over, those who wish to stay are more than welcome to settle down. We have plenty of room to build more cabins as needed. A simpler life is what we hope to establish here for future generations, and even though life is difficult right now, we have hope for that future.

"Some of my people will show you where you can rest and eat. Please, take the day to familiarize yourselves with the place. I ask that your leaders meet with me in the morning for breakfast. We have much to discuss." Damian nods to a small handful of Blackthorn women standing by. "Please, follow these ladies. They will show you everything you need to know of our sanctuary."

Zeke shifts uncomfortably next to me. "Is this all of them?" He looks around at the people falling into step behind their guides. "He said the rest of Charon. Is this all that is left?" There is sadness in Zeke's voice. "They didn't make it?" he asks sorrowfully after combing through the crowd again.

Realization hits me—his family. Because, of course, there was more to his family than Danny. I turn my head to scan the grief-stricken face of my friend.

There was a sister, right? Eliza, or something like that.

"I'm sorry," I say, placing a hand on his shoulder in an attempt at comfort.

"Yeah, me too," Zeke responds mournfully, shrugging off my hand as he stalks off to our shared cabin, shoulders hunched. I debate whether to follow him or not, but I am unsure of what to say.

Damian approaches, saving me the hardship of making a decision. "It isn't as many as I would like on the cusp of war, but they didn't think it was wise to pile everyone up in one place when they still don't trust us. There are about a hundred more waiting elsewhere, prepared to join us or defend their people here."

I perk up at Damian's words. "Do you know if Zeke's family is with them?" I ask, hopeful.

Damian shakes his head, staring after the large group of what used to be our enemy. "No, I don't know who is where. I barely know any of these people's names. That's why I need you," he admits. "You have somehow managed to gain respect on both sides of the line, whether you know it or not. These people are still wary of me. They were raised to believe that my family was only ever out to kill them. I need them to know that isn't the case."

"It isn't?" I ask, very aware that I am once again the person a Vance is going to when faced with uncertainty.

Damian shakes his head. "Not anymore. We need each other now. I'm not going out of my way to protect them, but I will do what I need to ensure that my people are safe—even if it means being friends with Charon."

I grit my teeth. *I knew it.* "If you need anything, just ask," I say with a nod.

"Good to hear," Damian says with a firm pat on my back. "I knew I could count on you. But don't share anything more with Zeke, will you?" he asks, voice dropping to nearly a whisper.

"Why?" I ask, stricken with a sudden conflict of interest.

Damian sighs, glancing around to see if anyone is around to overhear. "There is something up with him. Ysabel has been having dreams about him."

"Dreams? Those aren't real. Maybe she has a crush," I say, perplexed. Damian is a 'believe what you can see' kind of person, much like his sister. I find the words coming out of his mouth unbelievable.

Damian's jaw visibly tenses. "Ysabel's are," he says. "It runs in the family through the women."

"What are you talking about?" I ask.

"It's called the Sight. They can see things nobody else can, whether through dreams or visions. There isn't much known about it, except that when a woman in my family tells you she has dreams, you need to listen."

I frown, trying to filter through my memories. "Iylara mentioned a dream once, but she never went into detail. She was sure she was making the right decision based on it, and we are here now. You'll have to give me more than that to make me believe you."

Damian shakes his head. "Whatever Luther did to her will have twisted her Sight. Nothing she saw can be trusted if she even knows about it. Our mother was wary of it and tried to keep it under wraps."

I stare at Damian, lips parted and brow furrowed. "You know that sounds crazy, right?" I ask, skeptical of the entire thing.

Damian nods his head. "Oh yes. I reacted the same way that you are at first."

I huff out an exasperated sigh. "So what did Ysabel dream about?" I ask. I may not believe in the validity of dreams, but I want to know what Damian is basing his uncertainty of Zeke on.

"She keeps having dreams of this shadow surrounding him. It moves around and through him, controlling him."

"Kind of like the program in Iylara?" I ask with a shiver.

"No, not quite. We aren't sure what it is, and I'm not even sure Zeke is aware of it."

"If it's a real thing," I mutter.

Damian grits his teeth in frustration. "You don't have to believe in it; just trust me. Don't tell Zeke anything. I'm not sure if he has anything to do with Luther knowing where we are or not. If he is some kind of guardian, it would explain why he has done everything in his power to keep Iylara alive, *and* why he happened to be stationed with her."

I sigh in defeat as I nod my head. "I won't say anything."

Damian nods with a small, relieved smile. "Thank you. I will see you in the morning. Give him some menial task to keep him busy. He cannot have anything to do with our plans until I know for sure what is going on."

"Yes, sir," I say, withholding my feelings on the matter.

This entire thing is nuts.

Damian takes his leave, and I stare after him, the bitter taste of iron in my mouth. With a deep breath, I trudge off to the cabin I share with Zeke while racking my brain for something he can do without him asking questions I can't answer.

Why can't things ever be easy?

***

I enter the small meeting room, eyes downcast. Damian is the only one here so far. Plopping down into the chair next to him, I say, "Zeke's gone."

Damian turns in his chair to glare at me, anger darkening his previously relaxed features. "What do you mean? When was the last time you saw him?" he demands.

I sigh reluctantly. "After dinner last night. He was upset about his family not being with the convoy. He believes they are dead, but I couldn't tell him that might not be true. When I woke up this morning, his bed was made, and his bag was gone."

Damian grits his teeth but refrains from saying anything else as Ysabel slips quietly into the room.

"Well?" Damian asks, expecting something from his daughter.

"Spectrals," Ysabel says.

"Okay?" Damian asks, prodding for more information. I glance between the two of them in confusion.

Ysabel approaches and sits on the edge of the long oak table laden with breakfast to face her father. "The shadow that I have seen in my dreams. They can only be seen with the Sight in their manifested forms," she begins, talking dramatically with her hands. "They are black hovering shadows, absorbing the light around them. But technically, you can't even see them *with* the Sight, only the void they leave behind as they absorb the light." She pauses for a moment, her lips pulling into a tight line. "I think that it might be possessing him. If it's *in* him, it's why I haven't seen it in person."

My brow furrows as I try to grasp the craziness I am hearing. I look sideways at Damian, hoping for some explanation, but he appears to be as confused as I feel.

"How did you come to that conclusion?" Damian asks.

Ysabel pulls a small leather-bound book from her pocket. "Grandma's journal. She knew a lot more than anyone gave her credit for."

Damian's eyes widen as he reaches out, grabbing the book from Ysabel's grasp. "Where did you find this?" he asks, roving his fingers over the hand-tooled designs on the front. He doesn't even bother opening it. The designs his mother engraved herself are enough for the moment.

Ysabel shrugs. "In some of mom's things. I don't know where she got it unless she found it in the Apothecary somewhere. I thought it unlikely grandma would have given it to her, but it doesn't matter. What does matter is what it says."

"And what does it say?" I ask, unable to help myself.

Ysabel smiles at me, eyes bright. "Spectrals don't have much power, mainly messengers. They can influence the weak-minded and possess willing people to carry out their handler's agenda."

"So what exactly are they?" Damian asks.

"Grandma called them demons, but she wasn't too fond of the term. She seemed to believe they were something else, but 'demon' was the best word she could find to describe them."

Damian looks up from the journal at his daughter. "Did she say anything about where they came from?" he asks.

Ysabel nods. "Oh yes. They've been here since the Great War. They are the reason the bombs fell and destroyed everything. Whatever the people were trying to use to bring world peace backfired and set them loose. She says something about a portal to the unknown that they opened. Spectrals forced their way through and ended the world as the people before us knew it."

Damian raises a brow in consternation. "But you just said that they don't have much power. How could they destroy the world?"

Ysabel delicately takes the book back from her father with two fingers. She flips to a page about halfway through and begins to read. "There are many Spectrals, maybe a few thousand scattered around the world, that came through the portal all at once. No more have been able to come through, and the ones here haven't been able to leave since the portal was destroyed. It would seem that our plane of existence is not suitable for them long-term, and they have devolved over time, going from beings of great power to man's minions. There is a way to bind them to you to do your will, but grandma never mentions it other than to say the world will be safer with the loss of such knowledge."

Damian stares at his daughter, dumbstruck. "Have you ever seen anything like them before?" I ask in his silence.

Ysabel bites her bottom lip, eyes downcast in what I can only assume is shame. "On the night of the attack. It was my first glimpse of a vision, but I saw it hovering over Aunt Ray. I think it was marking her."

"Is that what you were trying to tell her?" Damian asks, finally finding his voice.

"Yeah," Ysabel says quietly.

"Why didn't you tell me about this before now?" Damian asks angrily.

Ysabel doesn't back down from the anger radiating off of her father. "I didn't know what was happening! And I didn't know what a Spectral was until today, so no. You wouldn't have believed me anyway, so it wouldn't have done much good."

Damian is about to retort, but Sartor enters, leading about a dozen Charon into the meeting room. Ysabel retreats from the room without another word, leaving the two of us blindsided by this new information.

"This is crazy," I mutter, reaching for a biscuit to finger at mindlessly.

"You're telling me," Damian says with a heavy sigh, rubbing his temples with both hands. He drops his voice to a whisper. "As if things weren't already difficult enough. Now we have to worry about demons? What the hell?"

I shove a large chunk of biscuit into my mouth with a shrug. "Maybe she is wrong," I say around my food.

Damian shakes his head. "I always knew my mother knew things, but she never spoke of them. And Nadia knew, but she was too much of a kiss-ass to say anything if mom told her not to. I need to get my hands back on that book and read it when we are through here. There is no telling what else is in there that we need to know."

A handful of Blackthorn follow in last, and Damian stands, motioning for everyone to sit down. "Thank you for joining us.

Please, help yourselves to anything you would like to eat and get settled in. Let's make some war plans, shall we?"

***

I scout the area with Kali, a Charon woman with copper skin and black braids pulled back with a strip of leather. We lay prone on the ground next to each other on the hillside overlooking the Vesper camp in the valley below us.

In the eyes of her people, Kali seems to be the closest thing to a Chief that they have left—what with her father being the Chief that Carnegie killed to take power, but their customs are a little different from ours. She was none too happy to learn the truth about him being with Vesper and very much alive.

Her heavy-lidded eyes sweep the valley through a pair of binoculars, and I follow her finger to the point of interest. My eyes land on auburn red hair blazing in the mid-morning sun peaking through gray storm clouds. The hair's owner drags a struggling woman from what appears to be a makeshift chow hall near the center of the camp, where a single fire burns under a deer carcass roasting on a spit.

"What is she doing?" I ask quietly, more to myself than Kali, but she has so far had an answer for every question I have asked, directed at her or not. I haven't decided if I like that trait yet or not.

"I think that woman stole food," she says in disbelief. "I could be wrong," she adds, "but I don't think this will end well." She hands me the binoculars, but I do not want to get a closer look. I can see enough as it is already.

Who I assume is Aella, not Iylara, points her gun at the woman's head. I will not watch. "We need to get back and prepare the attack while they are distracted," I say, stuffing the binoculars in my bag. I slowly back away from our vantage point, trying not to listen for the sound of a gunshot.

Kali follows, and we set off at a trot back to our camp. "That red-headed woman used to be your Chief?" she asks, turning her observant brown eyes on me.

I cannot even begin to explain what has happened to Iylara and only nod.

"Were the rest of her family as cruel? Damian seems alright, but I've heard stories," she continues innocently. Still, a flare of anger rises inside of my chest regardless.

I cannot let that idea stand. "No. They are *not* cruel. Something happened to Iylara to make her the way she is now. I'm not going to try and explain it, but they were and are great leaders. Their family has led Blackthorn from the beginning with pride and care. But we came up against something we weren't ready for," I say with an exasperated sigh. I know my following words are true, but I do not want to believe them. "But nothing lasts forever. Charon is an example as well, yeah?"

Kali is skeptical, but she does not press the matter. "Yeah, I guess not," she says, voice trailing off in thought.

As we enter the clearing where the rebel fighters sit preparing for battle, our conversation comes to a close. Guns are checked over, and swords are sharpened—all with looks of determination.

Attention turns from the weapons to us, and I stop at the camp's head. "They are distracted," I say as Kali nods next to me. "Get everything together. We march in ten." Activity erupts as tasks are finished and everyone prepares themselves.

The people begin to fall into formation, and I motion for Kali to step forward. According to Damian, letting her take the lead shows Charon that it isn't merely Blackthorn calling the shots. It says that we are in this together. I never thought he would give *any* power to Charon. I hope it isn't just for show.

Kali clears her throat and begins to review the plan. "Vesper troops are unsuspecting in the valley south of here. We only have one chance at this. Group A will go to the south end, Group B to the east, C to the west, and D to the north. Once you're in position, your squad leaders will give the signal. Then you will hear the whistle that signals the attack from Jai at D. Give it all you got because it is. No hostages except Carnegie and the General, but do not underestimate them! We will show them what happens when you try to take us on. When this is all over, we will display their corpses as trophies!" Kali ends her speech with a battle cry reciprocated by the crowd—except me.

Display their corpses.

There is no way in hell I can watch Iylara swing from the gallows like some macabre scarecrow left to rot. I may not have a hand in stopping her death because it is what she wants, but she will have the funeral she deserves.

"March out!" Kali yells as Damian appears from the mass of people with a nod. Everyone moves in unison.

I head off with Group D as Kali departs with Group A, and we make our way silently to our positions. I give the bird call that signals our readiness before settling in against a tree, picking at my thumb as we wait for the others.

Two more signals come, and I stand, breathing deeply to calm myself. I look around, meeting the eyes of the men and women around me. Determination shines brightly in their eyes, Blackthorn and Charon alike. I give them a nod and a reassuring smile.

A trilling bird call sounds from the south. I glance down into the camp, and Vesper doesn't even notice. I am hopeful that this could work. With a deep breath, I whistle the attack signal, and chaos ensues.

Twenty-eight
IYLARA

"Are you ready for this, my dear?" Luther asks as he sits leisurely in his high-back chair.

Standing in front of his desk, Aella replies, "Yes, Master," as I hold my head high.

"Good. Now one thing I want to make clear. We do not tolerate disobedience, but it can be tricky to weed out. When under stress, who a person truly is will be revealed. I find the battlefield is the perfect place to find those who are not as loyal as they say they are. So yes, I want you to go and destroy the rebels, but I also want your eyes on your own soldiers. The world we are building has no room for those who cannot follow orders," Luther says, voice stern. "We have had too much of that as of late."

I nod. "And if I were to find one of these people you speak of, what do you want me to do about it, Master?" Aella's voice is hopeful. Any reason for violence is a go for her, but I can't feel the disdain toward her that I should. Not anymore.

Luther grins knowingly. "Kill them," he says simply. "We do not have the time or resources to try and recondition soldiers who fail to follow orders at this point. They either learned how things work the first time or didn't."

"It will be done, Master," Aella says as I bow my head in veneration.

"Another thing," Luther says. I look up at him in expectation. "Carnegie takes orders from me. And you will take orders from him without question. Are we clear?" Luther asks.

Aella sighs. "Yes, Master." She can try to hide her aggravation from Luther, but it bubbles inside like simmering water.

"Good—now for business. Carnegie is preparing the troops as we speak," he says, sliding a map across his desk. It has arrows and lines drawn on it, pointing to a clearing on the map about three miles from the rebel camp. "This is your base camp. Close enough to those we seek to destroy, yet not so close as to raise suspicion until we are ready to strike." Luther grits his teeth. "Although your lovely host has already told them we know where they are, they do not know our plans. They will be unable to hold back our forces for long as you besiege their village. Your troops will converge from all sides and burn the place to the ground. Take no prisoners. Not even the children. Understood?"

"Yes, sir," Aella says happily. The prospect of spilling blood, innocent or not, excites her to a sickening degree, overriding her aggravation at Carnegie's position over her.

Luther nods with a smile. "Good, now get a move on. The troops should be ready to march out soon if they are not already waiting for you. Make me proud, my dear," Luther says in a fatherly way, reserved only for his favorite experiment.

"Yes, Master," Aella says with a low bow as I back away to the door. I grab the doorknob, and Luther clears his throat, halting our exit.

"Oh, and I don't need to remind you what will happen if you fail, no?" he asks, voice like silk.

The first feeling of fear from Aella reverberates through us, touching my psyche with reaching tendrils, threatening to infect me. “No, sir. You don’t,” she says meekly.

Luther’s smile turns deadly. “Good.”

***

“Please,” the malnourished woman pleads with Aella from the ground. On her knees, she grips the grass beneath her in terror, her black fatigues stained with dust from where I drug her from the food line.

“Why are you begging me?” Aella asks coldly. “You have nothing to bargain with.”

“I know, I know,” she pleads. “I am asking for mercy. Please, I have nothing I can give you. I’m just so hungry.”

“Whoever said I wanted anything?” I step forward, towering over the woman cowering in my shadow. “I have no mercy to give, darling. You were warned already,” Aella says in a low voice. I draw the revolver from its holster on my hip as Aella speaks, eliciting a terrified whimper from the woman. “You knew the consequences, yet you still acted against your better judgment.” Raising the gun, I level the sights on my mark between the woman’s eyes.

I don’t want to watch, but I cannot turn away in my mind’s prison. I see what Aella sees, feel what Aella feels, and sleep when Aella sleeps, which isn’t much. Everything she is overrides me, so I watch, letting the exhilaration rushing through her comfort me.

“Wait,” a voice says from behind me, halting my finger on the trigger.

“Why?” Aella asks Carnegie impatiently, never looking away from the woman on the ground. Her blood lust is disorienting. The need to kill is ingrained in her. She will jump at any chance that presents itself. “I have to put her down. She broke the rules,” Aella says, fully convinced of the need to pull the trigger as her conviction seeps into me. The woman does not deserve this fate over a few chunks of meat, but it doesn’t matter.

“Did she do something worth dying over?” Carnegie asks quietly.

At his words, I lower the gun, turning on him. "And who are you to ask that? Are you going to go against our Master's orders to weed out insubordination?" Aella asks dangerously.

Carnegie grits his teeth. Sparing the woman's life would be insubordination in its own right.

"Will you at least tell me what you are putting her to death for?" he asks, changing direction.

The woman whimpers on the ground, crying. Disgust rises in Aella at the woman's weakness in the face of death. "Oh, shut up," Aella growls at her. I turn to glare at Carnegie. "Stealing food, which is explicitly forbidden, is punishable by death." Aella pauses as I turn to face the woman on the ground again. "She thought she was worth enough to have a second serving."

Without asking if the woman has anything to say for herself, I raise the gun again. There is no hesitation as I pull the trigger, and the echoing boom of the gun silences the camp. The woman's head snaps back, and she crumples to the ground on her side, eyes unseeing but staring directly at Aella—*at me.*

I drop the gun as a tremor goes through me at the sight of the death stare. It stares past Aella and into my very being. I start panting as nausea hits me—a memory pushes its way through the catacombs of my mind.

Something snaps, and as the memory takes hold, I am in Aella's mind, seeing my memory from her perspective as if she were a bystander in my nightmare.

"Just watch. Don't move. Don't speak," Carnegie says with a strange quirk in his tone. Iylara looks around, and I follow her eyes as they land on a gray-haired man, with a long salt and pepper beard, near a table full of drinks and finger foods. He talks to a rather tall Charon with a tattoo-covered head. My brow furrows in confusion.

Jai Norris makes his way through the crowd opposite another figure making a beeline for the man next to the beverage table. Jai says something, catching the older man's attention. The tall Charon grabs Jai in a headlock as the gray-haired man looks around to find the figure headed for him, who draws a pistol from his jacket.

From the corner of my eye, Iylara twitches, seemingly trying to speak, but something stops her. The older man stares defiantly down the pistol barrel pointed in his face before a blast reverberates through the vast room I have no inclination to look at in detail. These few people are who hold my focus.

The room goes silent, and I look at Iylara, whose eyes have gone wide. I look back at the man now lying dead on the floor. His lifeless eyes stare straight at her, sending a shiver down my spine. "Go do what you must," Carnegie says, and Iylara comes alive, released from the invisible hold Carnegie has over her.

She rushes for the staircase as the room erupts into chaos, but my eyes travel back toward the dead man, and it hits me. That was Leeland Vance, her father. I take a step to the left, standing in the spot Iylara vacated, and his dead eyes find mine, searching my black soul even in death, and I cannot breathe.

Carnegie's hand grasps my arm, catching me as I stagger backward on unsteady feet. "Hey, whoa. What happened?" he asks.

Aella composes herself on the outside, but her raging emotions mirror my own. She must be feeling what I am feeling, and vice versa, volleying my torment back and forth between the two of us. I turn to look at Carnegie, finding a startled woman staring back at me in the reflection of his eyes. Whatever happened has jarred Aella like nothing else ever has.

"What did you see?" he asks, taking a different route of questions as if he knows what just happened. But of course he knows. He surely experienced the same things at the beginning of his turning. Aella and I may be one, but integration takes time.

"Leeland Vance's assassination," Aella says brusquely.

"What set it off?" he questions, searching my face.

I turn to stare at the dead woman on the ground. Her eyes still bore into us even with the quickest glance. "Her eyes," Aella says, barely above a whisper, as the emotions start to overwhelm her. She realizes what is happening before I do. "Iylara is fighting me," Aella says with a shaky breath.

A sharp pain behind my eyes sends me reeling, and I press the heel of my hands into them in frustration, making the world go black inside of my prison.

"Come on," Carnegie says, taking us away from prying eyes. The camp has mostly gone back to business as usual like nothing has transpired over the last few moments, but there are a few inquiring glances our way.

I take one last glance at the woman, and tears threaten to overcome Aella, but she is incapable of crying. It is me on the verge of breaking. Over the last horrendously long months, I had become numb to the things that transpired before everything went to hell, like my father's death, until now. Something has broken apart in my mind, threatening to bury me under the rubble.

Aella does not question Carnegie until we are a good ways away from that convicting death stare. "Where are we going?" Aella groans, the storm of my emotions still tormenting her in ways I do not understand, but I feed it, and her control slips a little more.

Carnegie does not answer as he stops, pulling the obsidian stone from under his shirt. Aella stares at it questioningly as the soft tinkling music emanates from it.

"This only works on Iylara. The closer she is to control, the more effect it has on her. It is a way of controlling her if needed, which is unnecessary with you."

He holds the stone up in front of him, and the energy of it pulses within me. Aella can feel it too, and I sink to the ground as the sensation snatches what control she has left away. My vision gets hazy, and I rise out of the prison cell in my mind.

"What's happening?" I ask, looking around in a daze.

"Iylara?" Carnegie asks.

"What is going on?" I ask. Aella thrashes inside like a caged animal, and I struggle to keep her at bay.

"You were triggered," he whispers as he kneels in front of me, eyes level with my own.

I look up into his blue eyes in bewilderment, void of the harshness I am used to seeing staring back at me. "What does that mean?" I ask.

"It means you still have some fight in you. Use it," he says, brushing a stray piece of hair from my face. "Aella will retake control soon, but never stop fighting. Please don't do what I did. I was wrong. You showed me that."

"Can she see this?" I ask, afraid of what could happen if she can.

"She shouldn't be able to right now, but she won't stop fighting for control," he says, placing a hand on my shoulder to steady me. "Listen, I finally found a way out, and I can't let you end up like me," he says.

"You say that like you care," I mutter, gazing up at the man I once swore to kill.

"Because I do. Maybe not at first, but I do now. You gave me a reason to fight my own demon," he says, taking my hand between the two of his.

I stare down at our hands, confused. "Are you Gryndale right now?" I ask. It is the only thing that makes sense.

He nods his head. "Yes. If Aella finds out, she will not hesitate to turn me in for a programming malfunction. If that happens, Luther will send me back to reconditioning, and I will forget who I am again. You can't let me do it in vain. Fight her. Fight him. Free us."

I bow my head under the weight of what he is asking of me, but I cannot say anything, even if I want to. Aella is taking more control back with each passing second. I look back up at him, and I am back in the cage in my head as Aella takes control once more. "I'm watching you," Aella says, my eyes narrowing at Gryndale. "You are up to something. Perhaps you aren't even Carnegie anymore," she accuses.

"Not like you could go to Luther without revealing you don't have as much control as he would want," Gryndale growls ominously, impersonating Carnegie most convincingly.

I grit my teeth while smiling inwardly at the small win. "Maybe so, but I won't let you hinder our Master's progress," she says. I hold my head up high as I stand to stare down at him in one fluid movement.

"Who said I was hindering progress? Did I stop you from killing that woman?" he throws back as he stands to face me, eye to eye.

Before she can retort back, a shrill whistle sounds, followed by a chorus of battle cries filling the atmosphere. Rebel soldiers appear from the trees, descending on the camp, followed by gunfire outside the boundary line.

"How?" Aella asks angrily, turning back to Gryndale as my internal smile widens.

Gryndale's face is listless as he shrugs. "Maybe Iylara told them more than we thought?"

"Impossible," Aella seethes. "She knew nothing of real importance."

"Maybe not," Gryndale says, watching as the rebels start overtaking the surprised Vesper troops in seconds. "But we don't have time to think about that right now." He unsheathes his sword with a ring as he speaks.

Blood lust takes over, and the momentary happiness at the situation is doused as Aella channels her energy into the oncoming fight. It is intoxicating. We rush into the fray, a sadistic laugh slipping from my lips as I slice through rebel fighters like butter with the thin blade of my sword.

At this moment, so overcome with the roiling emotions of Aella, we are truly one, flowing seamlessly as we cut a swath through the flood of fighters. I cannot see who they are, with their faces obscured from me by red vision as the fight takes over. The fact that I probably know some of these people does not even register on a level high enough to affect me.

The maniacal laugh from Aella resonates from my very being, and her power swells, fed by my own willingness to spill blood. It allows me to effortlessly shove back men twice my size without even a grunt of effort. Luther's farewell warning pushes us on, afraid of what may happen, but the numbers are too much. It is only a matter of time before we are overwhelmed.

Twenty-nine
JAI

Vesper soldiers are ill-prepared to defend against the hoard that swarms them. From all four sides, we make our way toward the center of the camp, cutting down any Vesper that gets in the way while the marksmen in each group pick off more from a distance.

It's like shooting fish in a barrel.

The few Blackthorn and Charon still under Vesper's thumb quickly realize what is happening and join us, shedding the star that marks them as the enemy.

"They have nowhere to run! Push in!" Kali yells out from the other side of the camp. A rallying cry erupts from the rebels, and Vesper starts panicking—the foot soldiers do, anyway.

I find General West swinging her sword with a fury, cutting down anyone that dares to engage her. I pause for a moment, caught off guard by the ferocity in the woman. Blood spray coats her face and neck, a snarl pulling at her lips. She is a force to be reckoned with. I know now what Damian meant by super-soldier as she strikes, quick as a snake, with the finesse and agility unmatched by anything I have ever seen from Iylara, or anyone else.

I am cut off from my reverie as a Vesper man runs at me, sword ready to strike me down. I block, sidestepping as the man's momentum carries him past me. Flipping my sword into a reverse grip, I shove the blade into the man's stomach as he turns to attack me from behind.

Pulling the blade from his belly with a gush of blood, I duck an axe swinging at my face. With a low swooping kick, I knock the woman's legs out from under her. I bring my sword down into her chest before she can get up off the ground and make my way closer to Aella.

Carnegie is not far away, cutting a path of his own as destructive as the General, but the duo is being driven back by the sheer numbers surrounding them.

Aella turns into a cornered animal, striking out at anyone who gets too close. "Hold!" I command the rebels encircling the pair. Aella's eyes turn on me; if looks could kill, I would drop dead where I stand.

Her ice-blue eyes are vicious and wild as she steps toward me, ready to strike me down. Past the adrenaline, the pain I feel looking at her is a dull pressure rather than a sharp sting, but I can barely breathe. I do not want to have to strike her down. Aella may be in control, but Iylara is still in there somewhere.

"Stop," Carnegie says to her, but she strikes out at me anyway. I barely block the whip-like strike, and our blades lock. She stares me down, her teeth bared over the crossed swords.

"I said, *stop,*" Carnegie says again from behind her.

With a growl, she concedes, pushing me away with strength I did not know she possessed.

Heightened senses, quick reflexes, super strong, blood-thirsty.

"It's over," Carnegie says, dropping his sword. There is something in his voice that I do not recognize, and there is no anger in his defeat.

Aella refuses to accept it. "No, it isn't," she hisses, chomping at the bit to strike me down.

"It *is*. Drop your sword," Carnegie orders, looking past her to me. The man staring at me is alien, lacking the malice I associate with him. I stare at him, puzzled. The energy of Carnegie's gaze is not the same as I remember from the few times I have met him, but he *looks* the same.

Iylara's words echo in my mind. *He is like me.*

Aella throws her sword on the ground in anger, conceding against what she wants. She would probably try to take on all of us if Carnegie would let her. After seeing her cut down fighter after fighter, I would not be surprised if she could survive the onslaught if she tried.

The crowd splits, and Damian steps into the circle surrounding the two Vesper officers. He stops in front of Aella, and something stirs behind her eyes. For the most part, she holds still—a stoic statue. However, the gears spinning in her mind are evident to those who know Iylara Vance. Something is waking inside the woman.

Shock is apparent on Carnegie's face. He surely did not expect to see a dead man.

"Ray." She shudders as Damian whispers his sister's pet name, breaking her stoic facade as she squeezes her eyes shut. Her hands clench at her sides, and I tense with anticipation.

"No," she growls, glaring up at Damian with renewed fervor. "You are dead!" she screams, and I am not sure who it is that speaks—Aella or Iylara. Regardless of who it is, there is anger rising in the woman. Violent anger.

She lunges at Damian, but Carnegie grabs her by the arms, barely containing her. "Where were you?" she asks, voice strained as she fights something within herself. "I did what I did because I thought you were dead!" she cries out. Tears fill her unnaturally blue eyes, streaking the charcoal around them as they spill over.

Iylara. I cannot help holding my breath as I watch the events transpire before my eyes. Her eyes remain blue, but the change in demeanor is shocking.

"Where were you?" she wails as Carnegie pulls her back a step.

"You did what you did because you are weak," Damian says, striking her with his harsh tone and words. Damian has been mournful of the entire situation, even if he has been trying to kill her. There is an entirely different emotion in his voice now, and I am not sure if he is goading her or if he has been keeping his true feelings to himself.

The effect is instantaneous. Iylara rips herself out of Carnegie's grip, hands going for Damian's throat. As Iylara fights, Aella seems to lose strength, and Damian grabs her by the wrists, holding her at bay.

Carnegie stays still, watching the woman in front of him flail against Damian's hold. "You could have told me you weren't dead!" she fumes.

Damian shakes his head. "No, I couldn't. It wouldn't have done any good."

"Any good? ANY GOOD?" she screeches. Damian pushes her back as she seethes. Carnegie grabs her arm, but she yanks it out of his grasp again.

Damian stares down sadly at his mess of a sister, genuine sorrow on his face despite his harsh words. "I'm sorry."

The dam of tears breaks in Iylara's eyes. Through her tears, I can barely understand her, but the pain and torment in her voice are evident. "D-do you k-know what he d-did t-to me?" Iylara whimpers through the tears, losing the will to fight as her knees give out.

Carnegie catches her around the waist before she falls to the ground. Rather than pushing him away like I thought she would, she leans into his chest limply, burying her face in his neck as she cries.

There is an uncomfortable silence in the camp. I am not entirely sure what is going on, but I at least have some kind of understanding of what has happened to the former Blackthorn Chief. I can only imagine some thoughts cropping up in the minds of those who haven't the faintest idea of what has been going on.

Damian turns to me. "Head back and have the gallows ready for our return."

"What?" I ask incredulously. I was sure Damian would go with a firing squad and get it over with despite Kali's words from earlier.

"That's an order," Damian says sternly.

I hesitate to follow his command. No matter what I believe, I will not have a hand in Iylara's death past what I have already accomplished. "I can't do that, sir," I say with finality, disregarding an order for the first time in my life.

Iylara jolts, looking up at me with wide eyes.

Damian frowns. "You are the one who said to let me do what I am going to do," he says.

I nod with a shrug. "Yes, but I won't have a hand in it past this point," I confess. I do not miss the confused look on Carnegie's face.

Is it Carnegie?

The eyes staring at me are the familiar ice-blue I associate with him, but there is something softer in them than I have ever seen.

"And yet you won't stop it?" Damian asks.

I glance at Iylara, the same broken woman who asked me to kill her only a short while ago. "No," I say. Iylara bows her head.

"Fine," Damian says with a growl. "Kali? You are the one who brought up hanging them. You do it."

"Yes, sir," she says, glaring spitefully at me. Suddenly, I do not like the woman as much as I thought I did.

Damian turns to look Carnegie in the eyes but addresses the man next to him. "Cuff 'em. We are going to have ourselves a hanging."

Thirty
IYLARA

My entire body trembles as I stand in front of the noose meant to end my life, my hands bound in front of me. Aella went silent after my brother appeared, yet I still cannot grasp my reality. Everything has been a blur, from the walk here to finding my niece standing quietly beside her mother upon our arrival, both of them very much alive.

Ysabel's face held a quiet sadness, but Keena's had a smugness that I could not help but feel I deserved. Maybe she knew what I would become all along.

I do not know what to make of any of it. Now that I am faced with the inevitability of my death, I do not want to die after realizing that I can fight Aella off. But then again, I do not know if she will rear her ugly head again or not. I stand quietly next to Gryndale as my brother speaks to the gathered crowd in front of us, but I cannot hear him over the ringing in my ears.

Zeke catches my eye from the shadows at the crowd's edge, but Jai is absent, having probably refused to witness my death. I resign myself to staring into familiar amber eyes as tears threaten to overtake me, but I will not cry. If I am to die today, I will die with dignity and not as a tearful child.

“Do you have any last words?” Damian asks Gryndale, who he still believes is Carnegie, but I know better. Gryndale stays silent, staring into space as he ignores everyone, including me.

“You?” Damian asks me, taking Gryndale’s silence as a ‘No.’

I nod slowly, scanning the crowd mixed with Blackthorn and Charon. “Yeah,” I begin, taking a deep breath. “I’m sorry—” I choke out, unable to finish the sentence without crying. I drop my head and take a few more deep breaths before finding my resolve. I lift my head, glancing around at the people I failed. “I didn’t mean for it to turn out like this.”

My voice is only loud enough for those in the front row to hear, but I find uncertainty in the eyes of the Blackthorn there. My words do not move the Charon who can hear me, and I find anger in many of their eyes, but it is mainly directed at Gryndale.

Damian stands by quietly as the woman, Kali, drapes the nooses around our necks. “This is for my father,” she tells Gryndale calmly. He drops his head, not saying a word.

I turn to my brother, regret in my eyes. “I wish this would have turned out different,” I lament in a shaky voice.

He walks up to me, an unreadable expression on his face, but his voice is sad. “Me too.”

Damian looks away, turning his attention to the man gripping the lever that will drop the floor out from underneath us, ending our lives, before he steps away. Damian nods at the man, whose grip tightens on the lever, his knuckles turning white before he yanks it back.

The floor drops out from under us, but there is no tension around my neck as there should be. I hit the ground hard, my knees giving out from the impact, my heart racing. Gryndale does the same, and we glance at each other, bewildered, as the gathered crowd yells out in surprise.

I glance up to find the ropes cut clean through, saving us from death by asphyxiation or a broken neck.

"Run," Gryndale says with a grunt.

He pushes himself off the ground. I look back as he grabs my bound hands, tugging on me to follow. Anger and confusion ripple through the crowd as they draw their guns. I do not have time to question who it is that has spared us as Gryndale pulls me away from the enraged mob.

Gunfire breaks out, bullets stirring up dirt around us as we run for our lives. The trees give the promise of cover as they loom ever closer in front of us. Gryndale cries out in pain, stumbling as a bullet hits him, but he regains his footing and continues to run. I follow after him on unsteady feet. The trees envelop us, but pounding footsteps still pursue us. We plow through the forest's foliage, only slowing down when thorns grab hold of us, tearing at our skin and clothing.

"Keep running," Gryndale says through gritted teeth as he rips off a thorny vine entangling him. I can only nod while batting low-hanging tree limbs out of my way with my bound hands.

Before long, I can no longer hear footsteps following us. But we do not stop running, pushing ourselves to exhaustion. Only when it starts to drizzle rain do we slow down, but we do not stop, even to free our hands, moving ever forward. To where I have no idea, but I do not care. I do not want to die anymore. Having come to this realization, I do not question what lies ahead, as long as it does not end with me dangling from the end of a rope.

We finally stop for a moment before we both fall out on the ground, and only one thought runs through my mind on repeat. *My brother tried to execute me.*

"We need to keep moving," Gryndale says, pulling at the ropes around my wrists with fumbling fingers. Once free, I do the same for him, and we are finally unhindered. We take off the nooses, and Gryndale tugs on my arm, pulling me to my feet. "We can't let them catch up."

I groan in assent, forcing my feet to move, one in front of the other. The mid-summer air weighs down heavy on us, the earlier rain having lasted only a few moments—long enough for the humidity to settle in.

"Who do you think saved us?" I ask breathlessly, trailing after Gryndale through the unfamiliar woods around me. The occasional drop of rainwater hits me in the head as they fall from the leaves above us.

"I don't know," he admits. "Probably Luther's spy, but I don't know who it is."

Thunder rumbles in the distance, and I lift my head, smelling the air as we continue to push through the forest. "It's going to start storming soon," I say, hating that I was right about a spy in the rebel's ranks.

He checks the air as I do. "It should hold off a few more hours," he says confidently.

"I give it ten minutes," I mutter under my breath. Gryndale glances over his shoulder at me with a contemptuous glare, but he does not respond.

"How is your wound?" I ask if only to keep from falling into my thoughts in the silence.

"It's healed. The bullet went through. I'm fine," he says, stopping to look at me. "Are you okay?"

I stop, contemplating the many emotions coursing through me. "No, I'm not," I admit quietly.

Gryndale begins to look me over, but I stop him. "It isn't anything physical that is wrong," I mutter, brushing past him in an unknown direction.

He falls into step with me, nodding his head in understanding. "You want to talk about it?" he asks.

"No," I say, harsher than I mean for it to come out. "We need to find shelter before that storm hits," I say, breathing in the humid, rain-tinged air deeply. The smell of dirt is strong after the little rain we've already had, but the sweet smell of the coming storm is more pungent as the wind picks up.

"What makes you so sure it is going to storm so soon?" he asks, glancing up at the sky through the trees. Specks of blue can be seen through the tree canopy, but dark storm clouds are swirling further away.

"I know what rain smells like. Will you please trust me on this?" I plead, not wanting to get caught in a thunderstorm or a possible tornado. The air is crisp, and the breeze has a nip through the humidity despite the summer heat that could spell disaster. The last thing I want is to be wet *and* cold. It will only make my dour attitude worse.

Gryndale grumbles, but it is not hostile. There does not seem to be any real hostility in him. From the little I have seen of Carnegie's host, he is quiet and thoughtful, erring on the side of caution with his words and actions. Meek is a good word for him, but it's weird to associate that word with his face. It makes my head hurt.

He pulls a map from an inside vest pocket, heavily crumpled from its time there. He stares at it a moment before pointing to the left of us. "There should be an outcropping that way, like a shallow cave. We can rest there if you believe the weather will get worse."

"I do," I say, following his finger without waiting for him to respond.

About a quarter-mile through the trees, we almost miss our shelter. I would call it a cave rather than an outcropping of rock, but it is indeed shallow. The opening is narrow, almost entirely concealed by hanging moss. I slide past the green curtain that Gryndale holds back for me, immediately shrouded in shadows. The little cave is pitch black, except for the sliver of light coming through the entrance, but in no time, we will be without any kind of light unless—

"You still have that stone?" I ask, eyeing his collar where the leather strap wraps around his neck, disappearing into his shirt.

Gryndale looks down, realizing what I am asking, and pulls it out. It starts to glow with its dark light, but it is enough to see our small shelter in full. The nearly inaudible music is ever-present and louder now that the stone hangs freely in the air. I can feel the energy from it, but without Carnegie's intention to use it to subdue me, its power withholds itself—despite the perpetual and eerie tingle the music sends down my spine.

"At least it's cozy in here," I say half-heartedly as I glance around the small space.

Our shelter is a simple area, thankfully free of any kind of animal that would try to make us into dinner. At the thought, my stomach rumbles as a clash of lightning strikes, bringing a ground-shaking crack of thunder, and the bottom drops out.

“Told you so,” I say quietly, my voice free of malice. My tone may be a little prideful, though.

“So you did,” he admits with a slight grin. “There goes our chance at getting supper,” he adds with an audible rumble of his stomach.

I shrug, plopping myself down onto the floor. “It isn’t like we have never been hungry before. We will survive.”

The wind picks up, whistling through the cave entrance, and I shiver. Gryndale sits down next to me, and warmth radiates off of him. I almost cannot abstain from leaning into him.

“What are we going to do?” I ask him. “Go back and pretend that we are still Luther’s play-things?”

“No. We failed. You know what he will do to us because of it. I also highly doubt you could trick him into believing you are Aella,” he says honestly, studying the rock wall in front of us.

“True. But why do you say I can’t trick him?”

“The two of you are nothing alike. How you hold yourself and talk is entirely different from Aella's, and you have not had enough time to get a feel for how she acts and reacts to things. I have had years to learn the ins and outs of Carnegie’s personality, but you haven’t had the same time with Aella.”

I look down at my hands, twiddling my fingers listlessly. “So again, what are we going to do?”

Gryndale shrugs. “I don’t know. Keep walking when the storm stops?”

“That’s a shit plan,” I mutter peevishly.

“You have a better one?” he asks. “We have no weapons, no supplies, nothing. If we keep walking, maybe we will find something or someone to help us, but we need to cut out our trackers before Luther can use them to find us. We only have so much time before he realizes something went wrong,” he says, motioning at my forearm.

I shake my head. “No, but it’s not true that we have nothing. I have a knife in my boot.”

He grins. “Of course you do,” he says, pausing a moment. “We could always be like, uh, Bonnie and Cletus?”

I chuckle darkly. “You mean Bonnie and Clyde, and I don’t think we want to be like them.”

"Why not?" he asks, full of curiosity. He must have grown up without a sufficient history teacher.

"Did you not hear the entire story?" *Of course not. He can't even get the names right.* "They went out in a hail of bullets." The mood in our little cave darkens at my words.

"Oh," he mutters, dropping his head.

I take a deep sigh. "Yeah."

Another strike of lightning hits right outside of our shelter, and I yelp in surprise. A cracking splits the stormy atmosphere, followed by a loud crash as an oak tree falls over the entrance of our hideout.

Gryndale throws himself into me, shielding me from the flying debris as limbs snap off in the entryway, piercing through our safe space. We freeze a moment, staring at each other with wide eyes, our faces inches from each other.

"How are—" I start to ask, but he covers my mouth with his hand, cutting me off.

Outside, through the clamor of the storm, I hear voices dangerously close to us.

They caught up.

My heart starts hammering in my chest, and I struggle to steady my breathing as Gryndale holds us still and quiet. The voices fade, and we sigh in relief. Afraid to speak aloud, I bridge the connection between us once again.

That tree probably just saved our lives.

He nods, pulling away to help me sit upright. A chill seeps in where he once was, and I shiver.

An act of God, if you ask me.

I raise an eyebrow at him. *If you believe in that sort of thing.*

Gryndale grins at me. *I don't believe in coincidences.*

***

"Hold still," Gryndale grumbles as I fidget.

"I'm sorry, I don't like getting cut on," I say nervously—like I have not dealt with worse pain before. I sit, listening to the pounding rain outside for a moment before sucking it up. "Fine, get it over with," I say, gritting my teeth.

Gryndale grabs my wrist in a firm grip, holding me still. My heart starts pounding as fight-or-flight tries to kick in. I breathe deeply, focusing on the sound of rain. He presses the dagger's blade into the skin of my forearm, and I hiss, trying to pull away as I scrunch my eyes tight.

"It will only hurt worse if you fight me," he warns, but he does not stop. The blade sinks deep into my arm. I open my eyes with a snarl and watch my blood ooze around the metal. Crimson runs over the sides of my arm like a macabre drip painting.

"Jeez, be gentle," I growl, clenching my fist as he digs for the tracking chip. At least I keep the thing sharp, or this could be worse.

"I'm trying," he says calmly, focused on his work. "Just relax."

I suppress a cry of pain as he pulls the chip out of the surrounding muscle tissue. He drops it onto the stone floor.

"Remember how you healed yourself with the cougar?" he asks. I nod. "Do it again."

I gaze down at the wound and picture the skin knitting together, becoming whole. Slowly, the shallowest parts start to come together before my eyes. I did not get to witness it when the wound was on my back, and I am amazed as I watch.

"You have to hold your focus," Gryndale reminds me upon seeing my progress slow with my bewilderment.

I stare up at him with wide eyes. "Sorry, I've never actually *seen* it happen." I look back down, drawing my focus back to me. The skin begins to come together once more, and the pain subsides to a dull ache. The deepest part in the middle takes the longest, but the pain disappears as the skin seals up, as if nothing ever happened. Only the blood remains.

"There. All done," Gryndale says with a gentle smile.

He hammers at the chip with the dagger's handle, its destruction liberating something inside of me.

Satisfied with his work, Gryndale sits back, gazing at me in the faint glow of his stone. "You feel it?"

His words jolt me, bringing me back to a life past on top of the Market roof when Carnegie asked me the same thing.

I *can* feel it, the sense of freedom coursing through my veins. "Yes," I whisper. The same answer I gave Carnegie, even if this situation is entirely different.

"Liberating, ain't it?" he asks with a smile.

I cannot hold back a genuine smile of my own. "It feels like freedom."

Almost.

Gryndale wipes the blood off the blade and flips the knife around, offering the handle to me. "My turn," he says, sticking his arm out for me. "Same spot, and go."

***

I lean against the window ledge of the dilapidated cabin, the high-noon sun lighting up the dusty room. We stumbled across it this morning after digging our way out of our cave, but our excitement was short-lived. There isn't much here.

I watch Gryndale pack some meager supplies into a bag he found under the rusting bed in the corner while I pick dirt from under my nails with my knife.

"I won't be gone long. I need to see what is close by. I've never been this far out," he says, securing the flap on the bag. He slings it over his shoulder and turns his eyes on me.

"The map doesn't reach this far. Are you sure we should split up? We have no idea where we are. What if you get lost?" I ask, trying to hide the worry in my voice. I feel like a nagging spouse.

With the raising of his brow, my concern has not gone unnoticed. "No, but it would be better for only one of us to get caught if we are too close to anyone searching for us."

"And what if they find me here? I am a sitting duck in this shack. I got one bullet in this gun we found that may or may not work, and only one exit," I say, motioning to the decaying door. "This window won't open, and I sure as hell can't climb through one of those tiny square window panes," I add.

"We can't cover all the 'ifs,'" Gryndale says tersely. "Please stay here. I will try to find us some food and water. I will be back as soon as I can."

"Fine," I say sourly, my dry throat throbbing at the thought of water. I push down the irrational and unfamiliar fear of being left alone.

Gryndale stops at the door, glancing back at me as if he wants to say something. We stare at each other for a moment before he nods once in farewell and disappears into the forest surrounding the cabin. I let out a shaky sigh, resigning to sit here and wait. It is not like I have anything else to do.

I settle down on the floor, hidden from the doorway by an overturned table, fiddling with the fraying edges of the newest hole in my worn pants leg.

***

A noise jolts me awake, and dread fills my heart. I did not mean to fall asleep, but I couldn't have been asleep *that* long. The clouds are back, and it has started to rain again, but that noise was not raindrops on a metal roof.

I peek around the table with my hand on the gun in my waistband, shirking away from the droplets of water leaking from the ceiling. I let out a soft gasp of surprise as my eyes fall on the figure in the doorway.

"Zeke?" I ask, taken aback by the amber-eyed man standing at the door. "What are you doing here?" I crawl out from my hiding spot, giving him a once-over. "I thought I would never see you again." My voice is almost shy.

Zeke drops his bag at the door and closes the distance between us in three long-legged strides, stopping in front of me. His likeness to Danny still makes my heart flutter, even after all this time. His vest is damp from the rain, and the smell of the wet leather is intoxicating.

I could pretend it is him if I wanted to delve into that pit. It's not like I have anything to lose.

"I came for you," he says in a low voice. I tremble, looking up at him with wide eyes.

His fingertips brush my cheek, and with a finger, he lifts my face to his. "I could be him," he whispers, lips hovering over my own. He speaks as if he knows the conflict raging inside of me. My heart thuds away in my chest painfully, and for a moment, I cannot move. I cannot breathe.

I want to feel something good again.

Disregarding the rational part of me, I close the space between us, pressing my lips against his for the first time. His other hand comes up, holding my face as he pushes back.

This isn't right.

I pull away with a shuddering breath. I stare into his eyes, and my knees weaken as they consume me.

Danny's eyes.

Resolve breaks apart inside me, and I reach up to comb my fingers through his thick wavy hair before my lips crash against his with renewed enthusiasm. Zeke wraps his arms around me, pulling me closer. A throaty groan escapes him, and our lips move together in unison.

He pulls away too soon, leaving me gasping as he gazes down at me. With hungry eyes, he pushes me up against the peeling wall. I use my arms around his neck to pull myself up, wrapping my legs around his waist.

Our lips meet again as he presses me against the wall. He trails kisses down my throat, nipping at the sensitive skin. I let out a quiet moan, tilting my head back. He bites down, and I arch against him with a gasp of pleasure and pain.

He growls against my neck, lessening the pressure of his teeth as his fingers trail the skin of my throat. Softly squeezing my neck, he descends on my mouth again, biting at my scarred lower lip. He pulls away, and I stare at him, breathing fast, with no intention of letting him get away.

My parted lips fall into a frown as the light goes out in his eyes. "Ze—" His hand tightens around my throat, killing his name on my lips.

I am stunned and taken off guard. His grip tightens, cutting off my air. I bring my arm down at the crease of his elbow, breaking his grip as self-preservation kicks in. Using the wall as leverage, I buck against him, knocking him off his feet. I land on top of him, the air whooshing from his lungs on impact with the hard floor. I roll off of him as he gasps for air.

Sinking into my fighting stance, I watch him with apprehension as he stands. "What are you doing?" I ask as he takes a step forward. My lips still burn with the passion between us, and I cannot understand what is going on.

He does not answer as he lunges with a jab at my face. I duck, throwing myself into a roll across the floor. My hand reaches out behind me, fingers wrapping around an old broom in the corner.

"Zeke!" I shout, trying to deter him, but he charges at me like a bull. I sidestep and whip the broomstick up, knocking his hand aside as he tries to grab me.

Zeke growls, shaking his hand, but he does not stop. He darts forward, and I swing again, hitting him in the side with a quick strike he fails to deflect. He only hisses in pain. I spin, building momentum for my next strike.

Zeke catches the broomstick inches from his head. He yanks it toward him, taking me with it. Before I can react, he head-butts me, and I stumble back with a painful outcry. Hot blood runs freely from my nose, and I lose my grip on my makeshift weapon. Disoriented, he strikes, hitting me in the ribs with the stick, and it snaps in half.

I yell out in pain and stumble back, but Zeke does not let up. He knocks me to the ground with a kick to the knee, and I land with a thump on my back, one arm twisted behind me awkwardly. I gasp for a breath as he pounces, pinning me to the ground. One hand goes for my throat again as the other restrains my free hand. I cannot break his crushing grip on my neck.

Please help me, I plead to Gryndale.

I'm on my way. You are going to have to kill him. Gryndale's voice is but a whisper in my mind.

"No!" I force out past Zeke's grip on my throat. I am prepared to hurt him but not kill him.

I twist, freeing my pinned arm. My dagger hides in my right boot, and with a little effort, I bend my leg enough to grab it. Vision starting to blur from the lack of oxygen, I drive the blade into Zeke's thigh. With a scream of pain, he lets go, and I use my hips to throw him off of me as he rages at the knife, knocking my hand away before I can retrieve it. I stagger to my feet, shaking. He pulls the knife out, holding it menacingly in front of him. It drips rubies of blood on the dusty floor.

"Zeke, please! What are you doing?" I ask desperately, backing away from him, but he is between me and the only exit.

There is no light in his eyes as he looks at me, and my heart plummets into the pit of my stomach as a thought occurs to me. "Fight it!" I cry desperately, assuming he is under a program similar to my own. What else could it be?

You can't reason with him. Kill him, or die. It isn't a program, Gryndale warns.

Tears pool in my eyes as I back away from Zeke, pulling the revolver from my belt, hand shaking like a leaf. Zeke lunges again, and a gunshot reverberates around the room, even though I did not consciously decide to pull the trigger.

I stare in horror as he stops mid-attack. A billowing black cloud bursts from his mouth, hovering behind him a moment before dissipating. Zeke drops the dagger, clutching at his chest. The faded black shirt he wears darkens as blood spreads.

"NO!" I scream, dropping the gun. Reaching out, I catch him as his knees buckle. "Oh God, no! No, no, no!" I cry, pulling him into my chest as the iron taste of blood seeps into my mouth from my freely bleeding nose.

"Ray," he says in a pained whisper. I pull back to find the light is back in his amber eyes but fading quickly. A wretched sob breaks from my throat as he goes limp in my arms.

"Please, no!" I sob, burying my face into his shoulder, holding him tight. "What have I done? I didn't mean to."

"When in danger, Aella will do anything to survive—to live. She is still holding on." Gryndale's voice comes from the doorway rather than in my head.

"To live?" I shudder out a breath. "What about me? How am *I* supposed to live with this?" I sob, the pain in my heart crippling me. I bury my face in the crook of Zeke's neck, my blood staining his skin. I let out a heart-wrenching cry that crescendos into an anguished scream.

Gryndale kneels, placing a gentle hand on my shoulder. "I can't answer that. Let him go."

Surely this pain will kill me, I say mentally, no longer able to form coherent words.

It feels like it, but you will survive this.

"No," I whimper helplessly, holding Zeke even tighter, his arms limp at his sides.

"We need to go. If anyone is with him, they will have heard that gunshot," he urges me.

I pull away hesitantly, laying Zeke down on the ground. I cannot take my eyes off his, staring sightlessly at the ceiling. Reaching out, I shut them for one last time and gaze down at myself, freed from the trance those amber eyes put me in. My leather bodice is slick with Zeke's blood, shining where the blood pools in the indentions of the black tooled designs in the leather.

Trembling, I look up at Gryndale. He stands, offering me his hand. I stare at the Vesper star and runes inked into it before taking it, allowing him to pull me to my feet. I wobble, and he steadies me. A tsunami of tears comes out of nowhere, and to my shock, Gryndale pulls me to him. Instead of fighting, I collapse into his chest, broken. “I can’t do this anymore,” I whimper feebly.

“Yes, you can,” he says, running a gentle hand over my hair.

“No. At least before I could ignore the pain. I don’t want it,” I sob, shaking my head against his chest.

He pulls away to look at me. “Don’t stop fighting.”

I let out an unsteady breath, shaking my head again. “I’m sorry.”

“Ray—” It is the first time he has called me that, and it almost makes me change my mind. But nothing matters anymore.

This way or that, I am the death of the people I love.

Before he can say anything else, an ominous chuckle rises in my throat as I let go, the pain in my heart disappearing instantly. With no more fight left in me, I go numb, overcome by my personal hell.

“Perfect,” Aella purrs with a dangerous grin spreading across my face as she takes over.

“No,” Gryndale breathes as he steps away from me—from Aella.

“Haven’t you been naughty?” she asks, standing to circle Gryndale like a cat stalking her prey.

“A little,” he admits lightly, but he is on guard.

“I don’t think our Master is pleased with either of us at the moment, but I can make it up to him. I can get back in his good graces if I bring you back with me. Clearly, this little gimmick was a shot at preserving his hard work,” she says knowingly with a wave at the corpse at my feet.

“What do you mean?” Gryndale asks, perplexed.

“Zeid, or whatever his name is, was important to this emotional wreck I call a host. He is almost identical to the man you murdered to set the trauma programming into motion in the first place. It is poetic, really. Force her hand to kill him, and she might snap. And she did—like a twig. So I'm back. And I need Carnegie's help to wipe out our enemy, not you, *Gryndale.*"

Gryndale cannot defend against the barrage of violent electricity forced his way from my fingertips. He collapses to his knees with a cry of agony, helpless against the overwhelming power coming from me that finally surpasses his own.

Thirty-one
JAI

"I told you we couldn't trust Zeke!" Damian yells. "I should have never let him in. I knew when I met him that he would be trouble—just like that damn brother of his! This was the last thing we needed to happen!"

I sit hunched over in the chair by the empty fireplace in Damian's cabin again, head in my hands while the man rages. I have no words for our current situation, and the tiny house is beginning to make me claustrophobic.

"Damian," Keena says, reaching out to her husband. He knocks her hand away.

"You don't understand what this means! Everything we have accomplished is for nothing if those two make it back to Luther. They know we have Charon's help now. They could drop bombs on this place and not think twice about it." I shudder, remembering the remains of Camp #1.

"We don't know that they will go back. I believe both of them managed to break the hold their programs had on them," Ysabel says diplomatically.

"How do you know that? Aren't blue eyes a sign they aren't themselves?" Keena asks calmly, shushing Damian before he can start yelling again.

"I don't know. Maybe it has something to do with that 'becoming one' thing Jai mentioned. Maybe it's permanent now," Ysabel says.

"Oh great, so now there is no way of telling who we are dealing with then," Damian says snidely. He yells out in frustration, flipping the small table next to him over. The glass of corn liquor on top of it crashes to the floor, shattering on impact as the contents spill out. The pungent smell of alcohol envelops the room, and Ysabel's nose scrunches in disapproval.

Keena huffs at her husband. "Do you think throwing a fit about it will help anything? We need to get everyone together. Tell them exactly what is going on," Keena says, surprising me as the voice of reason for once. "They will either stay to fight or flee for their lives. If they run, all of this was for nothing, but *this,"* she says, motioning at Damian and the spilled liquor, "is not going to help anyone."

Damian looks scornfully at his wife, but he says nothing. Keena holds his gaze, and he nods after a few tense moments.

Keena turns to Ysabel and me. "Can you two give us a little bit?" she asks politely. I can see the carefully contained anger boiling behind her eyes, so I nod, grateful for a reason to leave. Ysabel follows me outside with a sigh. As the door closes behind us, she catches my arm before I can descend the porch stairs. I look down at her quizzically.

"Follow me," she whispers. "I need to talk to you."

I grit my teeth, conceding to follow her away from the cabin despite my want to be alone. Ysabel stops under a large oak tree a short distance away. "What?" I ask wearily.

Ysabel sighs, sorting through her thoughts before looking up at me. "I didn't want to tell dad this, but I saw something new."

My heart sinks. Partly because I still don't believe in the Sight thing, and partly because if Ysabel is refraining from telling her father something, it can't be good. "What happened?" I ask. I might scoff at her if it weren't for the desperate look in her eyes.

Ysabel looks at me before diverting her eyes away. "I don't want—" Ysabel wrings her hands together as the stress of what she is withholding seeps out. "Please don't make me relive it, but you gotta find Zeke. I don't know if any of what I saw has happened yet or not."

"Can you give me a little more to go on?" I ask, my pulse pounding painfully in my head.

Ysabel chews on the inside of her lip, staring long enough to make me uncomfortable before she finally speaks. "I was right about the possession thing, and Aunt Ray's Spectral will stop at nothing to force her to give control back to Aella. It must be a failsafe."

"I'm still not convinced of all that woo-woo stuff," I say, shaking my head.

Ysabel rolls her eyes. "I know, but can you trust me this one time? Find him, or people will die. *Aunt Ray* will die." Ysabel closes her eyes as tears well up. "If she gives up control again, we will *never* get her back."

My heart sinks into the pit of my stomach, and I drop my head. For Iylara, I will believe Ysabel this one time, but there is a problem. "I don't know where Zeke went. He threw that blade that cut the ropes and disappeared," I say, staring back at the young girl, her eyes wise beyond her years.

"Follow Aunt Ray's path. There are bound to be clues as to which way they went that the tracking party missed. Zeke will have followed them. I saw an old cabin in my vision. It only had one door, and the window was rusted shut. It had nine window panels too small to fit a person—so one way in and one way out."

"That isn't much to go on," I say, perplexed at the specific details but no real direction.

"It's more than you had a moment ago, and it's all I got. I'm going to choose to believe that you can find it. Can you choose to trust me enough to at least try?" Ysabel asks, sounding so much like her late grandmother that I cannot deny her.

I nod, swallowing the lump in my throat.

Ysabel smiles ruefully. "Thank you."

***

The abandoned ropes are a good sign that I am on the right track, but I almost lose the trail not long after. It starts to rain again as I trek through the trees, scouring the ground and foliage for any little detail that might point me in the right direction.

Further along, a felled tree catches my attention. I would have missed it had I not noticed the narrow path carved through the branches leading to a small cave. I squeeze through the tangled tree limbs and into the dark space. Pulling a box of matches out of my pocket, I strike a flame to light up the area. Dried blood and bits of crushed debris shine in the dim light on the floor. I don't know what it means, but someone was here.

I drop the match before it burns my finger and leave the cave carefully. I look around the entrance and find two sets of shallow footprints leading away into the woods from the shelter. I follow them with rising hope. I find the occasional print and broken twig to guide me. Suddenly, a break in the forest opens up to a small dilapidated cabin with one door and a nine-paneled window. I stop in my tracks, my mouth falling open in surprise.

It's real.

I carefully approach the cabin, listening for any noise inside. There is silence except for the pitter-patter of rain hitting the cabin's metal roof. The door stands open, and I step inside cautiously. The afternoon sunlight peeking through the rain clouds illuminates the one-room cabin in a dim haze through the window. In the center of the room lay Zeke, dead. A fresh pool of blood surrounds his body from wounds in his thigh and chest.

"Dammit," I mutter as I sink to my knees next to my friend.

Zeke's eyes are closed, smeared with blood as if someone with bloody hands closed them for him. I look around, trying to determine what could have happened. I spot a lone bloody dagger lying on the floor, its familiarity pricking my subconscious mind.

My heart wrenches as I realize whose it is, once one of my own.

Iylara.

I drop my head, fearing the worst. The guilt would undoubtedly be enough to push her back over the edge if she killed Zeke.

If she gives up control again, we will never get her back.

No tears come, but a sense of urgency overcomes me. I pocket the knife and pick up Zeke's body, slinging him over my shoulder, his still warm blood soaking through my shirt. I will make the trek back with nearly two hundred pounds on my shoulders or else. No matter what Zeke did, he doesn't deserve to rot away in an abandoned cabin in the middle of nowhere. I just have to keep my rampant thoughts at bay or risk losing myself in the sea of horrible possibilities that finding him dead could bring.

Thirty-two
IYLARA

"You have done wonderfully, my dear," Luther says with a genuine smile. His eyes shine darkly in the dim light of room 101, illuminated by Carnegie's stone dangling in his grip. The music no longer plays in Luther's grasp.

"I am confident your host will no longer put up a fight. Iylara turned out to be stronger than I gave her credit for, but everyone has a breaking point," he says, speaking to Aella directly. "We finally found it. Love was her downfall. If she did not care so much for that man, this might not have worked, but here we are," he rambles on happily, fiddling with a syringe on the mayo table beside him in the dark.

I stand nearby with a smile, staring down at Gryndale, shackled in the void, as Alastair silently prepares him for reconditioning. "Thank you, sir. Iylara has gone silent. All the fight in her is gone. We are finally and completely one," Aella says, and she is not wrong. The fog has engulfed me, and I act and react in line with Aella's program without a second thought about the consequences or lack of morality.

The sensation of being one is so strange. The guilt and pain that drove me back here are nonexistent, and the memories do not affect me like they once did. Through the lens that is Aella, I am finally happy, if that is possible. Maybe content is a better word. Either way, it doesn't matter. I no longer feel the pain that haunted me.

Luther nods his head. "Of course it is. She realized it was much easier to let you take the reins and surrender everything," he says agreeably. Turning to Gryndale, Luther's face turns sour. "You, on the other hand, I did not anticipate—not after all these years. If we cannot get Carnegie back in control, I am afraid I will have to put you down. It would be such a shame," he admits, voice trailing off in thought as he hands Alastair the syringe.

My eyes widen. "But Master, I need his help," Aella says as a current of unease runs down my spine.

Her words drag Luther from his thoughts. "This would be much easier with him, yes, but I have faith that if needed, you can find the strength to complete our mission on your own. You have evolved even further than I had hoped you could in your powers already. In less than a year, you have surpassed Carnegie, and I have been working on him for over two decades. Only time will tell whether he will comply," Luther says as Alastair sticks Gryndale in the neck with the syringe, none too gently.

Gryndale grunts, fighting against the serum as it courses through his veins. Through glazed-over eyes, he looks past Luther. He stares into my listless eyes, a crease forming between his brows when he cannot find any sign of the woman he tried to save. "She is completely gone, isn't she?" he asks in a pained voice.

Gryndale's eyes shine with tears as I stare at him with a silent sneer on my face. He drops his head with a groan as the serum takes hold.

"Come, my dear. You don't need to watch this," Luther says, grabbing me by the wrist to guide me through the dark to the door.

"Yes, Master," Aella says with relish. I follow him like an obedient pet, but neither Aella nor I can help one last glimpse over my shoulder at the man kneeling on the floor.

Gryndale's body shakes as he fights to keep control, and a part of me wants him to give in. I do not want him to die. *Aella* doesn't even want him to die. Maybe she can feel something after all. Maybe.

The door cuts off Gryndale's scream of agony as the serum gets the better of him, leaving Luther and me in silence as I follow him up the stairs. Only the soft click of Luther's over-shined shoes pierces my ears. This place is always so eerily quiet.

Luther leads me through the bland white hallways to his office, holding the door open for me to enter. The curtains are pulled against the morning sun, and I stand quietly as he flicks on the light. Luther walks past me but doesn't sit down. He leans against his desk with a strange smirk I have not seen on his face before.

"What are you thinking, Master?" Aella asks cautiously.

"Nothing, my dear. I'm just admiring my work. I'm in awe of you," he says, looking me over.

I stare back at Luther naively, but Aella is on alert. After a moment, understanding washes over me like a shift in the atmosphere. I have always tried to evade this situation entirely, but not today. Today I will use it to my advantage, driven forward by Aella's urging.

I am very aware of a plan forming within Aella, even though I am not quite sure what it is yet, but the small dagger on Luther's belt should be almost too easy to grab if I could get close enough.

"Come here," he says, voice low and throaty.

I step forward obediently, but it is only for show. Neither Aella nor I am willing to give him what he wants. I'm glad we can finally agree on something.

Luther reaches out, running his fingertips across the scar he carved on my lips. A tremble of anticipation runs through me, but it has nothing to do with Luther's touch. My need for revenge surfaces, and in the moment, I feel like myself for the first time in a *very* long while.

"So completely perfect," Luther croons, pushing away from the desk to stand against me. I do not back away as time slows down, and a genuine smile of my own pulls at my lips. "So completely obedient," he adds.

My smile falls from my face.

Go for it, Aella whispers in my mind.

"So you would want," I say. Aella chuckles inside of me as the grin slips from his face. Anger replaces it.

"What are—" Luther starts, but I cut him off with a delicate finger against his lips seductively as I press myself against him.

I smile sweetly up at him, exhilaration swelling within me. "You aren't as strong as you think. You are just a man whose power has gone to his head," I whisper. A flick of my tongue against his ear lobe makes him twitch. I pull away, watching him. Luther looks flabbergasted, reeling in his surprise. He knocks my hand aside and grabs my chin painfully, trying to instill a fear I no longer feel toward him.

I stare up at him with a condescending smile stretching across my face as he speaks. "You will do as I say, and you will watch how you speak to me," he growls, trying to hold on to the control I am sure he thought he would have forever. "Or I *will* cut out your tongue."

I chuckle darkly. "No, I won't. *You* won't. I have finally realized that you have no power, and Aella doesn't like taking orders. Neither of us will take your shit anymore," I say boldly. My exhilaration sends my heart thudding away in my chest with anticipation. I bide my time to make a move.

His eyes narrow, and his fingernails bite into my skin. "You little bitch, have you short-circuited? You are *mine*, and you will *not* talk to me like that," he says threateningly.

"I may be an experiment, but you don't own me," I say, allowing him to grip my chin tighter to try to get me to comply, but the pain feeds the eagerness rising in me.

"You are *nothing* without me," he seethes. "It's why you came back time and time again," he says, trying to drudge up the past against me. It will not work. The past no longer has any effect on me.

Nothing else matters except this moment.

"I came here because you deceived me with lies and tricks," I hiss, pushing into his grip, our noses almost touching.

Luther shakes his head, an arrogant sneer on his face. "You came here because I wanted you to—because I *own* you. I control everything that you are, and you have the audacity to rebel against me?"

I'm done listening to this, Aella whispers.

Let me enjoy this, I tell her, almost pleading.

Shut up and do it.

I grit my teeth. "We're done," I say, drawing the dagger in one fluid motion from his belt. Luther strikes out faster than I thought he could, knocking the blade off course as I attempt to drive it home into his chest, but he cannot stop me.

I throw my head forward, striking him in the nose with my forehead. Luther screams out in pain with the audible crack of bone breaking. He grabs his nose as blood gushes forth and stumbles back into the desk, unable to go any further. I take my chance. I thrust the dagger into his belly, once, twice, three times, and twist. He cries out, wide eyes finding mine in shock. He crumples forward, and I step back out of his path. Luther hits the floor with a thud, groaning as he bleeds out on the floor, grabbing at his wounds piteously.

"Burn in hell," I say, spitting on him. Tears of relief burn my eyes as I watch him lay dying. A pool of blood grows around him, and streams of crimson trickle from the corners of his mouth. With a final gasp of air, his hands go limp, and life leaves him.

"He's dead," I breathe out in release, sinking to the ground on my knees at the edge of the pool of blood.

He is, Aella says with an outrageous amount of glee that rushes through me. *Now we can do this my way.*

I glance up, startled by the tone in her voice. "What do you mean?" I ask, a grimace forming on my face.

"I mean," she says smoothly, taking over my mouth with ease, "we wipe out these rebels and take control of this region ourselves."

What? I ask, unable to speak.

"Sorry, I meant myself. You will have no say. It took you all of two minutes to believe you had control. You gave in. You are done. I let you have your vengeance, and you get to exist without all that emotional baggage waiting in the wings to devour you if I were not here to numb the pain. Turn it into something you can find joy and comfort in."

I go still inside myself, my mental mouth gaping open, speechless, but the action does not transfer to my body as Aella completely takes back the reigns. I fall back, stunned, even more so now that I realize I did feel in control for a moment, but only because she allowed me to.

Luther wasn't the real problem. Prison bars fall around me in my mind, preventing me from fighting her.

"You said so yourself that he was just a man. I am more, and together we are unstoppable. Look on the bright side. You can't feel the pain and betrayal you think you should feel right now. Lean on that, and don't worry about what happens next."

What about Carnegie? I ask as Aella walks out of the office, leaving Luther behind to be found by someone who might care.

I'm not sure if he is fixable. Only time will tell, but I don't need his help to wipe out the rebels. If he comes round before we launch our attack, it will only be an advantage in an already won war.

Unable to do or say anything else, I mentally nod, and Aella's smile on my face could rival that of the Cheshire Cat.

***

No time is wasted in gathering the reserve troops, along with every toy Luther managed to get working to attack. If anything, it is a little last minute, but Aella does not seem to care that the entire thing is reckless. As we soar through the air to wreak havoc on the rebels, she is confident that we do not need Carnegie's help either.

The wind whips my clothes around me as I hang out the side of the helicopter, staring off into the trees. A grin from Aella pulls my lips tight at the thought of wary rebels scurrying around in fear as the metal beast encroaches on them from the darkness of swirling storm clouds.

Pulling myself back inside the hull, I prepare the Gatling gun bolted to the floor. Aella's anticipation of unleashing hell on the rebels sends rivulets of shaking excitement through me. I take a deep breath to steady myself as she nearly jumps for joy.

The convoy isn't far behind, but Aella insisted on getting first dibs in the massacre to come.

"Incoming missile!" the pilot shouts suddenly into his microphone.

An explosion rocks the back end of the helicopter, and the pilot fights to maintain control as I brace myself on the railing.

We begin to lose altitude, and the helicopter lurches as it reaches the top of the trees, breaking my grip on the door railing, slick with misting rain. The force knocks me off my feet, and I hit the metal floor with a huff of air. Sliding along the floor as the helicopter tilts, I grab the seat leg on the other side before it ejects me.

Tree limbs reach out, beckoning me closer as the engine fails and the metal bird plummets to the ground. Pine trees snap under the weight, barely slowing our descent's momentum. A large oak tree looms, and the sound of crunching metal accompanies a sharp jolt that throws me from the craft.

The under railing catches me in the side as the helicopter spins toward the earth, flinging me into a tree like a rag doll, and I plunge to the ground. I reach out, grasping for branches to slow my fall. I land on the hard-packed forest floor, the air whooshing painfully from my lungs. I cannot catch my breath. The helicopter hits the ground no more than a hundred feet from me with another crunch of metal and bursts into flames.

Steel and fire rain down, lighting the shadows with an eerie flickering glow. With a cry of energy, Aella reacts, reaching out to push a piece of railing off course before it impales my already aching body. It stabs into the ground only a foot from my face, and I shudder out a breathless sigh of relief.

With a groan, I roll to my side, taking in my surroundings. I try to get up off the ground, heaving for air through the respirator of my helmet, but it is beginning to become constricting. I hastily yank it off my head, throwing it to the side with a grunt.

I inhale the crisp, fresh air, now tinged with smoke I could not smell through the helmet's filter, and gasp in pain. I have a broken rib or two. Or three. I heave myself upright with a groan. Poking at my side, I find skin where leather should be. My fingertips come away stained red, blood slicking the leather of my fingerless gloves.

I look down to find a severe gash bleeding freely on my side. The railing ripped clean through the molded leather bodice of my uniform. I become faint at the sight of the wound, but Aella pushes forward unfazed, forcing me onto my hands and knees before unsteadily standing.

I take in the carnage of the helicopter, burning brightly under an ominously dark sky. The fallen pilot lay halfway ejected across the front of the aircraft, glass from the windshield protruding from his back. His blood coats the matte black metal, making it shine darkly in the light of the flames.

I take two steps before collapsing on all fours, gasping in pain for air.

"Over here!" a familiar voice calls out.

I attempt to stand to my feet by myself, ignoring the owner of the voice. Failing miserably, I crumple to the ground. I lay on my back, eyes closed, while I focus on knitting the skin on my side and broken bones back together. Footsteps rush toward me, and someone kneels next to my head.

"Ray?" Jai's voice asks, horrified.

I take a deep breath as my side stitches back together, and any internal wounds heal themselves, indifferent to the man kneeling next to me. My eyes open, meeting Jai's, but there is none of who I once was peering from the icy blue eyes glaring up at him.

"No," he whispers, recoiling as he shakes his head at the sight of Aella's cold, hard glare. "You can't have given in again," he says in disbelief, sorrow coating his voice.

"She did," Aella says as I sit up. "After she killed lover boy," she croons delightfully.

"No," Jai mutters, fear in his eyes as he stands and backs away.

"When he realized that she broke free, instead of protecting my host, our guardian was forced to take drastic measures to ensure I would regain control." Aella sneers at Jai as realization crosses his face. "Your dear Ray couldn't handle the pain when he forced her to kill him. It was quite exhilarating to witness." A flare of heat shoots through my body, and I am overcome by her excitement, nearing that of arousal.

"Are you in there, Ray?" Jai asks timidly, refusing to believe that I am gone.

"She is watching, but she won't stop me. She can't—not now," Aella says with a sideways smirk. I finally manage to stand to my feet, indifferent to the world around me. My body runs on autopilot, doing what it knows it needs to do without thinking about it.

Jai stares at me as if I am a ghost. And I am, in a sense—a ghost of who I once was.

Aella reaches for my sword, but my belt is gone. Aella sighs, irritated as she spots the belt lying twenty feet away, sword hilt gleaming in the firelight. Shock crosses Jai's face as he realizes her intention and barrels toward me. His arms catch me around the ribs, and we fall to the ground.

Aella growls as he pins my arms above my head. Jai notices the rip in the armor and the blood, and concern flits across his features. Taking advantage of his momentary distraction, Aella releases a battle cry with another rush of energy, and Jai flies backward, leaving me free to stand. A red fog clouds my vision as Aella's blood lust consumes me once again, and all that stands before me is a man to kill.

Palm out, the broken railing jutting from the ground nearby flies into my open hand. Jai's eyes widen in astonishment. I spin it a few times to get a feel for it as I stare down my quarry. Jai is hesitant, but he draws his sword, holding it out in front of himself defensively.

He does not want to hurt me, and Aella uses it to her advantage. "Your hesitation will be your downfall," she says softly.

I attack with a grunt, bringing the metal down toward his face. He deflects it, sparks flying as the blade slides against the metal. I push him away and attack again, jabbing for his middle with the jagged end of the railing. He deflects, and I bring it up and around my head, slicing down at him. He knocks it away at the last moment, but the power behind the hit sends him stumbling backward. Jai falls to the ground, eyes wide in fear.

I tower over him, ready to drive the railing through his sternum. My arm rears back to strike as a gunshot breaks through the stormy atmosphere. A familiar force knocks into me with searing pain.

"Argh!" I howl, stumbling to the side. I glance down to find a bullet hole in the front of my chest, barely missing my heart.

A failed kill shot.

I turn to look in the direction of the person who shot me, but they are hidden in the trees. It doesn't deter me. I draw my arm back and throw the railing like a spear toward the trees. A deep cry of pain rings out from the brush, and a shadowy figure of a man collapses. No more gunfire sounds.

Jai yells for the person in the trees, scrambling to his feet as he looks over my shoulder. His eyes flash back to me, bright with distress. I advance on Jai weaponless. He jabs at me, and I dodge, knocking his blade off course with the metal bracer protecting my forearm.

The hit is weak. Jai is still leery—afraid to hurt me. Aella chuckles, and I strike, grabbing his wrist with the sword in one hand, the other going for his throat. Electricity jolts from my fingertips around his throat, and he cries out in pain. I lithely pull the sword from his hand, pushing him back with another pulse of energy. He stumbles back, eyes shining with horror.

"Ray, please!" he begs, holding his hands out in front of him, trying to stay my hand. There is surrender in his eyes.

I bring the sword up, my muscles tense, ready for the killing strike.

"No!" Jai cries out.

But it is not directed at me.

Intense pain shoots through my back. I glance down in shock to find a blade tip protruding from my abdomen more than an inch.

"I won't be sorry," a familiar voice whispers in my ear. Another intense ripple of pain cuts through me as Damian pulls his sword out of my back.

I stand there in shock, looking up at Jai, who stares back with wide, tear-filled eyes. I fall to my knees painfully, hands going to the mortal wound. I try to concentrate enough to mend the damage, but this is past fixing. I cannot focus.

I lean forward, closing my eyes. The pain rattles the shackles of my mind. Despite Aella's desperate attempt at holding on, they fall open, freeing me from the prison in the program.

I gaze back up into Jai's eyes. Our eyes meet, and he falls to his knees in front of me. "Ray?"

His hands cup my face, holding me steady while he gazes into my eyes. They are green again—I felt the switch as Aella fizzled out, like a spent match. The world is clearer now, even with the smoke, and the fog dissipates in my mind.

"Hi," I say weakly, my strength under Aella's control quickly slipping away with her absence. I collapse against him, and he lowers me to the ground, propping me up on his knee. My head rests in the crook of his arm, and the smell of wood smoke I associate with him breaks through the acrid scent of the burning wreckage. I breathe it in as much as possible through the pain of my damaged body, letting it comfort me.

Damian kneels beside me. "It's her? Did I—" he starts to stammer, his success nowhere near as glorious as I am sure he hoped it would be.

"D-don't," I say, holding up a blood-stained hand to silence him. "Y-you f-freed m-m-me." I look back at Jai, my hand moving for his face to touch him one last time, but I cannot muster the strength. My hand falls limp at my side, eyes staring blankly up at the gray sky.

"Please, don't go," are the last words I hear as the sweet embrace of death engulfs me.

Thirty-three
JAI

"Please don't go," I plead as Iylara's body goes limp in my arms. "Please!" I cry out in anguish. Tears stream down my face as I lean over her, wrapping my arms around her thin frame, delicate in my desperate grasp.

Damian sits silently with a deep frown on his face, holding his composure in light of my breakdown despite what he has done. He was prepared for this. I refused to admit that it might come to pass. Now that it is here, I do not know what to do.

I lean back, gazing at Iylara's face, innocent in death. My fingers trace her sharp cheekbones and mouth, anything to help me remember her. Even that damned scar on her lips because it is a part of her.

I cannot bear the thought of her memory fading with time.

The roar of aircraft creeps up on us, crackling through the air like lightning, but I do not move. I cannot move past this single moment in time.

"We need to go," Damian whispers urgently, but I can barely hear him above the noise approaching us, must less the ringing in my ears.

"I can't leave her," I say, voice cracking as tears stream down my face with abandon.

"We have to," Damian says, his voice hard. "Leave her. We will return for her if we survive, but they are almost here." He stands, offering me his hand. "We have to warn the others. This is only just beginning."

I gently lay Iylara down, closing her emerald eyes devoid of the light of life. Her auburn red hair glows like fire in the light of the raging inferno of the helicopter. Damian pulls me to my feet, but I stare down at Iylara, unwilling to walk away.

She was all I had, and I left her—I am leaving her.

Damian grabs my upper arm with a firm hand and tugs, nearly dragging me away from Iylara's body splayed out on the ground, motionless. He holds his other arm protectively against his chest. Blood slowly oozes from the place under his collarbone where the railing hit him, but it doesn't look too bad. He roughly shoves me toward cover as I slow down, looking over my shoulder at Iylara. He obscures my line of sight, and I begrudgingly let him push me ahead without a fight as my body goes numb.

I want to be mad, but I cannot blame Damian for killing Iylara. She was gone until she wasn't. I will hold on to the memory of those green eyes gazing up at me sadly for the rest of my life, a single tear streaking the charcoal around them.

A fleet of helicopters appears like a cloud in the firelight of the burning wreckage, and Damian tugs on my arm once more, pulling me down behind a large bush at the base of a pine tree. We hunker down within the cover of the forest shrubbery, barely breathing as crafts slowly fly over. Through the leaves, I catch sight of a soldier pointing out the wreckage, but they do not stop.

A twig snaps directly behind us. Damian inhales sharply, and my blood runs cold at the sound of the familiar voice that speaks. "Well, what do we have here? You two are a little far from home, eh?"

I turn to meet ice-blue eyes. The demeanor of the man who escaped with Iylara has completely changed, and the cold gaze I associate with him is back.

"Carnegie?" I ask as Damian goes still behind me.

"Yes," he answers before turning his attention past my shoulder to Damian. "You have caused me a mess of trouble."

"What do you mean?" Damian asks.

"My connection to Aella has gone silent after one momentary cry of pain that nearly split my head in two. I can only imagine that means her host is dead." He says it so casually, but his words rip the fresh wound in my heart open wider. "And *you* couldn't have done it," he adds, eyes drifting to meet mine.

I rush at him, pushing against the tree, my forearm against his throat. But Carnegie doesn't fight against me. He merely stares at me with that infuriating smirk of his.

I growl in his face. Anger and grief coalesce, turning my voice high-pitched and shaky. "She is."

"Oh, and I see you are still emotional. *My bad,"* Carnegie says sarcastically. He holds his hands up in mock surrender, but something mournful glows deep inside those familiar eyes.

"He is only trying to get a rise out of you, Jai. Stop," Damian says quietly. I tense as he places a reassuring hand on my shoulder.

"This is his fault," I say, my arm pressing harder against Carnegie's throat.

Damian shakes his head. "It isn't. He is like Iylara was. Luther is the real enemy."

"Luther's dead," Carnegie says, voice strained by the pressure of my arm on his throat.

I stare at Carnegie in surprise. "What? How?"

Carnegie looks down pointedly at my arm, and I loosen the pressure so he can speak freely. But I do not let him go.

"After Iylara gave up control the last time, Aella overpowered my host in quite the fascinating show of power. Drug him back to Luther for reconditioning. After being released, I found Luther in a pool of blood on his office floor, his dagger jutting from his stomach." Carnegie pauses to glance between Damian and me. "He was stabbed multiple times, quite viciously, I might add."

"Aella killed him?" Damian asks.

"Iylara," Carnegie says simply, almost as if he is getting bored.

"You mean *Aella?"* Damian asks, taking a step closer to Carnegie.

Carnegie shakes his head. "No, it was Iylara."

"How could you know that?" I ask. "You said she gave up control," I add after a moment of thought, voice shaking.

Carnegie stares at me, brow raised as if I should know already. "Mind connection, remember? I know she told you about it. It opened wide through the fog of my reconditioning, whether she knew it or not. Aella let Iylara have her vengeance and then revealed that she never planned to be Luther's pet forever. We are programmed to protect him, not kill, so she let Iylara do it." Carnegie sighs. "Luther was planning on bombing the place, but Aella likes to be dramatic. Executing your entire population one by one is more her style. I hope your people are ready. At least you have a chance against soldiers. Bombs can't be reasoned with."

I step back, releasing my hold on Carnegie. "But now that she is dead?" I ask, voice breaking on the last word as my mind still refuses to accept the reality of it.

Carnegie stretches, popping his neck casually. "I'm the only one that has a chance at stopping them. Vesper soldiers are trained to follow orders or die. I am their last surviving superior, but I'm not sure if they will listen to me at this point. Lucky for you, Gryndale's morality is seeping into my programming, so I am willing to try if we can stop them in time."

"Why wouldn't they listen to you?" I ask, dumbfounded at the thought of Carnegie trying to help us. But he did the same with Iylara.

Carnegie shrugs. "I wasn't there when she gave them the mission. I'm not sure if they will recognize my authority or not this time without her explicitly telling them otherwise. Luther was very particular about how he trained them."

I try to speak, but Carnegie cuts me off. "If I succeed, you need to kill me. I will eventually follow my darker instincts and follow in Aella's footsteps to wipe you out. I am the last head on this three-headed beast. "But we are wasting time talking. Either trust me to do as I say or kill me now and forfeit any chance you may have to save your people. You don't have the numbers, even with Charon, to beat us."

"Maybe not, but how can I trust you?" I ask, stricken.

Carnegie bares his teeth at me. "Do you have a choice? If I'm lying to you, you will all die anyway."

"He has a point," Damian says quietly.

I huff in frustration. "Fine."

"Follow me then," Carnegie says. He takes off at a sprint through the forest, following the path the convoy took.

Damian and I follow hot on his heels, uncertainty stirring up doubt and fear in my belly. There is no way we will be able to run fast enough to catch up with the aircraft.

The rebel village comes into view, and my worst nightmare is in full swing. Vesper soldiers pull people from cabins, dragging them into the entrance square. Row upon row of our people kneel, shaking with fear. Those with weapons are disarmed, and gunshots ring out as others try and defend themselves, falling victim to Vesper bullets before they can do any damage.

But most have given up, and the hopelessness strikes me in the heart. We haven't been seen yet, but it doesn't matter. I catch sight of Ysabel and Keena on the front row of people with guns to the back of their heads, and Damian darts toward them without any thought for himself.

I stand in shock at what my life has come to. Carnegie walks forward casually, hands raised. "Lower your weapons!" he orders. The soldiers that can hear him look up but do not stop going about their round-up of rebels.

"No," I murmur to myself. They aren't going to listen.

Damian is wrestled to the ground and his rifle taken as he attempts to fight the Vesper soldiers off near his wife and daughter. His desperation makes him careless, and injured as he is, they subdue him quickly, throwing him next to Keena as she screams, but I cannot hear her. The ringing in my ears is back. Carnegie turns to look at me. He shakes his head before turning back to try and talk his soldiers down. But still, they continue to round up rebels, lining them up for mass execution.

This can't be how it ends. But I can see no other way. Two broad-shouldered Vesper men stalk toward me, grabbing me by the arms. I do not fight them as they drag me toward the kneeling rebels. Kali catches my eye, fear plain as day on her face. I drop my head in shame.

This isn't how it's supposed to end.

"I said drop your weapons!" Carnegie orders, but again, no one listens.

A Vesper woman walks up to him. "Sir, we were ordered not to stop, no matter what you said." Carnegie fumbles, speechless. "You have no power here, sir."

"But the General is dead!" Carnegie finally says.

"That doesn't matter, sir. I'm sorry."

There is something robotic in the way the woman speaks.

Are they all programmed?

The sound of crying women and children swirls into the atmosphere as fear and chaos settle over the village. Angry men yell out but are helpless to do anything without themselves or those close to them killed. Not that it matters.

No one can save us.

I stare at Damian, at a loss for any reaction, as he stares at his daughter in complete terror. I feel nothing as Ysabel closes her eyes, cowering in on herself as she cries out in fear of the gun barrel leveled at the back of her head. The world is a blur, and I cannot comprehend the truth of what is playing out before me—the click of a hammer behind me zeros in my focus.

I'm going to die.

"One," a voice begins to count. "Two!" My heart nearly stops beating, but another voice cuts in before they can get to three.

"STOP!"

Thirty-four

IYLARA

The darkness is disorienting, the silence impenetrable. No breath or beating of my heart can disturb the all-encompassing pressure of the silence, as if neither is existent. I grope at the warm, slick floor, the rough stones scraping against my bare fingertips.

Hello? I ask in my mind, unable to move my lips. My thoughts are not clear, as if muted by water surrounding me, but there is no other presence in my mind besides myself.

I am completely alone.

I force myself upright, straining to see anything through the darkness around me, hot and wet against my skin. A shriek breaks through the dark, and I jump with a silent yelp. No noise comes from my movement. The shriek cuts off promptly, leaving behind a silence somehow even heavier than before. Anxiety rises in me as the silence grows hotter.

Terror strikes as a chorus of echoing screams splits the thick and overwhelming atmosphere. Flames burst forth before my eyes, illuminating damp stone walls on either side of me that drip with something like blood. Prison bars separate me from a looming dark figure that appears from the flames. A man glows with a dark aura in the fire, casting an eerie light around him, but I cannot see his face under the large hood of his crimson robes.

"You don't belong here." The figure's voice is deep and sultry, cutting through the atmosphere with authority. It is both lovely and horrible all at once.

I glance around me, licking my dry and cracking lips with a sandpaper tongue, trying to gain some semblance of where I am, but there is nothing familiar in my dreary surroundings. If I could get even a sip of water, I might be able to set my mind straight.

"Where is here?" I ask, finally able to speak, but my voice is as muted and muffled as my thoughts. My throat burns under the assault of toxic smoke-tinged air as I inhale involuntarily, and my lungs begin to protest.

"Gehenna," he says simply, his low tenor voice sending a ripple of fear down my spine, but I have never heard of such a place.

"I don't know where that is," I say. Tears blur my vision, burning my eyes like acid as fear encroaches over my shoulder.

"The end of the line," he hisses like the sound of many snakes.

I shake my head, memories surfacing with his familiar words, wincing at the pain my tears bring. Dark shadows guarding an iron door and the number 101 burned into the metal flash before my eyes.

The end of the line.

It doesn't make any sense. "I don't understand," I say through my rising tears.

"You don't belong here," he says again, barely above a whisper, as if I have not even spoken. "You never did."

"I don't know how I got here!" I cry out in terror and pain, looking around for anything to explain to me what is going on.

Alas, there is only dark stone and bars that offer nothing to comfort me.

My throat constricts, and the need to breathe overcomes me. I begin to hyperventilate, unable to get enough oxygen from the polluted air that wafts into my cell as the thick atmosphere turns hostile. Deep growling and gnashing of teeth fill the air, making the hairs on the back of my neck stand on end as my lungs burn like a blazing furnace inside my chest.

I cough erratically, gasping for breath as the figure watches me silently. A whispering breaks through the chaos like a sharp breeze. The man turns his head to listen, but I cannot understand the words. He looks back at me from under his hood. His voice almost sounds disappointed. "I can only keep you if you choose to stay," he says, voice louder as the whispering fades.

"I don't want to be here! I don't understand!" I wail as I cough and gasp, shaking my head violently. I claw desperately at my clothes as if they are what suffocate me.

He reaches out through the bars between us, dropping a golden ruby-encrusted dagger on the stone floor in front of me. Flames engulf him, and he disappears without an explanation.

The flames subside, slowly taking the light with them. I relax only a little, and the need to breathe is not as strong as it was a moment before. The heat in my chest lingers, dying out slower than the flames the man disappeared in.

I look down at the dagger, mystified. The chorus of shrieks and wailing starts again, piercing my eardrums painfully. I cover my ears with my hands, curling into myself. It does nothing to staunch the horrendous noises permeating the darkness. Suffocating was not as horrifying as the current assault on my eardrums.

Where am I? I plead in my mind, but there is only silence within me.

I am alone in my head, but something inside me wishes I were not, as if I have not always been alone. And yet I cannot recall anything before waking up here other than Room 101, wherever that may be.

The dagger starts glowing in the darkness left behind in the fading of the flames, shining like a beacon. A horrid thought occurs to me, and I watch as I drive the blade into my stomach in my mind's eye.

"No!" I gasp. I begin to suffocate again, but I do not lose consciousness as the vision fades. I do not need the air I so desperately crave to survive here.

"GET OUT NOW!" I nearly jump out of my skin. The voice is booming, rising above the cacophony surrounding me, striking terror in my heart.

A looming, shadowy figure appears with a burst of flames at the end of the tunnel before me, standing more than twelve feet tall, horns curling up from its head. The beast lumbers toward me down the tunnel, flames following in its wake. I know instinctively that if it reaches me, it is all over.

This is the end of the line, but not without a choice. The man in the robes said as much.

I reach out, hands shaking as my fingers close around the ornate handle of the dagger. It is heavy and cold in my hand as I stare at it, unsure if this is what I am supposed to do, but I see no other way out.

What if it's a trick?

I glance up to find the creature creeping ever closer to my cell, the smell of sulfur assuaging my nostrils. I run a fingertip softly across the blade, easily drawing blood. It is razor-sharp—the only amount of comfort I can glean from my situation.

I gag at the smell of rotting and decaying corpses following behind the sulfur. I try to scramble away from the cell bars, hands slipping on the stone floor. My back hits the wall before I can put any significant distance between myself and the figure right outside my tiny cell.

I turn the dagger in my hand, the tip resting against my abdomen, covered only by the light cloth of a dirty, oversized tunic. I am still unsure if this is what the figure or my vision meant for me to do, but it will do no good to try and fight the beast in front of me.

A burnt, clawed hand reaches out, grabbing the latch on the cell door. My grip on the dagger tightens as the fear of the end clutches at me. I do not want to be ripped to shreds by those claws.

Paralyzed, I stare at the beast breathlessly as it snaps off the lock and latch of my cell with one fluid, effortless motion.

The beast steps into the cell, and I only have a moment to make my decision as the gnarled hand reaches out for me with a snarl from its owner.

With a cry of indignation, I do not think, only react. I push the blade into my stomach. No pain follows, only instant darkness.

***

I jerk awake, and the sting of icy rain pelts my face. I roll over with a groan, wiping water from my eyes. On my hands and knees, I look around. A fog coats the small clearing of trees I lay in, occupied only by the charred wreckage of a helicopter, but I have no memory of how it or I got here.

The only thing I remember is the looming figure reaching out for me. I flit around in horror, searching for the beast, but I am alone. More memories start to surface, and I look down at my abdomen, remembering the tip of a sword protruding from it, but there is no wound—only a slice through the leather where the blade would have come out and a rip in the leather on my side from some unknown injury. No blood mars the black leather or my pale skin underneath, washed away by the rain.

I stand up, unsteady on my feet, as a hearty chuckle sounds behind me. "I knew you wouldn't give up that easy," the voice says. It seems I should know the voice's owner, but it is unfamiliar.

I turn to find a man with shaggy, light brown hair and amber eyes. "Who are you?" I ask, unsure of myself and my surroundings.

He raises an eyebrow, thin lips turning down into a frown. "You don't remember?"

"Remember what?" I ask, looking around—hoping that something will trigger my memories.

"Me," he says with a curious expression. "Do you remember *anything?"* he asks, stepping forward hesitantly.

"Some things, but I don't understand them," I admit, turning back to him in question. He is beautiful in a dark kind of way as if made of more secrets and shadows than light. "Did I die?" I ask. It is the only feasible conclusion that I can come to.

The man walks up, stopping no more than a foot in front of me. "Yes," he says quietly, reaching out to tuck a stray piece of hair behind my ear. I cannot feel the soft brush of his fingers against my cheek. "What do you remember?"

I grimace, trying to remember back as far as possible. Calling my memories inadequate is an understatement. "The last place I woke up in was dark and terrifying. Worse than any nightmare," I say quietly, feeling safe near this amber-eyed man for some unexplainable reason. It feels like he understands me even though I do not understand myself. I have no proof of that, only a feeling, but it is an intense sensation in the pit of my stomach that I cannot ignore.

"Gehenna," the man states knowingly.

"Y-yeah," I say hesitantly as I look up at him, remembering the word. His eyes are soft and lovely, and warmth overcomes me through the icy rain and the cold that envelopes me.

"It is where the spirit and soul of evil ones are destroyed, lost forever in a sea of darkness and pain," he explains, searching my face for something.

I stare at him in thought for a moment. "There was a man—a dark figure in a red robe. He said I didn't belong there," I say after replaying the moment in my mind.

The amber-eyed man nods his head. "Because you didn't. Your spirit is not what was tainted, but your mind, only a part of your soul, against your will."

I stare at him, confused. "That doesn't make any sense."

The man watches me sadly. "No, it doesn't because you are ignorant of how things work, but you were never malevolent in your own heart. Things were done to you against your will, which carried you down the path you were on. You may have felt like you made your own decisions, but you didn't. They were always influenced by the thing placed inside you. Without it, you would never have done what you did, and without it, you can set things right."

"That doesn't help me understand," I say begrudgingly, trying not to become annoyed through my desperation to comprehend what he is telling me.

"And nothing probably can. Just know that you can have a second chance if you choose to return. *You* were never too far gone to be saved, even though it may have looked like it. *You* were meant for great things, not to fall into an early grave without having finished what was set out for you," he says, his eyes searching my face.

His gaze makes me vulnerable, and I hug myself as if it will protect me from the strange and unknown. "But this isn't real, is it?" I ask, knowing something is still off. The landscape around us is too summery to be as cold as it is.

"Oh, it's real, but not how you would think," he says, motioning behind him to a woman sprawled on the ground.

I approach her, mouth agape as I stare at myself lying dead in the helicopter's shadow, my blood soaking into the dirt beneath me.

"What—" I begin, unable to find the right words.

"Choose," he says. There is that word again.

"Choose what?" I ask, desperately trying to understand something—anything.

"To stay or go," he whispers, a longing in his voice.

"Why would I choose to stay here?" I ask, looking at the man carefully, and then it clicks. "Danny?" I ask incredulously.

He smiles that unforgettable smile that can light up a room. "So she remembers," he says to himself somberly, despite his brilliant smile.

I reach out to him, grabbing his face in my hands to pull him toward me. I can feel him now, warm and inviting. I hesitantly bring my lips to his, but as they touch, every memory I have forgotten comes flooding back.

I pull away, staring up at him with wide, tear-stained eyes. "What happens if I stay here with you?"

Danny looks at me, voice matter-of-fact, but his eyes glisten with the threat of tears. "Your people will die."

My breath hitches. "Then I can't stay—" I say, my voice fading off. I do not want my death to destroy lives as I did in life. "But I don't want to leave you," I say as tears creep down my cheeks.

"You have lived without me for some time. You know you will survive," Danny says, trying to comfort me.

"But I don't want to *just* survive. I want *you*. I only ever wanted *you,"* I cry, holding on to the front of his shirt for dear life. "I'm sorry for the things I said to you."

Danny wipes away the stray tears that escape my eyes despite me trying to hold them back. "I forgive you," he says with a smile. "If you choose to go back, you will not be alone. Even before me, the one who has always been by your side will never leave you again. You already know how he feels about you."

I look up at him for a moment, mind racing. "Jai?"

Danny nods, his eyes downcast but kind. "Deep down, you feel the same way about him. You've suppressed it all these years, even before we met. Then I died, and you became afraid to face your true feelings for fear of feeling as though you would betray me. You did a damn good job too. I bet you don't even know how you truly feel about him."

I shake my head, trying to absorb the truth. Realization finally dawns like a tiny ember that grows, igniting everything around it. "But what about Zeke? *That* wasn't a betrayal?"

Danny shakes his head, but he cannot withhold his frown. "You only thought you loved him because you let yourself *believe* he was me. But he wasn't. He gave himself over to that which inhabited him on his own accord, in favor of the promise of power he never got. He even betrayed me trying to attain it, but he was consumed. Your emotions are traitorous when you follow them blindly. They will always lead you astray, as his did."

"You had nothing to do with any of this?" I ask, wanting the sweet relief that little two-letter word could bring.

"Not willfully, no," he says, shaking his head. There is something in his voice I do not like, withholding the relief I so desperately crave.

"What is it?" I ask, searching his eyes.

Danny shakes his head, staring down at his feet shamefully, avoiding eye contact. "I trusted my brother and foolishly allowed him to lure me into a trap. None of this would have ever happened if I had seen the signs that something was off—if I had chosen differently," he explains, forcing himself to look back at me. "I'm sorry for that."

"You can't blame this on yourself," I say, shaking my head in defiance.

He chuckles, a sad smile on his lips. "If I can't blame myself, then neither can you."

I refuse to pin the blame for *anything* on him. I cast my eyes away to look down at our feet, our toes nearly touching, trying to accept his words.

"I will be here waiting for you when your time comes, but you should go back right now. Try to make things right, regardless of what happens," Danny says, lifting my chin gently to look me in the eyes.

Tears cascade down my cheeks freely, and I meet his gaze with a sniffle. "I love you. Always will."

"I know," he says with a smirk.

A peace I cannot explain comes over me. I nod, my smile taking over my face as I recall saying those two words to Jai once upon a time.

Once more, I reach up, pressing my lips to Danny's. He holds me steadfast before releasing me with purpose. "Go save them," he says, gripping my shoulders as he leads me to my dead body lying on the ground.

"Okay," I sigh, kneeling next to myself.

"Close your eyes," Danny coaxes, but I steal one last look at him, afraid of forgetting his face.

I let my eyes close with his face imprinted in my mind, and the sensation of cold water engulfs me.

***

I jerk awake with a gasp, eyes flying open. I no longer kneel next to myself but lay on my back where my lifeless body once was. The rain that falls is warm as it hits my face, and I breathe in the smell of smoke lingering in the air. I sit up, looking around for Danny, but he is nowhere to be seen.

I can sense a presence next to me, a cold whispering kiss of a breeze brushing against my cheek, and then it is gone. I savor the moment, taking a deep breath. I stand to my feet and give myself a once over. All my wounds are healed. Only the tell-tale sign of damage to my leather bodice remains.

My mind and thoughts are clear—no brain fog or voices. Glorious silence.

I bask in it a moment longer before setting my sights on the task laid out before me. I cannot let Aella succeed even after death and take off sprinting through the unfamiliar forest in the village's direction. Even as I get short on breath, I do not give up, pushing myself ever faster.

Please let me reach them in time.

Thirty-five
JAI

"Put down your weapons!" The woman's voice is filled with terror yet laced with authority that halts the army surrounding us where Carnegie's did not.

I would know her voice anywhere. But that isn't possible.

"Iylara?" Damian asks weakly. The threat of having to watch his daughter executed before his eyes has drained him.

I must be seeing things.

Iylara walks toward us carefully, hands raised. Despite the damaged leather armor encompassing her abdomen, she is very much alive. "Change of plans," she says. "I think we have made our point. Return to base. *Now.*"

The soldiers don't ask questions as they lower their weapons. They merely follow her orders without hesitation. In unison, they turn away from us and disappear into the trees. I stand in awe before staggering to my feet with tears in my eyes. I stumble toward Iylara in relief, stopping in front of her, and she looks up with a small smile.

"How?" I ask, softly touching her face. She shakes her head, green eyes shining.

"Later," she says quietly, patting me on the chest. Iylara side-steps me, eyes on her brother. Keena stares daggers at her but remains quiet as she holds her sobbing daughter.

"But—" I say, eyes darting around to take in the reactions of the people who have been spared death. They were all blessedly disarmed, or a few might not give her the chance to speak.

"Damian," Iylara says casually. There is no animosity in her tone or face, even though he killed her.

"Iylara," Damian mirrors her tone, but he stares at his sister, eyes wide in shock.

"You were dead," Carnegie interrupts, staring at Iylara with a mystified gaze.

Iylara looks at him with a poignant smile before turning her attention back to Damian. "I was," she says softly. She shakes her head. "But right now is not the time to talk about it," she says, looking around at the rebels. Some stand up while others still kneel, astonishment evident on their faces. A few comfort their loved ones. "They will want to know what is going on."

"And what the hell am I supposed to tell them?" Damian asks, angry. "I don't even know what's going on." I look at him, wondering where the hostility comes from. "You're supposed to be *dead,"* Damian spits out, taking a threatening step toward his sister. Her eyes widen as she takes a step back, assaulted by the venom in his voice.

I step between the two of them, facing Damian. "They don't know that."

Damian snarls. "What do we do? Part ways and say, 'Oh, my bad?'"

"Basically," Carnegie says curtly.

"Stay out of this," Damian snaps. "I don't need to hear anything from you." He glares at his sister. "Leave, now. Do not force me to kill you again. I think you have done enough."

Iylara grits her teeth, nostrils flaring. She looks at me briefly before grabbing Carnegie's hand, pulling him after her to follow their soldiers.

I stare at Damian, aghast. "What the hell? She is alive!" I hiss.

Damian turns on me. "And it's unnatural. She can't be trusted. That program probably reanimated her, biding its time before it strikes again."

I shake my head. "I don't believe that. And I don't think you do either if you are going to let her walk away."

"I will not kill her in front of my daughter. I have other ways to deal with this," he hisses.

I bite the inside of my cheek as my eyes flit back and forth between the trees where Iylara disappeared.

Damian sees the conflict in me, shaking his head in disgust. "Would you leave us for her after everything she has done? The people she has killed?" he asks in a low and threatening voice.

I stare at him, dumbfounded. "It wasn't *her,*" I say after a moment.

"If you turn your back on us now, you will not be welcome back," Damian says with finality.

"But dad!" Ysabel pipes up from her mother's arms. Damian raises a hand, silencing her.

"I can't believe you," I say, shaking my head in disbelief. "You aren't even willing to talk about this?"

"No!" Damian shouts, losing his temper. His uncontrolled anger solidifies my decision.

I speak through gritted teeth. "Fine." I look at the rebels in varying degrees of shock, anger, and confusion. They have no idea what is going on, and maybe it is worth it to stay and argue my point. Damian will surely make me out to be a traitor who worked for Vesper all along otherwise. But I can't do that—not now. Without another word, I turn my back on Damian and the rebels, following Iylara's trail into the trees.

"TRAITOR!" Damian screams after me.

The sound sends a tremor down my spine, but I do not stop walking and do not look back. I have to be able to look myself in the mirror at the end of the day, and letting Iylara walk away after feeling the way I did as she died in my arms will not let me do that. Whatever may come, I am ready for it.

***

“Jai?” Iylara asks, bewildered upon seeing me pushing my way through the foliage. “What are you doing here?”

She motions for the troops to continue loading into the helicopters in the clearing, but Carnegie stops a ways back, watching with a raised brow.

“I couldn’t leave you again,” I say, unable to second guess my choice. “I’m considered a traitor now, but at least I can live with myself.”

Iylara watches me for a moment, brows creased together before she reaches out. She grabs me by the collar, pulling me toward her. Her lips crash against mine, and for a moment, I am too stunned to react, frozen in place. Then everything fades, and all that exists in my mind is the two of us. I wrap my arms around her, holding her tight as I kiss her back through a smile I cannot contain. Never did I believe this would or even could happen. Not after today, but it is. I desperately hope that it is not some sort of horrible cosmic joke.

Iylara pulls away, watching me shyly, but Carnegie is the one who speaks, killing my moment of bliss. “I can still control this army.”

I turn to face Carnegie. Iylara looks between the two of us in confusion. “So?” I ask, trying to figure out what Carnegie is saying.

Carnegie saves me the effort. “Do it. Kill me. I know you want to. After all these years, my mind is fractured. There is nothing left in me to be saved in this life as I am. And you don’t want me to have *any* control of Vesper’s army. I already told you—I will follow my darker instincts eventually, and you will die. You do this now, and you live.”

“What? No! We can fix this.” Iylara pleads as she faces Carnegie.

He looks at Iylara. His lips are turned down in a sad smile. “You can’t fix me, my love. I want this. Please let me have it.”

Iylara’s lips tremble. She closes her eyes, tears leaking from the corners. After a moment, she nods once before shocking both of us by pulling Carnegie into a tearful hug. “I forgive you,” she says through her tears.

Carnegie wraps his arms around her, pressing his face into her hair. His voice is thick as he says, “Thank you.” He pushes her away, looking her in the eyes. "Maybe one day I'll see you on the other side."

Iylara sniffles as she nods her head again. "I hope so." A sob breaks from her throat, and she steps away, head in her hands as she tries to shut out what is coming.

I step forward, searching Carnegie's eyes for any hint of tricks. There is nothing but sincerity, leaving me to try and drudge up every bad thing the man has ever done to go through with it, including the fact that he once shot me in the back. It takes a moment to get past Iylara's quiet sobs that wrench my heart, but the man standing in front of me has done so much.

Almost lovingly, I grab Carnegie's head in my hands as the man stares back soberly. "I hope you find some kind of peace," I say, unsure of where I find it in me to say such a thing. My words are sincere nonetheless.

"Me too," Carnegie says softly. I am almost positive that I am talking to the real man inside, not Carnegie, but it makes it harder if I think about it. "Leave me here when it is done, no matter what she says," he whispers.

"You, of all people, should know that I can't make her do anything," I say with a sad smirk. Carnegie shrugs, staring me in the eyes. His face is stoic, but there is a faint smile in his eyes.

The muscles coil in my arms, and with a flick of my wrists, Carnegie's neck snaps. He crumples to the ground, dead. I step away from him with none of the relief that I thought his death would bring. Iylara sinks to the ground, and I turn away as she pulls Carnegie's limp body into her lap, smoothing down his hair as silent tears fall on his face. I do not understand what could have happened between Iylara and the man who killed her husband, but it wrecks me regardless.

"I'm sorry," I say, unable to look at her as tears threaten me.

Iylara shakes her head. "Don't. He wanted it. I know what that's like." Her voice is barely audible, but it pulls the tears from me against my volition.

"He said to leave him here," I say, tone half-hearted at best.

Iylara looks up at me with dangerously narrowed eyes. "He has told me to do a lot of things, and I never listened before if I could help it. Why would I start now? He deserves a proper burial. I don't care what anyone says, including him."

I cannot argue with that. "Okay."

Thirty-six

IYLARA

I stare out the window of Luther's office in silence. His bloated body gently swings in the breeze over the entrance gate, a macabre reminder of everything I have been through.

Contrary to what I thought I would feel at seeing the man dead, the sight is only a small comfort to me. My brother still wants me dead, and my entire life has been turned upside down. I am surrounded by strangers who call me leader, a title I am now confident enough to carry, but they aren't my family or my people.

After what feels like hours of standing in silence, I finally speak. "This isn't how I thought life would turn out."

Jai shifts in his chair. "Me either, but it could be worse. And we are alive. *You* are alive. That is more than I could have hoped for."

I look over my shoulder at him with the ghost of a smile. "Yeah, I guess so," I say, looking back out the window shyly. He took my retelling of death much better than I thought was possible. I still catch myself watching him, waiting for him to run for the hills, but I have not found any regret in his eyes.

Jai stands, and I look back out the window. He slowly approaches me, and I watch him in the window's reflection. I am not the same woman he knew or even fell in love with before. My stance is less haughty, and the skin of my forehead is beginning to show the stress from this past year. But there is a strength resonating from the woman staring back at me in my reflection despite it all—and Jai still chooses to stay, like Danny said he would.

Jai wraps his arms around me, placing his chin on my shoulder to look out the window with me. "I guess we run this place now, huh?" he asks playfully, trying to lighten the mood.

I chuckle, and Jai smiles against my cheek. "Yeah, I guess we do." I turn in his arms and clasp my fingers together behind his neck.

Jai searches my eyes and the deep sadness that is still there. "I may not be your first choice, but I hope you can learn to love me just the same," he says.

My eyes mist over. "But you were. You've been there since the beginning, but I was too blind to see. I'm sorry," I confess, searching Jai's eyes again for any sign of regret at his choice to stay by my side again.

Jai shakes his head. "There is nothing to be sorry for."

"There is plenty to be sorry for," I argue.

Jai shakes his head again with a soft smile. "But we are going to forget about it, okay? Start fresh with the time we have left."

I start to retort, but Jai holds up a finger against my lips to silence me. "And don't think about what *could* happen. We are here, *now*. Let that be good enough."

I bite my lip and stare down at his chest as I nod. My eyes meander back up to meet his as I speak, a smile creeping across my face. "Okay."

Jai lowers his head, touching his lips to mine softly. "Good," he says as he pulls away.

I give a mischievous, side-ways smirk as I say, "Good," right back and pull his lips down to meet mine.

A light tap on the door sounds, and we break apart with a huff from me and an entertained chuckle from Jai.

"Yes?" I ask, turning to the door, slightly irritated as Jai withdraws to look out the window, still smiling.

Yates sticks his head inside the office. "There are people here to see you, ma'am," he says before spotting Jai. "And Mr. Norris," he adds, looking at Jai perched on the window sill behind me.

I frown, not expecting visitors. "Send them in," Jai says. I look around at him, eyebrow raised in question. "I watched them come in earlier," he explains, motioning at the window.

I nod at Yates, and he bows out. "And you didn't warn me?" I ask Jai, peeved.

"I figured it would be a nice surprise—well, one of them anyway. But it took a while to vet them. I couldn't override the protocols already set in place. Only you could do that, and I didn't want to spoil the fun."

It is only a few moments before another knock sounds. "Come in," I say, gripping my hands together on the desk. I don't like surprises these days, but I can't kill the smile on Jai's face.

The door opens, revealing our first visitor—Ysabel steps inside the office. I dart out of my chair and around the desk. I hesitate in front of her, dropping my arms to my side, afraid of making the wrong move. Ysabel giggles excitedly and throws her arms around me. I hold her for a moment before she steps away to look at me with a bright smile.

I chew on my bottom lip. "Why are you here?"

"I wanted to know the truth. Dad believes you are still programmed, but I don't believe that. I may not know exactly what happened, but you're not the same as you were. You aren't the General. I can see it in your eyes."

"Oh," I say quietly, shrinking away to my chair. That truth hurts a little more than I would like it to, even if it isn't all bad. I might have died, but the mess I stirred up before will inevitably follow me forever. "So, what are you gonna do?" I ask as I sit down, motioning for her to take a seat.

Part of me wishes that she would stay, but she has a home to return to—a place she truly belongs. Not by my side as a traitor as Jai chose to be. Hell, Damian probably doesn't even know that she is here right now. I doubt he would have let her come.

Ysabel smiles apologetically. "I'm going back to my parents, but I won't buy into their ideas. Something happened to you. I don't want you to try and explain it," she says, holding up a hand to stop me from speaking. "I just needed to know that all the horrible things I'm hearing aren't true for either of you."

All the horrible things.

She probably wouldn't be standing here now if she knew everything. She is still so young. I cannot believe that Damian would have told her *everything.*

"I've done plenty," I say, looking away from her probing eyes.

"Maybe, but I wanted to know that when I try to persuade people to spare your life, I am doing the right thing."

"Spare my life?" I ask as Jai and I both sit up straighter.

"Dad is going to try to have you convicted and executed," she says. "I'm trying to petition against it."

I stare at my niece, flabbergasted. "Doesn't he remember that I already died?" I ask.

"Yeah, but according to dad, you should have stayed dead." Ysabel's voice is stern, more adult than it should be at her age.

Her words strike me, but she is only speaking the truth. I cannot blame her for that. I already know the answer to my next question, but I have to ask to make sure. "And your mom still hates me?"

Ysabel nods with a grimace. "Oh, for sure."

My shoulders slump as I sit back in my chair with a dark chuckle. "I figured as much."

An uncomfortable silence falls over the room, and Ysabel shifts. "I wanted to let you know that I have your back." She looks at Jai. "And to bring *you* this," she says as she shrugs off the duffel bag on her shoulder. "It's your stuff from the cabin. Dad tried to burn it, but I saved almost everything."

Jai takes the bag with a wide-eyed yet appreciative grin. "You didn't have to do that. I would have survived without this stuff."

Ysabel shrugs. "In unfamiliar times, it's nice to have something familiar to hold on to, yeah?" she asks, reaching into the pouch hanging on her side. "I also brought this," she says, withdrawing an ornately tooled leather sheath housing a familiar dagger.

I stare in shock at my mother's blade. "How did you get it?" I ask, believing I would never have anything from my old life to hold on to.

"Mom gave it to me, but she never thought I would give it to you. But you are the rightful owner of this blade. It is supposed to be passed down from mother to daughter. Grandma should have never given it to my dad or, in turn, my mom. Please take it."

I cannot help the smile on my face as she places my mother's dagger in front of me or the tears that surface as I stare at her in awe. "Thank you," I say.

I pull the blade from its sheath and watch it glisten in the light of the room. The last time I touched it was while holding it against Keena's throat. I never imagined it would be mine one day—my wildest dreams never even accounted for this moment, as simple as it may seem.

Jai grips my shoulder comfortingly, and I compose myself, looking back at Ysabel. I wish I had the energy to try and talk her out of going back, but she *needs* to go back. For now, at least. She will do what she wants eventually.

I have messed up so much, yet she is still willing to back me up.

I don't deserve it.

"I'm going to go now before they ask too many questions about where I went, but I wanted to tell you that I love you," Ysabel says with a sad smile.

I nod my head as I suck on my top lip. "Okay. I-I love you too."

Ysabel's smile is mischievous. "I will stay in touch." She nods in parting at Jai and turns, leaving the room with a soft snick of the door.

I bow my head, huffing out a heavy breath, fingers roving over the indentions of the tooled leather mindlessly. Thoughts racing, I am not allowed much time to deal with anything before two heavy strikes sound on the door.

"Come in," Jai says, graciously allowing me a moment to gather myself before I turn my eyes to the unfamiliar woman who enters now.

She steps into the office with purpose, fire blazing in her dark eyes. "So, did we miss something?" she asks before we can say anything.

I frown at her a moment, trying to figure out who she is before I put the pieces of Jai's previous stories together.

Kali.

Weariness creeps over me, and my foot starts tapping silently under the desk. She is the one who prepared the gallows for Gryndale and me.

Jai straightens up, shoulders stiff. "What do you mean?" he asks, moving to position himself between us.

"The war is over? Just like that?" Kali asks angrily. "Damian tried to explain things, but he is holding back. I'm getting sick of that bastard withholding information. I don't believe you are a traitor either, so did I join the wrong side?"

Jai withholds his retort, glancing back at me as I stand to my feet. "Luther is dead if you didn't notice. We are sending people back home to where they came from if they so wish to go, and no one will attack anyone anymore. You may live in peace," I say, but the explanation is insufficient.

"After everything you did? And Carnegie! Where is he?" she asks angrily. "I have an issue that needs to be settled with his blood."

I stare at Kali, heart pounding, but Jai steps forward to answer. "Carnegie is dead."

"And for some reason, I don't believe you," Kali seethes.

I huff, not wanting to drag this out longer than necessary. "Follow me," I say as I stalk out of the office, not bothering to wait for them to follow me. I walk toward the morgue with determined steps, but my breathing gets heavier with each footfall.

I do not want to see his lifeless body again.

But I have to do this. Kali won't believe me any other way.

We stop outside the door labeled *Morgue*. Kali turns on Jai, apparently refusing to speak to me, her nostrils flaring in anger. "Who did it?" she asks, clearly angry that she did not get to do it herself.

"I did," Jai says bluntly.

"Then show me," she says, glancing between us.

"Don't believe me?" Jai asks, his anger rising to meet hers.

"No, not really," she says, pushing past me to open the door herself.

A single exam table sits in the middle of the room, but it is empty. The white sheet on top of the table is thrown back haphazardly.

"Is this some kind of joke?" Kali asks, turning on me with a fury.

I shove past her, disregarding her demeanor in my shock. I stare at the empty table in disbelief.

I helped put his body up there myself.

"He was here," I say under my breath.

"Well, he isn't here anymore. Carnegie isn't dead unless I see a body," Kali snarls. "Now, where are you hiding him?"

I glance over at Jai, who has come to the same conclusion that I have.

"He *was* dead," I say thoughtfully, ignoring Kali completely.

Kali glares at me with a disgusted look. "What do you mean *was?"*

I shake my head. "He isn't anymore," I say, looking back at Jai. There is a dawning light in his eyes, but Kali does not understand the situation as we do.

"Dead people don't come back to life," she says, turning on me with malice.

I shake my head with a small hysterical chuckle. "No, most people don't."

"Most people?" Kali stalks toward me menacingly, but I stand my ground, staring her in the eyes. "Where are you hiding him?" she asks angrily.

I bare my teeth at her. "I'm not hiding him anywhere."

Kali bows up, but Jai steps between us. "He *was* here. I helped bring him in myself," Jai says.

"Like I would believe *your* word. Maybe you *are* a traitor," Kali hisses.

I snarl at the woman's words, and Jai pushes me back a step, but it does not stop my mouth. "So you're gonna believe everything Damian says now? You already said you don't trust him!"

“Shut up,” Jai mutters, and I clench my teeth together, but I hold my ground.

“This isn’t over,” Kali threatens. “I will be back.” She gives me a nasty glare past Jai before stalking off, leaving me to stare at Jai with an uncertain gaze.

“Where the hell is he?” I whisper.

Jai shrugs, still in disbelief. “Your guess is as good as mine.”

“Was it too much to ask for it to be over completely?” I ask warily.

Jai sighs. “Maybe, but I’m not going anywhere. We can handle whatever comes at us. Together.”

Epilogue

My past choices, good and bad, have impacted my present. Those choices shaped me into who I am now. When all was stripped away—and everything I tried so hard to hold together finally fell apart—how I reacted to the mess is what revealed who I truly am.

I forgot that what is important is how I allowed what I went through to shape my future—whether or not I allowed it to control me. And I did, for a time. The path I walked led me to my destination, but I chose which way to go in the end.

How many times will I look back on my life, searching, before I can finally find the meaning of it all? Too busy stuck on what-ifs and should-haves to see the treasure beneath the rubble?

Every choice in my life added a piece to the puzzle. Some were too insignificant to be worth recalling, but others were so magnificent that I cannot help but wonder in awe at them, even now.

I am still searching for that treasure, having lost my way for a bit, but as I sit on the soft floor of this familiar pine forest surrounding me, staring into the crackling fire in front of me, I can almost taste it through the chaos that is my shattered life.

What-ifs and should-haves will utterly ruin me if I give them credence. Sure, there are things I wish I could have changed, but that is in the past. I have no control over them now, but I do have control over whether I allow myself to wallow in them or not.

Fact: My choices, influenced by something other than myself or not, have brought me *here.*

Truth: I cannot say that I am pleased with my situation, but I am *alive.* I have a second chance to make the right choices. I died to who I was so I could choose a different path forward.

That has to count for something.

Danny told me to make things right, and I did that to the best of my ability. What is left of my family is alive and able to return to our home, regardless of whether I can be with them. The separation of clans no longer divides the region. What more could I want, after everything?

Vesper dissolved once I sent the people back to their homelands and brought our people back. More than I could have hoped for survived, even Eddie. He is missing an arm now, though. I am sure that mixing drinks is not the easiest thing in the world, but I was not around long enough to learn any different.

To my brother's great displeasure, the congregation chose to exile rather than execute me, and I have my niece to thank for my life and the hope that comes with it. After everything, I made it to the other side of what I thought would be my destruction with her help.

Not everything is okay or right, but I have hope that it will turn out for good eventually. In the years to come, I will look back and see how much I have grown from the wreck I once was to the redeemed woman I am now. And I will know better when the enemy comes knocking.

Together, Jai and I will face the unknown head-on and live without regrets as outcasts—because not all who wander are lost. In time, I have faith that we will find our home—a place with no memory of what I did or the people I hurt.

After every trial we have survived, and with every testing that will inevitably come, love is the only thing strong enough to carry us through. And I will be okay with that.

***

THE END

CPSIA information can be obtained
at www.ICGtesting.com
Printed in the USA
LVHW101337140922
728284LV00004B/28